New York Times and *USA Today* bestselling author

KAREN ROBARDS

"ROBARDS'S SINGULAR SKILL OF COMBINING INTRIGUE WITH ECSTASY . . . GIVES HER ROMANCES THEIR EDGE."
—*Lexington Herald-Leader* (KY)

"ROBARDS IS A STUPENDOUS STORYTELLER."
—*Midwest Book Review*

"ROBARDS HAS A TRUE FLAIR FOR CHARACTERIZATION AND EXCELS AT ADDING LARGE DOSES OF HUMOR TO THE SPICY MIX."
—*Romantic Times*

"ROBARDS IS EQUALLY GIFTED IN CRAFTING HISTORICAL AND MODERN ROMANCE."
—*Booklist*

Sea Fire is also available as an eBook

KAREN
ROBARDS

Sea Fire

Pocket Star Books

New York London Toronto Sydney New Delhi

Pocket Star Books
A Division of Simon & Schuster, Inc.
1230 Avenue of the Americas
New York, NY 10020

This book is a work of fiction. Names, characters, places, and incidents either are products of the author's imagination or are used fictitiously. Any resemblance to actual events or locales or persons, living or dead, is entirely coincidental.

First Pocket Star Books paperback edition March 2012

POCKET STAR BOOKS and colophon are registered trademarks of Simon & Schuster, Inc.

For information about special discounts for bulk purchases, please contact Simon & Schuster Special Sales at 1-866-506-1949 or business@simonandschuster.com.

The Simon & Schuster Speakers Bureau can bring authors to your live event. For more information or to book an event, contact the Simon & Schuster Speakers Bureau at 1-866-248-3049 or visit our website at www.simonspeakers.com.

Designed by Leydiana Rodríguez-Ovalles

Manufactured in the United States of America

10 9 8 7 6 5 4 3 2 1

ISBN 978-1-4516-4979-6
ISBN 978-1-4516-4982-6 (ebook)

To Doug,
with more love

one

❧⟐❧

In the waning days of the summer of 1844, Lady Catherine Hale was more beautiful than she had ever been before in her life. Her shining red-gold hair, a thick mass of waist-length curls when she loosed it, was worn for coolness' sake in a soft chignon. It formed a shimmering golden nimbus about her small face when caught by the rays of the hot South Carolina sun. Her face was hauntingly lovely, an almost perfect oval dominated by a pair of incredible sapphire eyes, dark silk fringed and slanting at the corners, which added a touch of the exotic to her golden beauty. For the rest, she had high cheekbones flushed a warm peach by the sun, a delicate, straight nose, full, rosy-red lips that her husband teased her about by saying they were made expressly for kissing, and a willful little chin that just hinted at her underlying strength of character.

She was a small girl, with fragile bones, but her body was as exquisite as her face. Her breasts were high and full and just the right size to fit into the palm of a man's hand (this, too, she had from her husband). Her waist was narrow, her hips deliciously curved above legs that were slender but shapely.

On this particular day in August, Cathy had dressed rather casually because of the heat. But the very simplicity of her low-necked muslin afternoon dress, full-skirted with the tiny puffed sleeves that were all the rage, became her vastly, while its pale yellow color set off the porcelain smoothness of her complexion.

Only nineteen, she was more woman than girl. Her naturally sweet expression softened even more as she glanced out of the back parlor window just as the man who had made her so strode into view. Clearly Jon had just left the fields. A fond smile hovered on Cathy's lips as she saw that her husband was filthy, his dark face sweat-streaked and his black hair urged by the afternoon's humidity into the deep waves that were the bane of his existence. His buff-colored breeches and white shirt were coated with a fine layer of grit, as were the high leather boots he wore and the wide-brimmed hat he carried in one hand. Jon worked hard, overseeing the cultivation of Woodham's vast cotton crop. Cathy knew that he did it solely for herself and their fifteen-month-old son, Cray. Secretly she guessed that Jon sometimes hankered after the wild, roving pirate life he had enjoyed before their marriage and Cray's birth had prodded him into respectability. But good as he had been at pirating, as she had often told him, it could have only one end: a hangman's noose. Jon had escaped it twice, and Cathy had no intention of allowing him to tempt the devil again.

Cathy's smile widened as she saw, rounding the corner of the house, Cray in the arms of Martha, his plump, grandmotherly nurse. Martha had been Cathy's nurse, too, almost from the moment of her birth. After Cathy's mother, Lady Caroline Aldley, had died when Cathy was only seven, Martha had completely taken over the job of raising the girl. Cathy loved the woman dearly, and Martha in turn was fiercely protective of both her and Cray. After some initial distrust on both sides, Jon had also been allowed into the magic circle of her devotion. Martha would have willingly laid down her life for any of the three of them, Cathy knew. But of them all, Cathy suspected that Cray was closest to Martha's heart, and she was glad.

"Daddy!" Cray shrieked happily upon seeing Jon. Cathy had to shake her head at the rather vulgar Americanism. Despite her own thorough Englishness, Cray was every inch an American, his father's true son. He even looked like Jon! The child's black curls, gray eyes, sturdy frame, and even occasional mulish expression were his father's all over again. Cathy sometimes wondered how on earth she was going to deal with another obstinate male when Cray was grown, then shrugged her shoulders. Needs must, as Martha was fond of saying.

"Daddy, Daddy!" Cray was struggling imperiously in Martha's arms. The woman obligingly set him on the ground. Jon hunkered down, laughing, opening his arms wide, as the little boy toddled across the smooth green lawn toward him. Reaching his goal at last, Cray gurgled with joy as he was caught and swung up high in his father's strong arms. Cathy felt her heart turn over with love as she watched the two of them. They meant more to her than all the world, and she thanked God every day for the twist of fate which had given them to her.

Jon tossed Cray high in the air and caught him while the baby shrieked with glee. Cathy shook her head, smiling as she watched her tall, muscular husband tussle with his tiny son. Then she hurried out of the house and onto the back lawn before anything untoward could occur. Cray had just finished his supper, and when over-excited had a tendency to lose it in a most disconcerting fashion.

"All right, you two, that's enough of your foolishness," she reproved with mock sternness as she walked across the grass to join them. Jon grinned at her cheekily. Cray, watching his father, did likewise. Cathy had to laugh. They were as alike as two watermelons!

"Yes, ma'am," Jon said meekly as he set his son down.

"Yes, ma'am," Cray piped an echo, clutching Jon's long leg for balance. Cathy laughed again, scooping the child up and giving him a quick hug. Cray cuddled into her neck while Jon's arm slid around her waist, pulling her close as he planted a quick hard kiss on her soft lips. Cathy returned it lovingly, feeling the familiar quickening begin inside her. It never failed to amaze her how, after more than two years together and the birth of a son, Jon's touch could still make her go weak at the knees. At first she had considered it shameful, thinking that a lady of her breeding, daughter of an earl and descendant of one of England's most illustrious families, should find a man's physical attentions coolly distasteful at best. "Close your eyes and think of England," was the way most ladies of her class described their approach to the marital act. For a long time Cathy had wondered a little fearfully at her own very different response, but repetition had accustomed her to it. Besides, she knew that Jon found her ardor in bed extremely exciting, and exciting Jon had very definite rewards.

"Hungry?" she asked her husband prosaically, to cover thoughts that were rapidly beginning to get out of hand.

"Starving," Jon replied with a devilish gleam, then leaned closer to murmur in her ear, "for you."

Cathy blushed, shooting him a laughing, reproving glance. Martha watched this little piece of by-play indulgently. For all Master Jon's wild ways, he made Miss Cathy happy, and that, in Martha's opinion, was the important thing.

"It's time the young master here was abed," Martha told Cathy stolidly, reaching out her hands for Cray.

"Don't want to go to bed!" Cray announced mutinously, then looked surprised as his small pink mouth opened wide in an involuntary yawn. Cathy chuckled, passing him over to Martha.

"You're tired, precious," she said, bending close to kiss his plump baby cheek. When he still looked unhappy, Jon leaned over to whisper something in his son's ear that made the child chortle with glee. To Cathy's amazement, there were no more protests as Martha bore him off, Cray's arms clutched contentedly around the woman's neck.

"What on earth did you say to him?" she demanded of her husband bemusedly as she watched Martha carrying the still beaming child away.

"Man talk," Jon answered with an aggravating grin. Cathy could only shake her head as Martha disappeared with Cray onto the long verandah that ran along the back of the pillared brick plantation house.

"Alone at last!" Jon breathed, his eyes teasing. Before Cathy could guess what he was about he snatched her off her feet and swung her around in a wide circle, then proceeded to kiss her with a thoroughness that left her breathless.

"Jon!" Cathy protested laughingly when she could again speak. "The servants!" She looked meaningfully toward the half-dozen or so opened windows which looked out onto the back lawn.

Jon's answering grin was wolfish.

"What do you mean, you shameless hussy, keeping me from my supper by your wiles?" he roared, his eyes dancing with amusement as they took in Cathy's discomfiture. When she would have opened her mouth to remonstrate with him, he whirled her about so that she was pointing in the direction of the house, administering a sharp slap to her rounded posterior. Cathy jumped, giggled helplessly, then allowed herself to be propelled toward the house by the hard arm that curved close around her slim waist.

They strolled for a moment in silence. Cathy breathed in deeply, loving the smell of the waxy white blossoms of the magnolia trees that stood sentinel by the back door. Pressed close against her side she could feel the sweat-dampness of Jon's shirt, and beneath it the work-hardened muscularity of his ribcage.

"You work too hard," she remarked seriously, stretching

up on tiptoe to press a soft kiss to his sandpaper cheek. His arm tightened around her waist at the loving little gesture.

"So reward me," he advised her, looking down with a smile at the lovely little face turned up so earnestly to his. At what he saw there one eyebrow quirked upward and he chuckled.

"You've got dirt on your nose," he said, flicking it with his forefinger. Cathy wrinkled the maligned member, her eyes crossing as she tried to see the offending streak for herself.

"It's no wonder. You're filthy. What have you been doing, wallowing in the dirt?"

"Just about. The ground is so dry from this drought that we kick up clouds of dust just walking through the fields. If we don't get some rain soon the cotton will be burnt to a crisp."

His tone was unusually serious. Cathy looked up at him, her expression troubled. She knew that making Woodham, inherited two years ago in deplorable condition from his estranged father, a paying proposition again was vitally important to Jon. Although she was a wealthy woman in her own right, Jon obstinately refused to touch a penny of her money, insisting on supporting her and Cray and the plantation on what capital remained from his years as a pirate captain and on what the plantation itself could produce. He had never said so, but Cathy was aware that Jon was determined that she, used to every luxury before her marriage, should not have any the less because of it. It was useless to try to persuade him that expensive dresses and jewelry and furnishings meant less than nothing to her compared with him or Cray. His fierce pride refused to let him believe her. His hardheadedness exasperated Cathy mightily. Still, she was deeply proud of him for his never-ending struggle to bring Woodham back to life again.

At Cathy's extended silence, Jon glanced down at her, his

brow wrinkled inquiringly. Noting her concerned expression, he mentally damned himself for worrying her, and promptly attempted to distract her attention by giving her luscious bottom a playful pinch.

"Forget about the drought," he advised as she squealed protestingly. "Woodham has survived worse, believe me. We're not quite at the point where you'll have to do without all your pretty gew-gaws. However, it *would* help if you could eat a bit less. . . ."

Cathy chuckled at his banter, and proceeded to repay his impertinence by digging him in the ribs with her sharp little elbow. He grunted as she made painful contact, then grabbed for her, intent on administering suitable punishment. She twisted away adroitly, giggling as she picked up her skirts and sprinted for the house. Jon followed close on her heels.

"You'll pay for that, minx," he threatened, coming up behind her as she dodged through the back door and scampered for the parlor. She shrieked as his warm breath on the back of her neck warned her of his closeness. But it was too late. His strong arms were around her, snatching her high against his chest.

"Mercy! Have mercy, oh captain pirate!" she gurgled between helpless peals of laughter as he growled with mock ferocity and bore her off toward the stairs.

"Never!" he hissed evilly, starting up the wide, curving staircase with Cathy still imprisoned securely in his arms. She struggled in mock fright, squirming and kicking up her legs in a froth of white petticoats. Happening to glance back down into the hall, her movements stilled abruptly. Petersham, Jon's wiry little valet and the household's mainstay, was looking up at them with amused resignation.

"Shall I tell Cook to put dinner back, Master Jon?" he asked in an extremely dry voice.

"Yes!" Jon tossed the word at his old friend with a twinkle, already halfway up the stairs with his now-quiet burden.

"No!" Cathy countermanded quickly. "Petersham, don't you dare! Jon, we're having guests, don't you remember?"

Then, in a muttered aside to Jon, she added, "For heaven's sake, put me down! What on earth must Petersham be thinking?"

Jon grinned. "I'm sure Petersham's thinking is right on the money, as usual," he replied, not even bothering to lower his voice, and continued on up the stairs without making any kind of move to suggest that he would comply with Cathy's demand.

Cathy, looking back down into the hall with pinkened cheeks, saw that Petersham had permitted himself an answering grin. With an indignant snort she glared at him. Really, these males! When it came to dealings with the fairer sex, they stuck together as if glued!

"Uh—the guests are scheduled for half past eight, if I remember correctly, and it is now gone seven," Petersham called after them, wiping the offending grin from his face as he encountered Cathy's darkling look. "Shall I have water for a bath sent up, Master Jon?"

"Later, Petersham, much later," Jon answered shamelessly, gaining the upper landing and striding off down the hall with his crimsoning prisoner.

"*Now*, Petersham," Cathy wailed over Jon's shoulder, already resigning herself to the inevitability of being disobeyed.

To her surprise, she wasn't. Jon had no sooner shouldered his way into their bedroom and snatched a lusty kiss than there was a discreet tap on the door.

"Who the hell . . . ?" Jon muttered belligerently, eyeing the offending portal with smoldering eyes. The tap sounded again, and he very reluctantly set Cathy on her feet, striding across to the door and flinging it open.

"Yes?" Jon snapped. The unaccustomed shortness of his tone nearly caused Tyler, the young black houseboy who stood there, to drop the steaming buckets he held in either hand. As it was, the sight of his tall, awe-inspiring master, clearly displeased at being disturbed, glowering down at him, made Tyler gulp, and take a hasty step backward. He was brought up short as he stumbled into Micah, the other houseboy who stood, similarly laden, behind him. Petersham, standing behind them both, clucked disapprovingly as the water in all four buckets sloshed alarmingly. Jon's eyes fastened themselves on Petersham.

"Sorry, Master Jon, but you did look dirty," Petersham explained hastily, shooing the boys into the room before Master Jon could explode, as he looked on the verge of doing. Jon looked his valet over slowly as the boys proceeded to fill the dainty porcelain tub that stood, discreetly shielded by a silk-upholstered screen, in one corner of the room.

"This isn't the first time my wife has incited you to mutiny, old friend. I'm getting rather tired of it." Jon sounded menacing. Cathy hastily muffled a smile. It was still something of a sore point with him that his pirate crew, of whom Petersham had been one, had been won over to a man by Cathy in the days before she had become their captain's wife. Before her arrival on board his ship, Jon had been accustomed to his crew's unquestioning loyalty and total obedience. He still felt slightly disgruntled when he remembered how easily his men had been converted to her cause.

"Sorry, Master Jon," Petersham said again, looking properly abashed. Then, as the houseboys, having completed their task, scuttled from the room, he added, "I'll send Martha along in a quarter-hour to help you dress, Miss Cathy, if that suits you."

"Thank you, Petersham," Cathy approved before Jon could say anything. Petersham, recognizing from long experience storm signals in his master's stiff stance, hurriedly took himself off. Jon glowered at the closed door.

"That old reprobate will go too far one day," he prophesied darkly, then grimaced with reluctant humor as Cathy, no longer able to control her amusement, laughed.

"Petersham's right. You're filthy," Cathy told him firmly as he made as if to reach for her again. "And I have to get dressed. There'll be plenty of time later for—for—*that.*"

"Oh, *that,* is it?" Jon grinned, ignoring her attempts to elude him and catching her around the waist. "And what makes you think I want *that?*"

Cathy looked up at him through her lashes, a roguish dimple appearing briefly in one cheek.

"The signs are unmistakable, my love," she said demurely, twisting away from him with a supple movement. "But you'll just have to wait."

"And if I choose not to?" he challenged, but Cathy only laughed as she whisked away into the adjoining dressing-room.

When she came back, a sky-blue silk dinner dress that was part of the new summer wardrobe Jon had insisted on having made for her hanging over her arm, he was already ensconced in the tub. Cathy eyed him with idle interest, taking in the broad bare shoulders and dark-furred chest, the steel muscled arms tanned to a teak brown by days of laboring shirtless under the broiling sun. His knees were drawn up almost to his chest to enable his big body to fit into the small tub. Water glistened on his hair and skin and lapped modestly around his waist, hiding that most essential part of him from her view. He looked slightly ridiculous and wholly adorable. Cathy smiled tenderly at him.

"Wash my back," he invited throatily, looking up in time to catch her eyes on him. Cathy considered, then shook her head.

"I fear for my virtue, sir," she teased.

"Coward," he grunted disappointedly, and, surrendering to the inevitable, proceeded to soap his arms and chest. Cathy watched him for a moment, weakening. At age thirty-six he was still the handsomest man she had ever seen, taller by far than average and corded with muscle, his black hair curling wetly around his head. His gray eyes were veiled at the moment by long silky eyelashes, the only feminine touch in an otherwise totally masculine face. Just the sight of that long mouth with its twisting smile was enough to make her heart beat faster. Jon looked up again then, and correctly interpreted the look in her eyes. He smiled broadly as he leaned back in the tub.

"Come here, sweetheart," he directed softly. Cathy flushed, and looked hurriedly away.

"Don't be silly. We're having guests to dinner in less than an hour." She busied herself by laying her dress out on the bed.

"An hour's plenty of time for what I have in mind. In fact, the way I feel right now, it won't take a quarter of that." Jon grinned wickedly at her hot cheeks.

"I have to get dressed," Cathy told him, but even to herself her voice lacked conviction.

"Not just yet." Jon drawled the words as he stood up. Water streamed down his body, flattening the fine black pelt which covered him, parting at his swollen manhood to flow down his long legs.

Cathy's eyes widened to saucers and she backed as he stepped out of the tub onto the highly polished wooden floor. Water formed big pools at his feet as he moved toward her.

"Jon, no!" she protested weakly, still backing around the foot of the bed. "We're having people to dinner! We don't have time! I don't want. . . ."

"Liar," he chided softly, his hands shooting out to capture her soft upper arms. "You do want, and I want, and, since you're my wife, I mean to take advantage of the fact. So shut your mouth, woman, and kiss me."

Cathy was pulled hard against his soaking chest, feeling the wetness and heat of it penetrate her thin gown, and looked up into his face with a mixture of amusement, irritation, and love.

"You're impossible," she accused severely, her hands coming up to rest on the wide expanse of his shoulders. A small girl, she didn't come much higher than that, and she had to tilt her head way back to see into his face. The blazing desire in his gray eyes fanned an answering spark in her. Cathy could make no further protest as he bent his head toward her.

"So I've been told," he murmured as their lips met, and then neither of them could speak for a very long while. His kiss was deep and gentle, reminding her of past, shared pleasures and hinting of even more wondrous enjoyment to come. Cathy returned it freely, her inhibitions lost in the wave of longing she felt for him. Seductively she pressed her curved shape against his larger, naked one, quivering as she felt the unmistakable proof of his passion prodding her belly. Eyes closed, oblivious to everything except the pleasure he was giving her and that she wanted to return, her hands stroked down his bare back, molding the strong spine, running teasingly over the hard curve of his buttocks. They tensed beneath her caress, his breathing quickening noticeably. He raised his lips a little away from hers. Cathy opened her eyes to find him looking down at her with a hot intensity that made her heartbeat quicken threefold.

"You're beautiful," he told her thickly. Cathy smiled.

"So are you," she answered with shameless honesty. Jon groaned a laugh before covering her lips with his once again. Cathy felt the tremor in his arms as he swung her up in them and deposited her in the middle of their big bed, following her down. His mouth took hers hungrily, seeking, exploring, while his hands ran over her body, palms flat as they found each soft, feminine curve beneath her dress. His mouth left hers to trail across her cheek, nibble on her ear, then slide down the quivering cord of her neck to feast on the rounded swell of her bosom just visible above the neckline of her dress.

Cathy's arms were locked around his neck and she pressed small, teasing kisses along the salt-tanged line of his shoulder as his arms went around her, his fingers busy as they tried to undo the numerous hooks that fastened the dress up the back. He succeeded with several without too much difficulty, but one halfway down seemed to defeat him. Silently he struggled with it until Cathy, finally becoming aware of his difficulty and his frustrated passion, giggled. Jon raised himself a little away from her, looking down into her face with something that was not quite a smile in his eyes.

"Laugh at me, will you, minx?" he growled "Well, I'll soon teach you better manners!"

With that he reached down with mock violence to grasp the hem of her dress and jerk it up around her waist. Then his fingers moved to the drawstring of her lace-trimmed pantalets, untying it and tugging them down.

"Jon, no!" Cathy protested, feeling duty-bound to do so. The way he was planning to take her was not proper, she knew. According to the tenets of the time, married people were supposed to make love with as much dignity as the act allowed, not couple in broad daylight with the woman still half dressed, like a wench being tumbled in a haystack!

"Cathy, yes," he answered mockingly as he dragged her pantalets off, leaving her naked from the waist down except for the hem of her chemise and her silk stockings, held around her slim thighs by lacy blue garters. A froth of yellow skirts and white petticoats nearly covered the upper portion of her body. Cathy gasped, wriggling, as Jon's hand slid to the blonde triangle of hair between her legs. Then, as he wouldn't let her go, his fingers caressing her, she quivered and went still.

"Still no?" he murmured teasingly after a while, watching her flushed face with pleasure. Cathy felt her color deepen, aware of his eyes on her but unable to control the instinctive movement of her hips.

"I love you," she told him softly, her eyes flickering open

to meet his. Jon's face changed, his eyes darkening passionately. At his expression Cathy felt a sudden fierce tightening in her belly.

Jon lowered his head to take her mouth in a devouring kiss, his tongue and lips telling her what he still found hard to put into words. Cathy clung to him unashamedly, her body writhing beneath his, eager for his possession. He groaned at the feel of her soft, undulating flesh, covering her body with his, his muscled thighs pressing her legs apart. Cathy opened them willingly, her nails raking lightly across his sweat-dampened back, returning his kisses with a passion equal to his. With a single hard thrust he took her. The exquisite sensation left them both gasping. Jon began to move, rapidly at first and then more slowly, pausing, teasing, until Cathy strained against him frantically, her eyes closed, her lips parted as she panted for air.

"Jon, Jon, Jon," she moaned his name over and over, unaware that she was doing so, her hands making beseeching little movements against his back as she urged him to finish. Finally, when she thought she couldn't stand it any longer, he withdrew almost all the way. Cathy squirmed against him, her eyes opening in protest. He was watching her, his eyes burning as they took in her desire.

"Want me?" he demanded huskily, his breath rasping hoarsely in his throat.

"Yes, oh, yes!" Cathy gasped, mindless with longing, her hands clutching his broad back, her body moving wantonly against his. With a strangled groan he thrust deep inside her. Cathy cried out, clasping him to her, while his arms tightened around her body like a clamp. She felt him shuddering inside her and gave herself up to ecstasy.

It was some little time later before Cathy became fully aware again. Her heart had slowly resumed its normal rhythm, and her breathing was once again regular. Jon still lay sprawled across her, his big body almost crushing her smaller one. His head was beside hers on the pillow. She turned to look at him, one finger coming up to lovingly trace his hard features. At her touch he opened his eyes, his own warming as they moved over her face.

"Wife," he said on a note of intense satisfaction, and kissed the slender finger she pressed to his lips.

Cathy smiled at him, opening her mouth to tease him about his reluctance to say the three simple words she wanted to hear. On the rare occasions when he did bring himself to the point of telling her how much he loved her, he was almost sheepish, embarrassed at having to admit to such a thing. Jon belonged to the world of tough, ruggedly masculine men; to confess to feeling an emotion as soft as love was difficult for him. But he had proved his love over and over again with deeds, and Cathy was content.

"Don't. . . ." she began, meaning to add teasingly, "you have something to tell me," when a sharp rap sounded on the door. Cathy started, for all the world like someone caught out in a misdemeanor. Jon grinned at her.

"Don't worry, love, what we just did is perfectly proper." He mocked her discomposure in an undertone, dropping a hard kiss on her mouth before levering himself off the bed. "We're married, remember?"

"Oh, hush," Cathy told him, blushing as his eyes kindled again as they touched on the wanton display she made, skirts raised around her waist, naked limbs sprawled across the flowered silk bedspread.

The knock sounded again, even more peremptorily. Cathy slid off the bed, hastily straightening her skirts and raising her hands to brush ineffectively at her hair, which was tumbling in a golden riot from its pins. Jon watched her efforts, still as naked as the day he was born, hands resting lightly on his hips while a faint smile curved his mouth.

"You look as if you just got out of bed," he observed, tongue-in-cheek. Cathy glared at him.

"Miss Cathy?" The voice on the other side of the door was Martha's, as Cathy had known it would be. "Miss Cathy, it's almost eight o'clock, and your guests will be arriving soon. Shall I help you dress?"

Jon chuckled softly as Cathy went, still struggling uselessly with her hair, to open the door. Before she reached it he padded away into the dressing room. As she let Martha into the room she heard him bellow loudly for Petersham.

Martha's eyes were twinkling as they touched on Cathy's flushed face and obvious deshabille before moving knowingly to the half-empty bath, the puddles standing on the floor, and the rumpled state of the bed. But for once the woman chose to remain tactfully silent. She walked over to the bed without casting more than a single look in Cathy's direction, straightened the covers, picked up Cathy's discarded pantalets and put them in the basket reserved for soiled clothing, then with an arrested expression moved down to the foot of the bed. Cathy watched, puzzled, as Martha worked to free something from the space between the mattress and the footboard.

"My dress!" she gasped, horror-stricken, as she recognized the crumpled folds of material that Martha was shaking out.

"You won't be wearing this one, I fancy. And just as well, if it's one of them indecent ones that you just had made up."

"They're not indecent!" Cathy defended hotly for what must have been the hundredth time. "The low-cut bodice is the latest fashion! And you needn't look so smug, Martha. I'll just wear another of my new ones, and they're all cut the same way!"

"I declare, Miss Cathy, sometimes you are a disgrace!" Martha muttered as she put the crumpled dress aside. Cathy ignored her, sluicing her face and hands with cool water from the pitcher on the stand near the bed.

Martha maintained a disapproving silence as she helped Cathy to undress, not even lowering her dignity enough to remark on the fact that the job was already half done. When Cathy had washed, Martha assisted her into fresh pantalets. The dropped shoulder, low-necked styling of the new evening dresses Martha objected to would not permit the wearing of a chemise. Martha, grim-faced, laced Cathy into her stays, tightening the strings with some satisfaction until Cathy was gasping and her waist measured no more than the fashionable hand's span. Then she dropped the required three petticoats over Cathy's head and rolled gossamer stockings onto her legs, all the while refusing to utter so much as a syllable.

"Oh, go get my dress. The blush pink one," Cathy was driven into snapping finally, naming another of the offending garments. With an audible sniff Martha did as she was bidden, while Cathy, draping a shawl about her shoulders for modesty's sake, sat down at the dressing table and proceeded to try to brush some of the tangles from her hair. Martha came back with the dress before Cathy had made much headway, and, after laying the dress on the bed, took the brush from her young mistress. She began to brush out Cathy's long hair without a word.

"Cathy, have you seen my razor? I can't seem to find it anywhere."

Jon stood in the open doorway between the bedroom and the dressing room, one shoulder propped negligently against the jamb. He was dressed in the sumptuous crimson brocade dressing gown that had been Cathy's present to him on their first wedding anniversary. Shaving lather obscured the lower third of his face. Through the dressing table mirror Cathy saw an appreciative glint appear in his eyes as they ran over her, dressed as she was in her underclothes with her golden hair hanging in loose waves to her waist.

"I borrowed it," she confessed guiltily, turning to face him. Jon straightened, coming a little further into the room.

"You borrowed it? What for?" He sounded surprised, as well he might.

Cathy cast a quick look over her shoulder at Martha. If she told the truth her old nurse would rant for hours; Martha's notions of what was and what was not proper behavior for a lady of good family were extremely rigid. The woman was already eyeing her with suspicion, while Jon waited for her reply with interest.

"I shaved my legs." Throwing caution to the winds, Cathy announced it defiantly. "According to *Godey's Ladies' Book*, it's de rigueur with the new sheer silk stockings."

The effect of this pronouncement on her audience was immediate. Martha visibly swelled, while Jon grinned, his eyes dancing.

"I can't say that I noticed the difference," Jon murmured outrageously, looking amused as he came to retrieve his property, which Cathy held out to him.

"Miss Cathy, are you shameless?" Martha demanded rhetorically as soon as she recovered her power of speech. "What would your sainted mother say? The only kind of ladies who do things like that are—well, they are *not* ladies!"

Jon was grinning widely as he vanished back into the dressing room. He found Martha's scolds hilarious. And so would she, Cathy reflected sourly as she listened to this seemingly endless one, if they weren't always directed at her.

"Oh, Martha, do hush!" Cathy finally was driven into snapping. "I'm a married lady now, and I can do as I please!"

"Married lady indeed!" Martha sniffed. "Yes, that you are, for all the good it does either of us! I must say that I'm surprised at Master Jon for letting you carry on the way you do. He spoils you, that's what it is. Any proper husband would put his foot down! Putting scent in your bath is bad enough—and yes, miss, I can smell it on you, so don't think to fool me—but shaving your legs . . . ! Well, it's all of a piece, if I may say so!"

After that Cathy listened to the monologue in fuming silence as Martha styled her hair. If only the woman would go away, she would very much like to put a dab of rice powder, which she kept hidden in a drawer of the dressing table, on her nose. But even more than scent, or low-cut dresses, Martha disapproved of a lady painting her face. *If I listened to her, I'd be a regular dowd,* Cathy thought resentfully, but could not quite find the courage to openly defy her old nurse by applying the powder in front of her.

When Martha had finished arranging her hair in the elegant looped style that Cathy had lately taken to preferring for evening, Cathy pushed the stool back from the dressing table and stood up. Martha, still grumbling under her breath, went to fetch the disputed evening dress from the bed.

"Stand still," she ordered Cathy, returning, and threw the dress expertly over the girl's head without disturbing a lock of her coiffure. As the dress settled Martha twitched it into place, then moved around behind Cathy's back to do it up. Her mouth was pinched disapprovingly all the while.

"And don't think I don't know about that powder in your dressing table, either," Martha said sharply out of the blue, just as Cathy was beginning to hope the scold was over for the night. Cathy sighed. Really, that was the trouble with servants who had known one from one's cradle, she thought irritably. They thought they owned you, and could do or say just whatever they pleased. She thought wistfully of how nice it would be to have a regular lady's maid, one who did as she was told and spoke only to say "Yes, ma'am" or "No, ma'am" in respectful tones. Then, regretfully, she dismissed the notion. Martha's scolds sprang from love and concern, and Cathy knew that she would miss the woman dreadfully if she ever had to do without her.

When the dress was fastened, Cathy moved to stand in front of the long mirror that stood on its stand near the dressing table, while Martha watched grimly. Cathy ignored the woman's sour look as she critically inspected her reflection. The dress was a little extreme, Cathy had to admit, although wild horses couldn't have dragged such a confession from her aloud. It bared her softly rounded shoulders, the neckline straight across, resting on, and seemingly held up by, the pointed crests of her bosom. Her creamy shoulders and the gleaming upper slopes of her breasts were left totally bare, and the shadowy hollow between the twin peaks was clearly visible. Except for the flowing flounce that edged the neckline, the bodice was perfectly plain, clinging tightly to the curves of her figure as it descended into the new pointed waistline before flaring out into an enormous, bell-like skirt that reduced her waist to nothingness. Even the color, deeper than the pastel pinks worn by young girls for years, was new. It seemed to shimmer with a life of its own, though the sheen of the silk was no smoother than her pearly skin, or more glowing than her golden hair. As a final touch, Cathy added her long rope of pearls which she wore looped twice around her neck, and matching pearl eardrops. Standing back, she knew that she had never looked lovelier, but still she felt—just ever so slightly—overexposed.

"A trifle—uh—revealing, wouldn't you say?" Jon had left the dressing room and crossed to stand behind her, his hands resting lightly on her shoulders as he studied her reflection. "Have you left something off? Like a blouse?"

"Very funny," Cathy retorted, thinking how handsome he looked in his formal black evening clothes. "You sound more like a husband every day. I remember a time when you would have loved this dress."

"You mistake my meaning, sweetheart. I do—uh—love it. What I *don't* love is the idea of our male guests ogling my wife, as they are sure to do." Here he slanted a glance at Martha, who stood silently by, the look on her face expressing more clearly than words could have her approval of what he was saying. "Don't you agree, Martha?"

"Oh, for goodness' sake, don't get her started again! That's all I've heard from her for weeks!" Cathy was half-laughing as she turned from the mirror. "Anyway, Captain Hale, kindly remember that it was you who insisted that I have a new summer wardrobe, much against my wishes, I might add. You have only yourself to blame if the style is too extreme for you. Besides, don't you think I look nice?"

"Very nice," he agreed lazily. "And far be it from me to stand in the way of fashion! But don't be surprised if old Mr. Graves pours his soup down his shirtfront instead of his throat, all from admiring your charms." He ran a teasing finger along the low neckline of the gown.

Cathy laughed, reaching up on tiptoe to plant a kiss on his curling mouth.

"There, what did I tell you? Jon's not so stuffy," she said triumphantly to Martha. The older woman sniffed.

"As I said before, he spoils you. I only hope he doesn't live to regret it." This last was muttered under Martha's breath, but, as intended, it was perfectly audible. Cathy, very much on her dignity, chose to ignore it. Jon, with a smile at Martha, followed Cathy's lead.

From downstairs came the sounds of the first guests arriving. Cathy hurried to pick up her gloves and fan. Then she gave Martha a quick, conciliatory hug before taking Jon's proffered arm.

"What a handsome couple we make," Cathy thought as she caught a glimpse in the gilt-framed mirror adorning one wall of the entryway of their figures descending the stairs side by side. Jon was so tall and dark, topping her head and shoulders. Beside his commanding masculinity she looked small and fragile, absurdly young to be his wife and the mother of a year-old son. She met his eyes in the mirror, and by his slight frown she knew that he was entertaining similar thoughts. She smiled at him, and after a moment he smiled slowly back.

Besides Mr. Graves, the elderly gentleman who owned the plantation nearest Woodham, there were his wife, Ruth, and daughter, Millicent, awaiting them in the reception room. Cathy was fond of both Mr. and Mrs. Graves, who had gone out of their way to make the Hales welcome to the area, but Millicent was something else again. Nearly thirty, and extremely plain, she had never married. She dressed as befitted a very young girl, and simpered endlessly in her desire to appear youthful. But what really rankled with Cathy was that Millicent never let an opportunity pass to make sheep's eyes at Jon. Jon, to his credit, blandly ignored the whole thing.

As Cathy turned from greeting these first guests, the remainder of the company began to arrive. In short order the room was filled with chattering people. Cathy and Jon separated, circulating and exchanging light small talk with the new arrivals. Cathy, watching Jon laughing politely over a matron's description of her daughter's many suitors, felt a rush of love for him.

Dinner passed smoothly, although Cathy was hard put to it not to laugh when Mr. Graves, true to Jon's predictions, spilled his soup all over his frilled white shirt. Cathy caught Jon's eye, saw his lips twitching humorously, and looked hurriedly away, biting her lip. For the next few minutes she concentrated her attention on Gerald Bates, a contemporary of Jon's who sat on her left hand. By the time she was once again free to turn to Mr. Graves, the urge to laugh had passed.

After dinner, the ladies left the gentlemen to enjoy their cigars and brandy in peace while they retired to the drawing room to sip tea and gossip. It was some half-hour later before the gentlemen rejoined them. As they strolled into the room it was immediately apparent that they had drunk more than was considered proper. Gerald Bates was laughing just a touch too loudly, while some of the other gentlemen were very red of face. Jon was smilingly urbane as always. Cathy marveled, as she sometimes did, at his apparent capacity for drink. The only time she had ever seen him the worse for it was after Cray's birth, and even then, according to Petersham, Jon had consumed enough straight whiskey to fell a team of horses before showing it.

Cathy threw a reproving look at Jon, blaming him silently for letting their male guests get in such a state. He intercepted it and correctly deciphered its meaning, looking so penitent that Cathy had to smile in spite of herself. He rewarded her softening with a lopsided smile of his own that he knew from experience she found hard to resist. When she still eyed him severely, he made as if to come toward her.

"Won't you play for us, Lady Cathy?" Gerald Bates' over-loud voice forestalled him. Cathy wanted to decline, but could think of no reasonable excuse for doing so. Instead, smiling at her guests' polite urgings, she crossed to the small grand piano situated in one corner of the room, and seated herself without fanfare on the padded bench.

"What would you like to hear?" Cathy turned her head to smile at the assembled company. When they assured her that anything she cared to play could not fail to delight them, Cathy launched into the lilting strains of a waltz. Gerald Bates came to lean over the side of the instrument, watching her with poorly concealed pleasure. As she felt his eyes caressing the white flesh exposed by her gown, she began to wish fervently that he would go away. If he kept up his disgraceful perusal, there was bound to be trouble. Jon was fiercely possessive of everything he considered his property, and in his estimation Cathy was just that. If he was aware of it—as how could he not be?—he would not at all like the way Gerald was eyeing her. And Jon, if pushed, was entirely capable of laying Gerald flat on his back, guest in their house or not.

Cathy ended the waltz with a flourish, thankful that it was over. But before she could get to her feet she felt a swathe of soft cashmere drop over her shoulders. Startled, she looked around to find Jon standing behind her, regarding Gerald with a smile that could only be described as tigerish.

"I thought you might be growing chilly," he said, transferring his attention to her after he was certain that Gerald had gotten the message.

"Thank you, darling," Cathy replied meekly, wrapping the shawl around herself so that it covered the most extreme parts of her décolletage and rising as Gerald silently melted away. "I was a trifle cold."

She took Jon's arm and allowed him to lead her back to her chair, all the while silently congratulating him on his self-control. He could be violently jealous, which Cathy forgave because she knew that it sprang from a deep-rooted insecurity bred by his earlier dealings with women. But she was hopeful that he was at last becoming convinced that her love for him was unshakeable, and his restraint in the face of tonight's provocation seemed to bear out this hope.

Jon remained at her side for the next forty minutes or so. Cathy had to smile at the spectacle of Gerald taking extreme care to stay well out of their way. But he was wise to do so, she had to admit. Jon as an opponent could be more than formidable. . . .

"Miss Cathy." Petersham stood at her elbow. Cathy blinked as she looked up at him. She had been miles away.

"What is it, Petersham?" Cathy's first thought was that Cray must be ill. Nothing less than that would induce Petersham to interrupt when they had guests.

"There's a man here with a letter for you, Miss Cathy. He says it's urgent."

"A letter?" Cathy repeated stupidly, feeling her heart begin to thump. An urgent letter could only mean that something was wrong. With a muttered word of excuse she got to her feet, following Petersham into the hall. As he had said, a man was waiting for her. Cathy paid scant attention to his voluble explanation as she took the letter with shaking hands and, tearing it open, scanned the contents. As she read, she turned as white as the paper in her hand.

"What's wrong, sweetheart?" Jon had come to stand in

the doorway between the drawing room and the hall. He was frowning as he probed Cathy's pale face. She looked up at him, her eyes tragic.

"Oh, Jon, it's—it's Papa," she choked, throwing herself into his arms and feeling them close comfortingly about her. "They say he's dying! I must go to him!"

two

England was certainly cooler than South Carolina, but that was about all that Cathy could say for it. It was raining as they drove through the streets, that dreary, never-ending drizzle so common to London in late September. Cathy, seated in a hired hack with Cray on her lap and Martha occupying the seat opposite, shivered as she huddled into the soft fur trimming of her cranberry wool pelisse. The steady clop-clop of the horse's hooves on the cobbled streets, the splash of the carriage wheels as they rolled through countless puddles, seemed to her to be the loneliest sound in the world. Does the whole country smell of worms? Cathy wondered dismally. Taking some comfort from the child's drowsy weight against her, she cuddled Cray closer. With every fiber of her being she longed for Jon.

He had had to stay behind at Woodham, of course. With the cotton so near to harvest it would have been pure folly for him to leave. Cathy knew that, had even pointed it out to Jon himself when he had suggested accompanying her. But the real sticking point, the incontrovertible fact that had caused Cathy to almost implore him to stay at home, was this: in England, Jon was an escaped felon, convicted of piracy and murder. If caught, he would be summarily hanged.

"We've stopped, Miss Cathy." Martha spoke for almost the first time since they had set out from the docks nearly an hour before. The sound of her voice jerked Cathy back to the present. She leaned forward to peer out the near side window, using her bare hand to wipe a little circle of glass clear of condensation. From the outside, her Aunt Elizabeth's, Lady Stanhope's, fashionable Grosvenor Square townhouse looked exactly the same as it had two years before. Three stories tall, made of red brick with a delicately wrought, black-painted iron fence separating it from the street, it was as imposing as the lady herself. And as Cathy remembered only too well from her one previous visit, the house was as strictly correct inside as out. Formality was the unbending rule in manners as well as furnishings. Cathy had stayed there for nearly three months while she was pregnant with Cray and had thought herself deserted by her husband. That visit had been distinguished only by its sheer misery.

"You gettin' out, lady?" The truculent tone of the cabbie as he stood holding open the carriage door, rain dripping from the brim of his hat, pulled Cathy from her reverie. She passed Cray, who had finally fallen asleep, to Martha and stood up. Martha was visibly bristling at the man's rudeness. Cathy, who didn't think that she could bear any additional unpleasantness, quelled her with a stern look.

"Cover your head, lovey, it's raining," Martha advised as Cathy prepared to descend, contenting herself with fixing the cabbie with one long, contemptuous stare. Cathy did as she was told, pulling the hood of her pelisse over her head as she stepped lightly from the carriage. Martha followed, a thick silk shawl draped over herself and Cray. The cabbie, having insisted on being paid in advance, barely took time to throw their baggage into the street before remounting his seat and driving away. Cathy looked with some dismay at the piles of luggage left standing on the curb, slowly becoming drenched. Then, with a resigned shrug, she turned her back on the depressing sight and marched firmly up to the door.

"Good afternoon, my lady," said Sims the butler, as he opened the door to her brief knock. He didn't sound at all surprised to see her. Cathy supposed that her aunt must have assumed she would come, and so informed her servants. There had been no time to reply to that fateful letter before setting out.

"Good afternoon, Sims." Cathy's reply was equally matter-of-fact. As the butler held the door wide she walked past him into the marble-floored foyer, closely followed by Martha with Cray. Martha exchanged cold glances with Sims as she passed him. They had been at war throughout the one previous time Cathy had stayed in this house.

"Lady Stanhope is in the small drawing room, my lady," Sims informed her in his funereal voice.

"And my father?" Cathy questioned softly.

"He is upstairs, in the green bedroom, my lady. I am sorry to tell you that his condition is not much improved. May I say how sorry we all are that such a thing should happen to Sir Thomas, my lady."

"Thank you, Sims. I will go up to him at once. Please show Martha where we are to sleep, and have someone bring in our things. I fear they are getting sadly wet."

"Very good, my lady." Not by so much as the flicker of an eyelash did Sims betray his surprise at Cathy's lack of manners. The correct thing would have been for her to greet her aunt, who was, after all, her hostess, and perhaps drink a cup of tea before going upstairs. Cathy was perfectly aware of her breach of etiquette, but truthfully she did not feel up to facing her aunt at the moment. She had not seen Lady Stanhope since Jon had stolen her away from this house in the middle of one snowy January night nearly two years ago, and she did not imagine that her aunt was overly eager to welcome her.

Left obviously pregnant after her notorious abduction by pirates, Cathy's first appearance in London society had caused quite a scandal. The story that her father and aunt had circulated about her being a grieving widow already carrying her late husband's posthumous child at the time of the kidnapping had been patently disbelieved. And then to have her disappear just when the talk was beginning to die down . . . ! Cathy's lips quivered with sudden humor. How on earth had Lady Stanhope managed to explain *that*?

"My dear!" Cathy's intention of going directly upstairs without seeing her aunt came to naught as the lady herself sailed into the foyer. Before Cathy knew quite what was happening, she was enfolded in a perfumed embrace. She returned it rather bemusedly. Whatever reception she had expected had certainly been nothing like this!

"Hello, Aunt Elizabeth," Cathy murmured politely when she was at last released, bestowing a gingerly peck on the rouged cheek that was presented for that purpose. "It's good to see you."

"Oh, my dear!" Lady Stanhope's voice was filled with emotion. Cathy blinked. Her aunt had always been reserved to the point of hauteur, a cold, majestic lady who cared for only two things: her son, Harold, who had acceded to the title of Lord Stanhope upon the death of his hapless father, and her position in society. Maybe she had been fonder of her only brother than Cathy had ever realized. Certainly that was the only thing Cathy could think of that might account for this bewildering volte-face.

"I see you brought the child." Lady Stanhope's expression was odd as she seemed to see for the first time Martha holding the still sleeping Cray. Cathy's chin went up at her tone. To Lady Stanhope and her son, Cray would always be nothing more or less than a disgrace. The thought made Cathy's blood boil.

"Certainly I brought my son! If it is not convenient, then

we would be more than happy to put up at an inn." The words were icy. Lady Stanhope looked taken aback. This self-assured creature bore no resemblance to the meek young girl who had stayed beneath her roof once before!

"No, no, I wouldn't hear of it! You are very welcome! Besides, you must want to be near poor Thomas!"

Cathy considered for a moment, then inclined her head. Lady Stanhope's slight emphasis on "you" when she said they were welcome had not escaped her. But for the time being her father's well-being must outweigh her pride.

"Thank you, Aunt. Now, if you don't mind, I should like to see my father. And if you would direct Sims to show Martha to a bedroom, I would be grateful. My son, as you can see, is already asleep."

"Oh, yes, my dear, of course," Lady Stanhope agreed hastily. Then she seemed to hesitate. "There is a matter of some urgency that I must discuss with you, Cathy. Perhaps we can talk first, and then you can visit Thomas. After all, it is not as if there is anything you can do for him."

"I would rather see my father first, if you don't mind, Aunt. Whatever it is can surely wait until after that."

"Yes, yes, I suppose it can," Lady Stanhope murmured without much conviction. "But, Cathy, there is something that should be made known to you. . . ."

"Later, Aunt, if you please," Cathy said firmly, turning away and starting up the stairs. Martha followed with Cray, and Sims, after a questioning glance at his mistress, brought up the rear. Lady Stanhope was left to frown thoughtfully after them.

"Miss Cathy! Oh, Miss Cathy, you came!" Mason, her father's valet for many, many years, opened the door to the green bedroom in response to her summons. The dapper little man was beaming, his eyes suspiciously moist as he greeted the girl he had known from her cradle. "Sir Thomas will be so pleased, Miss Cathy!"

Cathy, knowing that Mason was genuinely devoted to Sir Thomas and more than fond of herself, felt an answering dampness in her own eyes as she returned his smile.

"Did you think I wouldn't come, Mason?" she inquired gently as he stood aside to let her enter.

"I knew you would, Miss Cathy. It was Lord Stanhope who thought you might not."

"Well, Lord Stanhope was wrong, as he is more often than not." Cathy's voice was slightly tart. She had never liked Harold, and she knew the feeling was mutual. "How is my father?"

"Not very well, Miss Cathy, I'm sorry to say," Mason told her sadly, his voice dropping to a whisper as he trailed after her to stand beside the huge four-poster bed. "He had been feeling rather low for some time—missing you, he said—and then he came up to London for the races. He—he had the attack almost at once. In this very room. His whole right side is paralyzed, Miss Cathy, and he is rarely conscious for more than a quarter-hour at a time. It's pitiful, truly it is."

Cathy merely nodded in reply, the lump in her throat grown so huge that she didn't think she could speak. Gazing down at the frail outline, barely visible beneath the piled quilts, of what had once been her handsome, robust father, she felt her heart constrict. The hair that had been as golden as her own when she had last seen him was now flecked with gray, and the face turned into the pillow was pinched and white. He looked terribly old, Cathy thought, and for the first time she admitted to herself the possibility that he might die. All the way across the Atlantic she had refused to consider it, comforting herself with the notion that all Sir Thomas needed was the careful, loving nursing of his daughter to set him to rights again. Now she saw that the case was far more desperate than she had let herself believe.

"Oh, Papa!" she choked, dropping to her knees beside the bed and groping for her father's emaciated hand. "Papa, it's Cathy. I'm here, Papa."

The closed eyelids flickered open for a moment, and the faded blue eyes seemed to see her. His breath escaped in a rasping sigh. Cathy held his hand tightly, tears spilling from her eyes.

"Cathy." Her name was just a husky whisper, barely audible although she strained to hear. The hand she was holding squeezed hers for an instant, and then went limp. His eyes closed once more.

"Papa!" Cathy pressed a kiss to the paper-thin flesh of his hand, tears streaming down her cheeks. That her father could be dying seemed unbelievable, but she was very much afraid it was true. Sorrow formed a hard knot of agony inside her.

"Dr. Bowen said that sleep is the best thing for him, Miss Cathy." Mason moved to place a gentle hand on her shoulder. She looked around blindly to see that his cheeks were as wet as her own.

"Yes." Cathy gulped back her tears, and, with Mason's assistance, rose shakily to her feet. "Do you—do you have any idea what brought on the attack, Mason?"

Mason looked at her oddly. "Lady Stanhope has not yet spoken to you, Miss Cathy?"

"She wanted to, but I wanted to see my father. Why, Mason?"

"I hardly know how to tell you, Miss Cathy," he said unhappily.

"Tell me what, Mason?" Cathy's voice was sharp. A nameless dread was beginning to gnaw at her. Something was very wrong, that much was clear.

"Sir Thomas was writing a letter when he was stricken, Miss Cathy," Mason began slowly. "I—I think you'd better read it."

Mason crossed to the escritoire that stood beneath the damask-curtained windows, opened a drawer, and withdrew a piece of paper. He shut the drawer and came back to stand in front of her, his movements deliberate. Cathy took the paper from his outstretched hand without a word, saw that it was addressed to her at Woodham, and unfolded it with shaking fingers. Her mouth was dry as she started to read.

"Daughter," the letter began. "It grieves me very much to be the bearer of tidings I can only describe as ill, but I have just come into some information that I feel should be passed on to you without delay. It is my hope that you can rectify what has happened without too much harm to your spirits or station in life, or that of your son or husband.

"Cathy, my dear, when I arranged for your marriage to be performed by Captain Winslow on the *Lady Chester,* I naturally assumed that he was, as such officers are, duly authorized to perform a legal ceremony. I am certain that he assumed the same, so no blame lies at his door. But the unwelcome fact, of which I have just been apprised, is that Captain Winslow had been removed from his post by the Crown prior to solemnizing your vows. The ceremony, therefore, was not legal, and your marriage to Jonathan Hale has never, in actuality, existed."

The letter continued briefly, advising Cathy and Jon to marry again without delay in order to legitimatize Cray's birth. Cathy was so stunned by what she had read that she could barely take any of it in. Finally the writing trailed off into a long squiggle, and Cathy vaguely registered that it must have been there that her father had the attack.

"Jon and I are not married! Cray is—God forgive me—a bastard!" The words ran over and over again through her shocked brain. When finally she lifted her eyes from the paper to look at Mason, their expression was dazed.

"Mason. . . ." Her voice sounded strangled. "Mason, are you aware of what this says?"

"Yes, Miss Cathy," he answered compassionately as he met Cathy's ravaged gaze. "We found the letter after Sir Thomas had the attack. It must have been as great a shock to him as it is to you."

"Yes, of course." Cathy saw what must have happened

with great clarity. Her father, made aware of this information, must have been horrified beyond expression to realize that his only daughter, instead of being happily married as he had thought, was in fact living with a man as his mistress, however unwittingly. And Cray—Sir Thomas adored his grandson. He would have been devastated to realize that the child was illegitimate. As Cathy considered the ramifications, she blanched. If this news ever became public, she would be regarded as a fallen woman, no longer welcome in the homes of her friends and acquaintances. It would put her beyond the pale: society offered no forgiveness for women who had "gone wrong," as they put it. And Cray would no longer be his father's legal son, no longer his heir, but a bastard! Cathy felt sick.

"Are you all right, Miss Cathy?" Mason inquired anxiously as she swayed.

"Mason, please fetch Martha. I think I'm going to be ill," Cathy managed to say with some semblance of calm. Then, as Mason hurried to do her bidding, her trembling knees refused to support her any longer, and she sank down upon the rug.

❧

The next few days passed in something of a blur for Cathy. Her every instinct urged her to write to Jon, advising him of what had happened. Only the fear that such a letter would bring him post-haste to England stayed her hand. She would have to go home, she realized, to set matters right, but she hated to leave her father who, contrary to his doctor's expectations, was showing some slight improvement. Martha was as upset as she was, and together they discussed the problem at length. They both agreed that Jon, once the circumstances were made known to him, would immediately wed her again, and set about legitimatizing Cray. Cathy had no doubts at all on that score. But she could not feel comfortable until she was Jon's legal wife. She was torn between her fear for her father and an overwhelming urge to fly back to the love and security that only Jon could offer.

To Cathy's amazement, her Aunt Elizabeth was unexpectedly kind. She neither reviled her niece as a harlot, nor denounced Cray as something worse. Perhaps her brother's illness had mellowed the woman, who could say? One thing was certain, two years ago she would not have been so understanding. She would have considered Cathy and Cray a blot on the Aldley family escutcheon, and taken no pains to hide it. Cathy knew that her aunt felt no particular affection for her, so she was at a loss to explain the woman's seeming tolerance. Then, as days passed, Lady Stanhope began to drop subtle hints that gave Cathy the first inkling of what was in her mind.

"As I've always said, things tend to work out for the best," said her aunt with a sigh as Cathy took tea with her in the small withdrawing room one dreary afternoon.

Cathy looked up rather vaguely at this. Lady Stanhope, seeing that her niece was being annoyingly obtuse, pushed on a little further.

"I daresay you don't know this, my dear girl, but your father and I always shared this absurd fantasy. After Harold was born, and then you, we used to think that perhaps, one day, the two of you might marry each other. At one time it was Thomas' dearest wish, and mine too."

"As you say, Aunt, an absurd fantasy," Cathy responded, her attention sharpening. Why bring this up now? If Sir Thomas had indeed ever entertained such a notion, it must have been years before. And she tended to doubt that he ever had. He didn't approve of cousins marrying, as a general rule.

"Not quite so absurd as all that." Lady Stanhope gave an annoyed titter. "After all, you and Harold could almost be said to be ideally suited! He is just the right age for you, my dear, at seven years older—I always think it is nice if the man is enough older than his wife so that he may guide her! Both of you are from similar backgrounds, both attractive, charming people. . . ."

Here Cathy interrupted, taking just an instant to marvel at the blindness of mother love. For surely only his mother could describe plump, pasty-faced Harold as either attractive or charming!

"There is really no point to this discussion, is there, Aunt? After all, any hopes you and my father may have shared must have been abandoned when I married Jon, if not before."

"But that is exactly the point, Cathy!" Lady Stanhope, throwing prudence to the winds, replied eagerly. "You never really married that man! You have never been married! You are free to rectify the appalling mistake forced upon you by circumstances! Harold and I have discussed it, and we have agreed: it is the hand of God! He is giving you a second chance, Cathy!"

Cathy was torn between anger and amusement. "But I don't want a second chance, Aunt, although I thank Him very much if that is what He had in mind. As soon as I return to South Carolina, I intend to marry Jon without delay. I thought you understood that."

Lady Stanhope was experienced enough at getting her own way to know when to retreat. "It seems such a waste," was all she said, and then, to Cathy's relief, the subject was allowed to drop.

It wasn't until much later, when Cathy was keeping her nightly vigil in a chair drawn up beside her father's bed, that the conversation recurred to her. The more she thought about it, the more she realized that her Aunt Elizabeth had provided an explanation for what had been puzzling her: the Stanhopes, mother and son, were being so uncharacteristically tolerant of her unconventional situation because they hoped to persuade her to marry Harold! But why? She and Harold had despised each other from the time of their first meeting, and although Cathy had occasionally seen a hot gleam in his eyes as he looked at her, physical desire for her body was certainly not reason enough to make Harold want to marry her! His consequence was such that he would certainly feel himself slighted if the bride he eventually took to bed was not a blushing virgin from one of England's best families. It didn't make any sense. Still feeling uneasy, Cathy tried to dismiss the whole notion as something she had conjured up out of thin air and a touch of paranoia. But she resolved to ask Dr. Bowen the very next day about the possibility of leaving for the States in the very near future, and taking her father with her.

It was Harold himself who kept her faint suspicions alive. He was so polite, seeming to bend over backward to run little errands for her, bringing her the latest novels to read as she kept watch beside her father's bed, even purchasing a toy for Cray in a transparent attempt to ingratiate himself. Cathy received these offerings with a cool indifference that seemed to nonplus him. Instead of being grateful for the attentions of a high-born man-about-town, as Harold plainly considered himself to be, she quite frankly turned up her nose at him.

When Dr. Bowen reluctantly agreed that Sir Thomas could be removed to the States to convalesce, Cathy was inwardly jubilant. She was in a fever to go home again, to be held tightly in Jon's arms, to have this whole nightmarish episode behind her. Cray missed his father, and Cathy missed her husband—or husband-to-be, as it turned out. Feeling almost lightheaded with relief, Cathy giggled. Perhaps when they married this time, they could have a proper honeymoon. She would play the shy, modest bride to the hilt, while he—Cathy giggled again. This long separation would spur him to positive virtuosity in the role of the virile, desiring bridegroom!

Martha was strongly approving of Cathy's decision to leave for South Carolina as soon as arrangements could be made. Unlike Cathy, who had been too wrapped up in her worries over her father's illness and her non-marriage to see what was as plain as the nose on her face, Martha had noticed much that was not to her liking. For one thing, Lord Harold, when Cathy wasn't looking at him, watched the girl with an open lust that scandalized Martha to the roots of her gray hair. For another, Lady Stanhope, who Martha knew from experience was a conscienceless, self-serving, haughty lady at the best of times, was so sweet to Cathy it was frightening. And for a third, there were rumors below stairs that the Stanhopes were well on their way to being financially embarrassed. Add all that together, and in Martha's opinion it equalled trouble. It would be far better for all of them if they were to get Miss Cathy well away.

Mason, when Martha confided her worries to her old ally, agreed with her wholeheartedly. Together they contrived to keep an eye on Cathy as unobtrusively as possible. To Martha's way of thinking, there was no point in worrying the girl more than she was already, so neither she nor Mason said anything to her on the subject. But whenever Lord Harold was in the house, one or the other of them made it a point to stay at Miss Cathy's side.

Cathy, meanwhile, purchased accommodations for herself, her father, Martha, Mason, and Cray on a ship scheduled to leave London five weeks almost to the day after she and Martha and Cray had arrived. That done, she felt better, and was able to entertain with some equanimity her aunt's suggestion that she join the small gathering that Lady Stanhope was hostessing that evening. With less than a week remaining of her time in England, Lady Stanhope argued, it would be a shame if Cathy did not enjoy herself a little. Besides, "That old talk about your being still unwed while you were with child has not completely died," Lady Stanhope said severely. "And your disappearing like that certainly did nothing to help. It was all most embarrassing! Still, I don't mean to reproach you. But you must see that it does your reputation no good not to go about a little in society when it is well known that you are staying in my house. I wish you will think of me, and my dear Harold, a little. Harold is very desirous of obtaining a political appointment, you know, and that old scandal can do him no good. You wouldn't want to stand in Harold's way, would you, Cathy?"

To tell the truth, Cathy didn't mind standing in Harold's way at all, but it would hardly be polite to say so. As no other excuse occurred to her on the spur of the moment, she saw nothing for it but to agree to be present.

The rest of the afternoon Cathy spent with her father, who had longer and longer periods of consciousness. Although he was still incredibly weak, and unable to move his right side at all, he recognized Cathy and took great pleasure in her company. A visit from Cray was the highlight of his day, but Cathy took care to keep these short. Sir Thomas was still not out of danger, and the least bit of excitement, according to Dr. Bowen, might precipitate another attack. For that reason, Cathy made no mention of Jon, or her bogus marriage. Apparently the attack had blocked the events immediately preceding it from Sir Thomas' mind. He had no memory of the disaster that had befallen her, and Cathy was content to keep it that way.

When Mason brought his supper tray and Cathy got up to leave, explaining that she would be dining in company that evening, Sir Thomas was delighted. In his slurred speech he told her that it would do her good to see someone besides an old gentleman like himself, whom she was closeted with all day.

"You're looking peaky, daughter, and no mistake. You're young, should be having fun. Not looking after a sick old man. . . ."

"Oh, Papa, I love looking after you," Cathy reproached affectionately, touched by his concern for her. "Besides, you're certainly not a sick old man. When you get well again you'll have all the ladies in Charleston battering down Woodham's doors. We'll have to ask you to leave just to get some peace."

Sir Thomas chuckled. It was the first time he had laughed since his attack, and Cathy felt a sudden soaring of hope. Perhaps with time he would recover fully. After all, doctors weren't infallible. Already he was so much better than he had been when she came. Now all they had to do was spare him any more shocks. . . .

Cathy bent and kissed her father lightly on the cheek, feeling more cheerful than she had in days. Her step was buoyant as she crossed the hall to her bedroom, her smile bright as she greeted Martha and Cray, who looked up as she entered.

"Help me dress, Martha," Cathy directed gaily, moving to scoop up her son.

"Mama!" Cray squealed protestingly as she tickled him, and then, as she rolled with him on the bed, they both dissolved in a gale of giggles.

"You're awfully happy, lovey," Martha observed with a smile, arms akimbo as she watched the two people she loved best in the world.

"And why not?" Cathy retorted, grinning. "In less than a week we'll be on our way home! Every time I think of it I feel wonderful!"

"Me, too," Martha answered in a heartfelt way. Cathy looked at her curiously. But before she could ask the meaning of Martha's intensity, Cray distracted her.

"Cray wants to go home!" he announced, his little chin quivering ominously. "Cray misses Daddy! Daddy, Daddy!"

"We'll both see Daddy soon, precious," Cathy promised, looking quickly around for something to distract him. Her eyes alighted on her pretty crystal bottle of scent, cunningly formed in the shape of a wild bird. "Darling, play with this while Mama gets dressed. Then I'll tell you a story before you go to bed."

"Pretty," Cray said reflectively, taking the crystal bird in his chubby little hand and proceeding to pop it immediately into his mouth. Cathy looked at him for a moment, pondering the wisdom of taking the thing away from him. If that crystal were to break. . . .

"He'll be all right, lovey," Martha said comfortably. But Cathy continued to look rather doubtfully over her shoulder as Martha arranged her hair.

Selecting a dress to wear presented no problem, because Cathy had packed only one suitable for evening. It was a rich cream color with a satin under-dress overlaid by yards of Irish lace. Long-sleeved and tied around the waist by a twist of ivory ribbons, it was more severe in styling than most of the dresses that Cathy had worn recently. Looking at it, Martha signified her qualified approval.

"At least it covers your bosom," Martha sniffed, and Cathy wrinkled her nose at her.

Martha had left her hair loose, catching it up at the crown of her head with a single ivory ribbon into which she tucked a fragrant cream rose. Red-gold ringlets given form and shape by Martha's deft hand with a brush cascaded down Cathy's back. Her only ornaments were her wedding and engagement rings, and a delicate diamond necklet that had been Jon's gift to her on her last birthday. Martha, looking at her as she swished across the room and sank down on the bed to tell Cray the promised story, thought that she didn't look old enough to have a son.

By the time Cathy went downstairs, the other guests had arrived. Cathy could hear them laughing and talking in the large reception room at the rear of the house. She walked swiftly toward the open french doors, sniffing appreciatively at the sweet scent of the massed fresh flowers that the servants had arranged in such profusion. Crimson and pink and white, their colors were gorgeous against the sober brown of the rich walnut paneling.

"Cathy! There you are, my dear!" The gushy voice belonged to Lady Stanhope, who swooped on her niece as she hesitated just inside the french doors. Immediately all eyes riveted on Cathy. Cathy turned a glittering smile on the assembled company, knowing she was the object of considerable speculation: the black sheep of the Aldley flock, a real-life, in-the-flesh scarlet woman! Cathy read these thoughts in their faces. It was all she could do not to cross her eyes and stick her tongue out at them like a freak in a circus sideshow.

"Cathy, I believe you know the Countess of Firth?" Lady Stanhope had shepherded her over to an awful old harridan in a vivid puce gown. Cathy nodded politely, although she hadn't the faintest idea where she might have met the Countess before, if indeed she had. The Countess returned her nod with a glacial inclination of her be-feathered head.

"Lady Catherine," she got out in arctic tones. Cathy smiled coolly at her, determined to face down anyone who dared try to belittle her. Lady Stanhope, flustered by this icy exchange of civilities, hurried her niece on around the room.

There were a great many people crowded into the long room, too many for Cathy to remember more than a quarter of their names. Lady Stanhope soon left her to her own devices. Cathy circulated in the approved manner, chatting amiably about nothing, smiling at dull witticisms and generally behaving in an exemplary fashion. It was no wonder that her head soon hurt abominably; the room was stiflingly hot, the long windows closed in deference to the popular wisdom about the miasmas of night air. Candles guttered smokily in chandeliers overhead, the smell of melting tallow combining sickeningly with the scent of food and close-packed bodies. Cathy felt her stomach churn, and knew that she needed to find a quiet place where she could sit down.

She skirted the edge of the crowd with a smile pinned to her lips, nodding when people called or waved to her. She had to get out of this crush! Finally she found what she had been searching for: a crimson velvet curtain that concealed the entrance to a small anteroom. Cathy brushed through it, crossed the marble floor, and sank down onto the unyielding, horsehair upholstery of a prim, upright sofa. Its scratchy surface felt like silk to her skin. Cathy smiled a little, leaning her head back and closing her eyes. I must be more tired than I imagined, she thought, if this thing feels as soft as my featherbed. After a moment she put her feet up to lie on the sofa, and let her thoughts wander.

It was thus that Harold found her. He came quietly through the curtain and stopped, momentarily transfixed. She was so beautiful, with her white skin and golden hair, her slender, curved body clothed so demurely in creamy lace, that it took him a moment to remember that she had been a pirate's whore, and had borne a bastard child. His rather loose mouth curled in distaste even as lust shone from his eyes. His mother must be mad to suggest he marry her! Although he wanted her body badly, he didn't think he would have to marry her to get it. After all, she had been away from her so-called husband for almost two months now. Her flesh must be itching for a man. . . . But then, there was the money to consider. Her father was a rich man, and she was his only child. It stood to reason that he would leave it all to her. And in the meantime, there was all that lovely money in her trust fund, just waiting to be spent. And Harold needed money badly. He had gambled away his entire fortune, and creditors were dunning him on all sides. If he didn't find the funds to pay them soon he would be ruined. Maybe he would marry her, at that. She was certainly beautiful, and she had good blood in her, although somehow it had gone wrong. He could marry her and school her until she was a meek, obedient little wife, content to stay down on their country estate and let him spend his time in town. She would probably be so grateful to him for elevating her to her rightful station in life that she would do just whatever he said. Yes, maybe he would marry her. . . .

Cathy stirred, her breasts lifting as she inhaled deeply. Harold stared open-mouthed as those enticing mounds thrust at the fabric of her dress. All thoughts of money and matrimony immediately quitted his brain. He could only think of how she excited him. Automatically his hand came up to smooth the thinning strands of gingery hair that his man had oiled and teased into the latest fashion. Then, with a tug at the yellow brocade waistcoat made vexingly tight by his supper, he crossed the small room to stand over the sofa, looking down.

Pleasant dreams chased one another through Cathy's head, dreams of soft summer sunlight and herself laughing with Jon. She dreamed that she was home at Woodham again, lying out in the soft grass of the back lawn, protected from the view of the house by the tall apple tree. Jon came to sit on the grass beside her, smiling at her lovingly, his gray eyes twinkling as he began, ever so gently, to caress her. His hands touched lightly on her breasts, stroking the sensitive nipples into throbbing life, before sliding down to span her waist and then trace the curve of her hips and the long, lissome line of her thighs.

Deep in her dream, Cathy smiled. Jon smiled back at her, his dark face bending nearer. More than anything in the world she wanted him to kiss her. . . . She was starving for the feel of his lips against hers. With a low moan deep in her throat she lifted her hands to twine them around his neck, pulling his head down. When his mouth touched hers at last she gave a hoarse sigh of satisfaction, returning his kiss eagerly.

But something was wrong. The mouth that pressed hers so greedily was loose, and wet, and tasted of stale wine and onions. The hands that clutched her body so roughly were clammy. Never in all the time she had known him had Jon kissed her like this, clumsily, grinding her soft lips back on her teeth, thrusting his tongue so far down her throat that she feared she might choke. Repulsed, Cathy struggled out of her dream only to find that she was still being hotly kissed. Her eyes flew open.

To her horror she found herself looking into Harold's round, perspiring face. His eyes were closed, and he was breathing noisily through his rather large nose. His hands clutched hurtfully over her breasts, and it was this that galvanized Cathy back to full awareness. My God, what did he think he was doing?

Before she could clout him on that shuddering nose, as she had every intention of doing, there was a sound over by the curtain. Automatically her eyes swivelled toward the noise, and what she saw made her heart drop into the pit of her stomach.

"What the . . . !" The furious, bitten off exclamation hurt Cathy's ears. Angrily she pushed at Harold's shoulders, desperately wanting to free her mouth so that she could explain. There wasn't time. Harold was suddenly plucked away from her as though a giant hand had reached down from the sky and grabbed him. He was spluttering, his red face turning quickly white as he guessed the identity of the grim-faced man who held him by the collar, shaking him like a great dane with a rat between its teeth.

"Jon!" Cathy cried, wanting to stop him before the violence got out of hand. She might as well have saved her breath. He didn't even look at her. His anger was all focused on the quivering little man he held before him. As Cathy watched helplessly, Jon's large fist slammed into Harold's soft stomach.

"Ugghh!" Harold grunted, doubling. Jon raised his fist to repeat the blow.

"Jon, no!" Cathy shrieked, flying up from the sofa to catch at his arm. "Don't hurt him!"

Jon turned blazing gray eyes on Cathy for a moment. The look in them caused her to shrink back. He was angrier than she had seen him in years, angry enough to kill. She was almost relieved when he transferred his attention back to Harold.

"I'll teach you to lay hands on my wife, you bastard," Jon

said thickly, pulling Harold upright again so that he could land another blow to the man's jelly-like middle.

"She's not your wife!" Harold got out before the blow landed, and then he was too busy groaning to say anything at all.

Jon hit him several more times, hard, expert punches that reduced Harold to sobbing helplessness. Finally, with a contemptuous laugh, he released his hold on Harold's collar and let the smaller man slide to the floor. Then he turned to look at Cathy. His expression was menacing, but she met it bravely.

"What the hell did he mean, you're not my wife?" he asked heavily. Cathy swallowed. This was not, definitely, how she had planned to tell him. But there was nothing for it, and anyway he certainly couldn't blame her. She only hoped that he was not angry enough to wash his hands of her as a poor bargain after what had happened tonight.

"It's true—we're not married," she began nervously. His eyes widened incredulously.

"The hell we're not," he ground out. Then, his expression growing uglier, he reached out and grabbed her arm in a grip so hard it hurt. "Is that why you were letting him make love to you? Hoping to catch a lord this time, Cathy? What did you do, have the marriage annulled? If you did, you're a lying little bitch! It's been consummated more times than I can count."

"Of course I didn't have our marriage annulled," Cathy said indignantly, her eyes beginning to snap blue sparks at his unfounded accusation. "If you would just listen. . . ."

"I'm listening," Jon growled, but before Cathy could start to explain Harold began to scream like a creature demented. They both turned to look at him, surprised. For a moment they had forgotten his presence.

"God, help me! He's hurt me! Oh, he's hurt me!" Harold wailed at the top of his lungs. Almost immediately people began to thrust inquisitive heads through the curtain.

"Help me, help me! I'm hurt!" The room was filling with

people eager to watch any new scandal. Jon quickly crossed the room and grabbed Harold again by the collar. His intention to shut the man up by whatever means were necessary was obvious. Harold shrieked.

"For God's sake, don't let him hurt me! Summon the constables! The man's an escaped convict, sentenced to hang, wanted for piracy and murder!"

three

꒰ꔷ꒱

Newgate Prison was every bit as gruesome as Jon had remembered. Moisture dripped down gray stone walls that were green in splotches from mold. The odor of dampness mingled with the stink of human excrement to form a smell that was indescribable. Just as well that he had dined on nothing but a moldy slice of bread for the past three days, Jon thought with black humor as he sat huddled on the rough stone floor, arms wrapped around his drawn-up knees for warmth. If his stomach had been comfortably filled, he could not have been answerable for the consequences.

He was dressed only in his now torn and filthy breeches. The rest of his clothes had been confiscated while he was still unconscious from the beating he had received while trying to fight his way free of his captors. His bare arms and chest and, yes, even his feet were ridged with goose bumps. God, the damned place was cold! Maybe whoever had designed it had, in the spirit of economy, hoped that inflammation of the lungs would save the Crown the cost of many a hangman.

One of the few advantages of being under sentence of

death, Jon reflected wryly, was that he had the small cell all
to himself. It was no more than a dank hole measuring five
feet across by eight feet long and located deep in the bowels
of the prison, totally dark except when touched by the light
of a lantern held by a passing guard. He knew its exact size,
because he had paced it off countless times since his confinement began. Still, if he had been an everyday criminal,
a pickpocket, say, or a highwayman, there would have been
half-a-dozen or so other poor, unwashed souls crammed in
with him. As it was, because of the death sentence soon to
be carried out and his previous escape, he was left in splen-
did isolation. They meant to see to it that he did not get the
chance to escape again.

There was no furniture, not a bed of any description, not
even a pot to piss in, as the saying went. That last was literally
true. He had been forced to turn one corner of the cell into
a privy, just one of the many indignities witnessed with delight by the grinning guards. That corner, degrading and de-
humanizing, was something he preferred not to think about.
It reminded him too vividly of the half-crazed, starved, and
filthy creature that this place had reduced him to once before.
Oh, well, he thought with another attempt at humor, at least
he wouldn't have to worry about that; this time he wouldn't be
around long enough.

God, he was hungry! Unable to stop himself from drool-
ing, he pictured a huge Virginia ham, baked to a turn, with
all the trimmings: yams, fresh baked bread with butter. . . .
Suddenly he dropped his head to his knees, feeling queasy.
His stomach, so empty that he could feel its sides clinging
together, gave a loud growl followed by a dry heave. Grimly
he forced his mind away from the dangerous topic of food.

Cathy; her lovely face with its huge sapphire eyes and
trembling rose-pink mouth replaced the ham in Jon's mind.
But this image was even more painful. Since the night when
he had been dragged from her aunt's townhouse by a half-

dozen burly constables, he had not heard so much as a syllable from her. So she was not his legal wife—that smarmy little cousin of hers had made sure he knew the facts of that. Still, what of the love she had professed to feel for him? What of their son, and their home, and their plans for the future? Did they mean nothing at all to her? As much as the thought hurt, Jon was beginning to believe it must be true. She had not visited him, not written, not even sent him a message by one of the guards. It was as if, now that she knew that she was not bound to him by the chains of matrimony, she preferred to forget his existence. In less than a week now he would be dead, unless by some unlikely chance he could manage to escape; the thought that Cathy didn't even care enough to come and bid him a final farewell tortured him.

He had tried. God knows, he had tried! He had done his best to give her all the things she was used to, but he knew that life as the wife of an obscure, not particularly wealthy cotton planter could not compare to what she could have had if he had not turned her life upside down. If he had not abducted her and made her his mistress, she could have married anyone: she would have been rich and pampered, with an entrée into the most exalted circles of society. Ever since their marriage, the fear that she would one day regret her decision and leave him had haunted his nights. It was this fear, plus the knowledge that she was back in the midst of the glittering world she had once held so dear, that had at last broken through the barriers raised by his better judgement and sent him hot-footing it to England. Jon smiled bitterly. The threat of a hanging had seemed as nothing compared to the danger of losing Cathy's love. So now he was here in this stinking prison, his wife already lost to him, his life soon to be. God, what a blind fool he had been!

Still, he could not quite extinguish a last flicker of hope. Maybe something was keeping her from him—maybe her father was worse, and she didn't feel that she could leave him.

Jon knew just how pitifully forlorn this conjecture was, but he was loath to let it go. His love for her made him hope long after the time for hoping had passed, but gradually the harsh cynicism born of a lifetime of dealings with the so-called gentler sex surfaced. Women were by nature two-faced creatures whose one interest in a man was in his ability to provide them with fripperies, as he knew, and had always known full well. He could blame no one but himself if he had allowed a lovely face and soft, curved flesh to distort his judgement. Well, better men than he had made fools of themselves over a woman. But the blow to his pride—he no longer was prepared to admit that it might have struck clear through to his heart— was a stabbing ache that, try as he would, he could not banish.

The spectre of Cathy as he had last seen her, in the arms of another man—a wealthy, titled lord for all his fat stomach and thinning hair—haunted him night and day. It had the power to make his palms sweat and his teeth gnash with rage. She's mine! He wanted to cry, and came to despise himself for the wanting. But still he sat huddled on the cold stone floor, watching the iron-barred door hour after hour, hoping against all odds to see a woman who never came.

∼∾∾∽

Cathy, for her part, was nearly in despair. She had spent the last few days in a feverish race from one judge to another, from magistrate to magistrate as she made shameless use of her family connections, cajoling and promising and finally out-and-out begging with tears rolling down her cheeks for a commutation of Jon's sentence. Her pleas continually fell on deaf ears. To a man, the judges pronounced Jon a pirate and a murderer, well deserving of a hangman's noose. They were sorry for her and her son, they said, but there was nothing they could do. Jon's execution was scheduled for seven days hence, and it would be carried out.

Her father, although greatly improved, was still far too

ill to be of any help to her. Cathy was very much afraid that the shock of hearing of Jon's imprisonment and imminent hanging would kill the older man. Martha and Mason were horrified and sympathetic, but horror and sympathy were not what Cathy needed. She needed, as she was finally coming to realize, a small miracle if Jon were to be saved from death.

Six days before the scheduled execution, Cathy went to the prison as she had every day since Jon had been taken there, only to be once again turned away. The prisoner had escaped once, she was told grimly, and they were taking no chances on its happening again. He was to be allowed no visitors; even the hanging itself was to take place within the prison walls, on a scaffold specially constructed for that purpose.

Cathy returned to her aunt's house in tears. Only the day before she had seen the last of the judges with any jurisdiction over the case. During the interview, she had practically gone down on her knees as she begged for Jon's life. The man was not to be moved. Cathy had come away with a dreadful sense of helplessness: he had been her last hope. The only thing left for her was to somehow arrange for Jon to escape, but she hadn't the faintest idea of how to go about it. Panic threatened to swamp her, but she forced it back. Think, she told herself fiercely. Think!

She rocked back and forth in the small chair set before the sewing room fire, racking sobs threatening to choke her. Dear God, what could she do?

"Troubled, cousin?" Harold's smirking voice broke through her haze of agony. She turned to face him like a small wild animal, eyes flashing, teeth bared. She blamed him utterly for what had happened. If Jon died, he would have caused it as surely as if he had pointed a gun at him and pulled the trigger.

"Not crying over the pirate, are you?" he asked tauntingly. "Waste of time, you know, my dear girl. He's dead meat. Nothing in the world that can save him—unless. . . ."

Cathy, knowing that he had deliberately set out to tantalize her, nevertheless snapped eagerly at the bait.

"Unless what?" she demanded, eyes fixed with painful intensity on Harold's moon face.

"Unless you had someone very influential to pull some strings. Someone like Sir Thomas. . . ."

"You know the shock would kill him," Cathy answered resentfully, sinking back in the chair. She had known that Harold's mouthings would come to nothing, but still. . . .

"Or me," he added. Cathy's heart missed a beat.

"You?" she breathed slowly. "You could help me?"

"Oh, I *could*," Harold replied, negligently brushing a piece of lint from his maroon velvet coat. "If I wanted to."

Cathy thought quickly. Harold was, after all, a peer of the realm, and for some reason unfathomable to her seemed to be in high favor at Court. It was just possible that he could help—she was surprised that it hadn't occurred to her before. But why should he? He was not particularly fond of her despite their blood tie, and she suspected that he hated Jon. Her eyes narrowed. Whatever it took, she would persuade him.

"What do you want, Harold?" With great effort she managed to keep her voice reasonably cool. It would never do for Harold to guess how near to the end of her rope she had been. He was sadistic by nature; it would give him pleasure to watch her squirm. He might even refuse just for the pleasure of witnessing her pain.

"Well, let's see, what is a pirate worth these days? I imagine they must come pretty high. Not exactly two-a-penny, you know."

"I'll pay you anything, Harold. You can have all my money. I—I have quite a lot, and I've never touched a penny of it." The words burst from her before Cathy could control them. When they were out, she sat biting her lip, knowing she had made a mistake. Harold's eyes gleamed with satisfaction; his pursed mouth smiled at her.

"All your money—ah, that's quite a temptation. But you can't do that, you know. Your money's tied up so that you can't just give it away. Nasty little thing called a trust fund."

"I—I'll find a way to break it, Harold. Or maybe I could borrow against it." Cathy despised the humble tone of her voice, but she couldn't help it. She would do anything, anything, to save Jon.

"Well, now, I don't know. When I think of all the people the pirate is bound to have killed, the ships he's looted, my blood just runs cold. It might be a public service to let him hang—and, as you know, I am a great believer in serving the public."

"You're enjoying this, aren't you?" Cathy accused bitterly, rising from her chair to face him, hands clenched impotently at her sides. In the sober deep blue of her challis day dress, long-sleeved and buttoned close to the neck, she was a small, slender figure with flashing blue eyes. Harold stared at her, admiring the golden hair swept back into a smooth chignon, the soft skin glowing pink with temper, even the defiant way her little chin was tilted at him. She was most desirable, and he wanted her as well as the money. Suddenly he made up his mind.

"I'm going to do you a favor, cousin: I'm going to marry you. I'll even let you keep your bastard whelp, so long as he stays out of my sight."

It was a statement, not a question, and it robbed Cathy of breath.

"I—I. . . . You don't want to marry me, Harold," she said at last, moistening her lips with her small pink tongue. She felt as if her worst nightmare was coming true. "I'm not the wife for you. You need someone worthy of you, a young lady with an unblemished reputation. If the reason you want to marry me is for the money, I'll find some way of breaking the trust, I swear!"

"The money's a prime inducement, I'll admit," Harold answered smugly. "But I want you, too. You hate me, don't you, Cathy? Well, I don't like people who hate me. You're going to have to pay for that—in my bed!"

"I can't do it," Cathy said, feeling sick at the images conjured up by his last words.

"Not even for your pirate?" he taunted. "And I thought you loved him. It's the only way I'll help, cousin. Otherwise, he'll hang."

"Harold, please. . . ." Cathy was trapped and she knew it. She had exhausted all other avenues open to her. Jon would die in six days if she didn't do something, and Harold was offering her a way to save him. But if she married Harold, she would be cutting Jon out of her life for good. He would never forgive her for what she knew he would consider her betrayal, and, anyway, she would be another man's wife.

"Those are my terms, Cathy. But I can see you're not interested." Harold turned and began to walk out of the room. Cathy stared after him in an agony of indecision.

"Harold, wait!" she cried as he reached the door. Slowly he turned back to face her. He was smiling triumphantly.

"I—I'll marry you," Cathy said, her voice low. She felt as though her heart would break.

He returned swiftly to her side.

"I felt sure you would, my dear," he said. Cathy had to fight back an acute attack of nausea as he enfolded her in his arms.

His touch revolted her. She could feel the clamminess of his palms through her thin dress as he clutched at her back. His mouth was loose and wet on hers, and he kissed her as if he wanted to drain every last drop of sweetness from her mouth. Cathy went rigid in his arms, eyes tightly shut, fists clenched at her sides as she tried not to remember that by agreeing to marry him she had given him the right to kiss her like this. After the ceremony, he could do anything he liked with her. At the thought of the physical intimacies he would undoubtedly insist on sharing with her, she shuddered. "Oh, Jon!" her heart cried, but she knew that she had to endure Harold because, simply, she had no other choice.

"We'll be married day after tomorrow," Harold told her thickly, raising his head at last. "And after we're wed, I'll expect a little more cooperation from you, my dear. After all, it's not as if you were inexperienced."

The sneer in his last words made Cathy long to hit him, but she was at his mercy, and both he and she knew it.

"And Jon?" she asked unsteadily, struggling to remain composed under his taunting eyes.

"I'll see to it—after we're married," Harold said, and turning on his heel, left the room.

❧

*H*er wedding day—her second wedding day— was the most miserable of Cathy's life. As Martha helped her dress, tears stood in her eyes, eyes that were already red and swollen from the tears that had kept her awake all night. Every fiber of her being revolted at what she was about to do. To be married to Harold—to be his wife; the thought made her want to throw up. Martha, sniffling audibly behind her, was no help. Instead of her usual practice of looking for a silver lining to the blackest of clouds, the woman was clearly as upset as Cathy. Together, they were doubtless the most mournful pair who had ever made ready for a wedding.

Two things kept Cathy from breaking down completely: one was the thought of Jon's long body dangling from the end of a rope that was slowly choking him, his handsome face blue and swollen, his features contorted with agony; the other was the hope that, somehow, she might be able to evade Harold. If he kept his promise and arranged for Jon's release immediately after their wedding, then it was just possible that she wouldn't have to carry through her end of the bargain. If she could keep him out of her bed until Jon was free, then all bets were off: she would immediately petition for an annulment. That such a plan was strictly dishonorable, Cathy knew full well. She also knew full well that she couldn't care less.

The dress that Martha was helping her into was pale gray silk, almost the color of mourning. Its somber hue exactly matched her mood; if her choice disturbed Harold, then well and good. She cared not a whit what he thought as long as he kept his word about freeing Jon.

Martha drew Cathy's hair back severely from her face, arranging it in a sober knot at her nape. The tiny white frills edging the high collar of the dress framed her face, which was almost as pale as the lace. Cathy noted with satisfaction that she looked awful, her face colorless and drawn, her eyes swollen from weeping. If ever a girl had looked less like a bride she would not like to see her, Cathy thought starkly, and then when she could delay no longer she turned slowly away from the mirror.

"We'll be back right after the ceremony, I imagine," Cathy said evenly to Martha. "Unless Harold wants to stop somewhere to celebrate." She put bitter emphasis on the last word.

"Oh, lovey, I hate to see you go through with this," Martha choked, tears welling up in her eyes.

"Not nearly so much as I do." Cathy forced the joke, then grew serious once more. "Don't worry about me, Martha. Whatever happens—it'll be all right."

"I hope so, lovey, I surely do." Martha gave her a fierce, quick hug, which Cathy returned rather desperately. Then, while she could still summon the courage to do so, she went out of the room and down the stairs to where Harold awaited her.

Cathy became Lady Stanhope less than an hour later, in a dingy registry office on the outskirts of London's bustling business district. Her hand shook visibly as she held it out to receive Harold's ring. Looking down at her white, trembling fingers, she saw to her horror that she had forgotten to remove the gold and diamond bands that Jon had placed on her finger so many months before. Harold's face reddened angrily as he followed the direction of her gaze, and he made a gesture as though to snatch the rings from her finger. Cathy forestalled him, jerking her hand from his grasp and removing Jon's rings herself. For a brief moment she clutched them tightly in her palm; then, with a defiant look at Harold, she slipped them into her reticule.

After it was over, she endured her aunt's triumphant congratulations before numbly taking Harold's proffered arm and allowing him to lead her outside. It was a misty, gray day, with wisps of fog rolling along the cobbled streets. Cathy thought that she had never seen a place that depressed her as much as London, and then she ceased thinking at all as Harold ceremoniously handed her up into the ornate brougham that awaited them. As he released her hand she shrank back as far into one corner of the plush seat as she could, wishing desperately that Harold had not chosen a closed carriage. It would be just like him to try to make love to her on the way back to her aunt's house! And with Jon still very much at the mercy of Harold's whims, she would be forced to accept whatever he meted out.

When Harold clambered inside at last, he was smiling. Cathy looked at his white skin, nearly as soft and well cared for as her own, at his round cheeks and thinning red hair, at his pursed mouth and beady blue eyes, and felt hatred so intense that she fairly blazed with it. She was sickened at the thought that she now belonged to him, that this very night he was planning to violate her body, which he had every right to do. He was her husband—how the thought flayed her! But she was not beaten yet, thought Cathy with a defiant lift of her chin. If Harold thought that he was going to have everything his own way, he was very much mistaken!

Harold parted the tails of his truly magnificent morning coat, apparently so that he wouldn't sit upon and wrinkle them, then sat down heavily beside her. Cathy's lip curled at this display of concern for the state of his dress. Truly, as dazzling as his raiment was this morning, a little thing like wrinkled coattails would go completely unremarked! The combination of canary yellow breeches, so tight around his pudgy thighs that Cathy was in constant expectation of hearing them split, white satin waistcoat embroidered with tiny yellow daisies, white silk shirt frothing with lace, high-heeled black leather shoes with gleaming brass buckles, and that extraordinary coat made him look like a particularly garish species of tropical bird. Beside him, in her sober gray dress, Cathy knew herself to be positively eclipsed!

"Smiling, my dove?" he asked coldly, correctly interpreting the sneer she had not had time to hide. "Let me entertain you further. I'm sure you'll be most interested to hear the details of our honeymoon."

"Honeymoon?" Cathy repeated, feeling a chill of apprehension.

"You didn't think that I'd ask my lovely new wife to forgo her bride-trip, did you? When you know me better, Cathy, you'll realize that I would never be so thoughtless! I've arranged for us to board the *Tamarind* at Southhampton this evening. She sails on the morrow for La Coruña. I thought we would explore Spain for a while, then return to London via the Continent. Altogether, I expect we'll be gone for about six months."

Cathy's mind reeled beneath the weight of this unexpected information. All her hopeful plans for avoiding Harold would come to naught if she were to be alone with him for six interminable months. She had very much counted on her father's and Martha's, and yes, even her aunt's, presence to keep Harold from resorting to physical violence to consummate their marriage. But now . . . ! And there was Cray! She couldn't possibly leave him for six months. And her father. . . .

"You're joking, of course," Cathy said with as much composure as she could muster.

"I never joke, my dove," Harold answered, clearly enjoying her discomfiture. "After all, you must admit that it's only natural for a new husband to want to have his bride to himself for a while. There are so many aspects of marriage that are best enjoyed in privacy, don't you agree?"

The leering look he passed over her body made Cathy cringe instinctively. I can't go through with it, she thought. Every cell in her body urged her to jump from the carriage and run before it was too late. The imagined feel of Harold's hands on her naked flesh, of his corpulent body joined with hers, made her shudder with revulsion.

"I cannot possibly leave Cray," Cathy told him coldly.

"Your bastard is of no concern whatsoever to me, my dove. Be thankful that I allow you to keep the whelp at all. My initial inclination was to hand him over to one of the excellent institutions with which this country abounds. I certainly will not allow him to interfere with my plans." Harold dismissed Cray with a negligent wave of one pudgy, beringed hand.

Cathy's temper boiled at hearing her beloved son called "bastard." While technically she knew this was so, he had been made with love and born into what both she and Jon had believed to be a true marriage. She would not allow this fat, pompous toad to so slightingly dismiss her son!

"Why, you . . . !" she spluttered, rejecting epithet after epithet as being too mild for the loathing she wanted to express.

"I'd bite my tongue, if I were you, my dove," Harold advised maliciously, his pale blue eyes gleaming his pleasure at having provoked such a reaction from her. "There's still the pirate, you know. If you come the ugly to me, I won't lift a finger on his behalf. And he'll hang while you and I are enjoying the delights of our honeymoon."

Cathy quivered, her anger replaced by rage of another sort.

"You gave your word!" she spat contemptuously. "You

gave your word that you would save him if I married you!"

"And I fully intend to keep it—as long as you keep to your part of the bargain. But I think you should remember that, as long as the pirate remains in prison—which I imagine he will do for many years to come—it will take only a word from me to have him hanged. I would advise you to keep that thought firmly fixed in your lovely little head while you set your mind to pondering how best to please me!"

Cathy wanted to kill. Her fingers curled with the force of her longing, the long, smooth-buffed nails digging hurtfully into her palms. If Harold had been better acquainted with her, he would have recognized his danger from the glittery brilliance of her eyes. As it was, he saw nothing but a properly chastened bride, and congratulated himself on finding an excellent means of keeping her in line.

Cathy stared at him for a long moment, her blue eyes afire with temper. Then she forced herself to try to relax. As Harold had so gleefully pointed out, he had the upper hand. Jon was to all intents and purposes his hostage, and Harold clearly meant to use her love for him to insure her compliance with his every wish. With the threat of Jon's hanging held over her head, Cathy realized with a sense of horror that she would be forced to submit docilely to Harold's demands, possibly for years. A wave of black anguish threatened to engulf her. Why hadn't such a possibility occurred to her sooner? And, yet, if it had, what could she have done?

The carriage rocked to a halt. Cathy looked up, surprised. Maybe Harold had just been teasing her; was it possible that they had returned to her aunt's house in Grosvenor Square? Where else . . . ?

"See how I keep my word, my dove?" Harold asked jovially, rising as the driver swung the door open from the outside. Cathy stared at him blankly, not understanding. Then, through the open door, she saw the forbidding gray stone walls of Newgate Prison.

"I'm sure you'll excuse me while I arrange to save your pirate from his richly deserved fate," Harold continued smoothly. "And remember, I expect you to keep your side of our bargain as well as I have mine."

Cathy said nothing as Harold descended. When the door was closed behind him she scooted across the seat, lifting one hand to brush aside the curtain and stare out. The prison sat on a back street in one of London's slums; all about the carriage Cathy could see ragged and filthy children pawing through the garbage that filled the ditches running along either side of the street. Slatternly-looking women leaned drunkenly against the high prison walls, some clutching a bottle in one hand from which they would snatch an occasional swallow. All seemed totally oblivious to the steadily-falling drizzle. The guard at the gate paid scant attention to these denizens of the street, except to tell one who had sidled close to move along in a loud voice.

Cathy started when the door swung open.

"Out you get, my dear," said Harold with a smirk, holding up his hand for her to grasp and smiling evilly into her bewildered face. Cathy didn't move.

"Don't you want to bid your pirate a fond farewell? I assure you, you won't be seeing him after today. You really can't expect me to permit my wife to visit an incarcerated prisoner."

"Why are you doing this?" Cathy's voice was faint. More than anything in the world she wanted to see Jon, wanted to tell him she loved him and explain why she had acted as she had. But she knew Harold too well to suppose that he had her wishes in mind. No, his purpose had to be something nefarious.

"Quick, aren't you, my dove?" Harold said with every evidence of approval. "I have a little score to settle with your pirate. He hit me quite hard, you know. For several days I actually feared that he might have ruptured my spleen. Now I plan to inflict a little pain of my own."

"I refuse to be a party to such a thing," Cathy replied

slowly, impotently clenching her hands that had been resting lightly on her lap.

"You'll do just as I tell you, Cathy my dear. Remember, one word from you, even a gesture that I mislike, and he hangs. Besides, there is really no need for you to get into such a fret." Here Harold cast a glance at her clenched fists. "Having the pirate physically abused is the very furthest thing from my mind, I assure you. After all, one is, however much one regrets the fact, a gentleman. No, I merely intend to present him with the spectacle of our newly wedded bliss—and what I require from you, my dove, is the portrayal of my loving wife. For the sake of the pirate, I hope you are convincing. I am sure that hanging is a most unpleasant way to die."

Cathy stared at him, biting back with difficulty the words she longed to utter. Jon would be stabbed to the heart, she knew, when he learned that she had married Harold. But better by far to let him suffer a little emotional bloodletting than death. Besides, he would surely understand that what she had done, she had done out of love for him.

Harold was watching her gloatingly. Cathy's chin snapped up, and her eyes hardened. She would play Harold's little game, because he left her no choice. But one day there would be a reckoning! With icy dignity she permitted Harold to help her from the carriage.

Inside, the prison stank. As they were escorted by an obsequious guard along dark, clammy corridors, Cathy wrinkled her nose at the horrible smell, and was finally forced to extract a perfumed handkerchief from her pocket and hold it pressed to her nose. Harold did likewise; Cathy watched him sniffing fastidiously into his lace-edged handkerchief with loathing.

Almost worse than the smell were the sounds. Low moans of pain joined sobbing cries of despair to form a hellish chorus. Listening, Cathy shivered convulsively, sickened to think of Jon imprisoned in such a place. Surely Hell itself couldn't be worse than this!

By the light of the lantern held aloft by their escort, Cathy could just make out dozens of half-naked, filthy men and women jammed into tiny cells, forced to endure conditions far worse than even those afforded the wild beasts at the Exchange. Sunken eyes glowed at them darkly from the depths of cavernous faces; voices implored them to have pity. Poor souls, Cathy thought, tears rising to her eyes as Harold hurried her past. At their passage some of the prisoners leapt toward them, wailing inhumanly as they begged for help, clinging to the bars like apes. Cathy cringed instinctively. Harold shrieked, then immediately sought to disguise his display of cowardice by screaming to the guards that came running to their aid, "Whip them! Whip them!"

"No!" Cathy cried, aghast, but it was too late. The guards were inside the cells, laying about them with huge whips, yelling obscenities at the cowering, scuttling prisoners. Harold's arm curled roughly around Cathy's waist when she would have stopped, forcing her on.

It was still around her waist moments later when the guard abruptly stopped, raising the lantern high above his head to illuminate the interior of a small cell. Cathy barely had time to register the green slime on the walls, the moisture standing in pools on the stone floor, and, of course, the terrible stink, when her eyes fastened on the gaunt and filthy man slowly unwinding from a sitting position on the floor. He was blinking, as though the dim light had momentarily blinded him, and he leaned one hand heavily against that revolting wall for support. His black hair was overlong, matted and unkept, while the beginnings of a rough black beard covered the lower half of his face. Only the gray eyes, at first incredulous and then slowly filling with pleasure at the sight of her, were unchanged.

"Oh, Jon!" Cathy's heart cried, but a large knot of tears in her throat prevented her from saying a word.

"Cathy!" he said hoarsely, taking a faltering step toward her. "Oh, Cathy, sweetheart, I thought. . . ."

Here he broke off. His eyes hardened to fierce agates as they recognized Harold, took in the possessive arm around Cathy's small waist and her acceptance of the other man's touch.

"What did you think, Hale?" Harold asked with a gloating smile. "Pray go on. My *wife* and I would be most interested in whatever you have to say. Won't we, my dear?"

Cathy, watching Jon with agony in her own heart, saw him flinch as if from a blow. Harold, watching as avidly as she but for different reasons, saw that involuntary movement too, and practically crowed with triumph.

"Won't we, *wife*?" Harold asked again with a hard edge to his voice, his fingers digging warningly into her waist as Cathy didn't answer. Blinded by tears she feared for Jon's sake to shed, Cathy could do nothing else but agree.

"Yes, Harold," she said, her voice muffled in a way that she prayed he would mistake for docility. Her eyes stayed fixed on Jon, willing him to understand the reason behind her action, to have faith in her love.

"You . . . married him?" Jon was speaking to her, his eyes as they tried to search her face through the shadows leaping with fierce emotion.

Harold's fingers dug into her waist again, hurtfully, when it seemed she wasn't going to answer. In truth, Cathy wasn't sure she could; her throat seemed to have closed up. Closing her eyes, she licked her dry lips; then, hating Harold, hating herself for the pain she knew her answer would cause the man she loved, she said simply, "Yes."

Even in the poor light she could see the muscles in Jon's face clench.

"For God's sake, why?" Jon demanded hoarsely, those leaping eyes never leaving her face.

Cathy trembled, and knew she could find no answer to this. Harold, feeling the tremors that racked her, answered for her.

"She had the good sense to recognize a better bargain, Hale," he taunted. "Surely you can see that for yourself. I am, after all, a peer of the realm; you are a condemned pirate. Besides, she only married you in the first place because of the brat, you know. Why else would a lady of her background marry a man of yours?"

Jon said nothing, but his eyes slashed back to Cathy. She stared at him mutely, willing him not to believe Harold's farrago of lies.

"Cathy?" he rasped.

She felt Harold's eyes on her face, his fingers digging menacingly into her waist. If she broke down now, he would carry out his threat to have Jon hanged. She knew it, knew Harold would even be glad of an excuse to have it so. To call Harold's bluff would only result in Jon's death.

"He's telling the truth, Jon," she said in a low voice, and felt Harold almost purring with satisfaction beside her.

"Well, we must be off," Harold said with taunting gaiety. "We were just married this morning, you know. We're anxious to be away on our honeymoon. Tonight we sail for La Coruña—that's in Spain, you know—and after that we're going to take a leisurely tour of the continent."

He made a movement as though to turn away, then seemed to hesitate, and turned back.

"Oh, and one more thing, Hale. I must thank you for breaking my wife in to her marital duties so well. As I'm sure you remember, she's quite delicious in bed."

Jon's eyes blazed murder as Harold turned on his heel, taking Cathy with him. He practically dragged her back down the passage, a malicious grin on his face. The bewildered jailer trailed them, holding the lantern high so that they could find their way.

"Jon, oh, Jon, darling," Cathy sobbed inwardly as she stumbled along at Harold's side. Then she broke down completely as, just before they turned the corner that would take her from Jon forever, the blackness behind them was rent by the hoarse, tortured cry of a man in mortal agony.

four

~~~

Jon twisted miserably on the long wooden plat-
form, running his swollen tongue around his
dry, cracked lips. The hold of the *Cristobel* was
like an oven; prisoners were crammed into it like sardines.
There must have been more than two hundred of them, all
male in this section at least, chained lying on their sides to the
platforms that were arranged one above the other in layers so
close that Jon's broad shoulders barely cleared the one above
him. Shackles with a short length of chain between them had
rubbed away the skin on his ankles and wrists; for further security a chain had also been passed around his waist and that
of the man who lay sweating not more than a hand's width
in front of him, linking them together. O'Reilly, he'd said his
name was, when they'd first been locked into this hellhole.
Lately, no one had bothered to talk; they hoarded all their
energy just to survive.

The man directly behind Jon was dead. Jon had heard
him choking on his own vomit several hours before, and as yet
the guards had not discovered him. When they did, his body
would be pitched overboard without ceremony. After all, why

waste prayers on a convict, whose crimes had robbed him of all humanity? Jon heard the clatter of the hatch cover being removed, then the thud of footsteps as the guards descended into the hold. Closing his eyes, he muttered a brief prayer for the soul of the dead man behind him, thinking, Christ, I don't even know his name.

"All right, you bastards, on deck! Move!"

Jon heard a series of clanks as the long metal poles holding the prisoners in place were removed, felt the pole that had held his arms chained above his head slide free, and lowered his arms, groaning. Pain stabbed through cramped muscles as he rubbed them with both hands, trying to restore their circulation. O'Reilly, closer to the narrow aisle that ran between the layers of platforms set into either side of the hold, began to scramble for the open space after the man in front of him. Jon had, perforce, to follow. Behind him he could hear tired curses as men trapped by the dead man's inert form struggled to get out, then a slow scraping noise as they pushed the body before them.

After ten days on board, this early morning ritual was expected. The prisoners were herded up on deck just after sunrise for exercise and their one scant meal of the day. Muskets were kept trained on them from all sides, but so far there had been no trouble. Despite their vigilance, the crew didn't appear to expect any. As Jon shuffled after O'Reilly up the narrow stairs, he had to concede that they were probably right. After hour upon hour spent in that stifling hold, all any of the prisoners seemed to want was to breathe in the brisk sea air, drink their cup of water, and eat as much as they were allowed.

In response to a prod from one of the guards, Jon fell into line with the other prisoners along the rail for shackle inspection. The first mate, Hinton, a big, burly fellow almost as tall as Jon, inspected their chains link by link. He had been one of the contingent sent to fetch Jon and six others from Newgate, and while there had apparently been treated to an account of Jon's circumstances. Jon hated him with an intensity all the greater for being impotent. Every time that big, ugly face grinned knowingly at him, every time that slack mouth spat a stream of brown tobacco juice through the gap left by a missing front tooth, Jon had to fight an urge to smash him to bits. That he could have done it, he was sure. He was equally sure that such an action would cost him his life.

"Wonder what your lady-love is doing today, pirate?" Hinton grinned at him as he yanked on the chain that bound him to O'Reilly. "On her honeymoon with some fancy lord, ain't she? Bet they're in the sack right now, all warm and cozy. . . . Sailed on the *Tamarind*, didn't they, on the very day we started on our little voyage? Maybe we'll pass 'em, and you can give 'em a wave."

He chortled. Jon's muscles bunched in violent response, and O'Reilly gave him a warning look. If Jon caused any trouble, they wouldn't hesitate for an instant to shoot him down like a dog.

"Lock 'em up!"

The order was bellowed down from the quarterdeck. Jon's muscles slowly relaxed as Hinton became all business, sliding a long chain through his and O'Reilly's shackles before throwing it to another guard, who did the same. In this way fifty or sixty men were fastened together, and the chain secured to a ring-bolt set into the deck. This was supposed to prevent a mutiny, or any of the men from leaping overboard. So far, it had succeeded admirably.

"Jump!"

Came the command, as it did every morning. Painfully the prisoners began to jump up and down, waving their arms and stomping their feet. This exercise, which was kept up for some five minutes, was designed to insure that the men would be fit for work when they reached their destination. For work was what they were slated to do. Factories abounded on Africa's west coast, factories that supplied England with numerous goods and were run on slave labor. When the *Cristobel* docked along the Ivory Coast, the prisoners would be auctioned off to the factories. The money would go into England's coffers, less a tidy profit for the crew. Thus everyone—except, of course, the new slaves—would be happy.

When the exercise was over for the day, the men were herded around the half-dozen or so large black cauldrons that cooked the day's ration of food right there on deck. Hungrily they scooped the inevitable watery stew up in their hands, devouring it as quickly as they could until it was gone.

"Take 'em below!"

Jon was still eating when the order rang out. Hastily he scooped up one last handful of stew, gulped it down, and licked his fingers. He just had time to swallow his allowance of water before Hinton and another guard stood before him. The other man bent to unfasten the long chain from the ring-bolt, while Hinton walked behind Jon, prodding him painfully in the back with his musket in an unspoken command to move. Jon, along with the rest of the prisoners, obediently started to fall into line for the return trip to the hold. Suddenly a hoarse scream rang out: everyone on deck immediately craned their necks to see what was happening. Over by the open hatchway, two prisoners had each other in a strangle-hold. Four guards ran over to separate them, clubbing them viciously with their muskets. Over his shoulder Jon could smell Hinton's sour breath as the man moved closer so that he could watch the fun; his musket once again jabbed Jon sharply in the small of the back. Instinctively, without even taking time to think, Jon brought his two fists together so that the thick chain was bunched between them. Then in a lightning move he whirled, bringing the iron club thus formed down hard onto Hinton's unsuspecting head. The man crumpled without a sound. Jon looked hastily around: only O'Reilly's bulging eyes seemed to be watching. To his relief he realized that everyone else was too preoccupied with what was taking place near the hatchway to have seen what he had just done. It took only an instant to lean down and remove the ring of keys from Hinton's belt. Careful to keep well out of sight, he unfastened his shackles and the chain that bound him to O'Reilly. Then he passed the keys to O'Reilly who quickly loosed his own bonds and passed them on. Jon, meanwhile, snatched up the fallen guard's musket and began to move quickly and unobtrusively toward the stairs leading to the quarterdeck As he gained the top of them, the musket at the ready, he heard a sudden roar behind him, and above it the cry, "Mutiny!"

"No heroics, gentlemen, or I'll blow you all to hell!" he said calmly to the ship's officers; as they whirled to face him, a savage grin split his face.

❧

Cathy, on the *Tamarind*, was smiling equally savagely. Harold had just left her, in what, for Harold, passed as a towering rage; Cathy doubted that she could hold him off much longer. He had made it clear that tonight he meant to share her bed, whether she was sick or well. It was this that had occasioned Cathy's grin. She had been feigning seasickness for the past ten days, moaning and clutching her stomach whenever Harold was near. Harold, himself somewhat sickened by the movements of the ship, was revolted by the sight of Cathy's distress. But this morning, when she had seemed no better, he had accused her of play-acting, which had somewhat increased Cathy's opinion of his intelligence. For play-acting she was, and very skillfully, too, if she should say so herself; after her experiences with Jon aboard the *Margarita,* her stomach was proof against anything the sea could throw at it.

If Harold didn't believe her little act, Cathy thought determinedly, she would have to convince him in such a way as would leave him in no doubt. She hit on a plan, and smiled as she considered it. So far Harold had not been hard to dupe, and she expected tonight to be no exception. Their marriage was still unconsummated, and, if Cathy could possibly contrive it, it would stay that way.

As evening approached, Harold returned to the cabin. Behind him came a sailor bearing a loaded tray. While the sailor set the dishes on the table in one corner of the room, Harold crossed to the bed and stood looking angrily down at Cathy. She returned his look limpidly.

"I insist that you join me for dinner." His voice was harsh.

"But, Harold, I am not well," Cathy protested tremulously. "The motion. . . ."

"You heard me!"

"Yes, Harold," Cathy whispered, meekly casting down her eyes. Through her thick lashes she saw his triumphant smile.

Dressed in a charming bronze-green satin wrapper over a matching nightdress from the complete trousseau that had been waiting for her when she had come aboard the *Tamarind*, Cathy obediently sat down opposite Harold as he began to eat. Although her perfectly healthy stomach protested since she had had no more than tea and toast all day, she listlessly pushed the food around her plate with her fork. The impression she wanted to give was that she was too ill to eat; from the frowning looks that Harold was casting her way, she thought she just might be succeeding.

In truth, Harold was thinking that she looked utterly enchanting, pale from her long sojourn in their cabin (she had not been on deck since they had sailed; perhaps she really was ill). Her sapphire eyes seemed to glow like stars against the whiteness of her skin, while her golden hair, loose and waving about her shoulders, was lovelier than Harold could have dreamed. That silky outfit she wore became her extremely, as did the rest of the garments he had selected for her. For an instant Harold congratulated himself on his excellent clothes sense, and then Cathy moved her head in a way that set her breasts to jiggling entrancingly. He stared openly, wetting his lips. Since marrying her, he had come to desire her more fiercely than he had ever desired a woman in his life. So far she had managed to keep him out of her bed, but tonight he would put an end to that. He meant to have her whether she was willing or no. And, who knew, perhaps by the time they returned to England she might be as hot for him as he was for her. Certainly it was no use for her to even think about the pirate; he had seen to it that the man was put forever beyond her reach, while still keeping his promise to the letter.

"Not feeling ill, are you?" Harold queried sharply when she took no more than a bite of the delicious raspberry ice that had been provided for their dessert.

"Not—not really, Harold," Cathy whispered bravely, playing her part to the hilt.

"Good. Because I don't intend to allow you to escape me any longer. Tonight I'm going to take what is legally mine."

Cathy felt her temper spark at this deliberate crudeness, but she managed to hang on to her submissive facade.

"We're married, Harold. How could I possibly escape you? It's just—I've felt so ill." Deliberately Cathy let her voice die away.

Harold nodded with satisfaction.

"In a way, I'm glad you've decided to be sensible, although taming you would not have been without its rewards. But I'm sure you gained plenty of experience as the pirate's paramour, and I expect you to make good use of it tonight. If my bride is not the blushing virgin that I deserve, then she can at least pleasure me. So come here, Cathy, and make a start."

Cathy blanched as Harold pushed his chair back from the table and stood up, beckoning to her. She had not counted on this happening so fast. Her mind raced as she stood up. For the moment she had to obey him. To fight him now would only result in rape. No, guile was what she needed to win this battle, and guile was what she would use. . . .

Harold's touch was every bit as dreadful as she had known it would be. His arms clamped around her body, jerking her roughly against his protruding belly, his mouth attaching itself to hers like a leech. It was loose and wet as it moved against her lips; his tongue forced its way between her teeth, thrusting down her throat so that she wanted to gag. But she stood her ground, submitting as docilely as she could to his grotesque embrace, not flinching even when his hand thrust roughly inside the neckline of her wrapper to close hurtfully on one soft breast.

Cathy's fingers itched to slap him as he kneaded her bare breast with rough familiarity, making obscene grunting noises in his throat like a huge rooting pig. With an immense effort of will she managed to restrain herself. Jon's dark face swam momentarily across the screen of her closed lids; the thought of his reaction if he could see her now made her banish it hurriedly. If her plan was to succeed, she must concentrate solely upon saving herself.

When Harold began to rip at the bodice of her wrapper, Cathy pushed him away with what gentleness she could muster. He stumbled back a pace. She saw with inward contempt that his face was mottled with passion and his breathing was hard and irregular. For the first time she began to get an inkling of the effect she had on him. His physical reaction betrayed his desire, and she began to perceive that it was something that might later be turned to her advantage. He was not the only one to hold aces in their little game.

"Harold, please, let's do this properly," she whispered, lowering her eyes as if shy. "Why don't you go for a walk on deck while I bathe and get into bed? When you get back, I'll be waiting for you. . . ." her voice trailed off seductively. Harold gulped, his pale blue eyes bulging as he stared at her.

"I don't want to wait," he said thickly, nearly making her jump out of her skin as he reached for her. Smiling slightly, shaking her head, she still managed to look seductive while placing both hands on his pouter pigeon chest and holding him off.

"It will be better later, don't you see?" she beguiled him with her eyes. "I've been ill and I need a bath. I have the most delicious perfumed bath salts . . . and then we'll share a bottle of wine. . . ."

"All right," Harold agreed in a hoarse voice, much to Cathy's relief. She smiled at him, inwardly wishing that she had a sword so that she could run him through. God, how she despised him! Just the thought of him making love to her—if it could be called that—was enough to make her stomach churn, in truth!

He pressed a moist kiss on her mouth, and then, with one last, languishing look, left her. Cathy nearly crowed with triumph. It was going to work . . . it was going to work! She began to undress as quickly as she could, splashed herself with cold water and a little perfume, and climbed into a fragile nightgown of pure white silk that had obviously been designed with a bride in mind. She ran a quick brush through her hair and leapt into the bed, pulling the covers up around her waist as she lay back provocatively against a mound of pillows. At all costs she had to make this believable.

She was ready not a moment too soon. As she heard Harold fumble with the door latch she took a deep breath. Then, determinedly, she thrust a slender finger as far down her throat as she could reach.

Her timing could not have been bettered. Harold finally made it through the door to be greeted by the sight of his incredibly lovely bride, dressed in nearly transparent white silk with her golden hair loose and gleaming in the light of the many-branched candelabra, vomiting grotesquely all over the jade velvet of what was to have been their bridal bed. He recoiled against the doorjamb, feeling his own stomach heave at the gruesome sight. In a high-pitched, shaking voice, he began to call for the ship's doctor.

Over the next few days, Cathy was hard put to it not to laugh. She played at being desperately nauseated, and Harold believed her. Whenever he was in the cabin she had only to clutch her stomach and moan to send him scuttling from the room. His own digestion was delicate at the best of times, he informed her nervously, and just the sight of her being so ill had been enough to put him off his feed. He took good care to stay out of the way as much as possible, even going so far as to have the steward make up a bed for him in an empty cabin. Since he had previously taken care to inform everyone on board that they were on their honeymoon, this circumstance was greeted with hilarity by the ship's crew, and those male passengers in the know.

Ian Smith, the ship's doctor, was puzzled at Cathy's illness. He examined her only cursorily (it was not considered proper for a doctor to do more, unless the lady lay at death's door), and he had to admit that she had all the usual symptoms of seasickness: vomiting, listlessness, a refusal to eat or even suffer food near her. Still, something did not quite seem right. But he could not put his finger on it, and, when pressed, said reluctantly that Lady Stanhope appeared to be suffering from a severe case of *mal de mer*.

Cathy was well aware that she couldn't hold Harold off forever by pretending to be ill, but while they were still at sea it served very well. There was no possible way he could take reprisals against Jon, for the simple reason that there was no way he could send a message; besides, after she had had time to think things through, it had occurred to her that if Harold really did, as he had threatened, go ahead and have Jon hanged to punish her for her lack of cooperation, he would no longer have anything to hold over her head. She would then leave him so fast he wouldn't have time to blink. Since her freedom involved Jon's death, the very thought of which made her shudder convulsively, she hadn't yet figured out how to turn this deduction to her advantage, but given time she was sure she would. And that was what she was doing now—playing for time.

◦◦◦◦◦◦

Five days later Cathy was growing more than a little tired of her pretense. Staying in bed when one felt perfectly well was boring in the extreme; besides, it gave her too much time to think, and her thoughts inevitably centered on Jon and little Cray. By now Jon must know that he was not to be hanged, and she wondered if he knew how his reprieve had been achieved. She hoped desperately that he did; the memory of his last anguished cry, after Harold had told him that they were wed, tortured her. At least, if he knew, he would also know that her seeming betrayal had been prompted by her love of him. Perhaps it would serve to take away some of his hurt.

Thinking of Jon was too painful, so Cathy tried not to. But thinking of Cray was nearly as bad. Poor baby, how he must be missing her! Her heart constricted as she pictured him crying for her, not understanding why she wasn't there. As soon as they had boarded the *Tamarind*, she had dashed off a quick note to Martha, explaining what had happened as concisely as she could. She knew that Martha would care for Cray as well as, or better than, she could, but still that didn't help. Her arms ached to hold him, and her eyes filled with tears as she imagined his bewilderment at the sudden changes in his life. He wouldn't understand what had happened to her, or Jon. He would think they had abandoned him!

And then, too, there was her father. Cathy greatly feared that the shock of hearing what had befallen her would kill him. She could only trust that Mason had broken it to him gently, and try to put it from her mind. At present, a mere two days from the coast of Spain, there wasn't a thing she could do for anyone except herself.

It was on a sunny day in early November that the *Tamarind* dropped anchor at La Coruña. Cathy had dared to get out of bed for just long enough to peep out at the harbor. From where they lay in a line of ships docked close to the wharf, she could see the town through the porthole. It looked very gay and colorful, with brightly dressed men and women milling with donkeys and pushcarts as they tried to market their wares to the people just getting off the ships. Cathy opened the porthole slightly, unable to resist the lure of the scene. Immediately the sweet smell of bananas and mangoes reached her nostrils, while the sounds of laughing, Spanish-speaking voices assailed her ears. It was almost evening, yet the sun was still a bright yellow ball above the horizon.

"You've been playing me for a fool, haven't you, Cathy?" Harold's ominously lowered voice behind her sent her spinning guiltily about. He was regarding her in a way that boded no good, his small eyes made even smaller by anger and his loose mouth for once clamped into a tight line. Cathy could find no words to answer him. She was well and truly caught out. Only an hour ago she had moaningly told him that she was too sick to even think of getting out of bed, much less sally forth to explore the town.

"You haven't been sick at all, have you?" he continued in that frightening voice. "What you thought to gain, I don't know. All your little pretenses can't change the fact that you're my wife, however much you may dislike it. And I'm sick of being the butt of jokes from every man on this ship. I intend to take what I married you for, now."

"You mean my money?" Cathy sneered, realizing that the showdown had come. In a way, it was a relief to let her loathing show at last. Harold's ugly face grew uglier at her taunt.

"I mean your body," he corrected crudely. Cathy's chin came up as he moved toward her, her muscles tensing for fight or flight. If Harold thought that bedding his sweet little bride was going to be a pleasure, then he had better think again!

"I'm going to make you very sorry that you tried to trick me, my dear," he promised in a guttural tone as he continued to advance.

"You mean succeeded, don't you?" Cathy dared recklessly, uncaring of how she was infuriating him. Her eyes cast surreptitiously about for a weapon as she spoke.

"Why, you little bitch, you'll pay for that!" Harold bellowed, incensed, and leapt for her. Cathy dodged nimbly to one side. His reaching fingers caught the fragile silk of her tangerine wrapper as she twirled away, tearing it down the back from neck to waist. Cathy let it drop to her feet and then kicked it aside as she sprinted toward the door. Harold, cursing under his breath, was right behind her.

"You're going to be sorry," he told her as he caught her by her flying hair, winding it hurtfully around his fist as he pulled her back to him. "I'm going to teach you a lesson once and for all. You're going to beg me for mercy. . . ."

"Poor Harold," Cathy gasped breathlessly as she was dragged backward. "Does it hurt your little pride to know that I loathe and despise you? That your touch makes me sick to my stomach? When you kiss me, I want to throw up!"

With an inarticulate cry of pure rage, Harold yanked viciously on her hair, forcing Cathy to her knees. She went because she couldn't help herself, but her face as she turned it up to him mirrored her continued defiance. His chin quivered as he stared at her, a slender, fragile figure lightly clothed in a peach silk nightdress that revealed more of her charms than it concealed. She was glaring at him, her blue eyes blazing their contempt. It stung him, feeding his anger. With an oath he raised his hand, slapping her viciously across the cheek. Her head snapped back at the force of his blow. Tears of rage and pain filled her eyes, but Cathy refused to let them fall. She would never give the filthy little toad that satisfaction!

"Does it make you feel like a man, Harold, to hit a woman?" Cathy taunted softly, knowing that she was inviting more of the same but too angry to care.

"You God-forsaken whore!" The words weren't much more than a furious whisper. Cathy's eyes instinctively followed the movement of his hand as he clenched it into a fist, raising it in apparent readiness to knock her senseless. As it began to descend she couldn't control a flinch.

The blow never fell. Cathy was saved by a brisk knock on the door. Cursing, lowering his fist, Harold stared balefully at it.

"What is it?" he called, giving Cathy a warning look. She was silent simply because it would do her no good to be anything else. As Harold's legal wife, he was entitled to do anything he cared to do to her, including beating her if he felt so inclined. There wasn't a man on board who would lift a hand to stop him. All she would achieve by calling attention to Harold's brutality was her own humiliation.

"It's the steward, with your supper, sir," came the voice from the other side of the door.

"Take it away," Harold ordered harshly.

"But, sir, Cook's going ashore with most of the rest of the crew. If you don't eat now, you won't be able to get anything else until morning."

"I said, take it away!" Harold screamed. Cathy moistened her lips as she heard the scurry of retreating footsteps.

"Now, you whore, where were we?" Harold muttered. Cathy closed her eyes, expecting him to hit her and not wanting to see the blow as it fell. Instead, he released her hair to grasp her upper arm, hauling her to her feet.

He shoved her toward the bed. Cathy half-fell, hoping to slow him by her weight, but he dragged her ruthlessly forward. As they neared the bed, he released his hold on her arm to grab her around the waist, his stubby hands digging into her soft flesh. Cathy, seeing what he meant to do, began to struggle; but despite Harold's girth and lack of height he was more than a match for her.

Picking her up, he flung her onto the mattress. Cathy bounced back against the wall, hitting her head so hard that she saw stars. Momentarily, she was stunned. Harold took advantage of this lull in her defenses to fling off his clothes. Cathy could only watch dazedly as he undressed.

In a kind of frenzy he threw aside his peacock blue coat, his lace-laden shirt and cravat, and stepped out of his pale blue breeches. Cathy stared with horrified fascination at the pasty mound of flesh thus exposed to her view. The muscles of his arms and shoulders, if muscles they were, sagged loosely; his puffy chest was as white as her own, its center adorned by a single tuft of reddish hair. His breasts were as large and pendulous as many a woman's, while his belly protruded grotesquely. As he peeled off his long underdrawers, Cathy could only watch, transfixed. Automatically she compared his pale, flaccid body with Jon's hard, muscular strength. For just an instant she was conscious of a crazy desire to giggle.

At least it restored her to full consciousness. Still, she lay supine, thinking to gull Harold into over-confidence. Her lip curled slightly with contempt as he strutted toward her, ostentatiously displaying his nudity. Apparently he felt no lack in himself.

The cabin was dark now except for a faint gray light filtering in through the open porthole. Through it Cathy could smell the sweet scent of fruit, hear the faint splash-splash of a boat being rowed. . . .

Then Cathy's seeking eyes spied what they had been looking for. On the bedside table stood a heavy metal bust of the Queen. Cathy smiled, reaching for it. Victoria, with her known views on the subservience of a wife to her husband, would surely frown on the use to which Cathy intended to put her likeness; but at the moment Cathy didn't particularly care.

Reaching for the bust, she had momentarily taken her

eyes off of Harold. That was a mistake. With a triumphant grunt he flung himself upon her, knocking her head back against the wall while his weight pinned her to the mattress. Cathy, taken by surprise, turned into a tigress. She kicked and clawed and bit him, no longer thinking of anything except the fact that this loathsome creature was doing his best to violate her body. That he was her legal husband weighed with her not at all. She hated and despised him, and not all the vows in the world could change that.

He was biting at her breasts, making disgusting noises deep in his throat as his hands roamed her body. Cathy gave up trying to fight him frontally; instead, she reached over her head, feeling for the bust. If she could just get it in hand, she would give her bridegroom a night to remember!

Harold took advantage of her seeming acquiescence to push the hem of her nightdress up around her waist. Cathy felt his naked flesh touch hers, and shook with revulsion. Her hands abandoned their quest for the bust to fly to her nightdress, trying desperately to cover herself. She clamped her thighs so tightly together that they hurt; she would not give in! She would not. . . .

He bit viciously at her breast. Cathy gasped, pain bringing tears to her eyes. Her hands curved into claws which reached for his eyes, but he caught them in his, holding them so that they were helpless. His knee began inexorably to part her thighs.

"Dear God," Cathy prayed mindlessly. "Help me. . . ."

As Harold brutally forced her legs apart, his mouth sucking and biting on her breasts, she fleetingly remembered her first time with Jon; she had accused him of raping her, had held it over his head for months. Only now was she coming to realize the true horror that rape meant.

With a grunt Harold spread her legs wide. Cathy tensed all her muscles, hoping to hold off his entry for as long as she could. She felt him probe her softness, and in an instinctive reaction opened her mouth to bite him viciously on the neck. Suddenly, through the darkness behind Harold's head, she caught a blur of movement. Something silver gleamed faintly as it descended in a long arc. There was a muffled thud; Harold gasped, then went limp.

For just a moment Cathy lay there, stunned. What had happened? Then a sense of her own possible danger began to penetrate. Frantically she shoved at Harold's shoulders, trying to squirm out from under his dead weight.

From somewhere above her came the sound of a hard, unamused laugh. Over Harold's shoulder loomed the outline of a man's head. Cathy stared fearfully through the darkness at the apparition; her breath caught in her throat as she met a pair of very familiar, very icy gray eyes.

five

Jon!" she gasped, barely able to summon her voice at all.

"Well, well, if it isn't Lady Stanhope!" he drawled with awful affability. "Pray forgive me for interrupting your honeymoon, my lady."

The rasping emphasis he put on the word "honeymoon" brought color surging into Cathy's cheeks. Jon was furious: she could tell, although he was doing his best to conceal it. So he had believed Harold's lies! Cathy knew she should be furious as well that he had had so little faith in her. But she was so wondrously glad to see him, alive and apparently free, that her anger died.

"How on earth did you get here?" she gasped, that question surfacing from the dozens that hovered on the tip of her tongue. As she spoke she pushed impatiently at Harold's limp form. If she could only get up . . . !

"You weren't expecting me?" Seeing her frustrated attempts to shift Harold, Jon's lips curled sardonically. With easy strength he reached out and grasped Harold by one shoulder, flipping him over onto his back and away from Cathy. "Obviously not."

Hearing the freezing sarcasm in this last, Cathy followed his eyes. They rested, granite-like, on the bared lower half of her body before moving to touch on Harold's nakedness. Knowing what he was thinking, she couldn't stop herself from flushing guiltily. Which was absurd, as she had done absolutely nothing to be ashamed of! Damn the man for being so quick to jump to conclusions!

"It's not what you think," she began, hastily pulling her nightdress down so that she was decent as she scrambled into a kneeling position on the mattress.

"Of course not," he responded coldly, pulling loose a length of rope he had coiled about his waist and beginning to cut it into smaller sections with a wicked-looking knife he withdrew from a scabbard at his belt.

"What are you doing?" His actions momentarily diverted her. She watched, wide-eyed, as he turned the unconscious Harold over onto his stomach and proceeded to tie him up.

"What does it look like?" As a final touch, Jon pulled a rag from the pocket of his black cloth breeches and thrust it into Harold's mouth. He then proceeded to strip a pillowcase from the pillow he pulled from beneath Harold's body, and used that to tie the gag in place. "I suppose I should kill him, thus making you a widow, my sweet, but I find that I no longer consider you worth risking the death penalty—even a second one."

Cathy stared at him in dismay. Why was he always so ready to believe the worst of her? Surely she had proved her love over the past two years!

"Listen, you big oaf, I said it's not what you think!" She glared at him furiously, fueled by a sudden spirit of rage. He ignored her, reaching down to pull the coverlet up so that Harold was completely hidden from sight. Watching him, with his white shirt open carelessly halfway down his chest so that the pelt of dark hair covering his body was tantalizingly visible, the muscles in his arms and thighs rippling as he moved, Cathy was struck by a sudden sense of *déjà vu*. With his hard, handsome features set ruthlessly and stubbly blue-black bristles obscuring his jaw, he was frighteningly like the pirate who had abducted her two years before. Even the pair of silver-mounted pistols thrust into his belt added to the illusion!

"I presume you have a trunk?" His question was clipped. Cathy nodded, bewildered. What did her trunk have to do with anything?

"Where is it?"

"In the corner!" Cathy's tone was as short as his. He turned to look where she had pointed, then fixed those steely eyes on her face once again. "But I don't see. . . ."

"But then no one ever accused you of being overly bright, did they?" Jon was fast losing his facade of politeness. Cathy's eyes widened furiously at this insult; then, as she sat there killing him with her eyes, she had to smile at herself. For weeks she had been longing for the sight of him, doing everything in her power to see that he was unharmed. And now, when a miracle had brought him back to her, all she could do was quarrel with him! She shook her head at her own perversity. She would be sweetly reasonable. . . .

"Jon, darling, I'm really so glad to see you!" she sighed, clambering across the mattress until she reached where he was standing at its side. "If you'll just listen. . . ."

Smiling at him, she reached up to twine her arms around his neck. He caught her hands, holding her off. Her sweet smile turned to a glare of anger; the answering twist of his lips denoted satisfaction at her response.

"You really think you can have your cake and eat it too, don't you?" he asked as if marvelling. "Not this time, my sweet. You'll not get around me again with sweet smiles and kisses and your soft, seductive body. I've got your measure at last: you're nothing but a whore, for sale to the highest bidder. Or whoever can do you the most good at a particular time."

"How dare you say such a thing to me?" Cathy gasped, hurt mingling with her rage. "If you think that of me, then you can just leave! Go on, get out of here! I'd rather stay with Harold than you, by far!"

Jon smiled then, mirthlessly. His fingers tightened on hers so that she almost cried out with the pain.

"Very nicely done, Cathy," he applauded softly. "But you forget—I know you rather well. You can be quite a consummate actress, when it pleases you. And there is something else that you forgot to take into your little calculations: what is mine, I keep."

"I think it's *you* who's forgetting!" Cathy threw at him, incensed. "It's Harold I'm married to, remember? I am not yours, and if you keep this up, I never will be!"

"Oh, yes, you are," he said very softly. "You're mine for as long as I want you. When I tire of you, why, I might even return you to your precious Harold. Console yourself with that thought, my sweet, if you can!"

"What are you doing?" The question was jerked from her as Jon transferred both her hands to one of his, securing the wrists together with a piece of rope. Cathy tried to pull free as he tied the knot, deftly tightening it with his teeth.

"You're mad!" she cried with more anger than conviction as he turned her over onto her stomach on the mattress, affording her feet the same treatment he had given her hands. She struggled wildly, trying to kick him, but he held her down by the simple expedient of setting one muscular knee into the small of her back.

"If I am, you've driven me to it," he sounded grim as he knotted the rope about her ankles, then turned her easily over onto her back.

"If you don't let me go, right now, I'll scream. They'll

catch you and hang you for sure this time! I mean it, you filthy swine, I'll scream!"

"Will you?" The silky question should have warned her. That it didn't she supposed she should attribute to the fact that even after all that he had said and done, she couldn't believe that Jon would actually use her in such a way. But the cloth that was roughly thrust into her open mouth took her by complete surprise. While she was still spitting at the taste of it, he was securing it in place with his own neckerchief!

Cathy wriggled protestingly as Jon scooped her up, her blue eyes blazing fire.

"You bastard!" she tried to say, but the gag muffled all utterance. Jon grinned without humor at the strangled sound she made, as if he could somehow read her mind.

"Don't worry, I feel exactly the same way about you," he mocked harshly, and then he was laying her down on the floor. Cathy had only a moment to ponder his purpose before it was made crystal clear: he began rolling her up in the fringed Chinese carpet that adorned the floor beside the bed. She kicked wildly with both legs as she saw what he was about, but it was useless: he controlled her struggles as if she had been a child. Dust entered her nose and she sneezed, then choked on that horrible gag. Immediately Jon loosened the folds of wool swathing her face.

"Stay still, and you'll be fine," he told her roughly through the opening at the top of the rug. Cathy could only lift her head to glare smolderingly at him in reply.

She felt his arms go around her through the many thicknesses of wool, and then he was hoisting her to dangle ignominiously over his shoulder, as if it were in truth only a rug he was carrying! Fuming, she tried to kick, but his arms about her were like iron bands holding her helpless. Had he taken leave of his senses? she raged inwardly. He must have, to accuse her of such things, to dare to treat her in such a way.

She had lived with him as his wife for over two years, borne him a son, loved him, cared for him—and he believed her capable of throwing all that over at the earliest opportunity, just to marry Harold for his social position? It was almost funny, Cathy thought furiously. Strange that she felt not the smallest desire to laugh.

Jon stopped on his way out of the cabin to pick up Cathy's small trunk, which he tucked under one arm. The other arm was busy holding a wriggling Cathy firmly on his shoulder. Finally, as he climbed the stairs leading to the deck, she seemed to give up, and lay quite still. Jon could only hope that the rug hadn't suffocated her. Really, it was just as well that she was not, as he would have expected, fighting him like some tawny hell-cat. When he had first seen her, sprawled wantonly across the bed with her lover, rage had torn at his innards like a wolf with a slaughtered calf: his first instinct had been to throttle the pair of them. With considerable control he had managed merely to knock Harold senseless, and carry off his wife—no, not *his* wife, Harold's. He kept having trouble with that. But it wouldn't take much to stoke that banked-down fury into raging life, and woe betide Cathy if she managed it!

Luckily, an icy wall seemed to have descended over his emotions. Jon knew it for a fragile thing, but he was deeply grateful for its presence. It had stopped him from doing something he had known even then he would regret. The urge to strike her, to make her suffer as she had made him suffer, had been very strong. In that first shattering moment, when he had surprised her nearly naked in bed with her totally naked husband, the terrible reality of what she had done had seared through his mind and heart like a red-hot poker.

She had been his wife, before God if not legally before man, and she had betrayed him. Deliberately, wantonly, she had sold the body she had vowed to keep only for him to another man. And for what? Did he love her, that disgusting lump of suet she had taken to her bed? Would he work from daylight to dark for her, struggling to wrest a living from an uncooperative soil for herself and her son? Would he give his life to spare the smallest centimetre of her white skin from harm? Hell, no! Cathy had traded the gold of his love for the dross of wealth and a glittering London social life, just as he had always feared she would. In the process, she had proved herself to be just like every other woman he had known: like cats, they loved whoever fed them the choicest bits of fish, offered them the softest cushion beside the warmest fire. Their oft-protested affection went no deeper than that.

By now, that bastard cousin-husband of hers undoubtedly knew everything about Cathy's enticing little body that there was to know. As he strode along the dark, deserted deck of the *Tamarind*, looking like a sailor carrying his few possessions ashore to any who happened to glance his way, Jon tried and failed to banish an image of Harold's slack mouth and pudgy fingers crawling over Cathy's slender body. Had Harold made her cry out with pleasure, as he, Jon, had done time out of mind? Had he made her pant and beg and writhe, and brought her to an ecstasy she had never even dreamed existed over and over again? Jon ground his teeth. Doubtless Harold thought he had. The little bitch had probably put on a damned good show, knowing the way to bring men under her spell. He, Jon, had taught her well the secrets of how to pleasure a man. It flayed at him like a thousand cat-o'-nine-tails to imagine her using that knowledge to play the whore in her new husband's bed.

Jon's eyes were fierce and his jaw was clenched forbiddingly by the time he reached the *Tamarind*'s aft rail. O'Reilly, waiting with another former prisoner, Tinker, in a gig bobbing on the waves far below, thought that he had never seen a man look angrier than Jon did as he lowered the small trunk into the gig with a rope.

"Did you find what you were after?" O'Reilly finally summoned up the nerve to call guardedly, knowing a good bit of the story behind Jon's pursuit of the *Tamarind*. He had been surprised, when Jon had reappeared, to see him alone. The *Cristobel*'s new captain had come for a lady; in the brief time he had known him, O'Reilly had already learned that Jon Hale was not a man to fail.

"Yes." Jon gritted that and no more as he swung himself one-handed down the dangling rope suspended from the *Tamarind*'s deck, his legs wrapped snugly around it for leverage. His other arm he kept firmly about a rolled and tied rug that dangled over his shoulder. O'Reilly stared at it for an instant, perplexed. What in hell . . . ? Then, suddenly, light dawned and he understood.

"Let's go," Jon said briefly when he stood upright in the gig. O'Reilly and Tinker began obediently to row. As the little boat pulled away from the *Tamarind*'s towering side, Jon lowered the now-writhing rug very gently to the bottom of the boat. A muffled, angry-sounding noise came from the rug's depths. O'Reilly was amused to see Tinker cast it a startled glance.

"I said, be still!" Jon told the rug sharply, dropping to his knees beside it and adjusting the opening at one end. Tinker looked even more startled, his pinched cockney face turning to see what O'Reilly made of their captain's sudden eccentricity. O'Reilly reassured him with a broad wink.

When another muffled sound came from the rug, Jon set his teeth, and ignored it. He moved to the gunwale, and stared stonily out to sea.

The *Cristobel* was anchored at the very mouth of La Coruña's harbor, and it was toward her tall silhouette that the gig headed. A cool night breeze blew over the water, hinting strongly at rain soon to come. White caps rose in little flurries on the crests of dark waves. The sea was choppy, and the gig bobbed roughly up and down. O'Reilly supposed that the lady in the rug must be getting a severe jarring, but he told himself that it was none of his concern. Besides, if even half of the tale of what she had done to the captain were true, it was nothing compared to what she deserved.

When they reached the *Cristobel*, Tinker shouldered the trunk up the rope ladder flung from her deck by another of her makeshift crew. O'Reilly, his offer to help with the clearly rebellious rug curtly declined, followed. Jon, carrying his burden easily, brought up the rear, and the ladder was pulled up after them.

The deck was alive with men who were doing their best to get the ship ready to put out again to sea. Few of the former prisoners were experienced seamen; there were just enough of those to form a very skeleton crew. The rest were, at least, willing to learn and hardworking. Jon had ruthlessly weeded out those who weren't, and had put them ashore along with the vessel's former captain and crew and most of the women prisoners, who were quite willing to go. Jon knew that it would be only a matter of time before word of the mutiny got back to England and ships were sent in pursuit. But by that time, he hoped fervently that the *Cristobel* would be well away.

Jon strode briskly along the deck toward the captain's cabin under the quarterdeck. As the only man aboard who had ever captained a ship of this size, he had been selected by default. But from the first he had made it clear that he expected to be obeyed. The men had come to respect his knowledge, his fairness, and his sheer physical size, and there had been little trouble. Those who had seemed bent on making mischief had been re-imprisoned in the hold; they, too, had been put ashore with the others. Jon knew from his long years as a pirate captain that mutiny was like measles: contagious. It had happened once on the *Cristobel*, and he meant to do his utmost to see that it didn't happen again.

The captain's cabin was small and dingy, as was everything else on the prison ship. Besides the bunk, it had only an ugly, belching coal stove and a small square table bolted to the floor, with two straight-backed chairs for furnishings. The bunk was a hard, narrow shelf built right into the wall. That it was hellishly uncomfortable Jon knew only too well from the week he had already spent sleeping on it.

When he had entered and closed the door behind him, Jon lit a candle. Then he lowered a wriggling Cathy, still wrapped in the rug, to the dusty plank floor, setting her carefully on her feet. Slowly he unwound the rug from about her. She was very dishevelled, her golden hair tumbling over her shoulders to stream across her heaving breasts to her waist in wild profusion. That flimsy orange thing that was all she wore barely veiled her charms. The gag in her mouth effectively prevented her from speaking, but then, she didn't have to: her eyes said it all for her. If looks could kill, Jon thought, he would be lying dead at her feet. He took savage satisfaction from the realization. By the time he had finished with her, she would have good cause to feel that way!

"I'm going to take the gag off now, but I warn you: give me any trouble and I'll put it back. And leave it there! Do you understand?"

Those slanting sapphire eyes still looked murderous, but after an obviously reluctant moment she nodded. Turning her around, Jon worked the knot loose and removed the cloth tied around her head. Cathy spat out the wet and crumpled rag that he had stuffed in her mouth. Then, ankles and wrists still bound, she whirled rather clumsily to face him. The lower part of her face was pinkened from the chafing of the gag; her lips were dry-looking and slightly swollen. She was also quivering from head to toe with temper.

"This time I really do believe you've lost your mind, Jonathan Hale!" she spat, running her tongue over her dry lips. "How dare you manhandle me in such a fashion? You are a low-down, loathsome, stupid pig, and if I'd had any sense I would have let them hang you!"

"Why didn't you?" he drawled, his eyes narrowing dangerously at her abuse. "I admit, that part has had me in something of a puzzle. What happened, Cathy? Did the thought of me being hanged actually prick that very convenient little conscience of yours? Is that why you and Harold arranged to have me transported and sold as a slave instead? Neat, that. Your guilty past safely and permanently out of the way without a spot of blood on those lily-white hands. Tell me, just as a matter of curiosity, how did you propose to rid yourself of Cray?"

"That is a filthy thing to say!" Cathy was nearly speechless with fury. "You know full well, you ungrateful cad, that I love Cray more than anything in the world! I would never want to rid myself of him, as you put it. And I loved you! You notice that I said loved! Past tense! Because after the way you've behaved to me tonight, I begin to wonder if I've ever even known you!"

"Next I suppose you're going to try to tell me that you did it all for love of me?" he mocked, only a muscle twitching convulsively at the corner of his mouth belying his light tone.

"I did! I did! *I did!*" Her voice rose to a crescendo as she screeched the words at him.

"Like hell you did." He dismissed her claim brutally. Rage flared like a flash fire in Cathy's eyes.

"You have a mind like a sewer!" she said in a shaking voice. "You sicken me, did you know that? You've been warped beyond saving! You. . . ."

"That's enough!" he ordered sharply, his face grim. "I don't have time to listen while you spin your little web of lies. Unless we want dear Harold and his buddies to catch up with us, we have to sail with the ten o'clock tide. And we wouldn't want that, would we, love?"

The taunting way he called her "love" told her he meant just the opposite. Cathy, glaring up at him as he stood towering threateningly over her, nearly snarled with wrath.

"Oh, yes, we would!" she said venomously, and at that moment she almost meant it.

"The truth will out," he quoted ironically, then took her arm, pushing her ungently toward the bunk.

"What do you think you're doing now? Take your hands off me!"

At her attempted resistance Jon bent and scooped her easily up in his arms. Fiercely Cathy resented the overwhelming strength that made her helpless as a babe in arms against him.

"Oh, no, my sweet. We've been through this before, remember? I'm not taking any chances on leaving you loose in here, only to return to find that my pretty little bird has flown her not so pretty cage."

"You can't mean to keep me tied!" Cathy gasped indignantly, wriggling wildly in his arms. He controlled her struggles with little seeming difficulty, smiling down at her unpleasantly all the while.

"Can't I? Try me!" With that he dropped her without warning onto the bunk. Its thin mattress was hard as a board, and Cathy winced from the abrupt contact. She had been so knocked about already tonight that she ached all over, and this last jolt certainly did nothing to make her feel better! But she didn't have time now to worry about her aches and pains. Disregarding her still bound ankles and wrists, Cathy struggled to get to her feet.

"Oh, no you don't!" Jon was pushing her back with one hand against her chest. Then, to keep her in place, he straddled her, pinioning her bucking body between his knees.

Cathy lay on her back, twisting uselessly, her bound hands striking out at him until he caught them and drew them up over her head As he secured them with a piece of rope to the bunk frame, she called him all the filthy names she had ever heard. He ignored her, going calmly about his business. When he had her hands positioned to suit him, he stood up, moving down to the foot of the bunk. Cathy kicked at him, aiming viciously for his groin. Jon caught her flailing feet by the rope that bound them, and despite her efforts accorded them the same treatment he had her hands. Cathy was left lying helpless, her arms bound together at the wrists and stretched above her head, her ankles bound and secured to the end of the bunk. Her knees were raised and slightly bent, her nightdress hitched up around her slim white thighs. The long, pale length of her legs gleamed invitingly. Golden tangles of hair streamed across the bunk to spill in an unruly mass toward the floor. Spots of angry scarlet color burned becomingly in her cheeks, while her eyes threw sapphire daggers at him. She seemed to have run out of invective at last, for she lay panting and glaring silently at him. Jon stared down at her for a long moment, his expression unreadable. Then his eyes flickered. With an almost savage gesture, he reached down and twitched the hem of her nightdress into its proper place about her ankles. Then, without a word, he turned on his heel and stalked from the cabin, pausing only to blow out the candle as he went.

Out on deck, Jon drank deeply of the rapidly cooling night air, hoping that it would help to clear his mind. The little bitch's fragile beauty and pitiful mewlings were, unbelievably, beginning to cloud his judgement once more. Was it possible that she had done what she had done for love of him, as he had asked her so sarcastically? No! He ruthlessly extinguished that tiny flicker of hope. If she had truly wanted to save him from the gallows "because she loved him," he mocked mirthlessly, there were any number of things she could have done that did not involve marrying a wealthy lord or letting that lord use her body. Her father would have helped, for Cray's sake if for no other reason. That mangy-looking butler who had admitted him to the house on Grosvenor Square had said that Sir Thomas was much improved, out of danger, in fact. So the lying bitch needn't think that she could plead her father's illness as an answer to that! Or she could have bribed a guard to let him escape, or. . . . Besides, out of her own mouth she stood condemned. That day she had come to Newgate she had admitted everything, then walked calmly away, leaving him shattered. He had actually howled out his grief like an animal in pain. No, it was only now, when she feared that he might exact some sort of revenge, that she was once again bleating about her supposed love for him. Jon tried to convince himself that it was a desire for revenge that had sent him sailing after her into La Coruña, carrying so much canvas that sometimes even he had questioned his sanity. Painful as it was, it was time he faced facts: like better men before him, he had been taken for a ride by a two-faced little slut who was perfectly prepared to trade her body for whatever she wanted. Surely he was not such a besotted fool as to let her wrap him around her little finger again!

"Hale—I mean, uh, Captain—could you take a look at this? Somethin' don't seem to be workin' quite right."

Glad to escape from his own thoughts, Jon followed the man to the mizzenmast where he saw that, in the act of unfurling the cross-jack, the lines had somehow gotten snarled. The sail hung pathetically, like a woman with her petticoat half torn off. Jon sighed, then climbed the mast himself, clinging to the rigging with one hand while he patiently untangled the lines with the other. He then proceeded to demonstrate for what must have been the dozenth time the proper way to unfurl a sail. Under his eye, the inexperienced men in the rigging with him managed to do a creditable job. He told them so, then lowered himself back to the deck, leaving them to their work. God help all aboard the *Cristobel* if they should run into a storm! With her crew of amateurs, prayers were the only way they would survive it!

"Cold, Jonny?" The studiedly girlish voice belonged to Sarita Jones, as she called herself, a black-headed, black-eyed gypsy of a woman who had been sentenced to transportation for the crime of prostitution. She was one of the few women prisoners who had elected, and been allowed, to stay on board. O'Reilly had an eye on her and had pleaded her case, which was why Jon had permitted her to stay. But since then Sarita had made it clear that she found the *Cristobel*'s new captain far more to her taste. Jon sighed inwardly as he looked down at her, posturing and preening before him, her ample breasts nearly bared by the low-cut peasant blouse she wore. Women on shipboard were nothing but problems, he thought, harassed. And one thing was sure: he had enough woman problems of his own without adding this one to them!

"Females aren't permitted on deck after dark, Sarita. I've already told you that." His voice was patient, but he clearly meant what he said. Sarita fluttered her eyelashes at him.

"But I brought you a bottle of grog, Jonny. Surely that's allowed, to bring you up a bottle of grog, when it's chilly out?"

Jon looked down at her for a moment, not speaking. It was impossible to get really angry at Sarita, exasperating as her behavior was. She was slightly stupid, a tart from the gutters of London, but there was no real harm in her. And at least she was what she was, which was more than he could say for some.

"Thank you, Sarita," he said, accepting the bottle from her outstretched hand. He pretended not to notice when she caressed his fingers with hers as she passed the bottle over. "Now get below. Scoot!"

"Oh, Jonny!" Sarita protested sulkily; then, to his secret relief, she flounced away, her full hips swinging provocatively beneath their covering of full black skirts. Clearly she expected him to watch her go, and, watching, to lust.

"Women are the very devil, aren't they, Cap'n?" O'Reilly spoke rather wistfully beside him. The shorter, stockier, florid-faced man clearly envied Jon his dark good looks. Jon grimaced at him.

"They are that, O'Reilly, and no mistake," he answered in heartfelt tones. "Here, have a drink."

Jon passed the bottle over to the other man, who accepted it, took a swig, and handed it back. Feeling the need of some fortification before facing what was likely to be a very long night, Jon wiped the bottle on his shirtsleeve and then raised it to his own lips, swallowing healthily. The two men stood on the quarterdeck for the better part of two hours, talking only desultorily as they killed the bottle of rum between them. By the time the moon came up, a shimmering white crescent playing hide and seek with drifting gray clouds on a field of black velvet, the *Cristobel* was once again well out to sea. Jon stared somberly at the milky path cast by the moon across the dark water, knowing that he was ever so slightly the worse for wear. Not drunk, mind you, but not precisely stone sober either.

"I think I'll turn in," he said to O'Reilly, who nodded, and then, recollecting that Jon had a lady waiting in his cabin, grinned. Jon saw the grin with a slight twinge of annoyance. O'Reilly clearly imagined him to be heading in for a long night of passion, when he was likely to be greeted with a tantrum instead.

Jon turned over command of the ship to Mick Frazier, one of the few on board who knew what to do with it. He issued some instructions about their course and the correct amount of canvas to carry. Then he went to his cabin.

Cathy had fallen asleep from sheer exhaustion in the midst of her useless struggles. She awoke abruptly when Jon came through the door. He closed it after him, leaning rather heavily against it for a moment while his eyes adjusted to the gloom. From where she lay, Cathy could smell the odor of liquor that clung to him. So he had been drinking, had he, while she had lain here suffering? But as he moved toward her, she could detect no outward signs of drunkenness except for the too-bright glitter of his gray eyes.

"Do you think that you could untie me?" she requested tartly as he stood towering over the bunk. "Now that you're here to make certain I don't escape, of course!"

Jon seemed undecided for a moment, then sat down on the edge of the bunk. He said nothing as his hands moved to loosen the knot that tied her hands to the frame. That done, Cathy lowered her arms, not even trying to suppress a slight groan. If he felt guilty about the discomfort he had caused her, well and good! He deserved worse than that!

It took him a little longer to undo the rope binding her wrists. When he finally succeeded, Cathy flexed her fingers, then shook them. Finally she spread her arms wide. Pins and needles shot through her entire upper body, making her gasp.

"Arms asleep?" Jon asked with what could almost have been gruff sympathy. Cathy was in no mood to accept it.

"Oh, no," she said in a sugar-wouldn't-melt-in-her-mouth voice. "Why should they be?"

Jon shot her a hard look. She could see him glowering at her, clearly misliking her answer.

"Best keep a lid on that hot little temper, sweet. I can always tie you up again."

"You're awfully good at making threats, aren't you?" Cathy taunted, the hot little temper he had disparaged hitting flash point. "Let's see how good you are at carrying them out!"

Her hand connected with his face with a satisfying smack. Jon's head snapped back at the force of her blow, his hand flying automatically to his abused cheek.

"You damned little hell-cat!" he snarled, grabbing for her hands and imprisoning them in his. "You need a beating! And if you give me much more trouble, I'll give it to you!"

"Oh, lawsy, more threats!" Cathy mocked recklessly. "Dear me, I'm all a-quiver!"

Jon ground his teeth, his hands moving up to seize her by the shoulders. He shook her until Cathy's head was reeling. She fought, trying her best to pull her feet free and roll off the bunk. With her ankles still tied, it proved impossible.

"Let me go, you brute!" she snapped when she could again speak. Jon had stopped shaking her, staring down into her face with an expression that should have given her pause.

She was too angry to heed it. How dare he treat her like this? Her hand shot out again, slapping him hard across his other cheek.

"You bitch!" he roared, capturing her hands in a grip that made her wince. "I've had all I'm going to take from you! I ought to slap you silly!"

"Do it, you big, brave man! Go on, do it!" Cathy dared furiously. Jon's gray eyes blazed down at her dangerously, but he didn't take advantage of her invitation. For all her bravado, Cathy had not really thought he would. She knew him too well, or at least she thought she did. . . .

Instead he pushed her forcibly back down against the mattress, one knee nearly crushing her chest as it held her there. She squirmed and cursed as he tied first one hand and then the other to the bunk frame. She was as helpless as a baby by the time he stood up, his eyes gleaming with satisfaction.

"Untie me, Jonathan Hale! You untie me right now or I'll make you sorry! I'll scratch your eyes out when I get loose! I'll . . . !"

"Temper, temper, little girl," Jon chided with an edge to his voice, moving down to the end of the bunk. He reached for her feet, and Cathy was momentarily silent, thinking in some surprise that he meant to untie her, after all. But when her feet were free at last, he quickly tied them again; only this time her legs were tied separately—and apart.

"What are you doing?" she gasped.

Jon smiled nastily.

"It just occurred to me that I deprived you of a bridegroom. But don't let it worry you, sweet. I intend to replace him."

Cathy gaped at him as the import of her position, helpless and spread-eagled across the narrow bunk, became suddenly all too clear.

"Don't you dare!" she warned in a fierce, shaking whisper. "Jon, don't you dare! I'll hate you if you do! I mean it: I'll hate you!"

"Hate away, Lady Stanhope," he drawled nastily. "You couldn't possibly hate me any more than I hate you!"

While he was speaking he removed that wicked-looking knife from his belt. Cathy stared at it fearfully, shrinking into the hard mattress as its sharp edge approached her throat. But its target, as she realized with some relief, was the neckline of her nightdress. Catching up the fragile silk in one hand, Jon slid the knife under it, running the long blade the length of the material. The garment slit from neck to hem. Cathy felt the cool night air touch her skin as he pulled what was left of the gown from beneath her, wadding it up and throwing it on the floor. Watching the savagery of his movements, she shivered convulsively.

"Jon, don't do this! Please!" she gasped as he bent purposefully over her. Her anger had fled, to be replaced by a kind of horror. She couldn't bear it if he took her like this, brutally, with hatred between them where there had once been love. It would be rape as surely as what Harold had tried to do to her earlier would have been.

"Jon, no! Please!" she tried again, squirming as his strong, warm hands with their calloused palms slid with slow familiarity over her body.

"She begs so prettily," Jon said to no one in particular. "Is that how you begged Harold, Lady Stanhope? Before you let him take you?"

"No!" Cathy cried, shaking her head from side to side. But Jon was no longer listening. He had straightened, staring down at her fixedly as he divested himself of shirt and breeches. Her naked body gleamed through the darkness, a pale X against the darker background of the coverlet. Her breasts were soft and full and very white, twin peaks crowned with impudent little nipples blushed a dusty pink. They quivered as he looked at them. Her waist was incredibly narrow, her belly that had housed his son smooth and flat. Her legs were long and curved, jerking now against the ropes binding her feet. The soft, golden nest of hair between her thighs beckoned to him, promising him remembered delights. She was spread before him like a feast, and Jon suddenly knew that he was starving. He hadn't had a woman for months, not since she had left him at Woodham to go to her father. (More fool he, for being faithful to vows that she couldn't wait to discard!) During the long voyage across the Atlantic to England, he had dreamed of her endlessly, picturing her delectable body, imagining himself making passionate love to her. And in the even longer days and nights that had followed his imprisonment, his fantasies had grown more erotic. In his mind he had taken her every way in which a man could take a woman, but a mental seduction was a very unsatisfying exercise. But tonight—ahhh, tonight! She lay before him as helpless as a virgin served up for sacrifice, his for the taking. And take her he would. Her pleas and feeble little struggles moved him not at all.

"Jon, don't do this!" Cathy begged again as, naked, he stretched his length on the bunk beside her.

"Pretend I'm Harold," he whispered harshly back. Cathy cringed from the words.

He made a move as though he would kiss her; she turned her face away. His hand closed hurtfully on her chin, forcing her head back around. He held her chin tightly as his mouth closed over hers. His tongue probed between her lips, touched her teeth, which she kept tightly clenched. She would not, would not, submit to him!

"Don't fight me, Cathy, or you'll make me hurt you," he warned in her ear. When she continued her stiff resistance he bit her soft lobe punishingly. Cathy gasped with pain, her eyes and mouth flying open at the same time. At that instant his thumb came up to press against her cheek in such a way that, if she tried to close her mouth, she would bite the inside of her jaw. Then, with her mouth opened to his satisfaction, his lips closed on hers again, kissing her hungrily. His tongue penetrated the sweet depths of her mouth, exploring the dark cave, tickling her tongue with his. It stroked her lips and teeth and the roof of her mouth.

Cathy, hating him for what he was doing to her, for using force, took no pleasure from his touch. When he put his hands on her breasts, softly caressing her nipples, she tried to pull away. Tied as she was, she could move only a few inches. His hand followed her, continued with its play. To her shame she felt the soft peaks tremble, and grow hard.

His mouth took over from his hands, suckling gently at her breasts. Despite herself Cathy felt a burning ache begin in her belly. As if to assuage it, his hands slid over that silky surface, then moved down to rest lightly on the secret place between her legs. After a moment, his fingers began to move. Cathy heard a hoarse rasping sound, and realized with a sense of shock that it was her own breathing. Jon heard it, too, and raised his head to shoot her a triumphant look.

"Jon, if you do this, I'll never forgive you," Cathy whispered in a shaken voice as he raised himself above her.

Jon laughed.

six

When he had exhausted himself at long last, Jon lay sprawled on top of her, his big body limp and heavy. His flesh was still imbedded in hers as his breathing slowly resumed its normal rhythm. Cathy, feeling both humiliated by his harsh possession and bitterly ashamed of her own body's instinctive response to his practiced use of it, lay beneath him as still as death. His weight threatened to crush the air from her lungs, but she barely noticed that. Her whole consciousness was focused on the horror that had been done to her. Her eyes were closed tightly, and she was doing her best not to think at all. But her mind stubbornly refused to go blank. "I will never forgive him," she thought numbly, feeling the warmth of his seed still trickling between her forcibly spread legs. "Never, never."

His violence had taken the sweet flower of her love and twisted it into something ugly. That his perception of her actions might have provoked him, she realized but refused to condone as an excuse for what he had done. For years she had battled with his jealousy, with his deeply ingrained distrust of the entire female sex. Tonight, finally, she had lost. And she no longer cared enough to pick herself up, brush herself off, and rejoin the battle any further. He was simply not worth it, as she saw now only too well. Jon equated love with sex, and saw all women as latently promiscuous. Even if this unfortunate series of events had not occurred, he would sooner or later have accused her of infidelity. Well, she was sick and tired of fighting his insecurities! Legally she was no longer bound to him, and by his own act he had severed every last one of her emotional bonds. At long last, he had set her free.

Cathy felt icy cold as she remembered how he had taken her. He had not been physically abusive—with her tied, there had been no need. But when he had roused in her response that she couldn't control, he had sneered, calling her all manner of filthy names even as he had penetrated the last of her barriers. She had not even been able to close her thighs against him. . . .

To her shocked amazement, she felt a giggle begin to bubble in her throat. A near rape and a completed one all in the same night—and by two different men! That must be some sort of a record! Maybe she should feel flattered. After all, not every female could boast of having inspired such savagery. There must be something about her that drove men beyond the limits of normal decency, transforming them into ravening animals. She pictured Jon as a lean gray wolf and Harold as a fat pink pig, and the giggle burst trillingly forth.

Jon couldn't believe his ears. She was laughing! The little bitch was actually laughing! He raised himself on his elbows to peer down into her face with disbelief. After what had just taken place between them, the light-hearted sound stunned him. She must be even more depraved than he had thought!

Her eyes were tightly closed, her lashes laying in thick black crescents against the startling whiteness of her skin. Her pink mouth, swollen from his kisses, was open, and the laughter was spilling in long, irregular spurts. As he watched her, taken aback, two glistening silver tears worked their way from beneath her pale, closed lids to trickle pathetically down the sides of her face. Against his will, Jon's conscience smote him. Maybe he should not have taken her as he had, however much she had asked for it and deserved it. But he had been angry, and slightly tight, and the image of Harold stroking and kissing the body that was driving him, Jon, into such frenzies had sent him slightly off his head. As he remembered the names he had called her, even while her body was driving him wild with desire, he felt the first twinges of shame.

Cathy opened her eyes, the deep blue of her irises staring for a moment directly into his. Jon got the eerie impression that she didn't even see him even as his conscience flicked at him again. She looked so helpless, and so damned young. . . .

"You do look like a wolf," she murmured incomprehensibly, and then that appalling giggle sounded again.

"Cathy. . . ." Jon said, shaken by the sound. Then he broke off. The words that had leapt to the tip of his tongue had been an apology for his treatment of her, and he was damned if he would apologize for that, or try to explain! Why should he? She had given her body to Harold easily enough, and without, he would wager, all these heartburnings!

Jon rolled off the bunk and onto his feet, fists resting lightly on his naked hips as he stood staring frowningly down at her. Her slender body was glistening with his sweat, and dotted here and there with his dark hairs. Her legs and arms were still spread in the ignominious position in which he had tied her.

Cathy was staring at him, her eyes quite blank. Jon felt a frisson of alarm shiver down his spine. What the hell ailed her? As he watched her, half angry, half concerned, giggle after giggle began to ripple from her throat. Her eyes were soulless as they met his; she was laughing as though she would never stop. Jon felt the hairs lift on the back of his neck. It was the most frightening sound he had ever heard.

She was hysterical, of course. Jon realized that with a

tremendous sense of relief. For one horrible moment, he had feared that she had lost her mind. He bent to untie her, working as quickly as he could, resolutely dismissing the little voices that chided him for treating her in such a way. As that awful laughter continued to flutter around him like dry, crackling leaves born on intermittent bursts of wind, his hands grew clumsy. It was some little time before he had her loosed. Even then she made no move, but lay in the same position in which he had taken her, laughing.

"Cathy, that's enough! Stop it!" His voice was sharp as he grabbed her by the shoulders, unable to stand that hideous sound another second. Ruthlessly he yanked her into a sitting position, shaking her until her head snapped back; still her eyes were wide and staring, and that awful trilling laughter sprang from her throat.

"Cathy!" Desperate to silence her, Jon lifted a hand and slapped her with deliberate force across the face. Instantly the laughter stopped. As her eyes came back to focus on him, he was glad to see that they had regained a little of their awareness. Then, to his torment, she began wrenchingly to cry.

Her sobs tore at Jon's heart, harden it against her as he would. Cursing inwardly, he sat down heavily on the side of the bunk, attempting against his better judgement to draw her into his arms.

"No!" she screamed, pushing him away with such force that he almost fell off the bunk. "Don't touch me! I can't stand it if you touch me!"

"Cathy. . . ." His voice as he said her name was husky. He cleared his throat, not knowing quite what else to do. Obediently, afraid of bringing on another outburst of that spine-chilling laughter, he dropped his hands to his lap, where they rested rather awkwardly against his bare thighs.

"I'll never forgive you for what you did," she told him tonelessly, her sobs drying up as if suddenly dammed. "Never as long as I live. As far as I am concerned, whatever was between us is dead. You mean absolutely nothing to me. It's funny, but I find that I don't even hate you anymore."

Jon stared at her without speaking. She looked lovely and fey and a little wild sitting there with only her tangled red-gold hair veiling her nakedness. Oddly, her words stabbed him. Then, slowly, healingly, he felt anger begin to rise again, and welcomed it. At least it would stop him from making a fool of himself one more time.

"If you think that you can bring me around with tears, you can think again," he rasped, rising abruptly to his feet. "You've given as much to me, and Harold, and God knows how many other men, as I took tonight. That's what women like you were put on earth for—to pleasure men. I feel not the smallest shred of remorse for putting you to the use for which you were intended!"

Jon was savagely pulling on his breeches as he spoke. Cathy watched him stonily, unspeaking. While he shrugged into his shirt, their eyes clashed in a silent duel. Then, still without a word, he turned on his heel and stalked from the cabin, slamming the door behind him. Cathy stared frozenly at the still-reverbrating panel for a long moment, then collapsed sobbing into the bunk. It was a long time before she cried herself to sleep.

~∞~

"Cathy!"

She was awakened by rough hands shaking her. Resentfully she opened her eyes to find herself looking into Jon's dark, unshaven face. Sunlight streamed in through the small portholes, illuminating the cabin. For just a moment Cathy forgot where she was, forgot that this man had taken her by force in the night, brutally killing her love for him. She blinked at him owlishly, her blue eyes wide and still dazed with sleep. Then with a small moan she turned over on her side, presenting her curved bare back to him as she faced the wall, snuggling deeper into the unyielding mattress in a vain attempt to find a comfortable spot.

"Go 'way!" she muttered drowsily.

"Cathy, wake up!" His harsh tone and ungentle hands pulled her relentlessly back from the brink of renewed sleep. Her eyes blinked open again as he rolled her over onto her back. For a puzzled moment she stared up at him, wondering why he looked so cross. She saw his eyes kindle as they roved the length of her body. Cathy followed his gaze, a slight frown corrugating the pale skin of her brow, to discover that she was stark naked, her white body left totally exposed by the faded coverlet that was twisted somewhere down around her feet. The sight of her own unaccustomed nakedness brought the events of the previous night flooding back. With an angry gasp Cathy sat bolt upright, her breasts quivering with the suddenness of her movement as she grabbed for the errant cover and jerked it up around her neck.

"Your little display of modesty is quite charming, if a trifle overdone," Jon remarked sardonically. Cathy met his eyes, blushing furiously and glaring at the same time. Last night's blessed emotional numbness had completely worn off, she found. This morning she could feel again, and what she felt was rage.

"Come for your morning jollies?" she taunted angrily, tilting her chin at him. Jon's eyes narrowed to piercing gray slits at her crudeness.

"Thanks for the invitation," he drawled, infuriating her. "But I fear I must decline. I prefer my goods to be a little less—shopworn."

"Why, you . . . !" Cathy gasped, enraged as he had intended. Without stopping to think, she swung her fist in an arc toward his face. This time he forestalled her, catching her hand in midair and squeezing until she gave a little cry of pain.

"I'm warning you: hit me again and I'll hit you back," he

said through his teeth, his eyes menacing. "I've had just about enough of your spoiled-brat tantrums. Now, get out of that bed!"

With his hand still crushing hers, he jerked her precipitately from the bunk. Cathy would have fallen to the floor if he had not caught her, his strong hands closing about her bare waist as he set her on her feet. Fairly spitting with anger, Cathy shook off his touch.

"Why don't you leave me alone?" she snapped, straightening her spine as she faced him. "Isn't there anyone else on this ship that you can bully?"

"Get dressed," Jon ordered tautly, pointedly ignoring her goad. To punish her, he let his eyes run over her with blatant insult. Standing naked before him, her pink-tipped breasts quivering with temper, the skin of her slender little waist and lissome long legs gleaming silkily in the sunlight, she was so lovely she almost took his breath away. But he hid his reaction well, managing a derisive sneer. Those sapphire eyes flashed with fury as she took in his expression, and her cloud of golden hair seemed to shoot off fiery sparks.

"Go to hell!" Cathy replied with admirable succinctness, fixing him with a stony glare. She refused to even try to cover up her nakedness. That was what he was waiting for, she could see! So that he could use her very real modesty as a target for more of his poisonous barbs! Jon's jaw clenched at her terse response to his order. With a smothered oath he reached out to grasp her by her creamy bare shoulders, his gray eyes glinting warningly down at her.

"Something else you'd do well to remember," he grated, "is that on this ship I am the captain and I mean to be obeyed. Give me any of your tantrums out on deck, and you'll force me to respond in a way that I can promise you you won't like!"

"Impressive as that little speech was, *Captain*," Cathy sneered, "there was really no need for it. I haven't the slightest intention of setting foot on your precious deck!"

"Haven't you?" Jon smiled slowly at her, his expression unpleasant. "Then I very much fear that you're doomed to disappointment: you *will* go out on deck, and very shortly, too. And while you're out there you'll do just exactly as you're told. Contrary to your evident belief, this isn't a luxury vessel like the *Tamarind*. On the *Cristobel*, everybody works."

"Works?" Cathy was so taken by surprise that the question came out quite normally.

"That's right, works," Jon said with evident relish. "Something you're unaccustomed to, I know. But surely even someone as useless as you can do something. In fact, I insist on it."

Cathy knew full well that he had just dreamed this up as a way of teaching her a lesson. Her soft mouth tightened. She was not taking orders from him!

"I won't do it," Cathy stated, folding her arms over her breasts and giving him a mulish glare. "And furthermore, you can't make me!"

Jon's eyes glinted at this last, and Cathy had an instant to reflect that perhaps issuing such a challenge had been a trifle unwise. Then he smiled tigerishly at her, those gray eyes gleaming like a predator's, and Cathy was certain of it.

"I think we both know that that just isn't so," he said almost pleasantly. "I can make you do any damned thing I please, as I thought you would have learned last night. Now, I'm going to leave you to get dressed; like you, I have work to do. But if you're not on deck within fifteen minutes, I'll come fetch you. And if you put me to that much trouble, I'll take a great deal of pleasure in making you regret it!"

"I wish you were dead!" Cathy flung at him, knowing that the reply was childish but too furious to come up with anything better on the spur of the moment. In any case, it was doubtful if he even heard. He was already on his way out the door before Cathy had regained sufficient control of herself to speak.

She was of two minds whether or not to do as he had ordered. Part of her screamed no, but another part, the cool, rational part, told her that he had been pushed as far as he would go. Any more defiance on her part, at least until he had had a chance to cool off, would be summarily, and humiliatingly, dealt with. Finally, after about five of her fifteen minutes had passed, prudence won the day. Whether she liked to admit it or not, Jon was physically strong enough and determined enough to make her do just about whatever he wished, and it was clear that, at the moment anyway, he would take a great deal of enjoyment from forcibly bending her to his will. At least, if she did as he said, she could deny him that.

Sullenly Cathy crossed to her small trunk which had been pushed into a corner, knelt before it, and opened the lid. It contained just a few of the clothes that Harold had ordered prepared for their honeymoon. Cathy winced a little as she considered what Jon's reaction would be when he discovered, as he inevitably would, the source of her new wardrobe. Then she resolutely squared her shoulders. She was not afraid of Jon, she told herself stoutly—and if that was no longer strictly true, she vowed that at least he would never know it.

There was one problem with the dresses in the trunk: they were all made of the finest materials fashioned into the latest styles. Certainly none of them had been designed to work in. Work was something far removed from the world of ladies and gentlemen, and the modiste who had created these gowns would be appalled to know the use to which they apparently would be put. Cathy wrinkled her nose. If Jon said she was to work, then work she undoubtedly would, but at what she couldn't imagine. Knowing Jon, and his temper, she reflected that it would probably be at the most repugnant task he could devise, like scrubbing the decks, or emptying slops!

Cathy selected a dull blue silk afternoon dress almost at random. With its heart-shaped neckline set off by a tiny frill of white lace and its stylish puffed sleeves, it was every bit as lovely and frivolous as the rest of her garments. But at least the color was fairly sober; anyway, it was the best she could do. If Jon expected her to work, then he would have to provide her with suitable clothes if he didn't like those she had!

Seeing that her time was nearly up, Cathy quickly sluiced her face and body in the tepid water she found waiting for her in a tin bowl, then began to pull on her underthings. In deference to what she suspected would be a very hot day, she put on only a thin lawn chemise, pantalets, and a single petticoat under the dress. For coolness' sake (and also, to be honest, because she knew Jon wouldn't like it) she left off her stays, and the other two petticoats that were *de rigueur* for a properly attired lady. After an instant's reflection, she also decided to leave off her silk stockings. The only shoes she had with her had high, dainty heels. Somehow she felt that these would be less than suitable on a deck.

Her hair posed something of a problem. Jon had not thought to scoop up her hairpins when he had stolen her away so abruptly, and she had none on her, nor were there any in her trunk. The best she could devise was to brush out the curling mass as severely as she could, and then secure it away from her face with a scrap of pale blue satin ribbon. It flowed down her back with a life of its own, but without pins there was no way she could arrange it in a more circumspect style.

It was a beautiful but somewhat odd-looking lady who stood blinking in the strong sunlight some few minutes later, shielding her eyes with one hand as she tried to get her bearings. Contrary to all established modes, bare pink toes peeped from beneath the hem of a dress that was made in the latest fashion, but was just a trifle too long without the high heels with which it was intended to be worn. And trailing masses of golden hair, fetching as some might argue them to be, were certainly not the coiffure recommended for a female of quality! But Cathy, standing rather gingerly on the deck, was aware of none of these things. As her eyes adjusted to the brightness, it was all she could do not to run back to the comparative safety of Jon's cabin. The deck seemed to be positively crawling with men! They were everywhere she looked, all seeming to get in each other's way as they stumbled clumsily about, apparently trying their best to see to the business of running the ship.

Cathy stared, thinking that they were totally different than she had learned to expect Jon's crews to be. When she had sailed with him before, he had insisted on his men performing with clockwork efficiency. Humor twitched at Cathy's lips. These men certainly could not be accused of that!

As Cathy stared, so, one by one, did the men. Gradually the whole crowd of them fell silent, and stood gaping at her, open-mouthed. Under the regard of so many masculine pairs of eyes, Cathy felt suddenly nervous. Quickly she turned toward the narrow wooden stairs leading to the quarterdeck. She had not meant to go up there, planning to give Jon as wide a berth as possible while still obeying the letter if not the spirit of his order to present herself on deck. But she suddenly felt the need for his protection. However loathsome and brutal he might be to her himself, she was quite, quite certain that he would not permit anyone else to offer her the slightest hurt.

The quarterdeck, Cathy saw as she ascended to it, was small, hopelessly cluttered, and in need of a good sweeping. A scrawny little man with a head as bald as an eagle's was steering the ship, while Jon stood with another, stockier, man directly behind the bowsprit. He appeared to be explaining the intricacies of navigation to his companion, for he held a compass in one hand and a sextant in the other. Then the stocky man moved slightly, and Cathy saw, to her amazement, that a woman was standing with them!

"Uh—Captain." The scrawny man at the wheel cleared his throat loudly. When the three by the bowsprit looked inquiringly at him, he nodded his head wordlessly in Cathy's direction. Three pairs of eyes turned to look at her with very different expressions.

Cathy had no idea of the lovely picture she made, poised at the head of the stairs, one hand resting lightly on the narrow wooden railing that enclosed the quarterdeck. Against a background of blue skies and billowing canvas, the sun glinted off her hair, making the long, curling mass of it seem ablaze with golden fire. The bodice of her silk dress clung tantalizingly to her figure, emphasizing her rounded breasts and the narrowness of her waist, while the full skirt opened around her like the petals of some exotic flower. Above the dress the skin of her shoulders and bosom glowed pearly white, while the deep blue of the silk enhanced the sapphire of her eyes.

Beside him, Jon heard O'Reilly suck in his breath in wordless admiration, while on his other side Sarita, completely eclipsed by Cathy's beauty and knowing it, slowly stiffened.

"Jonny, who's that?" the woman demanded petulantly. Her possessive tone caused Cathy's chin to jerk up. With a haughty lift of her eyebrows and a cold look at Jon, Cathy moved forward, delicately lifting her full skirt out of the way of her bare toes.

"Yes, Jon, who is *that*?" Cathy asked icily, clearly referring to the smoldering Sarita. Jon grinned, suddenly amused. Despite her own two-timing, Cathy plainly did not care for Sarita's presence, or her familiar "Jonny." Savagely he hoped that jealousy would raise its ugly head to torture her as it had been torturing him for weeks.

"Sarita, let me make you known to my . . ." wife, Jon nearly said without thinking, but caught himself in time. "Lady Stanhope," he finished with just the suggestion of a bite. With a taunting smile at Cathy, he added, "Lady Stanhope, this is Miss Sarita Jones. Beside me is Tom O'Reilly, and over there at the wheel is Mick Frazier. All, like me, newly liberated prisoners."

Cathy nodded her head curtly in acknowledgement of these introductions, not liking the way the other woman was clutching at Jon's arm, for all the world as if he were her property! Not that he meant anything any longer to her, Cathy, but really . . . ! Sarita, for her part, was staring hard at Cathy, her expression hostile. Cathy stared just as hostilely back.

"Where'd she come from, Jonny?" Sarita's shrill voice grated on Cathy's ears. Jon smiled fatuously down at the simpering thing, patting the hand that clutched at his arm.

"I—uh—acquired her in La Coruña," Jon said smoothly, shooting a malicious smile at Cathy. Schooling herself to betray no trace of anger, which the swell-headed beast would doubtless misconstrue, Cathy smiled just as maliciously back.

O'Reilly, watching this exchange which reminded him of nothing so much as the salute of swords before a duel, thought with inward relief that he no longer had to worry about the captain making time with Sarita. No, sir, as much as the black-haired wench appealed to him, O'Reilly, she wasn't a patch on the captain's lady, and that was a fact. That little blonde was the prettiest thing he had seen in years, and he would wager anything you liked that he wasn't the only one to feel that way. The captain was watching her in a possessive way that shouted "keep off" as clearly as words, and a body would have had to have been deaf, dumb, and blind to miss the crackle in the air when their eyes met. One thing for sure, with the lady on board and the captain feeling about her the way he did, sooner or later there was bound to be fireworks. O'Reilly just hoped that he wasn't around when they were set alight!

"Ready to go to work, Lady Stanhope?" Jon asked with an edge to his voice.

"Quite ready," Cathy answered coolly, staring him down. Jon's mouth tightened, and he turned pointedly to Sarita.

"Lady Stanhope here has very kindly volunteered to help you and the other ladies with the cooking," he explained sardonically. Cathy shot him a dagger-look, but he was too busy smiling down into Sarita's coarse-featured face to see it. "I would appreciate it if you would show her what to do."

"Yes, Jonny." The cloying way the older woman was looking up into Jon's face was sickening, Cathy thought furiously. That and her everlasting "Jonny" was getting on Cathy's nerves. For that reason and no other, Cathy told herself, she felt the most overwhelming urge to knock the swarthy-faced wench back onto her too-plump behind!

Sarita led the way down from the quarterdeck and across the deck, her hips swaying exaggeratedly. Cathy, gritting her teeth at the woman's blatant provocativeness, had perforce to follow. She was determined to let Jon see not the smallest sign of weakness. She knew that he was just waiting for her to beg him for mercy, and then he would jeeringly let her off. But Cathy was not about to ask for quarter from him! Whatever Sarita set her to, she would do!

As Cathy picked her way across the deck in Sarita's wake, she felt herself to be the cynosure of all eyes. Men stared at her from every angle, men of all sizes, shapes, and descriptions. Some of them were admiring, some curious, and some frankly lewd. But none of them accosted her. Cathy supposed dryly that word must have gotten round that she was the captain's private stock, and as such, she merited their grudging respect.

The work Sarita set her to, fetching water from the barrels stored beneath the poop to fill the big cauldrons used for cooking, was exhausting, to say the least. Cathy suspected that Sarita had chosen to give her such an arduous task out of pure spite. But no matter, Cathy was determined to carry it through. Jon had told her to work, and work she would. And if he was waiting for her to collapse sobbing at his feet, she vowed, he would be mightily disappointed!

Despite the ever-rising heat, Cathy labored manfully. The buckets which she lugged to and fro were heavy, and grew heavier with each succeeding trip. It seemed as if it would take forever to fill the cauldrons. Soon sharp pains were stabbing through the muscles of her shoulders and arms, and the metal handles of the buckets were cutting into her soft palms.

Finally Cathy was forced to stop to tear the bottom ruffle from her petticoat to make pads for her sore hands. As she did this, she twisted the fine material savagely, wishing that she could do the same to Jon's strong brown neck!

When at long last—thank you, Lord!—no more water was needed, Cathy sank down in a shady spot on the deck. Leaning back against the rail, she fanned her flushed face with her skirt, hoping to get some relief from the stifling temperature. The other women—there were, perhaps, eight not counting Sarita—were busy stirring the mixture of salt pork and vegetables that the men were to have for lunch. Cathy felt not the slightest pang of guilt for sitting when the rest were working. She had done her share—more than her share—and she needed a break. Already she could feel her skin burning from its unaccustomed exposure to the near-tropical sun; her head hurt as well, and her stomach felt queasy.

The men came to eat in shifts, holding out tin plates for the women to ladle food into. Cathy watched the proceedings without much interest. The mixture looked unappetizing in the extreme, and Cathy was sure she could not eat it. But the men seemed to find nothing amiss. Greedily they gobbled what was put on their plates, for the most part using their fingers instead of spoons. Then they went back for more. By the time the second wave of locusts descended, and began to eat, Cathy was feeling nauseous just from watching. Finally she closed her eyes to block out the disgusting sight. She was so hot she had gone beyond sweating, and every muscle in her body was starting to ache.

Jon, when he came to eat with the last of the men, found her like that, her skirts spread in a wide circle around her as she sat in a patch of shade, her head resting back against the rail, and her eyes closed. She looked for all the world as if she were taking a nap. From the sweat streaking her brow and the disordered tendrils of her hair that curled around her up-tilted face, Jon concluded that she had been doing something.

Whatever it was, she obviously was doing it no longer. Plainly she felt that she could defy him with impunity. Well, he had told her to work, and work she would! His mouth tightened as he moved purposefully toward her.

"Lady Stanhope," he drawled with mock deference when he stood before her. Cathy opened her eyes, having to tilt her head back even further than it was already to see his face as he towered over her, his broad form blocking out the sun. He was frowning, she saw, and her own lips compressed in response. It was clear that he was in no very good humor, but bully for him! If it came to that, neither was she!

"Did you want something?" she asked ungraciously.

"Pray forgive me for disturbing your rest, my lady," Jon murmured, his eyes belying the pseudo-respectful tone of his voice. "I'm sure you need it after your exhausting labors."

"You're right. I do," Cathy answered with unhidden hostility.

Jon's eyes narrowed at her tone. "Napping must be very tiring," he murmured sardonically.

"Did you come over here just to make yourself objectionable, or did you want something?" she snapped.

A muscle twitched warningly in his jaw.

"Oh, I want something," he said. "My dinner. You can fetch it."

Cathy stared at him disbelievingly.

"You're joking," she answered at last.

"Not at all," Jon replied coldly. "As I believe I told you once already, no one on the *Cristobel* gets a free ride. Well, I agree you're not good for much, but you can fetch me my dinner."

"While you do what?"

"Take a well-deserved rest. Unlike you, I've been working very hard all morning."

"Unlike me . . . !" Cathy spluttered angrily. Then she bit back the catalogue of her morning's activities which had threatened to burst from the tip of her tongue. If he wanted to believe that she had done nothing but sit in the shade, then far be it from her to disabuse him!

"I'm not going to stand about bandying words with you all afternoon," Jon said shortly, his eyes hardening as they took in her indignant face. "I told you to go fetch my dinner. And I'd appreciate it if you'd be quick."

A whole range of emotions chased themselves across Cathy's expressive face. First there was disbelief, then anger, then defiance, followed by anger again. Her face flushed even rosier than it was already, and her blue eyes as they met his gave off glittering sparks.

"You actually mean for me to wait on you?" she asked as if she still couldn't believe that she had heard correctly.

"That's right," Jon told her. Tired of the discussion, he reached down and took hold of her upper arm, hauling her to her feet. When she was standing, Cathy faced him angrily, jerking her arm from his grasp.

"Now," Jon ordered grimly. Cathy stood glaring at him for an instant as if undecided, but apparently she remembered that discretion was the better part of valor. Contenting herself with an indignant sniff, she went to do as he said.

Jon grinned as he watched her go, his taut features relaxing in some amusement. She was openly flouncing, clearly furious with him. Her skirts swayed around her like a bell. The effect was entrancing, and Jon sank down into the place she had vacated by the rail to watch the show. Slut she might be, but she was certainly easy on the eye, and he saw no reason why he should deny himself whatever pleasure she could give him. After all, he had certainly paid a high enough price for it!

Cathy's eyes were glittering dangerously as she held out a plate to be filled. Clara, the stocky middle-aged woman in charge of that particular kettle, gave her a keen look.

"Brought you with us for a maid, did he?" she observed with sly humor, her head jerking in Jon's direction. Cathy's nostrils flared, but she had no intention of adding to Clara's enjoyment.

"Apparently," was all she answered, but as she returned to Jon her eyes were flashing fire.

He was sprawled where she had been, his long legs stretched out before him as he took his ease. The slight breeze was ruffling through his over-long black hair, which the heat had caused to wave in a way she knew he detested. His face and the strong column of his neck were very dark, burnt to a leathery toughness by constant exposure to the sun. The arrogant lines of his jaw and mouth were partially obliterated by several days' growth of blue-black, stubbly beard. Beneath his sweat-dampened white shirt she could see the faint dark outline of the fine black pelt which covered his chest. His shoulders as they leaned against the railing were formidable in their breadth, while his forearms, bared by the rolled up sleeves of the shirt, were tanned to a teak brown and corded with muscle. He was a handsome animal, Cathy had to admit, but she thought with a sniff that animal was the operative word.

"Your slave is back, master," Cathy sneered when she stood before him again. "Would you like me to feed you, too?"

Jon opened his eyes; those gray irises darkened to the color of gunmetal as they rested contemplatively on her face. Cathy met that considering look with a defiant glare. To her surprise he said nothing, just held up his hand for his plate.

As he began to eat, Cathy started to turn haughtily away. One brown hand shot out to catch a fold of her skirt, detaining her. She looked back down at him, her eyebrows lifted in icy inquiry.

"Stay," he directed briefly, as he would have to a pet dog. Cathy bristled, her arms crossing over her breasts. Jon eyed her belligerent stance speculatively, then returned his attention to his food without another word.

Cathy watched with growing indignation as he consumed

the unappetizing mess with what looked like relish. He was paying her no more attention than he would have a piece of wood, not even having the common courtesy to inquire if she had eaten, which she emphatically had not! No, he thought he could keep her standing before him like some odalisque from a Sultan's harem for as long as he wished! And he hadn't bothered to say even a word of thanks for the service she had done him, either.

When at last he had scraped the plate clean, he looked up. Seeing the raging anger in her eyes, he smiled slowly. The gesture was a mere thinning of his lips, in no way signifying amusement.

"I'm still hungry," he said meaningfully, and held up his plate. "You can fetch me some more."

Cathy spluttered angrily, her blue eyes flaming.

"Remember what I told you about tantrums," Jon warned softly, his gray eyes bright as if he were looking forward to having to quell one.

Cathy took his empty plate without a word. Her anger growing with every step, she went back to have Clara refill it. Then she retraced her path to stand before Jon, the filled plate in her hand.

"That's a good girl," Jon told her with mocking approval, and reached out to take the plate from her. Cathy smiled at him, her mouth curving sweetly to reveal the rows of small, gleaming white teeth. Then she lifted the plate just out of his reach, and proceeded to very gently tilt its contents all over the top of his arrogant black head.

seven

"*D*amn it!" Jon roared, his hand going up to dash the slimy mess from his hair and face as he sprang to his feet.

Cathy could not prevent a triumphant grin. It quickly disappeared as the full extent of his rage became apparent. His face was suffused with dark red color and his mouth twitched furiously as he towered over her. His hands were balled into huge fists at his sides. Cathy swallowed, suddenly nervous. It took every ounce of courage she possessed to stop her from taking to her heels. People had been telling her for years that one day her spitfire temper was going to get her into very serious trouble; Cathy very much feared that today was that day. Then, behind her, she heard a hastily muffled guffaw from an onlooker, and she was sure of it.

She risked a quick glance over her shoulder to find that she and Jon were the center of goggling attention. Activity on deck had been completely suspended as everyone craned their necks to see what would happen next. Would the new captain, who thought nothing of laying low the brawniest of men for so slight a cause as an insubordinate smile, meekly take such abuse from a little chit of a female, be she ever so pretty? And if not, how would he reply?

"I wager he knocks her back on her cute little ass!" Cathy overheard one excited comment.

"Nah, he'll pitch her overboard for sure," came the answer. As her eyes fearfully searched Jon's face, she felt the second fellow just might be right. Jon looked entirely capable of throwing her overboard. Those gray eyes blazed with an unholy light.

"You stupid little bitch!" he ground out finally, the words muttered half under his breath. Then he reached for her. Cathy, reading bloody vengeance in his eyes, felt her courage abruptly desert her, like the yellow-bellied turncoat it was. With a little gasp, she gathered her too-long skirts about her and turned to run. She never made it. Jon caught her by the arm, his long fingers biting viciously into her soft flesh, spinning her back around to face him. His face was a dark, furious mask, with only those glittering gray eyes providing twin pinpoints of light.

"I—I'm sorry," Cathy gasped, hoping to propitiate him. In the face of his rage, her pride had fled along with her courage.

"Too late," he bit off, and then he jerked her toward him. Before Cathy knew what he intended she felt herself twisting through space. With a jolt her stomach came into hard contact with his bent knee. As his arm clamped down over her back, imprisoning her, Cathy began to kick wildly. From her position, bent face down across his knee, her long hair trailing the dusty deck and her bottom ungloriously upended, she realized that he intended to publicly spank her!

"Let me go!" she cried, knowing even as she said it that it was useless.

"Oh, no!" he replied, sounding as if the words were forced out from between clenched teeth. "You asked for this, you little bitch, and you're going to get it!"

Cathy kicked and writhed, her struggles fueled by the

cheers and laughter that had greeted Jon's apparent intention. Then her cheeks crimsoned as she felt, to her shocked amazement, Jon lifting her skirts!

He pushed her skirt and one petticoat up around her waist, leaving her writhing bottom clad only in the thin muslin of her ruffled, lace-trimmed pantalets. Whistles and catcalls from the assembled crowd followed this action, and Cathy could feel her whole body flushing fierily. Her struggles intensified; she hurled invective at Jon's booted feet. Then the breath was knocked temporarily from her body as his large hand descended with painful force on the softness of her behind.

Whap! The blow was repeated unmercifully until Cathy's screams of rage were reduced to sobbing whimpers. Her bottom felt as if it were on fire. She had stopped kicking, sensing that it was just fanning the blaze of his temper, and finally lay quietly across his knee. Guffaws and admiring comments assailed her ears.

"That's the way to learn 'em, Cap'n!" Cathy heard respect in the man's tone.

"Yay-ah, we got to show them females who's the boss!" another man called out.

Jon's hand bestowed one more hard slap on Cathy's behind, then thankfully ceased its punishment. Roughly he hauled her to her feet. Her skirts were still caught up and she pushed them down with a swift movement, hot embarrassment flooding her face from neck to ears. For a moment her long golden hair shielded her from the grinning crowd. Then she shook it back proudly, her eyes glaring, her chin raised as she faced them. Damn it, she wouldn't feel shame before this assembly of jailbirds and gallows' bait! And Jonathan Hale was the chief one!

Before Cathy could do more than cast a venomous glance in Jon's direction, he scooped her up in his arms. Cathy, stunned by his action, lay quietly against his chest as she tried to work out what he meant to do. If his intention was non-violent, she didn't want to risk re-igniting his anger by putting up a fight that would almost certainly be a waste of energy in any case. But, on the other hand, if he was set on something dastardly, like throwing her into the sea. . . .

Whatever Cathy expected, it was certainly not what she got. Jon's rolling stride stopped abruptly. Cathy just had time to register that they were a good, safe distance from the rail when her knees were lifted high into the air and her head was allowed to drop. With an instinctive scream of fright she felt the same warm, gooey mess she had dumped on Jon's head reach up to caress her trailing hair. The no-good bastard was lowering her headfirst into one of the kettles which still held the remnants of lunch!

When Jon pulled her back out, her hair was coated with the sickening stuff. He had not dipped her in any further than her forehead, for which Cathy supposed she should be grateful. But she was too furious for anything but thoughts of murder. Her fingers curved into sharp talons as he hauled her back into his arms, letting the gruesome mess that he had made of her head rest with careless indifference against the clean white linen covering his broad shoulder.

"Better think again," he advised dryly, seeing the involuntary movement of her fingers. Cathy, her eyes promising a terrible retribution, did as he suggested. She would gain nothing by attacking him except her own further pain and humiliation. She could wait. . . .

He was openly laughing at her as he walked with her across the deck. The assembled men parted to let them pass, exactly like the Red Sea must have before Moses, Cathy thought resentfully. They were laughing too, deep, gurgling chortles that bespoke genuine amusement. Ha, ha! Cathy mocked furiously to herself. *Ha, ha, ha!*

"Perkins, better bring us some water. I think Lady Stanhope here would be much improved by a bath!" Jon said to a gangly boy as they passed. This remark occasioned more hilarity. Cathy bit down so hard on her lower lip that she felt blood seep into her mouth. He would pay for this humiliation, she promised herself, if it took her the rest of her life to arrange it!

Jon shouldered his way into his cabin, a taunting grin still splitting his face. As he shut the door behind them, he let Cathy slip to the floor. It was all she could do not to reach up and box those bronzed ears, but with truly heroic self-control she managed to restrain herself. He would get no more amusement out of her! Turning her back on him, she walked with stiff dignity to look out a porthole. Only the glitter in her eyes and the involuntary clenching and unclenching of her fingers betrayed her inner rage.

But Jon had known her too long and too well to be deceived.

"I warned you about throwing tantrums on deck," he reminded her, humor quivering in his voice. That was too much! Cathy whirled to face him with a snarl, her dripping hair whipping around her body. The horrible feel of it added fuel to the inferno of her anger.

The hot words bubbling in her throat were forestalled by the briefest of taps on the door. Jon grinned at her mockingly, then opened it. Perkins stood outside with his arms wrapped around a huge, iron-bound barrel. Over the top of his head someone had jokingly placed a dented tin tub. Jon took the barrel from the boy, set it inside the cabin, then lifted the tub from his head. Perkins grinned at him rather shyly.

"Thank you, sir. I—I thought you might need rather a lot. . . ." he stuttered.

"Good thinking, Perkins. You were exactly right," Jon said dryly, then as the boy still stood there, not seeming to know what else to do, Jon shut the door.

"Strip!" he said briskly to Cathy. She gaped at him, her anger temporarily forgotten.

"What?" she asked.

"Strip!" he said again. "The only way you're going to get that mess out of your hair is to wash it. I aim to help you out!"

"You can go to hell!" Cathy said between her teeth. Jon laughed.

"I've been there, thank you very much, and while it was well enough, I don't think I'd care to go back. Now, are you going to do as I say, or. . . ."

"I loathe and despise you," Cathy hissed, knowing that she had no choice but to obey. If she didn't, she knew full well that he would strip her himself, forcibly.

Knowing that to ask him to either leave or turn his back would be an exercise in futility, Cathy turned her own back as she began to unfasten her dress. Jon snorted.

"Why you continually pretend to a modesty you can't possibly feel is beyond me," he remarked laconically. "I've seen every inch of your admittedly delectable body—more than seen it, in fact. I've touched it, tasted it, watched it come to quivering life under my hands. . . ."

"Oh, shut up," Cathy snapped, annoyed and embarrassed at the same time. Her fingers were still shaking with temper, and she was having trouble with the dozens of tiny hooks that did her dress up the back.

"Need help?" That drawling voice spoke right behind her shoulder, making her jump involuntarily. Pride ordered her to refuse, but Cathy realized that she really did need help to get out of the blasted garment. Besides, as Jon said, he had seen her naked more times than either of them could remember. It was ridiculous to feel embarrassed now, but she did. Maybe it was because he was no longer her husband, but a bad-tempered, mocking devil of a stranger who seemed to think he could use her body as he chose. And he didn't love her anymore—if he ever had, which she was seriously beginning to doubt. If you loved someone, you trusted them, and you certainly weren't cruel. Besides, she no longer loved him: she hated him now, and that made all the difference.

"Thank you," Cathy's voice was cold as she allowed him to take over. He struggled with the stubborn hook for a moment, then cursed.

"The problem is, you've got that damned mess all over your back. There's only one thing for it." With that his hands closed around her waist and he picked her up, carrying her bodily the few paces it took to cross the room. When he set her down, she saw that her feet were firmly placed in the center of the tin tub.

"Do you have any soap?" he asked brusquely as her eyes widened questioningly on his face.

"By the washstand," Cathy nodded, then frowned. "But, Jon, I can't take a bath in this dress. The water will ruin the silk!"

"At a guess I'd say it was ruined already," Jon answered, moving to get the soap. When he came back Cathy took it from him mutely, knowing that what he said was true.

"Thanks to you," she said bitterly, her mouth hardening.

"No, thanks to *you,*" Jon replied equably. "I told you not to throw tantrums on the deck. You deserved far worse than you got. You weren't hurt—just had that haughty pride of yours dented a little. Would you have preferred a bout with the cat? Because that crossed my mind. You have to understand, these men aren't seamen. They don't obey me as captain because it's natural to them to do so. They do as I say because they know I'll knock their teeth down their throats if they don't. Some of them are just waiting for me to show a hint of softness, and then they'll try to close in. What you did today was damned stupid, and if I'd let it pass it could have been just the sign some of those jackals out there are waiting for. Besides, I warned you. And I'm warning you again: pull another stunt like that, and I really will take the cat to you. I swear it."

"I'm not afraid of you," she spat, the hold she had on her temper dangerously slipping.

"Then you should be," Jon said softly, and effectively curtailed any reply from Cathy by picking up the huge barrel and dumping a quarter of its contents over her head. When she opened her eyes again, sputtering, it was to find Jon peeling his stained shirt over his head. While she began to rather sulkily lather her hair with the soap, he sat down on a chair and pulled off his boots. Then he stood up again, peeling off his breeches.

Cathy's eyes widened so much at this that she got soap in them.

"What are you doing?" she demanded, rubbing the stinging orbs with her fists.

"What does it look like?" he asked coolly, stepping into the small tub with her as he spoke. They were standing facing each other, so close that Cathy could feel his body heat, smell the musky male odor of him. His tall naked body towered over her small, still clothed one. Cathy felt curiously disturbed at his proximity.

"Let's get you out of that dress," Jon said before Cathy could speak. With his hands on her shoulders, he turned her around. Obligingly she held her sudsy hair up out of his way while he grappled with her hooks.

Without the impediment of her greasy hair to hamper him, Jon managed to get her dress unfastened. Still standing in the tub, Cathy let him pull it over her head and toss it aside. She stood for a moment in her soaking petticoat, undecided about whether or not to remove it. To stand so close to him with both of them naked would only invite trouble.

The decision was taken out of her hands. Jon's hands reached around her, coolly unlacing the ribbons that held the front of the petticoat in place. When that was done, he removed that garment too. When his hands came back to feel for the drawstring of her pantalets, Cathy pushed his fingers aside and mutely did the job herself. While she was stepping out of them she felt his hands in her hair, gently massaging suds through the long strands.

"I can do that, thanks," she said with chilling courtesy when she was naked at last. His hands obediently left her head. Cathy kept her back to him, but they were so close that she could feel every muscle and sinew in that long body. She knew when he lifted his hands to his own head, rubbing the soap vigorously into his hair. And she knew when his body began to harden with desire. . . .

At that unmistakable sign, Cathy made a hasty move as if to step out of the tub. Jon's arms slipping around her waist forestalled her. Cathy strained futilely against their iron strength.

"Where are you going? You haven't finished your bath yet." His voice was disturbingly husky.

"Let me go. You're bothering me," Cathy said sharply, wanting to get out of his arms before she shamed herself as she had done last night.

"Is that what I'm doing? Bothering you?" The words were lazy, the tone seductive. "Now, I would have called it something quite different. . . ."

"You're a conceited thing," Cathy said on a note of desperation as one big hand began to work soap into the soft skin of her belly. He was arousing reluctant tremors of feeling inside of her, tremors that she knew she mustn't, for the sake of her own self-respect, allow him to suspect.

"Am I?" he breathed in her ear, moving closer until his warm, hair-roughened body was pressed tightly against her soft, curved back. One hand moved up to gently soap her breasts, still holding her firmly against him. The other moved down between her thighs. . . .

After a moment of this, Cathy could no longer control the quaking of her treacherous body. She knew he had to feel the long shudders that racked her, just as he felt the swelling of her breasts beneath his caressing hands. Only moments ago she would not have believed she could want him like this, not after the way he had treated her, the humiliations he had forced on her, and she would have been horrified to think that he was aware of her desire. But now, with his drugging hands on her quivering flesh, with his breath warm in her ear and his tall, hard body pressed so intimately against her buttocks, she was past thinking, past caring. She wanted him so badly that it was a physical pain in her belly. With a long, ragged sigh she relaxed back against him.

His arms tightened around her, his fingers pinching gently at the hard pebbles of her nipples. The hand between her legs was daring further, further. . . . Cathy's eyes were closed, her head resting back against the hard cradle of his chest. Her breathing sounded labored in her ears.

Jon bent his head to kiss her neck, his mouth and tongue tracing the taut cord, his teeth lightly nibbling at it. Cathy felt her knees weaken until she could hardly stand. His hard strength was all that held her upright. If he had let her go, she would have fallen into an ignominious heap at his feet.

"God," he gasped hoarsely in her ear; some recess of her being rejoiced that he was as much a victim of passion as she. Then he was turning her in his arms, gathering her against the steamy heat of his body, his hands sliding intimately down to close on her bottom and press her to him so that she could feel his throbbing need of her.

"You feel good," he murmured, his eyes dark with passion as he looked down at her. His hands still clasped intimately around the soft cheeks of her behind, he rubbed her against him, grinding their flesh together. Cathy felt a tremor all the way down to her toes. His body was hard and hot and hairy, all rippling muscle and wet bronzed flesh. She half-closed her eyes, her hands sliding up to clasp his shoulders. She ached for him. Despite everything, he could still make her want him so much that her desire was like a physical pain. Soap still clung to him, making his skin slippery to her touch. She loved the sensation, her hands moving of their own volition in seductive little circles along the width of his shoulders and down to his chest. She concentrated all her attention on that black-furred expanse, running her fingers through the soft curls, lightly scratching with her nails along its length. Finally, her eyes closed, her lips slightly parted, she pressed her mouth to the warm, soapy wetness of it. Jon's hands clenched convulsively on her buttocks. He groaned. Then he was lifting her, his hands still holding her bottom; they slid down along her thighs to wrap her legs around his waist.

Cathy was beyond thought. She was aware of nothing but the feel of his body entwined with hers, of the warm, soapy, musky man-smell of him, of her own spiralling desire. Deep in the recesses of her mind, a little voice was warning her that she would live to regret this total abandonment to passion. But Cathy was beyond heeding it. No matter the price, she wanted him as much as he plainly wanted her. If he did not take her soon, Cathy thought she would be consumed by the flames of her own throbbing need.

"Put your arms around my neck," Jon directed hoarsely. Cathy did as he said without opening her eyes, clinging to him almost desperately. She could feel the heavy thud of his heart against her breasts, hear the harsh rasp of his breathing. Her own heart was pounding so hard that she could feel it beating against her ribcage. God, she wanted him! Would he never . . . ?

His big hands still cupping her buttocks lifted her a little. Cathy could feel the rock-hardness of him as he probed for her opening. She gasped with pleasure when he found it, the pulsating length of him thrusting upward until he was deep inside her. Then for a long moment he held her perfectly still, her softness pressed all the way down against the taut muscles of his belly. Cathy couldn't stand it. She began to writhe, and moan, as she sought the pleasure he refused to give her.

Her body undulated against his, her long nails unconsciously digging into his strong nape. He was gasping, his breath rattling in his throat as though he were dying. Cathy looked up through heat-glazed eyes to see that his dark face was rigid with passion, his lashes laying like black fans along his cheeks, the muscles of his neck and shoulders and arms bulging as he sought his own release. He was thrusting deep inside her now, and Cathy matched his movements with her own. She was panting for air, her legs locked tightly around his waist, her head thrown back and her eyes closed. The whirlwind of passion within her was moving faster and faster, twisting and turning as it took her with it. Cathy felt him shudder against her, the hardness of him quivering as it spurted hot seed inside her. She cried out, falling spinningly into the vortex of her own ecstasy.

They clung together like that for some few minutes, slowly recovering their senses. His mouth was buried in the curve of her neck, and his breath was warm against her damp skin. Her own head rested wearily on his broad shoulder. Her hands were still clasped loosely around his neck, her legs hugged his waist. After what seemed like an eternity he lifted his head, his hands sliding from her buttocks to untangle her legs from about him. Gently he lowered her until she was standing somewhat unsteadily on her feet. Her hands clutched his shoulders for balance. Then, as she met his rapidly cooling gray eyes, she felt a hot tide of color begin to wash into her face.

"That was fantastic," he said, his long mouth curling sardonically. "Did you learn that from Harold?"

Cathy felt as if he had struck her. She stiffened, her eyes beginning to glare.

"I hate you," she whispered venomously. His sneer became more pronounced.

"My dear, I love the way you hate," he taunted, and she stepped away from him, her hands clenched into impotent fists at her sides.

"You make me sick!" she hissed, and he laughed, his gray eyes hard.

"You acted sick," he leered, his eyes sweeping comprehensively down her body. "You were making sounds like you were dying. I bet they heard you all over the ship."

"Why, you . . . !" Cathy lunged at him furiously, her nails going for his mocking face. He caught her easily, laughing softly as he held her off with one hand.

"I think you need to cool off, Lady Stanhope," he said, and with his free hand swung the barrel up to rest on his shoulder and emptied the contents over Cathy's unsuspecting head. Cool water poured over her in a sudden rush, rinsing away the last of the soap, and with it her momentary weakening toward him.

"Bastard!" she called him ferociously when she could speak, her blue eyes with their spiky black fringe shooting daggers. Jon's mouth was smiling, but his eyes were cold as they looked at her.

"Let's not start calling names," he said, his voice soft. "I wager I could come up with a few that would make any you could dream up for me seem pale."

"Get out of here!" Cathy hissed furiously.

"Oh, I'm going, sweet. Now that you've served your purpose, do you think I'd spend the rest of my afternoon locked up with you? Not a chance!"

Cathy was so mad that she could have bitten nails in two, but she managed to preserve a seething silence. To scream at him as she longed to do was useless: her harsh words bounced off him like water off a duck's back. To throw something at him, as she wanted to do even more, would be foolhardy in the extreme. So she said nothing, drying herself on a towel with hands that shook from temper. As she wrapped the towel around her head and moved across to the trunk for something to put on, she saw him sluice what water remained in the pitcher from her morning wash over his head to rid his hair of the last of the soap. Then he stepped from the tub and briskly toweled himself dry, stepping into his breeches and reaching for a clean shirt.

When he turned around Cathy had already donned fresh pantalets and petticoat, and was tugging a dull gold crepe afternoon dress over her head. Like all the clothes Harold had provided, it was far too grand for any but the most social of occasions. But the contents of that trunk were all she had.

"Nice dress," Jon observed when she had it twitched into place, his eyes ominously narrowed. "I don't believe I've seen it before?"

"You haven't seen a lot of my clothes," Cathy snapped back with perfect truth. Fervently she hoped that he wouldn't guess the source of her garments. She didn't feel up to another scene.

"Part of your trousseau, Lady Stanhope?" he asked unpleasantly.

"If you want to think so." Her voice dripped icicles. Calmly she turned her back on him and began to comb the snarls from her long, damp hair.

"Damn you, don't turn your back on me," he rasped, crossing the space between them in two quick strides and grabbing her by the shoulders, spinning her about. Cathy glared up at him furiously.

"Don't you manhandle me!" she hurled back, her chin jutting at him defiantly.

"I'll treat you however the hell I please," he growled. If Cathy had hoped her anger might divert him, she was mistaken, as she soon saw. "Did Harold buy that dress?"

"What if he did?" Cathy challenged, her eyes taunting him.

"By God, he bought everything you have on," Jon breathed, his eyes darting furiously over her. "He meant to pay you well for services rendered, did he? Well, too bad, Lady Stanhope. I'll see you in hell before I let you wear clothes he paid for when you're with me!"

His lips parted in a savage snarl. Before Cathy could guess

his intention, his hand shot out, closing over the neck of her gown and pulling downward with a hard jerk. The material gave with a loud rip. Cathy saw to her horror that the dress had split completely down the front. Even as she registered that, he was tearing it from her back, then did the same with her petticoat and pantalets. Struggling furiously, she was left naked, while he stalked across the cabin to her trunk. Dropping to one knee beside it, he rummaged through the contents, throwing out her brush and comb set and her other toiletries. It was when he was stuffing the torn gold dress and the rags that were left of her once-elegant underclothes inside it that Cathy's control deserted her. With a feral growl she launched herself at him, leaping onto his back, her little fists pummeling him with every ounce of her strength behind them.

"Hell-cat!" he bellowed, rising and spinning to catch her. His hands closed around her wrists with such force that Cathy could feel her fingers growing numb.

"Let me go, you . . . !" Cathy raged, unable to think of a name bad enough to call him.

"Run out of names?" he taunted, his fingers pressing cruelly into her soft skin. Cathy tried to jerk her hands free of his hold, and a stray sunbeam wandering mistakenly through a porthole glinted off the enormous diamond that was Harold's ring.

Cathy froze, but it was too late: he had seen it. His face hardened into a granite mask, his eyes leaping with anger.

"By God," he said slowly, drawing out the words in a way that made Cathy shiver. She would rather by far that he had ranted and raved and threatened her than just stare at her hand with that deadly look in his eyes.

"What happened to the rings I gave you?" he rasped after a long moment. "Did you pitch them out with the other garbage?"

"Yes!" Cathy hurled breathlessly, too angry to consider the consequences.

"You bitch!" he snarled, and then with a savage movement he was dragging the rings from her finger. That done, he pushed her away from him roughly, and turned to pick up the trunk crammed with her clothes.

"Where are you going with my things?" Cathy cried, recovering her balance just in time to keep from falling and clinging to the foot of the bunk for support.

"I'm going to pitch them overboard," Jon answered grimly, heading for the door.

"You can't!" Cathy protested frantically. "They're all the clothes I have! I don't have anything else I can wear!"

"You won't need clothes for your new job." He had turned to look at her, his eyes traveling insolently over her naked body. Cathy, suddenly becoming very aware of her state of undress, blushed from her toes to her hairline under that scathing perusal. Instinctively she snatched the cover from the bed, holding it in front of herself. Jon's lip curled.

"I've decided that your only value lies in your abilities as a whore, and for that you're perfect just as you are," he grated. Then, as Cathy gasped indignantly, he turned on his heel and stalked to the door.

"Be ready to commence your new duties when I get back," he threw tauntingly over his shoulder, and then he let himself out of the cabin.

"Filthy swine!" Cathy hurled at the closed door. Then she sat down abruptly on the end of the bunk. Her knees were shaking so badly that she feared they would give way at any moment.

Jon had said her new job would be as his whore, and Cathy soon found to her fury that that had not been an idle threat. He kept her naked, and locked in his cabin, coming in to take his ease of her body whenever it suited him. Days passed, and still he showed no signs of relenting. Cathy's hatred of him grew until it was almost a living creature inside her: she pictured it as a great fiery dragon, steam shooting from its nostrils and its tail continually lashing. Jon paid no attention to the abuse she heaped on his head at every opportunity. Instead, he merely picked her up, pitched her over onto her back on the bunk, and pumped out his lust between her legs. After these encounters, which were devoid of any feeling except impotent fury on her part and physical need on his, she wanted to kill him so much that she could taste the blood-lust in her mouth. He had called her a whore, and now he had made her feel like one. She would hate him forever for that.

He slept beside her too, of course. Certainly he was not gentleman enough to allow her the sole use of his bunk. It was usually late at night when he came in: he would strip off his clothes, wash, fall into bed, take her body or not as it pleased him, and promptly roll over and fall asleep. Most of the time he didn't even bother to speak. Cathy felt thoroughly humiliated by his treatment of her, and as her humiliation grew, so did her rage.

One night he woke her from a sound sleep, his mouth closing over hers, his hands parting her legs and his body thrusting between them before she was even totally awake. Cathy gasped a little at the pain of his taking her when she was not ready, lying stiff as a board in his arms as he moved over her.

"You're hurting me!" she cried as his mouth roughly ravaged her sensitive breasts.

"So?" he grunted insolently, barely pausing in what he was doing. "Getting hurt is part of the job for whores. You should have thought of that before you became one!"

"Get off me, you insufferable swine!" She pummeled at his broad shoulders with her fists, kicking and bucking as she sought to be free of him. "Get off me, do you hear?"

Jon merely laughed unpleasantly. He controlled her struggles with shaming ease, and in his own good time finished what he was about.

When he rolled away at last, Cathy lay fuming in the bunk

beside him. Her whole body was sore, her breasts tingling where he had practically swallowed them whole, the sensitive place between her legs aching at his harsh possession. But worse than any physical pain was her sense of mortification. It was intolerable that he could treat her like this! He took her body where and when he pleased, with no thought of either her pleasure or consent. And the truly horrible thing about it was, there didn't seem to be any way she could stop him. Her strength was puny next to his, and screeching at him was just as useless. What she needed was a weapon, to make him see that she meant business.

Cathy propped herself up on one elbow, looking reflectively down at the sleeping face of the man beside her. He was lying on his back (selfish swine, taking up all the room!), one arm flung above his head, the other curled at his waist. The top sheet was pulled carelessly up around his middle. His face, half turned away from her, was dark against the white of the bed linen. His lips were slightly parted as his breath rattled through them in a gentle snore. His black hair was wildly tousled, probably from the way she had pulled at it in an effort to make him let her go. Black stubble roughened the lean lines of his jaw and chin; Cathy could feel her own skin rubbed raw where it had touched her. For a moment her heart stopped. She thought, He looks like Cray! and an indescribable softness began to steal over her. Then the memory of the way he had treated her, the things he had said, came rushing back. His resemblance to Cray was only a surface likeness. Inside, he was warped by his insecurities, like a shiny apple that you bite into only to discover rot around the core. She thought of the night he had tied her, of the uncaring way he had forced himself on her tonight, and her heart hardened. He needs a lesson, she thought grimly, and as her eyes wandered around the dark cabin she began to get the glimmer of an idea.

She was up before him, the faded plaid cover wrapped sarong-fashion around her body, sitting in one of the hard chairs with her feet propped in the other. A small smile played around her mouth. As Jon muttered, and stirred, his hand searching the bed for her, Cathy's smile widened. Now, my fine captain, she thought triumphantly, is when you get your comeuppance!

Jon's eyes blinked open when he found no trace of what he was seeking, a faint frown corrugating his brow. Those gray eyes were still not totally alert as they searched the small cabin for her. When they alighted on her at last, they were sleepily warm, with not the vaguest hint of suspicion.

"Come here," he ordered, his voice husky from sleep. When Cathy made no move to obey, he shook his head a little as if to clear it, then propped himself up on one elbow.

"Did you hear what I said?" he demanded, the last softening traces of sleep vanishing.

"Oh, I heard you," Cathy answered softly, smiling. Jon stared at her for a long moment, his eyes narrowing.

"Then come here. I've a fancy for a little exercise this morning," he said.

"No." Cathy was really enjoying herself. It was all she could do to hold back a small chuckle. He was in for a surprise.

Jon's eyes widened as if he couldn't believe that he had heard aright. Then they narrowed again, the gray gleam of them hard as they rested on her flushed face.

"What—did—you—say?" he spaced the words out ominously. Cathy had to restrain herself from sticking her small pink tongue out at him.

"I said, no," she returned with studied nonchalance. Jon stared at her for a long moment, his frown deepening. She looked like the proverbial cat that had swallowed the canary: her blue eyes were shining with excitement, and her small face was flushed pink with it. Her golden hair was swirling about her with a life of its own. His eyes made a quick survey of her small form, draped in that ridiculous cover. At a glance nothing appeared amiss, but he had known Cathy long enough to know when she was up to something.

"If you put me to the trouble of getting up and fetching you, you'll be sorry," he threatened silkily, his eyes faintly wary as they watched her every movement.

"I wouldn't do that, if I were you," she told him, triumph lighting her eyes.

"But you're not me," he answered, and threw back the sheet.

"Stay where you are," Cathy ordered as he swung his legs over the side of the bunk. As he looked up she drew back the edge of the cover wrapping her to reveal the gleaming silver snout of one of his own dueling pistols. The mouth was pointed right at his mid-section.

Jon stayed where he was, his eyes contemplative as he mentally reviewed the situation. Damn himself for leaving the blasted pistols out where she could get hold of them! He should have guessed, with his long knowledge of the way her mind worked, that sooner or later she would try something like this. But he'd been angry—so damned angry he hadn't been thinking straight. And this was the result. But the more he thought about it, the more certain Jon became of one thing: Cathy wouldn't shoot him. Beneath all that fire and temper she had the softest of hearts, and she had once had a fondness for him. No, he didn't think she would go through with it. Besides, what else could he do but call her bluff?

He stood up. Her hand holding the gun wavered alarmingly, and her blue eyes widened until they were enormous sapphire pools.

"Stay where you are!" Her voice was high-pitched. "I mean it, Jon, I'll shoot you! I will!"

"Methinks the lady doth protest too much," he quoted ironically, and took a step toward her. Cathy, alarm growing in her breast, jumped to her feet, knocking over the chair in the process. She paid no attention to it as it fell to the floor with a crash, her eyes never leaving Jon. Both hands now held the pistol, and her aim never wavered. Blast him, he couldn't mean to ignore a gun, could he? Cathy thought frantically.

Apparently he did. He advanced on her steadily, his hand outstretched for the pistol. Swallowing, Cathy backed. Her hands were sweating profusely.

"Jon, I'll shoot!" she warned again desperately as her back came up against the paneled wall. He smiled tauntingly, his step never faltering.

"Shoot then," he directed calmly, and reached for the pistol.

Cathy gasped, and dodged away from him. The pistol wobbled alarmingly in her hands. He was laughing now, and Cathy registered that fact with a sudden lift of her chin. As he moved toward her again, she raised the pistol, said a brief, silent prayer, and tightly shut her eyes. Then she pulled the trigger.

eight

~~~~~~

The sound of the shot reverbrated through the tiny cabin; its force knocked Cathy backward. Her eyes flew open as she half-fell, and the smoking pistol dropped from her suddenly nerveless fingers. The acrid smell of gunpowder seemed to sear her nostrils.

To her horror she saw that Jon was staggering, his hand clapped to a spot just below his left shoulder. Bright red blood welled beneath his long brown fingers; crimson droplets were spattered on the dark pelt covering his chest. The stunned look on his face would have been almost comical under any other circumstances.

"Damn it, you shot me!" he muttered, his gray eyes lifting from his shocked contemplation of his wound to fix disbelievingly on Cathy's equally shocked face.

"I told you I would!" she cried accusingly, hurrying toward him. When she stood directly in front of his tall, naked body she stopped, hovering helplessly. In truth, she did not know quite what to do.

"Does it hurt?" she asked inanely. Jon flashed her an irritated look.

"Hell, yes, it hurts! What did you expect?" he growled, gingerly moving his injured shoulder. Cathy saw his face grow very pale beneath its tan.

"You'd better lie down," she exclaimed, thinking that his long body seemed to sway. "You look like you're going to pass out."

"Thanks to you, I probably will," he gritted. He tried to shake her off when Cathy eased an arm around his waist, but she hung on tenaciously. His weight was just beginning to rest against her when a knock sounded at the door. Immediately Jon's good hand came out to squeeze her shoulder hard. Cathy was horrified to see the gaping, oozing hole she had made in his shoulder.

"Just keep that too-quick tongue of yours still, will you?" he ordered softly, then raising his voice, called ungraciously, "What is it?"

"You okay in there, Captain?" O'Reilly's voice boomed. "We heard a shot."

"I was cleaning my pistols and one of them discharged. What were you expecting, an insurrection?" Jon shot Cathy a hard, warning look when she made a move as if to demur.

"Shouldn't we send for a doctor?" she whispered, her eyes fixed on the blood that was running freely from the wound in his shoulder. Bright crimson streaked his chest and belly and even his bare, muscular thighs. Cathy was beginning to be very much afraid that she had done him a serious injury.

"No," he answered fiercely. "Now shut up."

Cathy stiffened at his rudeness, but did as he said. From beyond the door, O'Reilly's voice came again.

"Just checking, Captain. Enjoy yourself." The chuckle in these last two words turned them into a bawdy comment. Cathy was too concerned about Jon's injuries to take offense. When she heard O'Reilly's footsteps move away, she turned on him angrily.

"Why didn't you tell him what happened? You need a doctor!"

"To begin with, there's not a doctor on board. And even if there were, I wouldn't call him. Good God, you still don't have a clue about the situation on deck, do you? The men out there are convicts, all of them. Some of them would slit my throat, and yours, for no other reason than they're here! What do you suppose would happen to you, to say nothing of me, if those men were to find out that I'd been shot? They'd close in like a pack of wolves, that's what. And I don't think you'd enjoy their idea of a good time. Although I could be mistaken. I have been before." Jon flashed her a sardonic look. It left Cathy in no doubt as to his meaning.

"You're hateful!" she hissed. "I'm glad I shot you! You deserved it!"

She glared fiercely at him. He glared back just as angrily, and then he closed his eyes, his face whitening even more.

"I think—I'd better—sit down," he muttered, and Cathy could feel his hard body sagging against her side. Immediately her arm tightened around him, and she supported him as best she could over the few paces to the bunk. He was too heavy for her to be of much help, but at least, she thought, she was there to catch him if he should fall. As he sank down in a sitting position on the hard mattress, Cathy felt like a murderess. She hadn't really meant to shoot him, God knows, just take his arrogant self down a peg or two. Deep in the recesses of her brain had lurked a vague but pleasurable picture of him down on his knees before her, begging her to spare his life. Knowing Jon as she did, she'd known from the first that she couldn't hope for that, but still, she hadn't expected him to laugh, and reach for the gun. . . .

"Shouldn't you lie down?" she asked, concerned, as he continued to sit slumped on the edge of the bunk.

"If I lie down, I'll never get up," he said abruptly, his eyes closed. "Do something for me: look at my back and tell me if there's an exit wound. You know, a hole like the one you made in my front."

"I know what an exit wound is," Cathy answered with haughty dignity. If he wasn't so very obviously in pain, she thought, she would have left him to his own devices. Then, as she was about to do as he had directed, a thought occurred to her.

"What happens if there's not an exit wound?" she asked suspiciously. Jon cast her a darkling look.

"Then that means the ball's still in my shoulder, and you'll have to get it out," he gritted. "God, did you always talk this much? Get on with it!"

Cathy ground her teeth, but said nothing further. Instead, she looked at his back. To her profound relief, there was another oozing hole piercing his shoulder blade; the broad planes of his back were transversed by flowing crimson rivers.

"There's an exit wound," Cathy gulped. Jon let out his breath in a sigh of relief. Cathy continued: "You—you're bleeding pretty badly. I—I'll get something to bind you up. I don't suppose there's anything like bandages on board?"

"Tear up a sheet," Jon answered. "But before you do, look in that box under the bunk. There's a bottle of whiskey: hand it to me."

Cathy got down on her knees, feeling under the bunk. Sure enough, there was a box, and as she dragged it out she saw that it contained, among other miscellaneous items, a three-quarters full bottle of whiskey. Without a word, she handed it to Jon. He took it with a grunt, and proceeded to pull out the cork with his teeth and down fully a third of the contents in a series of gulps.

Biting back a comment about the evils of strong drink, Cathy took the top sheet from where it was crumpled at the foot of the bunk. She stood looking at it rather doubtfully. As far as she knew, it was the only one available: the *Cristobel* did not boast a surfeit of bed linen. But although it had been washed several times since she had come on board, the sheet could hardly be termed sanitary.

"Isn't there anything else I can use for bandages? This isn't very clean."

"Well, it will have to do," Jon answered shortly. "I'm bleeding like a stuck pig. Can't you hurry up?"

"Listen, you ungrateful oaf, it would serve you right if I let you bleed to death!" Cathy was so annoyed that she tore the sheet straight across with one vicious jerk. Quickly she ripped the halves into manageable strips, and dropped to her knees before him.

"Wait a minute," he said when she would have pressed a cloth pad to the sluggishly bleeding wound. "First use this." He passed her the bottle of whiskey. "For disinfectant," he explained.

Cathy took it rather gingerly. She had heard of whiskey being used in that way, of course, but she had never actually seen it done, and she had certainly never done it. Jon maneuvered himself so that his back was to her, the black hole with its trailing crimson aureole uppermost. Cathy stared at it for a moment, feeling faintly sick. It looked awful. . . . Then, resolutely catching her lower lip between her teeth, she tilted the whiskey over it.

Jon gasped as the golden liquid poured over the wound; what she could see of his face turned as white as paper.

"Soak a pad in it and press it to the wound," he directed through gritted teeth. Cathy's hands were shaking, but she did as he told her. Then, while she held the wet pad in place, he moved again so that she had access to the front side of the wound. As she poured the whiskey over him this time, Jon made not a sound, but sweat beaded tellingly on his upper lip and forehead. His skin was so pale. . . . Cathy moaned herself as she soaked another pad and pressed it to the crusting hole.

"What are you whimpering about? You're not hurt." Jon's sarcasm sounded so nearly normal that Cathy felt a quiver of relief. His gray eyes opened and she met them, her own contrite.

"I'm sorry I shot you," she said low. "I never would have done it if you hadn't laughed."

Jon grimaced, then a faint smile tilted up the corners of his lips.

"I know," he admitted. "Don't feel too bad about it. You haven't killed me."

"I'm glad," Cathy whispered, surprising herself as much as him. The way she had felt about him lately, she should have enjoyed seeing him suffer, wanted to see him dead. But if he died, the thought occurred to her, what would become of her? She would be left entirely at the mercy of men that Jon himself was wary of. So she convinced herself that this, and this alone, was responsible for her nearly overpowering feeling of remorse, and set about binding his wound. Jon, for his part, cast her a sharp look. For some little while nothing more was said.

He sat in a half-reclining position while Cathy dressed the wound, his black head resting against the paneled wall of the cabin, his long bare legs stretched their length across the floor. His face was still very pale, making the stubble on his jaw and chin seem almost blue-black in comparison. He usually went three or four days without shaving—probably, Cathy guessed, because he knew she liked it better when he was clean-shaven, and hoped to annoy her. His mouth was set hard against the pain, and his eyes were closed. Blood was matted in the dark hair on his chest and belly. When she had secured the bandage Cathy began to gently sponge it away with a wet cloth. He said nothing, submitting docilely to her ministrations.

For just a minute after she had finished and sat back on her heels, he stayed as he was, unmoving. Against her will, Cathy's eyes ran the length of that long, naked body. Injured or not, he looked formidable; Cathy realized that, had she been a man, she would now be in quaking fear for her life. Broad of shoulder and wide of chest, with a tautly muscled belly and long, powerful-looking legs, there was no doubting his strength. And when he was in a black rage. . . . Cathy shivered. She was suddenly very glad that she was not a man.

Jon's eyes opened, and as they met her own Cathy saw with a sense of inevitability that they were as hard as the rock they resembled.

"Help me get dressed," he directed tersely, easing into a sitting position. Cathy gaped at him.

"You can't be serious," she said.

"I've never been more serious in my life. Now get me my breeches." From his voice there was no doubting that he meant what he said. Cathy stared at him for a moment, helplessly. His eyes were closed again, and she knew that he must be suffering a great deal of pain. As she watched him, frowning with concern, his eyes flashed open and seemed to bore down into hers.

"Go on, get me my breeches," he said impatiently. "If I stay in here much longer, the men will know for damn certain that something fishy's going on. I've had time to hump you fifty times over."

Cathy felt her cheeks crimson at his crudity. So that was how he thought of their lovemaking! She flashed him an angry look, then got to her feet and went to retrieve his breeches from the floor by the stove, where he had carelessly discarded them the night before.

"Bring my shirt, too, while you're about it," he directed. Cathy picked up that coarsely woven linen garment, one that Jon had clearly managed to acquire since taking over the *Cristobel*, and his boots. Then she carried her load back across to him.

"Breeches first," he directed. Cathy knelt at his feet, her lips compressed. She looked up to find him regarding her ironically.

"Jon. . . ." she began, only to be silenced by an impatient wave of his hand.

"For God's sake, don't argue," he snapped. "Accept the fact that I know what I'm doing. And you can stand up. I didn't mean for you to dress me like some puling infant."

"If you're determined to get dressed," Cathy replied coldly, "I'll help you. Now, would you mind lifting your feet a little?"

Jon flashed her a sardonic look, which Cathy ignored, then obediently lifted his feet. Cathy slid his breeches over them until his feet came out the end of the pant legs. Then she pulled the garment up over his knees to his thighs, where she was stopped by the fact that he was sitting very firmly on his hard-muscled bottom.

"You'll have to lift yourself up," she said, annoyed as she realized that his mouth was twitching. Then, as her hands came in contact with the black material of his breeches once more, she added disgustedly, "These breeches are filthy. Don't you have any clean ones?"

"No, Lady Stanhope, I don't," he replied, the humorous twitch vanishing as if it had never been. "Unlike you, I didn't come on a pleasure voyage. I was a prisoner sentenced to transportation, as you may recall. I was lucky to be allowed to keep the clothes on my back. Since then, I've managed to acquire a few shirts, ill-fitting though they may be, but breeches that are a reasonable size have been beyond me."

"Well, these need to be washed," she told him shortly, pulling the breeches up over his hips and beginning to button them. Her hands brushed the hardness of his belly, were tickled by the soft mat of hair that curled around his navel. The sensation was pleasurable. Cathy frowned irritably as she tried to dismiss it.

"Maybe you could get Sarita to do it for you," she added, her tone waspish.

"Maybe I could," he answered equably. Cathy fastened his last button with a twitch of her sharp-nailed fingers that made him wince.

Cathy stood up when this was done, undecided.

"Boots," Jon said. Cathy frowned at him, but turned to pick up his boots. They were high-topped leather ones, meant to shine softly but now scuffed with hard use and stained with sea water. And they were devilishly hard to put on. Cathy struggled over them for fully five minutes, her face flushed with effort, curses hovering on the tip of her tongue. That she didn't utter them was due entirely to the fact that she was born and bred a lady—and besides, Jon would have roared with laughter, and she had no wish to afford him any amusement.

Finally she straddled one long, muscular bare leg, hitching the trailing sarong-cover up crossly. She stood with her back to Jon, bent over as she finally succeeded in fitting the boot over his long foot. Then she grasped the cursed object by its top and pulled with every ounce of strength she possessed. It dragged upward a mere few inches. She was bending again for another effort when she felt a hand creep under the hitched-up ends of her garment to fondle the softness of her bare behind with intimate familiarity. Cathy choked, nearly tripping over Jon's long leg as she whirled. The devil was laughing, she saw with a sudden spurt of rage, and she lifted her hand to him threateningly. He pretended to cower away from her, raising his good arm to ward off possible blows.

"It was such a tempting target," he explained with a grin, and then, when Cathy raised her threatening hand a little higher, he added persuasively, "Now, you wouldn't hit a wounded man, would you?"

Cathy wouldn't. She scowled at him, her hand dropping reluctantly. He studied her for an instant, his eyes touching on the turbulence in her blue eyes, the tangles of her golden hair that swirled about her like a lion's mane, the belligerent set of her little chin, and the tenseness of her lovely body. He smiled suddenly, a sweet and charming smile such as Cathy had not seen on his face since she had left him behind at Woodham.

"You're a bloodthirsty little minx," he told her softly.

While she still gaped at him, he reached out and drew her down on his knee. Cathy stared at him warily, surprised and not entirely trusting of his sudden softness. His hand slid beneath her chin, tilting her face up to his. Cathy was too thrown off balance to do anything but acquiesce as he gently covered her mouth with his. The kiss was brief, but exquisite in its tenderness. For a moment Cathy was passive beneath it, but then she began to return it with wild hope. It was Jon who broke it off, lifting his head and pushing her gently until she slid off his knee to sit beside him on the bunk. She was still dazed from the kiss as he stood abruptly.

"Help me with this shirt. I have to get out on deck," he said gruffly, not looking at her as he picked up his shirt. Cathy stood up, bewildered. She took the shirt from him and gently helped him ease it over his injured arm and shoulder. Then, when he had put his other arm into it, she buttoned it for him as she would have done for Cray. Dozens of emotions were whirling crazily inside her, but finally one thought emerged from the confusion: she had to make one more attempt to convince Jon of the truth about her marriage to Harold. For the sake of the love she had once borne him, and for their son, she at least owed both of them that.

"Jon. . . ." she began, her hands clutching his shirt front as she looked up into his eyes. Their gray depths were unreadable as they stared down at her, but at least he no longer seemed actively hostile. Cathy moistened her suddenly dry lips with her little pink tongue, and saw his attention focus on that small movement.

"Jon, I. . . ." she began again.

"Later," he said brusquely, his hands coming up to free his shirt from her clutches. Cathy was left staring after him helplessly as he turned on his heel and strode from the cabin.

All through the day and long into the night Cathy waited for him as nervously as any bride. She would go down on her knees, if necessary, to convince him that she had done what she had for him. Despite his distrust of her, and his anger, which she suspected stemmed from pain, if he thought coolly and reasonably on the subject he could not help but be convinced: after all, he merely had to compare a mental picture of Harold with himself. Would any female in her right mind trade Jon's hard, virile masculinity for Harold's pasty mound of flesh? Certainly not. Cathy smiled a little at the images this conjured up. Persuading Jon of the truth of her argument might be most enjoyable, at that.

Cathy hummed as she washed herself, faltering only a little as the water in the basin turned a dingy brown from Jon's blood which had streaked her shoulders and hands. Perhaps shooting Jon had not been such a dreadful thing, after all. It had certainly provoked him to more tenderness than he had shown her since they had come aboard the *Cristobel*. Maybe it had needed a shock like that to bring him to his senses. Cathy frowned, considering the possibility that his wound might cause him some problems. He would certainly be weakened, both from shock and loss of blood, and his arm would be sore. But aside from that, it had been a clean, self-contained hole, and the blood had run freely from it, hopefully cleansing it of any impurities. Infection was the big worry; Cathy remembered the horrible putrification which had set into Jon's leg when he had been stabbed there years ago, and paled a little. But this wound was nothing compared to that dreadful jagged tear. He would survive it, she told herself consolingly, without much more than a few twinges of pain. And surely he deserved that for his suspicions of her!

Cathy scrubbed the blood from the floor and walls, and then turned her attention to the bunk. Blood stained the coarse white sheet and smeared the wooden frame. The frame was easily taken care of with water and a rag, but the sheet posed some problems. Since she had torn up the top one to use for bandages, it was the only sheet that was left. Cathy grimaced as she considered sleeping on it. Impossible! It sickened her just to think of it. No, the sheet would have to be washed if there were no more to be had, and she would have to do it. Grimacing, she stripped it from the bunk and set to work.

It was hours later, long after sundown, when Cathy finally could wait no longer. Where was Jon? Surely he was as anxious to work out their problems as she. And he must have sensed that she had something to tell him. He should have been back long before this. Cathy refused to even consider the possibility that perhaps he just didn't want to know. Something about the sailing of the ship must be delaying him, she told herself stoutly, or maybe he was just plain shy. Cathy grinned a little at the thought of Jon being shy. On the surface it seemed ridiculous, but one never knew. Maybe she should go and fetch him in, Cathy thought. It was after dark, and if she wrapped the cover securely around herself there would be nothing for anyone to see. Surely even Jon himself could not object. Making up her mind with a nod, Cathy rearranged her sarong so that it more closely resembled a toga, and let herself out of the cabin.

It was a velvety black night; the moon had not yet risen, and only a few tiny stars winked against the darkness of the sky. The sea was calm, one gently rolling wave following another. Only the slap-slap of water lapping against the hull and the creaking of the rigging broke the silence. The deck was deserted as far as Cathy could tell, and while she knew that couldn't be true it imparted a wonderful feeling of peace. The night air was warm and heavy as it caressed the skin of her face and one bare shoulder. Cathy breathed deeply of it, loving the salt smell which, combined with the odor of fish and the scent of tar, would forever remind her of the sea. For a long moment she stood motionless, savoring the night, and then she turned to the stairs that led to the quarterdeck. It was a safe bet that Jon would be up there, and that was where she would begin her search.

At first she thought the quarterdeck was deserted too, and she frowned disbelievingly. Jon would be furious if he knew. One of his strongest maxims was that there must always be a man on watch. Her frown deepened as she saw that the wheel was lashed. Where was everybody? Had something happened that she should know about? Then, as she came around the wheel so that the port side of the quarterdeck was visible to her for the first time, she stopped as if she had been pole-axed. Her eyes narrowed and her teeth clenched as she suddenly perceived the reason for the silence.

Just as she had expected, Jon was on the quarterdeck. He was busy kissing that hussy Sarita, who was wrapped around him like a particularly sickening species of clinging vine.

Watching them, Cathy felt a rage so fierce that it seemed to pierce her vitals. Her fingers curved into claws, the nails digging deep into her palms. Cathy didn't even feel the pain. Her whole attention was focused on the two silhouettes outlined against the night sky, so close they might almost have been one. The sight hurt so much that she could scarcely breathe. She wanted to scream, to cry, to run across and tear them apart. But she did none of those. She was rooted to the spot, her eyes fixed with dreadful fascination on the source of her agony while it seemed as if every drop of blood in her body had turned to ice.

She must have made some slight sound, because Jon raised his head. Over Sarita's black hair his eyes met hers. Cathy would have at least expected him to push the woman away, to attempt to make some sort of explanation. Instead a curious kind of triumph lit those gray eyes. Cathy could almost feel him savoring her agony. Then Sarita's hand came behind his head, pulling him down. Without another look at Cathy, he bent over the woman once more.

For what seemed like an eternity but must in reality have been only seconds, Cathy stood frozen while a horrible choking feeling gripped her throat. Then she turned, and stumbled blindly down the stairs and into the cabin.

She was still in a daze as she sank down onto the bunk. Thankfully, her emotions had gone numb. She felt as if some vital part of her had been destroyed; rather, she suspected, as she would feel if she had an arm or a leg amputated. How could he do such a thing, was the thought that kept pushing to the forefront of her brain. How could he do such a thing— to me?

It was foolish in the extreme to feel so betrayed. Cathy knew it, but she couldn't help it. Reminding herself that Jon was no longer her husband—had never been her husband— did no good at all. Illogically, she still considered him her own exclusive property. To see him like that with Sarita had been a killing blow to the chains that still bound him to her heart. She huddled into a little ball on the bunk, her arms wrapped around her knees, rocking back and forth like a bewildered child who suddenly finds itself alone in the dark. At any moment she expected Jon to come bursting through the door, full of apologies and explanations. "That bitch Sarita kissed me, I didn't kiss her," he would say, and when he saw how he had hurt her he would take her in his arms and kiss her, and tell her that she was the only woman in the world for him. Cathy prayed that this would come to pass with an intensity she had never felt before. But, as hours passed, and the night slowly lightened into dawn, she had to face the brutal fact: Jon was not coming to bed. At least, not to hers. He had doubtless been cozily ensconced in Sarita's lo these many hours past. Finally, as orange feelers began to grope their way across the violet sky, suspicion crystallized into certainty. Tears had marbleized on Cathy's face when exhaustion lulled her to sleep at last.

*J*on awoke feeling lower than a snake's belly. His shoulder ached like hell, his mouth felt like it was stuffed with cotton, and his muscles were protesting loudly at being forced to spend the night on the hard boards of the deck. But worse than any physical pain was his sense of self-disgust. He had used Sarita solely to get back at Cathy, and it had backfired. He had gotten no enjoyment from the act at all. If the truth were known, he had barely been able to function, and only his male pride had kept him from backing out at the last moment. The sight of Sarita's over-ripe body had sickened him: with every look he had mentally compared it with Cathy's silken perfection. Cathy. He groaned at the thought, rolling over onto his back and throwing his arm up to shield his eyes from the just rising sun. The stricken look in her eyes which had afforded him so much satisfaction last night returned in the sober light of day to haunt him. Against all reason, he felt as guilty as hell.

Which was stupid, he castigated himself. He was a free agent, not bound to Cathy by matrimony or anything else. He was a bachelor—briefly Jon savored the thought, which had just occurred to him—and there was no reason in the world why he shouldn't take his pleasure with any woman he pleased. Pleasure: now that was a word! Certainly he had felt none with Sarita, despite her almost embarrassing avidity. It was Cathy he had wanted, Cathy he had taken in the end when his mind refused to allow him to perform with Sarita as his partner. Finally, when he had spewed his seed into Sarita's writhing body, he had pictured soft golden hair and softer skin, black lashes lying like shadows against pinkened cheeks, a sweet voice moaning his name. . . . God! Whatever the little bitch had done to him, she had done it well. She had entwined him in silken threads as a spider imprisons a fly. Ever since he had first made her his—an eternity ago, it seemed—he had felt desire for no other woman.

Oh, he had tried. At first, when he was trying to fight his way out of her web, he had deliberately sought out the most attractive females he could find for the purpose of bedding them. But he had never been able to go through with it. No matter how enticing their charms, they had been eclipsed when he had compared them with the dazzling sun that was Cathy. Until last night, he had been ever faithful, like an old dog who has been abandoned by its master but still sits by the road, hoping and hoping he will return, Jon thought savagely.

Yesterday, she had shot him: any reasonable man would have been furious. But her action, and her obvious remorse afterward, had fired in him a tenderness that he had thought long dead and buried. Who but Cathy would have dared, and who but Cathy would have tended him so gently afterward? As he watched her struggling to dress him, when he was perfectly capable of doing it himself, he had felt the icy knot of rage that had dwelt for so long in his belly begin to melt. She had disarmed him, the minx, almost brought him to the point where he was trapped again and glad of it. But luckily he had caught himself in time. She had betrayed him once, and when she got the chance she would likely do it again. It wasn't in him to hold his heart out for rejection a second time.

The experience with Sarita had been sordid. She had been naked and all over him like an octopus, and he had not even bothered to remove his breeches. He had just unbuttoned them. The whole thing had been over in less than five minutes, and then he had left the still-clinging Sarita to spend what was left of the night in solitary splendor on deck. Jon grinned sourly. If word of last night's happenings ever got out, as it probably would, his reputation as a lover would take quite a beating. Jackrabbit Jonny, they would doubtless call him; to his faint surprise, the thought troubled him not at all. The only woman whose love he wanted, for better or worse, knew better. And he would see to it that she at least had no doubts about his sexual prowess!

She would be furious, Jon acknowledged to himself, but he was confident that he could overcome her anger. He had almost gone directly to his cabin to face her wrath last night after he had left Sarita, but the guilt that was already strong in him had held him back.

But why should he feel guilty? he thought, suddenly remembering his grievances against her. What she had done had been far worse than his one brief encounter with Sarita. She had sold herself to another man knowing that he, Jon, loved her, knowing that he still considered her his wife. And she had let that man bed her over and over again. . . . Jon's teeth clenched at the thought. He hoped she was angry. He hoped she suffered one-tenth the hell she had put him through!

Jon rolled abruptly to his feet, a black frown marring his face. He would go to his cabin and wash, and if the little bitch had the gall to castigate him for taking Sarita, then well and good. Because there were any number of things he wanted to say to her.

The sound of raised feminine voices checked Jon briefly as he strode toward his cabin. One woman was screeching something, and then he heard the unmistakable sound of a slap. The noise was coming from inside his cabin, Jon realized with an ominous sense of foreboding, and he was ready to swear that the voice he had heard screeching was Sarita's. Good God, what now? Then, as one awful possibility occurred to him, Jon hurried forward.

Cathy had been awakened from a troubled sleep by two hands dragging her roughly from the bunk. For a groggy moment she thought that Jon had returned at last. Opening her eyes, prepared to freeze him with an icy blast of indifference, she found to her bewilderment that the face bending over hers was not his at all: the eyes were large and black, the skin faintly coarse, the nose and mouth thick, and the whole distinctly female. Sarita! Even as the identity of her assailant popped into Cathy's brain, so too did the searing memory of how she had last seen her. Brushing the sleep from her eyes with one hand, Cathy jerked free of the fingers that dug into her shoulders so painfully.

"You get out of here!" Sarita stormed before Cathy had a chance to speak. "I'm moving in! Jonny's my man now, not yours!"

"You're welcome to him," Cathy snapped, her eyes disdainful as they took in the woman's dishevelment. Apparently Sarita was not long out of bed herself. "But I move out of this cabin when Jon tells me to, not you."

"You move out when I tell you: now! Jonny doesn't want you anymore! Last night he made me his woman, and from now on I'm going to be sleeping in his bed!"

"Indeed." Cathy drawled the word in her best Great Lady manner, her eyes traveling over Sarita with conscious hauteur. "How gratifying for you!"

"Don't you talk to me like that! Like you're some fine lady and I'm nothing! Jonny's told me all about you: you're no better than me!"

"A slut, you mean?" Cathy asked unpleasantly.

"Don't you call me that! You've got no right to call me that, you with your light skirts and easy ways! You whore!" Sarita followed this with a whole string of filthy epithets that Cathy had never even heard before. She listened calmly to the abuse, one eyebrow raised superciliously. She had learned long ago that the best way to deal with abuse by a person who secretly considered himself an underling was to play the highborn lady to the hilt.

"You get out of here!" Sarita finally ended her tirade. Cathy looked her over as if the woman were a particularly distasteful bug that had just crawled out from under a rock.

"No." The word was soft, and Cathy smiled as she said it. Only her eyes betrayed her rising anger. The more she thought of how Sarita had spent last night, the harder it was for her to control an almost overwhelming impulse to claw the woman's bulging black eyes out!

"Eeeh!" Sarita cried furiously, and her hand rang out against Cathy's cheek in a stunning slap. Cathy, taken by surprise, automatically clapped her hand to her bruised face. Her eyes began to glitter dangerously. Then, as Sarita reached for her, obviously intending to eject her from Jon's cabin by brute force, Cathy drew back her hand and returned the woman's slap with interest.

When Jon burst into his cabin, the two women were rolling around on the floor like Japanese wrestlers. Sarita had a big handful of Cathy's blonde hair wrapped around her fist and was pulling on it mightily. Cathy's hands were closed around Sarita's throat. Jon stood transfixed for a moment, staring at the pair with a mixture of consternation and amusement. He had rushed to his cabin for fear that Sarita might do Cathy an injury. Sarita must have outweighed the younger girl by two stone: she was far taller, and heavier of muscle. Plus, she had been raised on London's most squalid streets; she was no stranger to brawls, whereas Cathy had had the gentlest of upbringings. She was born and bred a lady, and fighting was not generally included in a lady's education. Jon would have laid money that Sarita could have torn Cathy limb from limb. And what was amusing him was that he would have lost: even as he watched, Cathy managed to roll on top of Sarita, straddling her as she pinned her to the floor. When Sarita's long nails went for Cathy's face, Cathy raised her clenched fist and delivered a blow to the chin that would have been worthy of boxing's finest. Sarita screamed, and the sound galvanized Jon to action. He hurried to separate the two, before Cathy could do Sarita real damage.

"That's enough!" His voice was sharp as he caught Cathy around the waist, lifting her bodily off Sarita. Cathy dangled from his arms like a small spitting kitten, and Sarita immediately took advantage of her rival's situation to surge to her feet. She came at Cathy with nails bared. Jon, seeing what Sarita meant to do just an instant too late, swung Cathy behind him only after the woman's nails had scraped a raw path down the side of Cathy's neck. Cathy gasped, and then as Jon released her to grab Sarita, she launched herself from behind him, her nails raking Sarita's plump shoulders, bared by the low-cut peasant blouse. Jon swore; one hand closed over Cathy's arm, the other over Sarita's. It was all he could do to hold them apart, and he was sorely tempted to knock their hot heads together and be done with it. Instead, in desperation, he bellowed for O'Reilly.

O'Reilly, when he arrived, sized up the situation at a glance. He locked both arms around Sarita's waist, dragging the woman bodily from the cabin. She screamed curses at Cathy as she went.

Cathy, for her part, was trembling in Jon's arms. As he swung her around so that he could see her face, he thought she might be suffering from a case of delayed reaction. But her blazing eyes told him otherwise: she was furious, plain and simple, and now that Sarita had been gotten out of the way, all that fire and brimstone temper seemed to be directed at himself.

"How dare you send your—your *paramour* to tell me to move out!" Cathy raged, her sapphire eyes flashing storm signals and her soft pink mouth trembling with anger. She had apparently slept in one of his discarded shirts; the garment was miles too big for her, falling down past her knees, the trailing sleeves pushed up in thick rolls above the elbows. In it, with her long golden hair and heaving breasts clearly outlined beneath the linen, she looked small and fragile, and completely, unmistakably, female.

"Jealous, Cathy?" Jon taunted softly, not liking the way she was making him feel. Cathy's lips drew back into what was almost a snarl; she tossed her head like a wild bull before the charge, and Jon could almost feel the heat of her anger.

"Of her? Don't make me laugh!" she spat. Jon, still securely holding her arms, smiled mockingly.

"I think you are," he said softly. "I think you're so jealous that your insides are rotten with it. I think that's why you attacked Sarita. . . ."

"*I* attacked *Sarita*?" Cathy gasped. "You really must think an awful lot of your abilities in bed! Frankly, my dear, you aren't worth it!"

"Is that right?" Jon's voice was silky smooth; only the narrowing of his eyes revealed that Cathy's dart had gone home. "That's not what you say when I hold you naked in my arms: 'Jon,' you sigh, and then you pant and beg for more. . . ."

"You conceited swine!" Cathy hissed, feeling her cheeks flush hotly at this all too accurate reminder of the way he affected her. "I'll never let you near me again! You'd have to kill me before I let you lay a hand on me!"

"I don't think so," Jon drawled meaningfully, his gray eyes taking on an ugly gleam. And then he proceeded to prove that he was right.

nine

⤜⤛⚬⤜⤛

$\mathcal{C}$hristmas came and went, and then New Year. Due to the intermittent squalls that kept the men fully occupied with sailing the ship, Cathy thought that she must have been the only one to note their passing. Briefly she remembered last year's holiday season, when she and Jon and Cray had celebrated as a family at Woodham. But the pictures conjured up were too painful, so she forced herself to dismiss them. That brief period of happiness was beginning to seem more and more like a dream; harsh reality was the never-ending rocking of the *Cristobel*, Jon's growing coldness, and the fact that her son was many, many miles away.

The *Cristobel* was sailing south. The weather was hot and sultry, with rain liable to fall at any time. Jon had grudgingly told her, in response to her equally grudging question, that he was heading for Tenerife. He had many friends from his pirate days on the island, and he would need their help to insure that the *Cristobel* was completely seaworthy before setting sail across the Atlantic for the States.

Cathy had finally obtained some clothes, courtesy of Angie Harrow, another of the former female prisoners. Cathy rather liked Angie, who was small like herself but much thinner, and as completely colorless as a piece of brown paper. Angie had been a lady's maid until she had been accused of stealing her mistress's diamond ear-bobs. The girl stoutly maintained her innocence, and Cathy was inclined to believe her. Not that it mattered. Angie appeared to have adopted Cathy as her new lady, and Cathy found it very pleasant to have someone around who took real pleasure in performing those tasks which Cathy had never expected to have to do for herself.

Jon looked askance on this new friendship, but he said nothing. It was as natural for Cathy to have someone to wait on her as it was for flowers to bloom in the sun. He only insisted that Angie stay out of his cabin when he was in it, and that she not neglect her other duties. Otherwise, since both girls seemed content with their arrangement, he let it stand.

The clothes that Angie had provided from her own meager store were the same type of simple blouse and skirt that had been issued to all the female prisoners. Cathy had only a single petticoat to wear under this simple outfit, but that did not stop her from donning it, and going up on deck whenever she got the chance. On the hottest days it was far more refreshing to stand out on deck, where there was almost always at least a faint breeze, than to swelter in the close confines of the cabin. For coolness' sake she took to wearing her hair in a single thick braid; with her bare feet peeping out from under the short, full skirt and the kiss of the sun across her nose and cheeks, she looked every inch a pirate lass. Jon, watching her as she lent a hand around the deck, thought that she had never looked more beautiful, and cursed himself for the desire that grew in him like a weed that refused to be uprooted.

Jon's eyes weren't the only ones that followed Cathy around the deck. Many of the men lusted after her openly, but not quite openly enough to let Jon see. And Sarita watched the younger girl with evil malevolence. Since that one night, Jon had not come to her pallet, and that lady-bitch was still in his cabin. Sarita smoldered, and bided her time.

The situation between Jon and Cathy could best be described as a state of armed neutrality. He took her body when he could resist it no longer, and she didn't fight him. On that one memorable morning when he had accused her quite rightly of jealousy, he had taught her once and for all that her physical responses were his to command. Rather than risk further humiliation by putting up a fight only to have him reduce her to a clinging supplicant in his arms, Cathy preferred to submit from the beginning. At least that way only she was aware of the totality of her own defeat.

They barely spoke; they lived together like outwardly courteous strangers except for the time they spent in that too-narrow bunk slaking their hunger for each other. Cathy was bitterly ashamed of herself for responding so completely to a man who had openly betrayed her with another woman, a man who made no bones about treating her as the whore he plainly thought she was. But she couldn't help herself. Her traitorous body had only to feel the touch of his hands or lips to melt like butter set too near a fire. She wanted him, God help her, and he wanted her. On that one subject, if no other, they were in complete accord.

The wound she had inflicted in Jon's shoulder was almost completely healed. Jon had tended it himself, holding her off with a cold stare when she had offered to help. It was as if he wanted to keep her at arm's length in as many ways as he could. By the middle of January there remained only two red, puckered circles to show where the hole had been, and Jon had almost completely recovered the strength in his arm and shoulder. For this Cathy was profoundly, if secretly, glad. The inexperience of the *Cristobel*'s crew meant that Jon had to spend much time in the rigging, setting canvas and securing lines. Every time she watched him pull himself hand over hand up a rope high above the deck, her heart was in her mouth. If he fell. . . . But Jon was incredibly strong. At full strength, it was most unlikely that he would make such a mistake, and he was almost at full strength again.

For some time now Cathy had noticed that her stomach was inclined to get upset if the ship pitched too much, or if she stayed too long in the heat of the day. At first she had put her symptoms down to the deplorable food that was all that was available to eat, and let it go at that. But gradually an appalling fact began to dawn on her: she had not had her monthly courses for—oh, for a long time. Horrifying as the thought was, it was more than likely that she was pregnant.

When Cathy admitted the possibility to herself, late one afternoon as she stood at the taffrail, the sun an enormous fiery ball beating down on her bare head, she couldn't believe that she had not realized it sooner. As she thought back, she could see that her stomach had been most unreliable for months. And as for her monthly time—Cathy concentrated. She had not had it since before she left Woodham. That meant she was—dear God, she was nearly five months pregnant!

Cathy went numb with shock, her hand flying automatically to curve over her stomach. Now that she thought about it, she could feel a slight roundness there, but surely not as much as there should be for a pregnancy so far advanced. Maybe she had miscalculated the dates, or maybe the child was to be exceptionally small. Cathy contemplated what Jon's reaction would be to the news that he was to become a father for the second time, and felt herself pale. He would be far from pleased, she knew. He would blame her. . . . Cathy tilted her chin up in a gesture of defiance. It took two to make a baby, and he was certainly every bit as responsible as she. Besides, it really had very little to do with him. In the eyes of the law, Jon would not even be the child's father. Harold would be, because Cathy was legally his wife. She had to fight a strong urge to giggle hysterically. Jon would turn murderous when that aspect of the situation occurred to him. His child legally claimed by Harold! If it was a boy, it would inherit the title, and all of Harold's dubious honors and assets. Cathy pictured Harold's outrage if informed that the wife he had never even bedded was due to present him with an heir, and this time she did giggle. God, was there ever such a mess?

"What's so funny?" a deep voice growled in her ear. Cathy started guiltily, and cast a quick look over her shoulder to see Jon towering tall behind her.

"Nothing," she said hastily, knowing that she must have time to ponder the situation herself before breaking the news to him. "I was just—just laughing."

"I wish you'd share the joke," he said sourly. "I could do with a good laugh."

Cathy turned another, more searching, look on him. He looked as if he were tired, or under a strain. The lines carving his face from nose to mouth were cut deeper than usual, and his gray eyes were hooded. His hair had grown so long that it was curling thickly over his collar in the back, and Cathy thought, "I must persuade him to let me cut it," before turning her attention to more serious matters.

"Is something wrong?" she asked quietly, half-turning to face him. Jon grimaced.

"Nothing more than usual," he said, not looking at her but over her shoulder at the deep blue sky. "What I came to tell you is, I think we're getting ready to run into a storm. A bad one. All the signs are there. I'm going to be working my ass off keeping this ship afloat, and I won't have time to be worrying about you. I want you to promise me that, no matter what happens, you'll stay in the cabin until I tell you it's safe to come out. Agreed?"

Cathy cast him another inquiring look through the thick screen of her lashes.

"If I didn't know better, Captain, I'd think that you were worried about me," she murmured provokingly. Jon snorted.

"Let's just say I'm not ready to see sharks feast on that delectable little body—at least, not yet. For the time being I can think of so many more enjoyable things to do with it." Cathy stiffened indignantly at this drawling speech.

"You can jump overboard," she told him icily, and turned her back on him, meaning to flounce away to a more private spot. Jon caught her arm, holding her in place. Cathy shot him a hostile glare.

"Promise me," he said softly. "Or I swear I'll lock you in. And if something should happen to me, and the ship were to sink. . . ."

Cathy gulped a little as she pictured this dreadful eventuality.

"Oh, all right, I promise," she said ungraciously, and he allowed her to pull her arm from his grasp and escape.

She stayed out on deck until long after dark, sitting with her back against the mizzen and her arms wrapped around her drawn-up knees. Jon was busy on the quarterdeck, and Angie had disappeared below. No one else bothered her, and Cathy was left to her own thoughts. They centered almost entirely on the coming baby. She would have to tell Jon: there was no way around that. Being with child was something that a woman could not hide indefinitely. At first she was fiercely resentful at the idea of an infant coming into her life at this time, when her world had turned upside down almost overnight. She wasn't even married to the baby's father, which was what made the situation so impossibly difficult. But worse than the absence of words written on a piece of paper were the lack of heart-ties that should have bound her to Jon. He didn't love her, he'd made that abundantly plain. He wanted her, and that was an altogether different—and to Cathy's mind insulting—proposition. And she—did she love him? Her emotions were in such a tangle she couldn't be sure. Sometimes she did, when he was the Jon she remembered from Woodham, her gentle considerate lover, Cray's father. But other times, when he was a sneering, sadistic brute intent on punishing her for an infidelity that she had never committed, she loathed and despised him. And every time she thought of that night he had spent with Sarita, hatred rose in a thick gray fog before her eyes. That incident topped the ever-growing list of things for which she could never forgive him; other items included his distrust of her, his refusal to believe in her innocence no matter how much she protested, and his callous taking of her body whenever it pleased him. So, in answer to the question, did she love him? Cathy had to be honest with herself and admit that she didn't know. If she did, it was a curious, twisted kind of love, a deformed ghost of the joyous flowering of passion that had once existed between them.

The sea was growing increasingly choppy, and the wind was beginning to pick up. The *Cristobel* plowed up and down through the rolling waves. Overhead, a thick canopy of black clouds had blown up, completely blocking out the pale sliver of moon. A cold salt spray borne over the ship's side by the wind caught Cathy full in the face; she sputtered, jerked from her thoughts by the cold shock of it. As she wiped the moisture from her face, a sail caught the wrong way by the wind began to snap and crack like a bullwhip gone mad.

"Drop that canvas!" she heard Jon's voice roar, the authority in it unmistakable. Cathy slewed around in the direction whence it had come, her eyes searching for and finding his dark form as he strode the length of the deck. He stopped at the foot of the mainmast, repeating his instructions to a man high in the rigging in a voice that rivalled the thunder that was beginning to boom.

"Hell and damnation!" Jon swore, and to Cathy it was apparent that the man was not following Jon's instructions adequately. Her eyes widened as she saw Jon catch hold of the pole with both hands and begin effortlessly to shimmy his way up it. By the time he had climbed less than a third of the way she was standing beneath the mast, her head tilted as far back as it would reach as she fixed him with fearful eyes. He was not alone in the rigging; there must have been a dozen other men up there with him, some dangling precariously from poles, others clinging to the ropes for dear life. Their mission was plain even to a landlubber like herself: to get the sails furled before the storm hit.

He was up there for a good quarter-hour, and Cathy thought that her neck would break by the time he came sliding down. His expression was a mixture of exasperation with his men's inexperience and grim determination to get the job done. When he saw Cathy waiting beneath the mast for him, apparently oblivious to the large rain drops that had just started to splatter the deck, exasperation won out.

"Damn it, I thought you promised to stay in the cabin during the storm!" he yelled at her. Cathy, not over-fond of his tone, made a face at him.

"What storm?" she asked impudently. "All I see are a few drops of rain."

Jon audibly ground his teeth. Reaching out, he grabbed her arm in a grip that hurt.

"What I see is the tail end of a hurricane," he said between clenched teeth. "And in about ten minutes, all hell is going to break loose. I don't have time to play games with you. You'll go to the cabin, and by God, you'll stay there, or I'll tie you to the bunk until we've ridden the storm out!"

"A hurricane?" Cathy breathed, appalled. The very name conjured up images that were terrifying. It would be bad enough to face such a tremendous storm on land, but in the middle of the ocean, with only a small, not particularly seaworthy ship between the souls on the *Cristobel* and a watery grave, the prospect brought goose bumps to Cathy's flesh.

"Yes, a hurricane," Jon growled, his fingers digging into her arm with so much force that the limb was actually going to sleep.

"I didn't realize—I'll stay in the cabin," Cathy said, but Jon was no longer prepared to take a chance on her word.

"O'Reilly!" he bellowed, and when the other man appeared beside him, directed: "Escort Lady Stanhope here to my cabin. And damn it, see that she gets there! No little excursions on the side, understand?"

"Right." O'Reilly nodded curtly in response to Jon's command. In an aside to Cathy, Jon added fiercely: "And if I see you out on deck again, I'll take my belt to you! And that's a promise!"

Cathy was too shaken by the prospect of an imminent hurricane to take umbrage at this threat. Obediently she allowed O'Reilly to take her arm. They had moved only a few paces when Jon called to O'Reilly again.

"Send the other women to my cabin, too," he ordered. "They'll be safer, and I think it's better that we know where they all are. I wouldn't put it past one of the feather-brained creatures to decide to go for a stroll in the middle of the bloody storm!"

"Aye, sir," O'Reilly said, grinning at this furiously uttered last. Cathy bristled, but O'Reilly was already hustling her off, and she was too aware of the steadily rising wind to want to linger. He saw her safely inside and then left; Cathy lit a candle and waited for the other women to appear.

"Cap'n says no candles—too much danger of fire," O'Reilly told her tersely when he returned with Angie, Sarita, and the others. They filed silently past him to huddle in a tight little group inside the room.

"You ladies stay put!" he added forcefully, singling out Sarita in particular with his eyes. Then he blew out the candle, and as the cabin plunged into darkness, left them.

If Cathy had thought that she and Sarita couldn't stay in the same room for five minutes without coming to blows, she was soon proved wrong. Penned together in pitch darkness while the ship was tossed crazily hither and yon by the wind, the muffled but still terrifying sound of the wind howling and wood snapping in their ears, they became allies in fear. The ten of them clung together, sometimes sitting on the bunk, sometimes pitched onto the floor if the ship bucked unexpectedly. All thoughts of class or rivalry were forgotten: each of them merely wanted to survive.

The storm raged for forty-eight hours, and many times during those two days Cathy thought a specific hour might be her last. Once the *Cristobel* seemed to stand on her head, caught in the deep trough of a huge wave. Cathy saw the black ocean race to cover the portholes, and said a fervent prayer. From the hastily moving lips around her, she realized that the other women were doing the same. Another time a wave broke over the deck, sending floods of water washing beneath the cabin door. Several of the women screamed; the only reason Cathy didn't join them was because terror had strangled all utterance.

Jon didn't return to the cabin at all. Cathy worried about him even more than she did herself. There was only jerky to sustain him, and out on deck he was exposed to the full fury of the hurricane. He must be chilled to the bone, wet and hungry and exhausted, and still working to bring them safely through the storm. Cathy said a prayer for his safety. For love or for hatred, she wanted him alive.

With the storm's blackness raging all around them, it was impossible to distinguish night from day. Cathy had no idea whether it was noon or midnight when the wind began to drop at last, but she welcomed its surcease with profound thankfulness. It seemed that their combined prayers had been heeded, and the *Cristobel* would be spared.

When Jon appeared at last in the door, he was drenched to the skin, and swaying on his feet from exhaustion. Forgetting their differences, and their audience, Cathy ran to his side. Beyond him she could see that the rain had lightened to a drizzle, and that the sky, while still gray, was bright compared to the blackness that had gone before.

"Are you all right?" she asked him, her hands coming

out quite unconsciously to rest against his soaked chest. He looked down at her for a moment, his eyes unreadable, while he supported himself with both hands braced against the doorjamb.

"I'm fine," he answered, then spoke over her head to the others: "You can all return to your quarters now. The danger's past."

"Thank God! And thank you, Captain!" Angie breathed, her eyes closing in relief.

"Yes, Jonny, it is thanks to you! You were wonderful, I know it!" Sarita exclaimed dramatically, and would have thrown herself at her savior if Cathy hadn't turned on her with a glare so fierce it would have stopped an army dead in its tracks.

Sarita returned her glare, but, when Jon moved out of the doorway, she walked by without attempting to touch him. Cathy thought fiercely that she was wise: it wouldn't have taken much provocation to send Cathy clawing at the other woman's eyes!

When they were alone, and the cabin door closed behind them, Jon made his way over to the bunk, shrugging Cathy away when she would have offered him her support. She followed anxiously behind him.

"God, I'm tired," he sighed, sinking heavily into a sitting position on the bunk. Cathy eyed him worriedly. He was very pale, his skin gray from water and fatigue.

"When did you last eat?" she asked quietly, brushing his hands aside when he started to unbutton his shirt and doing the job herself. He leaned his head back against the paneling, submitting with weary docility to her ministrations.

"Yesterday sometime—I think," he said, closing his eyes. "Tinker brought us all some dried beef."

"And you haven't had any sleep for the past two days, either." Cathy made it a statement rather than a question. Jon said nothing. Cathy took his silence for agreement.

"Here, lean up." Cathy pulled the wet shirt off when he did as she asked. He bent to pull off his boots himself, then hoisted himself to his feet, unbuttoning his sopping breeches and stepping out of them. He shivered as he stood there naked, and Cathy saw that his tall body was ridged with goose bumps. Quickly she caught up a rough towel and briskly rubbed him dry. Then she pulled the coverlet from the bunk and wrapped him in it. His hand came out to clutch it to him automatically; Cathy, looking at him as he stood there swathed in the faded plaid cloth, thought that he looked like some enormous Indian.

"Don't fuss. There's nothing wrong with me that a nap and something to eat won't fix," he said irritably as Cathy pushed him back down onto the bunk. "Besides, I'll wager that you haven't had much to eat—or much sleep—yourself."

"No," Cathy agreed. "But at least we were in here out of the storm, and we did manage to eat something regularly and even doze a bit. Now, I'm going to light the stove and get you something to eat, and then you can go to sleep. And not just a nap, either."

"Bossy little thing, aren't you?" he asked with a faint grin, but Cathy noticed that he did not argue. She turned to smile at him, but his eyes were closed again. Quietly she let herself out of the cabin to go in search of coal and food.

As she picked her way across the deck, Cathy was appalled at the destruction which met her eyes. The tip of the foremast had been broken off, and lay leaning drunkenly against the wall of the quarterdeck like a discarded Christmas tree. What was left of the sails hung in tatters from the spars. Ropes dangled everywhere. Bits of wood and cloth and other debris littered the deck, which was still thoroughly awash. Over by the poop deck, an emergency infirmary had been set up: perhaps half-a-dozen men lay beneath the shelter afforded by its wooden overhang. None appeared too badly hurt, although one kept clutching his leg, which was swollen to about thrice its normal size, and moaning. Another of the men, who she vaguely recognized as a quiet, scholarly type known as Dougan, was moving about amongst them, having apparently taken on the role of doctor.

"Do you need help?" she asked him quietly. He looked around, saw who was addressing him, and his rather thin face pinkened.

"Oh, no, ma'am, I mean, my lady," he stammered. "One of the other ladies—uh, females—has offered to help out. Angie, you know. She's a good girl. And none of these chaps are badly hurt. Except Croomer, who has broken his leg. Clumsy idiot tripped over a coil of rope."

Croomer, plainly the man who had been holding his leg and groaning, swore roundly at Dougan for this impudence. Dougan looked scandalized.

"Watch your tongue, you blasted fool, there's a lady present," he snapped, then looked flustered himself as he clearly wondered whether "blasted" was too strong a word with which to sully Cathy's ears. Cathy was barely able to hold back a grin. Did Dougan but know it, she had heard far, far worse, not only from Jon, from whom such a thing would be expected, but from several of the very genteel ladies who graced many a London drawing room.

"You looking after the Cap'n, ma'am?" Dougan asked. When Cathy nodded, he made a gesture of approval. "He's a brave man, my lady. He was everywhere, doing everything. Fighting the wheel, up in the rigging, chopping up the mast when it fell on Grouse. He brought us through almost single-handed, and that's a fact."

"I know," Cathy said quietly, and moved away. But as she searched out the supplies she needed and then retraced her steps to the cabin, she felt a warm glow of pride.

Jon had fallen asleep, she saw as soon as she entered the cabin. He was still in a sitting position, his head and broad shoulders leaning back against the wall, his lips parted as a slight snore rattled through them. Cathy looked at his pale, black-stubbled face, at the wildly mussed hair dulled by rain and sea water, at the long body huddled into the tattered cover and the strong brown feet protruding from its end, and felt a rush of tenderness. He looked so vulnerable, so entirely without defense, that Cathy wanted to care for and protect him as she would Cray. Just at the moment, she was prepared to forget all that had lately passed between them. He was tired, cold, and hungry. He needed her, and she would do her best for him.

She piled the coal in the stove, lit it, and watched until it was burning steadily. Then she closed the small grate and crossed the room to Jon. He would probably feel better for a wash, Cathy thought, seeing the salt bloom that marked his face and hands. But she thought that he needed sleep more. Gently she caught hold of his shoulders and tried to maneuver him so that he was lying prone. It was a harder task than she had anticipated: Jon was heavy, and asleep he was a dead weight. By the time she finally had his head on the hard, flat pillow, she was panting with exertion. Luckily his feet were easier to manage. She merely grasped them about the ankles and swung them up on the bunk. With some amusement she noticed that they protruded several inches over the edge. Jon was well above six feet in height and the bunk had obviously been designed for a much smaller man.

Still cozily swathed in the cover, he slept through the whole operation. As those faint, rasping snores continued to emerge with undisturbed regularity, Cathy had to smile. He had always slept like the dead, and Cray had inherited that tendency from his father. Lord help them all if ever an emergency arose while the Hale men were asleep! Unless she beat them over the head with a broom handle, Cathy thought, she would be left to face whatever it was alone! And suddenly she wondered if the new baby, the one sleeping even now in her womb, would be the same. It made the child seem more real, a person instead of a thing, and she suddenly felt a rush of love for it. No matter the problems it might create, it was hers, and she wanted it even if no one else did! Another little boy like Cray, or maybe a daughter. . . .

Cathy made herself a cup of tea and sat down in one of the hard chairs, absently contemplating Jon's sleeping form. She was tired herself, but she didn't want to climb into the bunk and risk disturbing him. He needed his sleep far more than she did, because she could sleep any time, and he was forced to snatch what rest he could between the various tasks involved in sailing the ship. He looked supremely peaceful despite his dishevelment. Cathy smiled faintly as she watched him.

She would have to tell him about the baby very soon, Cathy thought suddenly. Although he had been absent during most of her pregnancy with Cray, he was no stranger to the way a woman's body works. Sooner or later he was bound to notice the conspicuous absence of her monthly flow, or the slight but unmistakable roundness of her belly. He was even more intimately familiar with her shape than she was; Cathy was surprised that the increased fullness of her breasts and belly had not attracted his attention before this. Likely he had been too busy slaking his anger to pay his usual close attention to the contours of her body.

For the sake of the coming child, and for Cray, Cathy realized with a sense of inevitability that she and Jon would have to patch up their differences and try again. Their child—children, Cathy corrected with a tiny thrill—deserved a real, loving family, as she and Jon and Cray had been before Harold and his machinations had entered their lives. Her marriage to Harold was a problem, but she fully believed that it was not irresolvable. After all, the union had never been consummated. An annulment, while difficult to obtain, should not be impossible. She was not exactly a nobody, and her father, if he were still alive and somewhat recovered by the time she was once again in touch with him, should be able to use his considerable influence on her behalf. It was possible that Harold might object, or even lie about the consummation of their marriage, Cathy knew. But somehow Cathy didn't think that even the desire to be revenged on herself would outweigh in Harold's mind the idea of a bastard child of a convicted pirate inheriting his title. He was too full of pride.

The cabin had grown damp and chilly during the storm. Even now, with the little stove's round mid-section glowing warmly, Cathy could feel the pervading cold. She shivered, drawing her knees up under her chin and wrapping her arms around them for warmth. Except for the pool of light around the stove, the cabin was shrouded in deep gray shadow.

A sudden yawn caught Cathy by surprise. She was getting so sleepy! For some time she sat there, battling the effects of fatigue, and then finally she surrendered. Getting to her feet, she padded across the room to the bunk, and quickly shed her clothes. She still did not feel entirely comfortable about sleeping naked, but when one had only one set of garments, there wasn't much choice.

She stood for a moment staring down at Jon. He was sprawled on his stomach now, his face buried in the pillow and his arms and legs spread-eagled. The cover was wrapped around and caught under his big body. He looked bronzed and very strong lying there against the white sheet. He also looked immovable. Cathy sighed and began to push him over so that she could get into bed. Like a statue he lay unmoving until Cathy had the happy idea of blowing in his ear. At first he ignored it, then he frowned and brushed at the annoyance with his hand, and finally, with a grunt, turned on his side facing the wall to hide the maltreated ear from its tormentor. Quickly Cathy slid into the bunk beside him, drawing the freed coverlet up over both of them and snuggling up against his broad back for warmth. Her arm slipped cozily around his muscular waist, and with a little sigh she fell asleep.

The feel of a warm hand gently fondling her breast awoke her. Cathy lay quiescent for a moment, still groggy with sleep. The hand continued with its erotic movements, cupping and stroking and caressing the hardening nipple. Then, as if satisfied that one breast was fully aroused, the hand moved on to its twin, and repeated the motions until that breast was quivering like its fellow. Cathy gasped, opening her eyes to find Jon lying on his side beside her, one arm pillowing his head while his other hand toyed with her yielding body. His gray eyes were somnolent as she met them, and in something of a daze Cathy noticed that the shadows hemming them in were now almost pitch black. It must be the middle of the night.

"Go back to sleep," Jon whispered, his voice drugging her senses. That caressing hand slid down to gently stroke her belly, and Cathy obediently closed her eyes. It would be easier to pretend that this was all part of her dreams. . . .

His fingers traced a tingling path from her belly to her silken white thighs and back again, drawing teasing little circles, their texture coarse against the smoothness of her skin. Deliberately he avoided the one place, the secret place, that was aching for his touch. Cathy began to moan, a low sound deep in her throat, and her head moved from side to side on the pillow. Silently, with her movements, she implored him. . . .

Her eyes still closed, she refused to let herself think that, not so very long ago, he had been touching Sarita in just this same way. A demon of jealousy struggled to rise inside her, but she resolutely closed her mind to its influence. It was so pleasant just to lie here, to accept the rousing touch of his hands without protest, to know that soon he would cover her body with his own and make her his. . . . His mouth began to nibble seductively along the silken cord of her neck, and then his tongue came out and tested its way across her collarbone to the softness of her breast. Cathy moaned as it brushed wetly across the sensitive peak. Her breast swelled under the rousing contact. Gently, tantalizingly, his tongue made tiny circles around her eagerly awaiting nipple, until Cathy could stand it no longer. With a little cry she reached up and caught his black head, drawing it to the throbbing pebble that seemed the very center of her desire.

"God, you drive me crazy," he whispered in her ear, his mouth moving up from its titillation of her breast to lovingly explore the inner recesses of the shell-like structure. Cathy could only moan her reply, because his hand had at long last moved to the place where she wanted it most: the warm golden nest between her thighs. For an instant her thighs clamped together, wanting to deny her the enchantment that only Jon knew how to give her, but as his finger unerringly found all the right places her legs slowly spread wide for him. Still he didn't take her, although the feverish thrashing of her body begged him.

Jon pressed butterfly kisses to her closed eyelids, her temples, her cheekbones, and even her soft mouth, but he refused to linger. Cathy's hands curled restlessly against his broad shoulders, then moved down to run mindlessly through the thick black hair that covered his chest. Its roughness rasped at her soft palm. Cathy loved the sensation. Unthinkingly her fingers followed the dark trail over the taut muscles of his belly to the thick bush that surrounded his fiery hardness. Cathy, gasping and writhing under the tormenting caress of his hands, determined to practice some torture of her own. Her fingers closed gently around the throbbing member, then tightened.

"Oh, God. Oh, Cathy!" he groaned, as her hand began to move up and down. His breathing deepened and thickened until he was panting. Still Cathy showed him no mercy. She toyed with him as he had with her, until he lay flat on his back, groaning, with her leaning over him.

"Am I better than Sarita?" she demanded fiercely, the little demon breaking through the guard she had set around him.

Jon's eyes blinked open, and his lips parted for a reply. Cathy gave him no chance to speak. Instead, driven by a smoldering rage that was not red in color but a bright, bilious green, she bent swiftly until her mouth took over where her hand had been; she was determined to make him totally, completely hers, to leave her mark on him for all time.

"God, don't stop," he groaned when she lifted her head at last. Cathy remained poised over him, her blue eyes glittering cat-like at him through the gloom.

"Am I better than Sarita?" she demanded again. Jon sucked in his breath with a rattling shudder.

"God, yes," he muttered thickly. Triumphant, Cathy lowered her head once more.

When his seed spewed hotly forth, she felt as if she had won a prize. Gloating, she released him, to sink back against the pillows. Beside her, she could feel his sides heaving as his breath slowly fought to regain its normal rhythm. A small smile curved her lips, and she closed her eyes for sleep.

"Not so fast," said his voice softly in her ear, and Cathy was jolted awake by the feel of his hands parting her thighs.

"What . . . ?" she stuttered. She could feel her face turn fiery red as he moved so that he was kneeling between her spread legs, his hands drawing them with steely strength over his shoulders. God, he couldn't mean to . . . ! She had never permitted him to do such a thing before, and he, intent on pleasing her, had not forced the issue. It was indecent, it was obscene. . . .

It was also heaven. Cathy gasped and quaked under the hot tutelage of his mouth. Writhing, crying out her pleasure, she was soon lost to all shame. When he would have lifted his head, her hands came up to clutch his rough black hair, holding him to her.

"Am I better than Harold? "he demanded throatily in his turn. Cathy, half out of her mind with longing, sobbed out her answer.

"Yes, oh, yes. Oh, God, yes!"

His mouth returned to its work with a vengeance, and he took her almost savagely. Cathy went over the brink again and again and again. If he would only stop, she thought once, exhausted by the violence of her body's response; then, as the tremors began to build once more, she changed that to, If he would only never stop: if this ecstasy could just go on and on forever. . . .

Finally he lay for a moment between her legs, not moving. Cathy, eyes closed, skin still quivering, felt as if she had died. When he heaved himself up and over onto his side of the bunk, she seemed to sense the movement from a great distance. She felt as if she was floating, floating. . . . She scarcely noticed that he didn't even bother to say good-night.

The next thing Cathy knew, she seemed to be swimming through dark, tropical waters. She was far beneath the surface, and she knew she had to get to the top or drown. With all her strength she tried, and just as she thought her lungs would burst from lack of air, she made it: gulping, she sucked in great breaths of air, and opened her eyes.

For just a moment Cathy didn't know where she was. Instead of lapping waves, she was surrounded by soft beams of sunlight filtering in through smeared glass portholes. Beside her a warm body breathed rhythmically, plainly deeply asleep. Cathy moved her head until she could see that body, and immediately she recognized Jon. And hard on the heels of that recognition came mortifying memories. The whole appalling night replayed in her mind. She thought of what she had done, and turned bright fiery crimson from the tips of her toes to the top of her head. Then she remembered what he had done, and she wanted to curl up and die.

After a few moments of trying, she realized that it was impossible to die on command. She was going to live, and to live with that night as an inerasable part of her past. She thought of facing Jon, and felt butterflies flutter wildly in her stomach. Never before in her life could she remember feeling so embarrassed.

And sticky. Cathy felt sticky all over. Her skin seemed to adhere to the sheet, to Jon's bronzed flesh beside her, to itself. She felt positively unclean. She had to have a bath, now. Quietly she rolled out of bed, wanting to delay waking Jon for as long as possible. Until she actually saw his knowledge of the night they had just passed in his eyes, she could refuse to think about it. She could just push it out of her mind.

The water in the pitcher was cold, but Cathy didn't mind. Standing in the center of the tin tub, she slowly poured it over herself. Then, taking the cake of soap from its place on the washstand, she began to carefully rub it into her skin. She worked with deep concentration, willing herself not to think of anything except the task of getting herself clean.

How long Jon had been watching her when she became aware of it, Cathy didn't know. Her naked body silhouetted against the light streaming in the portholes, she merely turned her head to find his gray eyes fixed on her. The expression on his face puzzled her, and she frowned inquiringly. His mouth was bracketed in harsh lines, his lips set cruelly straight. And his eyes were hard and filled with a terrible light as they met her innocent gaze.

"How long did you think to keep me in ignorance of the fact that you're pregnant, Lady Stanhope?" he gritted. Cathy realized with a sinking sensation that he was blazing with uncontrolled rage.

ten

~~~
❧❧❧
~~~

J—I. . . ." Cathy stuttered, caught completely un-
prepared.

"Pray continue, *Lady Stanhope*," Jon sneered
softly, drawing out the title until it seemed to flay her.

Cathy swallowed, knowing that she had left her explanation too late. She should have broken the news to him, not left
him to find out for himself. Quickly she poured the remaining
water over her body to rid her skin of the soap, caught up the
towel, and wrapped it around herself as she stepped from the
tub. The cloth barely covered her most intimate places, leaving her long slender legs and creamy shoulders bare. Cathy
didn't even consider the brevity of her attire as she combed her
fingers abstractedly through her long hair, letting it tumble in
a thick golden mass down her back. All her thoughts were
concentrated on how best to propitiate Jon's clearly sizzling
anger. Surely he would see, once she had pointed it out to
him, that for the sake of their children it was time to bury the
animosities of the past, and get on with the future together.

"I'm waiting," Jon growled ominously. Cathy bit her lip,

brought abruptly out of the reverie she had inadvertently fallen into.

"And don't try to deny it," he added, his voice harsh. "It's as plain as the nose on your face."

"I wouldn't dream of denying it," Cathy said quietly, her blue eyes meeting his stormy gray ones with apparent serenity. "I'm proud of it. I want this child."

"You—bitch!" Jon grated, the lines around his mouth whitening angrily as he heaved himself into a sitting position. He sat there, on the edge of the bunk, naked, his black hair wildly mussed and his lean face dark with several days' worth of unshaven beard. "You stupid whoring bitch!"

Cathy's eyes widened angrily at this uncalled-for abuse. She glared at him, her soft mouth set in a straight line, her little chin tilted defiantly. As he stared furiously back, he almost audibly ground his teeth.

"I won't be spoken to in that way!" Cathy informed him haughtily, growing angry in her turn. "I'm sick of your filthy mouth! Why shouldn't I be glad to have this child? It's mine!"

"That's the one thing that's not in doubt," Jon muttered angrily. Then, louder, his eyes boring into hers, he added: "Did Harold know of your interesting condition before you— uh, took leave of him so abruptly?"

"No, of course not," Cathy answered impatiently, her temper subsiding a little. After all, it was only natural that he be shocked, and first reactions are apt to be unreliable. Why, she herself had been appalled when she had first realized that she was with child. When he had had time to consider, he would undoubtedly view the prospect of fatherhood with more equanimity. Look how he doted on Cray. . . .

"I didn't know myself, then," she added.

"Poor Harold," Jon remarked unpleasantly, his gray eyes glittering like twin knives. "You'll have to write and let him know. He'll be delighted."

Cathy felt her jaw drop. She stared at Jon for a moment, speechless as his implication sank home.

"You're not suggesting," she squeaked when she could once again form words, "that this child is—is *Harold's*?" Her voice rose incredulously on the name.

"You're right—I'm not suggesting it. I'm stating it."

"You swine!" Cathy breathed, blue fire seeming to shoot from her eyes as they fixed him. "Harold never touched me! The child is yours, damn you!"

Jon rose to his feet in a sudden lithe movement. He stood glowering at her, his hands clenched into fists at his sides.

"You don't expect me to believe that, surely?" he asked with a bite. "I think you must be forgetting that I saw with my own eyes Harold—uh, not touching you."

"He was trying to consummate our marriage," Cathy hissed. "Which I never let him do. I pretended to be seasick—*seasick*, do you hear?—from the first night of our marriage until you came and dragged me away like the brute you are! Only the night when you came, he had found out that I was not really sick at all. He was trying to force me, but you got there before he succeeded. Believe me, there is no possible way this child is Harold's!" She underlined the last sentence. Jon's lip curled.

"I wouldn't believe you if you swore it on a stack of Bibles!" he snarled. "If—and you notice I say *if*—what you say is true, why the hell didn't you tell me before? Why wait until I find out that you're with child? Mighty convenient, that."

"You made me angry," Cathy told him, striving to hold onto her temper. In her wildest imaginings, she had never dreamt that Jon would refuse to acknowledge paternity of her coming child. If it weren't for that child, and Cray, she would tell him to take a long walk off a short pier, and take a great deal of pleasure in doing it! How dare he continually think such dreadful things of her?

"You were so ready to assume that I had betrayed you,"

she continued bitterly. "Why should I set your mind at ease? If you didn't know me well enough and trust me enough to know that I wouldn't do a thing like that, then there wasn't any point in trying to convince you otherwise. You said you loved me: what a joke! When you love someone, you trust them, you don't immediately believe the worst of them, like you did with me! Ever since you first took me—I was a virgin, I might remind you, and you did it very much against my will—you've suspected me of infidelity if I so much as smiled at another man! I'm sick of reasoning with you! Believe what the hell you like!"

"Oh, I will," he said nastily. "I've listened to your lies for long enough to know that you spew them as naturally as breathing! You'll never convince me that Harold didn't bed you. God, I doubt that you even put up a token protest! You forget, I know just how much you enjoy being ridden by a man: you're hotter than any whore I've ever had! You can't go for two days together without spreading your legs. I'm surprised Harold even bothered to marry you: I'll wager anything you like that he didn't have to wait until the ring was on your finger before sampling your charms. I know I didn't!"

"You low-down dirty bastard!" Cathy cried, incensed. "The only reason you didn't have to wait is because you raped me, you cad, and you know it! Otherwise I would never have come within arm's length of you—a pirate, and a criminal! You weren't—*aren't*—fit to hold the door to my carriage. You're nothing but scum!" She was so angry she was visibly shaking.

"And you're nothing but a high-born whore who gives herself the airs of a lady!" he yelled back, dark red spots of color staining his cheekbones. He reached for his breeches as he spoke, stepping into them and jerking them up. Cathy's hair practically stood on end with rage.

"If you feel that way, why don't you let me go?" she spat, barely able to keep herself from flying at him and raking her claws down that sneering dark face.

"And return you to Harold?" he jibed, his eyes belying his mocking tone as they seared her. "Now, I might just do that. You're certainly of no more use to me. That's the problem with whores, you know: a man soon grows tired of them!"

"You bastard!" Cathy breathed, and throwing caution to the winds launched herself at him. He saw her coming and caught her by her soft upper arms, his long fingers biting deeply into her white flesh. He smiled savagely as he held her, seeming to take pleasure from the pain he was inflicting. Cathy threw her head back, glaring up at him with impotent fury. God, how she hated him! What she wouldn't give to be a big, strong man for just five minutes, so that she could wipe that smirk from his face!

"I wouldn't try it," he advised softly, reading blood-lust in her eyes. "Because nothing would give me more enjoyment than to beat you until you begged for mercy. It's what I should have done years ago: maybe then you wouldn't have the morals of an alley cat!"

Lightning flashed from Cathy's eyes. Her face contorted with rage.

"You make me sick!" she hissed, and without considering the consequences she spat full in his face.

Black anger leapt from Jon's eyes, scorching her. Cathy knew she should be afraid, should cower before the awful menace she read in his face, but she was too damned mad. She wanted to kill, and if he felt the same, then well and good! She would die before she would cower before him! She could give as good as she got!

"Now, that wasn't very smart," he drawled after a long moment, his hands tightening on her arms until she wanted to cry out with pain. "I should slap you silly—and if you ever dare to do anything like it again, I will. And that's a promise. Just because I've never laid a hand on you before, doesn't mean I won't!"

His eyes gleamed ferally as he lifted Cathy from the floor

by her arms, turning her around so that her back was to the bunk and he stood between her and the door. Temper emanated from him in perceptible waves. Cathy could not prevent a little frisson of fear from shivering down her spine. He was so very big, easily twice her size, and he could break her in two with his bare hands if he wanted. And in the mood he was in, it might not take much to make him want to do just that.

Almost gently he pushed her down until she sat on the bunk.

"Sit!" he said, his fingers digging warningly into her arms before slowly releasing her. Cathy, refusing to admit it, was cowed. She sat, seething.

He impaled her with those burning eyes while he fastened his breeches and shrugged into his shirt. Cathy, still clad only in the small towel, read a savage challenge in his eyes: move, they seemed to say, and I'll make you sorry. She had just enough judgement left not to put that silent threat to the test.

"Smart girl, aren't you?" he taunted after a moment. Cathy, still not quite daring to get up, felt hatred tear at her innards. She wanted desperately to make him suffer.

"Oh, yes, but not half so smart as you," she purred through gritted teeth, summoning up a false smile. "How very clever of you to guess that the child I'm carrying is Harold's! I should have known that it was quite, quite useless to lie. . . ."

For a moment Cathy thought she might have pushed him just that fraction too far: his eyes came alive with bitter violence, and he visibly had to restrain himself from hitting her. She faced him proudly, refusing to back down. After a sizzling instant, he seemed to get his fury under control.

"Yes, you should have, shouldn't you?" he grated, and, pivoting, stalked from the cabin. As the door slammed shut behind him, Cathy leapt to her feet. Her hands found the china pitcher and hurled it at the still vibrating portal. With savage satisfaction she heard the crash as it hit, then shattered into hundreds of tiny shards at her feet.

Jon didn't return to the cabin that night, or on any of the succeeding nights. Instead he sent Perkins to retrieve his few belongings. Upon hearing Perkins' halting explanation of his errand, Cathy, tight-lipped, packed up Jon's razor and shaving mug and brush, his one spare shirt, and what was left of the bottle of whiskey, and thrust them into the boy's apologetic arms. Perkins was still stammering excuses when Cathy slammed the door in his face.

Left to enjoy the captain's cabin in solitary splendor, Cathy's rage grew every day. She refused to speak to Jon when she saw him on deck, and he seemed to go out of his way to avoid her. Where he was sleeping she couldn't be sure, but if she were placing a bet, Cathy thought savagely, she would bet that he didn't lack for female company. Sarita's gloating self-satisfaction was so evident as to be sickening!

The crew viewed this unmistakable falling out between their captain and his mistress with a combination of amusement, curiosity, and speculation. The cause was unknown, but whatever the fight had been about, it must have been a dilly! And what was even more curious was that the captain was allowing the lady to remain in his cabin, while he himself bunked elsewhere. In the ordinary way of things, they would have expected the lady to have been thrown out on her ear if the captain felt inclined to switch partners. Something was up, they decided amongst themselves, but they could reach no consensus on what. One afternoon Cathy overheard them making wagers on the cause of the rift, and practically ground her teeth with rage. Two-to-one odds were being given on the supposition that she was cold in bed!

While all this was going on, the *Cristobel* was limping toward the nearest port. The storm had blown her way off course. According to Jon's calculations, they were now far to the east of Tenerife, and considering the shape that the vessel was in, it would be insane to head anywhere except toward the nearest shore. With the sails in tatters and the hull battered, it was a miracle that they were still afloat. If they ran into another storm, or even one oversized wave, they would likely sink to the bottom like a stone, never to be heard from again.

The weather continued very hot and sultry. The sun beat down relentlessly, and even if there had been any canvas left, there wasn't enough breeze to propel a child's toy windmill. The *Cristobel* seemed to mark her journey by inches instead of knots, and Jon, eking out the few feet of canvas remaining with what cloth was going spare amongst the crew, could only mutter a prayer that they would reach land before their provisions ran out.

As days passed, tempers shortened. Jon had ordered that the food be carefully rationed, and had put O'Reilly in charge of this task. Empty bellies and incessant heat led to outbreaks of fighting amongst the men and even sometimes the women. The principals in these disputes were impartially locked in a makeshift brig deep in the hold, and after a few hours in that stifling place could usually be trusted to behave. If not, Jon took positive joy in cracking heads together. His temper was so erratic that even O'Reilly began to stay out of his way.

If Jon was surly, Cathy was cross. More than once her sharp tongue reduced the faithful Angie to tears. Cathy always apologized afterward, but the memory of her remorse was never enough to stop her snappishness before it escaped. Between the heat, the increasing discomfort of her pregnancy, and her fury with Jon, she was as grouchy as a bear with a cub. And when Angie practically seemed to tiptoe around her, it only made things worse. Cathy knew it was unreasonable and unfair, but the girl's very faithfulness was enough to set her teeth on edge!

At least she had enough to eat. Jon had quietly given orders that her plate was to be filled, as Cathy had found out when she had questioned Clara about the amount of food the woman was ladling out for her consumption. Cathy, knowing that she had her pregnancy to thank for this special treatment, supposed that Jon expected her to be grateful. Well, she wasn't! She had neither asked for nor expected any favors from him, and if it wasn't for the well-being of her unborn child, she would take a great deal of satisfaction in hurling her plate in his teeth!

Water was being hoarded even more carefully than food. Certainly there was none to spare for bathing. Cathy was reduced, like the other women, to washing in sea water, and as a result she never felt entirely clean. The salt in the water stiffened her clothes until they chafed unbearably at her tender skin. Cathy scratched, sweated, and smoldered, and prayed that the dreadful voyage would come to a speedy end.

One consequence of Jon's vacating his cabin was that some of the men began to eye Cathy in a way she couldn't like. "Is she available?" they were clearly asking themselves, and without Jon to protect her, Cathy foresaw trouble. Sooner or later one of them was bound to put his luck to the test. Of course, she could always scream for Jon, and she didn't doubt that he would take sardonic delight in defending her, thus proving to her how very dependent on him she was. Cathy supposed if it really came down to it, she might have to do just that, as much as she hated the thought. But she hoped it wouldn't come to that. . . .

Her hope was in vain. Late one afternoon, when the sun still hung over the horizon like a fiery red ornament, Cathy was seated on the poop deck, where she had taken to spending most of her time. She had chosen the poop deck for two reasons: one, it provided a modicum of shade, and, two, it was at the opposite end of the ship from the quarterdeck, where Jon spent most of his days. Seated on an overturned barrel pushed up close to the taffrail, Cathy stared out over the flat, glittering blue of the sea and wished fervently for rain. Not a storm, of course, just a gentle, cooling rain of the sort she had so despised in London. What she wouldn't give to be standing in the midst of that once-scorned drizzle! Cathy closed her eyes, picturing it. She could almost feel the blessed moisture on her skin. . . .

"Lonesome, lady?" a gruff voice asked close to her ear. Cathy's eyes opened slowly, reluctant to abandon her daydream. She looked with some annoyance at the man who stood smiling fatuously at her. He was called Grogan, and a more repulsive specimen would have been hard to find. Big and hairy, with long arms like an ape's, he was considered very handsome by Clara and some others among the women. Cathy found his coarse features and the habit he had of bubbling his spit between a gap in his front teeth repugnant in the extreme. Still, he had never been other than polite.

"Not at all," she responded with cool civility, her eyes just brushing his face before returning to their contemplation of the sea. "Enjoying the solitude."

If she had hoped he would consider this a hint, she was wrong. It sailed right over his head. He grinned at her, and came a little closer.

"Me and the boys thought as how you might be wishful of a little company," he persisted. "Seeing as how you're on your own now."

The portent of this speech was not lost on Cathy, but she thought it best to ignore it. Rising with conscious dignity to her feet, she favored Grogan with an unsmiling look.

"You're very kind to be concerned about me, but I prefer to be alone," she said, and without another look at him turned to go to her cabin. She could sense him following her down the stairs and onto the main deck, but she refused to hasten her steps, or in any other way betray her growing concern. Men were like dogs, she thought with disgust and not a little apprehension. Let them once get the idea that you fear them, and they would immediately pounce.

"Wait, lady," Grogan said behind her, and reached out to

grasp her arm. Cathy, deciding that her best course of action would be to go on the offensive, whirled to face him, her eyes bright with indignation.

"Please take your hand from my arm," she demanded icily. Grogan's eyes widened at her vehemence, and then he began to smile.

"Well, now, so you ain't so cold after all," he grinned, making no move to release her. Cathy stiffened, regarding him with cold eyes.

"Please take your hand from my arm," she said again. Grogan winked at her.

"Okay, lady, I will—if you ask me real nice. Like with a kiss." A growing crowd had begun to gather around them, and several snickers greeted this outrageous suggestion.

"I will ask you once more to release me," Cathy gritted, controlling her temper with an effort. Her best bet, she knew, was to remain coldly dignified.

"Uh-uh." Grogan slowly wagged his head from side to side. "Leastways, not 'till I get that kiss."

"When hell freezes over," Cathy hissed fiercely, on the verge of abandoning her icy dignity in favor of all-out rage. "You'd better let me go, if you know what's good for you. Or I'll. . . ."

"You'll what?" he sneered, beginning to show signs of anger in his turn. "Cry 'help' to the captain? Lady, he ain't interested. He's found him a new woman, and I calculate that leaves you for me."

With a quick jerk on her arm, he pulled her forward, enfolding her in a close embrace. Cathy, pressed up against his mountainous form and forced to endure the assault of his lips, had had enough: she was ready to scream for Jon, and to watch him beat the man into a bloody pulp. The approving guffaws she heard on all sides only added fuel to the fire of her anger. She shoved hard at Grogan's shoulders, wanting to get her mouth free so that she could summon help. Her eyes were wide open as she struggled; suddenly, over the man's shoulder, she saw Jon join the crowd of spectators. She practically sagged in relief. Grogan's arms tightened enthusiastically at what he perceived as her submission.

Any second she expected Jon to bellow with rage, to pluck Grogan away from her and knock him sprawling on his back. To her stunned amazement, he did none of these things. Instead, he stood at the very back of the crowd, his arms crossed casually over his chest, a sardonic smile curving his mouth as he observed her predicament. As Cathy's widened eyes met his granite-hard ones, he very slowly lowered one lid in a taunting wink.

"You bastard!" Cathy screamed at him inwardly, knowing that he didn't mean to lift a hand to rescue her until she was reduced to begging for his help. At the realization that he was actually prepared to just stand there while another man mauled her about right under his nose, Cathy's temperature soared. She could feel bright scarlet heat flood her body. He thought to teach her a lesson, did he, to demonstrate that without his strength to guard her she was as helpless as a newborn babe? Hah! She would show him!

Grogan was greedily devouring her mouth, pulling her as close to him as he could with the slight protuberance of her stomach between them. Cathy's hands rose to grasp his shoulders for balance, and then, with a quick, vicious movement, she jerked her knee up so that it came into thudding contact with his soft groin.

"Yeow!" Grogan screamed, releasing her as if she had suddenly turned red-hot. Thus unexpectedly freed, Cathy stumbled backward while Grogan bent double, both meaty red hands clutching the injured spot. She caught herself, standing proudly upright as the assembled spectators roared with laughter at Grogan's expense.

"By God, Grogan, ain't you man enough to handle a chit of a girl?" one fellow called between chortles.

"Girl, hell! She's a she-devil!" Grogan moaned in his own defense, still stooped like an arthritic old man as he tried to rub the agony away.

Cathy tossed her head proudly so that her thick golden braid swung like a horse's tail behind her. With her cheeks flushed pink and her eyes a bright cobalt blue from temper, she stared them all down. The loose white peasant blouse and full black skirt she wore concealed her pregnancy, and she looked very beautiful—and also somewhat dangerous—as she glared impartially at every man-jack of them.

"And let that be a lesson to you all," she said clearly, meeting Jon's bemused gray eyes with triumph. "The same will happen to any man who dares to lay a finger on me, I promise you!"

With one final defiant tilt of her chin, she turned on her heel and marched away, leaving the gathered men gaping after her, humor and respect mingled in their faces. Not the least surprised of them was Jon; he had thought to humble her by making her call out for his assistance, but, by God, she had very neatly extricated herself from a situation that would have had most females, let alone ladies of her background, swooning dead away. Admiration rose unbidden in him. Damn, she was a woman in a million! At least, in some respects.

He shouldered his way to the front of the crowd, his jaw tightening as he met Grogan's wounded gaze. His instinct urged him to knock the man flying, but he had left it too late. He should have done it when the man had first laid hands on Cathy; to do so now would be redundant, and, what was worse, would make him look like a jealous fool. Which he probably was, he acknowledged angrily to himself, but he'd be damned if anyone else, most especially Cathy herself, was going to find it out!

"Any man who bothers Lady Stanhope answers to me," he told the still-chuckling men. "And you can pass it on. Now, get back to work, the lot of you."

Jon swung around and stomped back to the quarterdeck. The men exchanged speculative looks, then did as they were told and got back to work.

Over the next few days, Cathy was surprised at the renewed deference with which the crew treated her. They went out of their way to see to her comfort without annoying her at all. Puzzled, she pondered the volte-face: surely her besting of Grogan hadn't had such a wide-reaching effect? Grogan himself eyed her with smoldering resentment, but he made no move to approach her again and Cathy was careful to stay well out of his way. Jon, too, she avoided; she was at pains to show him that she didn't need him one little bit!

Angie found out about her pregnancy not long after this incident, and Cathy was resigned to the fact that the girl, who seemed to be congenitally incapable of keeping a secret, would soon spread the news throughout the ship. The most embarrassing part of this was that Angie automatically assumed that the child was Jon's. Since the girl did not know of their long and convoluted relationship, instead believing, like almost everyone else aboard, that she and Jon had somehow met in La Coruña, she spent most of her time commiserating with what she was sure must be Cathy's sense of shame. Cathy was not in the least ashamed of being pregnant by Jon, despite the fact that she had come to thoroughly despise him, but she did not feel up to explaining this, with its ensuing ramifications, to Angie. Thus she braced herself for knowing looks and snickers from the crew, and she was right: within twenty-four hours of Angie's discovery, every soul on board followed her movements like a cat watching a rat.

It took a little longer for Jon to become aware that the whole ship was privy to Cathy's condition, for the simple reason that no one dared to say anything to him about it. They assumed, correctly if for the wrong reasons, that Cathy's pregnancy was the cause of the ongoing state of armed warfare between her and Jon. To their thinking, of course, the captain was mad because his mistress had gotten "caught," and was thus no longer available for fun and games. Even O'Reilly, who knew much of Jon's history, thought that this must be the case. He even ventured to congratulate Jon on his coming foray into fatherhood. Jon did not disabuse him, but he accepted the other man's jovial comments and back-slapping with a clenched jaw. It would serve no purpose to air what he was convinced was the truth: that Cathy's child had been fathered by Harold, Lord Stanhope, her legal husband.

Since the incident with Grogan, he had hardly seen Cathy. She was clearly deliberately avoiding him, and when they did happen to pass each other on the deck her glance seemed to look right through him. The sight of her, blooming with impending motherhood despite the deprivations of the voyage, stabbed at him like a razor-sharp knife whenever he set eyes on her, so he, too, took care to stay out of her way. The knowledge that she was to bear another man's child tortured him continually, making him more and more morose as the *Cristobel* drew ever closer to land. Try as he would, he could not banish a picture of the child's conception from his mind.

The *Cristobel* was down to a half barrel of water and her last, stale rations of food when the crew finally sighted land. The joyous cry of "Land, ho!" brought everyone on board running to the rail. At first it was no more than a darker shape against the clear blue of the horizon, but as hours passed it gradually resolved itself into a dazzling white beach reaching out into the sparkling bay with the outline of a town the only thing marring a seemingly endless vista of sand.

"Where are we?" Cathy questioned eagerly, turning to find O'Reilly standing beside her at the rail. It was so wonderful to see land again, to know that soon she could have fresh food and water and, miracle of miracles, a bath, that she could have embraced the world.

"Cap'n says it's most likely Rabat, in Morocco," O'Reilly answered, looking down at the small, golden-haired girl beside him and feeling himself almost bowled over by the brilliance of her smile. Despite his friendship with Jon, he could not help but admire her. She was a beauty, and no mistake!

"Rabat," Cathy repeated wonderingly, never having heard of the place before. Then she turned her eyes back to the scene before her. The closer they came to it, the more truly unbelievable it appeared.

The harbor was filled with boats, just as it would have been in Charleston or London. But what boats! They were like nothing she had ever seen before: brilliantly painted, almost flat vessels with intricately carved prows and sterns rising proudly to face the brilliant sun. The masts were short and stubby, the sails themselves almost square. Perhaps half-a-dozen long oars extended from either side of the hulls. Dark-skinned men in baggy white trousers and tall white turbans swarmed over the decks to the rails to gape at them as the *Cristobel* glided past. Clearly the English ship was an oddity. Suddenly it occurred to Cathy to wonder if, perhaps, the natives might be somewhat less than friendly.

"They don't look very pleased to see us," she remarked doubtfully to O'Reilly.

"They're not. Sheikh Ali Ben-Kazar, who rules here, is not over-fond of visitors. Luckily, he and I have met," Jon's voice remarked from just behind Cathy's shoulder.

She turned to look up at him. It was the first time she had looked at him, really looked at him, for weeks. His skin had darkened until he was almost the color of the natives watching them. His black hair, gleaming with blue lights under the relentless sun and blowing gently on the breeze, added to his likeness to an Arab. Only the gray eyes, cold and clear, and his towering size told the truth of his ancestry.

"You've been here before?" His revelation that he had met the ruler of this exotic locale intrigued her sufficiently so that she was prepared to declare a temporary cease-fire in their private war.

"Yes." His answer was short, but it was an answer. Apparently he, too, was willing to call a halt to hostilities for a little while.

"When?" Cathy asked.

"Long before I met you," was all he said, but from that Cathy gathered that his previous call in this port had been under a pirate flag. She swallowed a trifle nervously. She didn't know if that was a good thing, or not. Perhaps this Sheikh Ali whoever was not partial to pirates.

"Ali is a friend of mine," Jon told her, correctly interpreting her doubtful expression. "At least, to a point. So long as we don't cause any trouble, he'll be glad enough to welcome us. Which is what I wanted to see you about: as long as we're here in Rabat you're to stay out of sight. All the other women will be confined to the ship as well, but you in particular, with your blonde hair, will attract attention of the sort we don't need. Do you understand me?"

"I can't go ashore?" Cathy cried, more aghast than angry. She had so looked forward to standing once again on dry, firm land.

"No." Jon must have read her disappointment in her eyes, because he softened the harsh monosyllable slightly. "At least not at first. Later, when I'm sure of the lay of the land, I might take you. But under no circumstances are you to go without me!"

He punctuated this last with a fearsome glare. Cathy returned his look sulkily.

"You enjoy cracking the whip, don't you?" she asked bitterly. His mouth tightened.

"You enjoy baiting me," he retorted grimly. "And one of these days you'll do it once too often. Now, get back to the cabin. As of this minute, you're confined to quarters."

Cathy glared at him mutinously. He was just doing this to punish her!

"Don't make me lock you in," Jon warned softly, for her

ears alone. Cathy cast a quick glance at O'Reilly, who had tactfully turned aside during this exchange. For her own pride's sake, she knew that now was not the time to challenge Jon's order. But later. . . .

With her little nose lifted high in the air, Cathy favored Jon with one long, contemptuous look. Then, her body held proudly erect, she swept away.

It was hot in the cabin. Cathy alternately raged and pouted, and finally smashed a dish as a means of venting her temper. After that, she felt slightly better—until she had to start picking up the shattered pieces. A long shard stabbed her finger; as she sat, sucking resentfully at the drop of bright red blood that oozed from the puncture, she got mad all over again.

It was late afternoon by the time the *Cristobel* finally dropped anchor. Cathy, watching the activity on the dock from a porthole, thought that one certainly couldn't tell it: the sun still beat down as hotly as ever, and shimmering waves of heat rose visibly from the gleaming white sand. The town itself, seemingly composed entirely of long, low, white buildings, appeared as insubstantial as a mirage through the haze of heat. Along the shore, people—she couldn't tell if they were male or female—idled, clad in long, loose white robes like shrouds. Even their heads were covered! From time to time a camel would amble past, its rider seated upon the odd-looking beast as securely as if he were riding the finest of saddle-bred mares in Rotten Row. Then, from her vantage point, Cathy saw one of the *Cristobel*'s gigs head for shore with Jon in its prow and perhaps six men manning the oars. As she watched the little boat disappear from sight, she felt aggrieved. Jon certainly wasn't planning to deny himself the pleasures to be found on dry land!

"When the cat's away, the mice will play." Cathy had heard Martha say that time out of mind. Now, for the first time, she truly considered what it meant: she certainly felt very much like a plump gray mouse as she crept out of the cabin. And she didn't feel guilty in the least, she told herself with a toss of her head. After all, why should she? Jon was merely being despotic as usual when he had ordered her to stay in the cabin. Certainly she need not regard his words.

The men were clearly excited at being in such close proximity to the first land they had seen in weeks, and they paid no attention to Cathy as she strolled along the rail. From their conversation she gathered that they were to be permitted to go ashore in small groups, with the understanding that they were to keep to themselves and not cause trouble. According to the captain, as Cathy overheard one grizzled old man say, the Berbers, as these folks were, and not to be confused with Arabs, which were something entirely different, had very strict laws on drinking and women and such: the consumption of even one drop of alcohol was punishable by a public flogging, while if a man dared to touch a woman not his own he could expect to be summarily put to death. Cathy, listening to this, wondered that the men wanted to go ashore at all under such conditions. Usually, in her experience anyway, women and liquor were, in that order, the two things disembarking sailors craved. For herself, she would love to go ashore just to put a foot once again on something that didn't rock up and down, but *men*—here her lip curled—men were like animals: their wants overrode all else, including caution. She wagered that the *Cristobel*'s crew wouldn't be able to resist temptation, and then there would be the devil (in the person of Jon, if nothing else) to pay.

The sun was beginning to hover over the horizon like a pigeon over its nest. Cathy surmised that it must be early evening. Already the air was growing noticeably cooler. Vaguely she remembered learning that nights in the desert states were often bitterly cold. Still, she felt that a chill would be more than welcome after the stifling temperatures she had lately had to endure aboard the *Cristobel*. Idly she seated herself on the taffrail, breathing deeply of the freshening air.

"Pretty full of yourself, aren't you?" a sneering voice hissed in her ear. Cathy stiffened, recognizing Sarita's far from dulcet tones. She had barely exchanged a word with the woman since they had shared a cabin during the storm, but she had been aware of Sarita casting her venomous glances from time to time. Why, she didn't know. Surely the woman wasn't jealous. After all, possession was nine-tenths of the law, and by that reckoning Jon was surely all Sarita's!

"Thought you were real smart, lettin' him get you with child, didn't you?" Sarita continued, when Cathy refused to respond to her first taunt. "But it backfired on you, didn't it? Now you're fat as a pig, and he wants me! And my fine lady will be left to bear a bastard child with no man to claim it!"

Cathy could feel the hair begin to prickle on the back of her neck. Sarita, whether she knew it or not, was treading on dangerous ground. The bare mention of the word "bastard" in connection with Cray had long been enough to make Cathy see red. She found that she was equally protective of this new child.

"If you don't watch your tongue, I'll pull it out," she said with a saccharine smile, turning to look at the older woman for the first time since the one-sided conversation began. Sarita looked clearly taken aback. Then, as her eyes ran over Cathy's small form, clearly swollen with Jon's child, her expression turned ugly.

"Oh, is that right?" Sarita snarled, and reached out a hand to give Cathy's braid, which hung casually over one shoulder, a hard yank. Cathy, outraged, leapt to her feet, and gave the larger woman a shove which sent her reeling. Then, as Sarita fell heavily onto her amply-padded rear end, Cathy favored her with a long, cold look, and turned away. Head held high, still seething with anger, she marched along the deck toward her cabin.

She was so furious that she failed to note the little group of men standing just to the left of her path until she was almost upon them. Running her fingers through her hair, partially unbound by Sarita's yank, she sought to separate the long strands, all the while muttering angrily under her breath. It was not until she felt the force of several pairs of interested eyes that she happened to glance around.

Three white-robed Berbers were regarding her closely, but Cathy hardly saw them. Her attention was entirely focused on a pair of furious gray eyes. Meeting them, she swallowed convulsively. From the look of him, it was clear that Jon was in a fine rage. And she didn't have to be psychic to guess that its focus was herself!

eleven

❧❧❧

The setting sun, sending out one last vanguard of rays before retiring for the night, caught Cathy in its sights. The orangey brilliance was trapped in her bright hair, making it glitter like living fire. The Berbers, used to only dark-haired, dark-skinned women, visibly gaped. Jon, impaling Cathy with his eyes, was nevertheless aware of his companions' reactions. Silently he ground his teeth.

"Who is this?" breathed the white-robed man at his left. Mustafa Kemal was his name, and he was the Sheikh's trusted servant. Jon glared at Cathy one last time, then turned courteously to the speaker. As desperately as they needed the Sheikh's help, it would never do to offend his man, and through him the Sheikh himself.

"She is my woman," he said, his eyes meeting Cathy's, daring her to deny it. She had halted uncertainly several paces away. Her eyes widened at his words, but for once in her life she was prudently silent.

"Very beautiful," Kemal approved, while the other two Berbers nodded their heads in vigorous agreement, their eyes never leaving Cathy. One of them said something in Arabic to

Kemal, and the other apparently seconded it. Kemal replied in the same tongue, then turned back to Jon.

"It is permitted that we touch?" he asked, his eyes gleaming darkly beneath the corded white headdress. Jon was nonplussed for a moment, then following the direction of their eyes, realized that they were referring to Cathy's hair. He had known that if the Berbers ever got a glimpse of that golden glory they would be entranced, which was why he had ordered her to stay in the cabin. Damn her for a disobedient bitch, and damn himself for a fool! He should have known that she would defy him the minute his back was turned! Next time he would lock her in. But for now the only thing to do was brazen it through.

"Certainly. I will tell her what it is that you desire, so that she will not be frightened." With a polite nod to Kemal, Jon detached himself from the men at the rail and took the few steps needed to bring him directly in front of Cathy. Standing with his back to the Berbers, he completely blocked her from their view. Cathy, looking up at him guiltily, was left in no doubt of his wrath.

"They want to touch your hair," he hissed between tight lips. "And you're going to let them. You're going to cast your eyes modestly to the ground, and not look at them. And you're not to speak. They're used to a very different sort of female than you, and I'll be damned if you're going to offend them. Understand?"

Cathy didn't much like his tone, or the hot anger in his eyes, but she knew that in this instance Jon had to know best. Already she had been disturbed by the intensity with which the strangers were regarding her. Moistening her lips with a quick flick of her tongue, she nodded.

"Good. Stay behind me." With a last warning look at her he turned on his heel and moved back toward the three men. Cathy followed meekly in his wake.

He stopped and stood slightly to one side of the men, his

hand reaching around to draw Cathy forward. She was grateful for the hard reassurance of his touch as one after the other the Berbers began to finger her hair.

As Jon had directed, Cathy kept her eyes cast modestly down and said nothing as she endured this odd inspection. Talking volubly amongst themselves, the men first touched her long tresses reverently, as if afraid they might vanish before their eyes. Then, as nothing happened, they began to run their fingers through the silken strands, pulling painfully at Cathy's scalp. She winced, but conscious of Jon's warning grip on her arm remained quiescent. Finally they touched her smooth white skin with their brown fingers, appearing to find its soft paleness marvelous.

"She is most unusual, most beautiful," Kemal said to Jon at last, signaling the others to call a halt to their exploring fingers. Cathy shivered with relief as they stood a little away from her. For a short while she had been almost frightened, nervous of where all this might lead. Vividly she now understood why Jon had told her to stay in the cabin.

One of the Berbers said something in Arabic to Kemal, who pursed his lips, then slowly nodded. Kemal turned to look at Jon, his white teeth gleaming in his dark face as he smiled.

"The Sheikh would be most pleased with such a woman. We will buy her for him," he stated. Cathy, horrified by this calm pronouncement, looked up. Jon met her appalled gaze with hard purpose for just an instant before smiling urbanely at the man. His hand tightened on Cathy's arm, and he pulled her around so that she stood in front of him. One hard arm slid around her waist, pulling her back against him. His long-fingered hand spread possessively over her rounded stomach.

"I would be most honored to make a gift of her to the Sheikh," Jon told Kemal politely, "were it not for the fact that the woman carries my son. I am sure that you and he will understand if I am reluctant to part with her under the circumstances. Please accept my deepest regrets, and believe that, were it otherwise, she would grace the Sheikh's seraglio this very night."

Kemal, with an inquiring glance at Jon which was answered by a slight nod, reached out a hand to pat Cathy's stomach, as if testing the truth of Jon's claim. What he felt appeared to satisfy him. With a gesture of regret he removed his hand, while Cathy shrank as close against Jon as she could. Being pawed about like a slave on the block was not only humiliating, it was terrifying.

"She is with child, as you say," he sighed, then said something to his companions. They looked sad.

"Go back to the cabin, and stay there," Jon said in Cathy's ear, his arm slowly releasing her. Cathy cast him a quick, grateful look as she slipped away. To save her, he had claimed the child he was convinced was Harold's as his own. It had cost him a great deal of pride to do so, she knew, and yet he had not hesitated. Perhaps he was coming to believe it himself, or perhaps he was, despite everything, fonder of her than he'd admit. Whatever his reason, he had done it. Cathy resolved to accept the harsh strictures he would doubtless rain down on her head for her disobedience without protest. She had to admit that they were richly deserved. If Jon had not had the wit to use her pregnancy as an excuse, it was very likely that she would now be well on her way to becoming a member of the Sheikh's harem. At the thought, Cathy shivered. Angry and disillusioned as she was with Jon, at least he was familiar.

Shaken by what had occurred, Cathy meekly stayed in the cabin until Jon came to her. It was some hours later, and she had begun to feel truly nervous. What if the Berbers, after thinking the matter over, decided that their Sheikh would want her despite her pregnancy? Outnumbered at least one hundred to one, with no guarantee that the *Cristobel*'s crew would even be willing to raise a hand in her defense, what could Jon do but hand her over? Butterflies flitted about in her stomach as Cathy realized how completely at the mercy of these strange people they were. In her battered condition, the *Cristobel* would not last another week at sea. If Jon were faced with a choice between herself and the lives of the eighty-some others in his care, what could he do but fall in with the Sheikh's wishes?

She was in such a state by the time he entered the cabin that she was trembling. Wide-eyed, she looked up at him with mute appeal. He was regarding her strangely, yet he did not seem particularly angry.

"What—what happened?" she quavered when it appeared that he wasn't going to speak. Jon's mouth twisted.

"The Berbers were much impressed," he said dryly. "They carried word of your beauty back to the Sheikh, who was likewise awed by the idea of a female with hair the color of the sun and skin as white as goat's milk. When he learned you were with child—a child I was forced to claim, I might add, lest they decide that you were an adulteress and stone you to death, as is their custom—he expressed much solicitude for your well-being. In fact, he offered me the use of one of the houses in his complex while the *Cristobel* is refitted, so that you would no longer be forced to endure the discomfort of life aboard ship."

"A house?" Cathy gasped, sifting through this information for the part that most appealed to her. "How wonderful!"

"Isn't it?" Jon grimaced. "The last time I was here I was offered no such courtesy. It seems that you are not totally useless, after all."

Cathy smiled at him, relief and pleasure combining to form twin imps in her eyes. It would be so marvelous to actually live in a house for a while, even if the thing was just four mud walls and a roof! She was sick to death of this squalid ship!

Her obvious delight touched Jon, when he had sworn that he would never permit himself to be moved by her again. In consequence, his voice was harsh when he spoke.

"It won't be as much fun as you seem to think," he warned, his eyes narrowing on her excitement-flushed face. "You will have to live very much retired, not even so much as showing yourself out-of-doors without my company. And even then you'll have to behave as their women do: covering yourself from head to toe at all times; keeping a respectful pace behind me when we go out; and never looking a man—who is considered a superior creature—in the face. Is that clear?"

Cathy looked at him doubtfully, her joy dimming noticeably. "Are you serious?" she asked, chewing her lower lip. Such servility was humiliating even to contemplate.

"Absolutely," Jon told her, and his tone left her in no doubt that he meant it. "And I warn you, their laws are very severe: if they decide a woman is immoral—and flouting any of their conventions could bring about such a decision—she is immediately put to death."

"I think you're trying to frighten me," Cathy accused after a long moment.

"Think what you like," he said coldly, turning away. "But you'll do as I say."

⟨⟨◦⟩⟩

The house that the Sheikh made available for their use was not, as Cathy had pictured, four mud walls and a roof. Instead, it was a veritable palace, made of thick white stone with huge, airy rooms and marble floors. Inside it was cool even in the blazing mid-afternoon heat, and Cathy found it no hardship to remain indoors. The house was shaped like a hollow box, with all four inner walls opening onto a small courtyard. Here she could sit in perfect privacy when she felt the need of fresh air, which was most often at dusk. It was in that courtyard, surrounded by the sweet scents of exotic flowers and the lush greenery that was only allowed to bloom by virtue of constant watering, that she spent her most enjoyable hours. Seated on an elegantly carved stone bench near the gushing fountain that formed the garden's centerpiece, she found the trials and tribulations of the outside world very far away.

Servants had been provided as a matter of course. They were small, dark-skinned, and unobtrusive, and ran the house so well that Cathy was left with nothing to do. Which suited her very well. Going into the seventh month of her pregnancy, she was tired almost all the time. Each afternoon she succumbed to an overwhelming compulsion to nap. By the time she awoke, bathed, and dressed, it was time to eat supper, which she usually took alone, or with Angie, who occasionally came from the ship to bear her company. Cathy would have invited the girl to stay with them, but Jon had firmly vetoed that idea. The more people from the *Cristobel* who lived ashore, the greater the potential for trouble, he told Cathy grimly. It was bad enough that her foolishness had forced them into a position where they had to come in daily contact with the devoutly Moslem native Berbers.

Jon himself was absent every day and usually long into the night. Overseeing the repairs to the *Cristobel* took up a great deal of his time, and in addition he was occupied with teaching some of the Sheikh's sailors the finer points of navigation. This he had promised to do in return for the materials needed to get the ship in seaworthy condition, and for the victuals needed before they could set out on a trans-ocean voyage. Both parties to the deal considered that they had struck a good bargain, which Cathy supposed they had.

For appearances' sake, she and Jon shared a bed. The servants, while polite to a fault, no doubt reported their every movement to the Sheikh as a matter of course, as Jon informed Cathy dryly when she objected to this arrangement. Unless she had a fancy to be one of the Sheikh's many concubines, she had better make a pretty convincing show of belonging to Jon. And even if the thought of joining a harem didn't trouble her, Jon added nastily, she had better give a little thought to what the Sheikh's likely reaction would be if he discovered that they had lied to him. He would be displeased, to say the least, and while the *Cristobel* lay as helpless as a beached whale, the Sheikh's displeasure was something they could ill afford.

Since he had discovered that she was with child, Jon had not tried to make love to her. Cathy, piqued by this omission, would not admit it even to herself. She was positively thankful that he found her expanding body repulsive, she told herself fiercely, and tried not to spend most of her waking moments speculating on whether or not Jon was taking Sarita to bed in her stead.

As weeks passed, her coming *accouchement* began to occupy Cathy's mind to the exclusion of all else. This child was not as active as Cray had been, and she was nowhere near as elephantine, but still she could anticipate the birth with nothing but dread. Having a baby in a foreign land without a doctor was not going to be a picnic, she foresaw. Still, it was better by far than giving birth on a ship in mid-ocean. Fervently she began to hope that Jon meant to stay in Rabat until after the child had put in an appearance. When she ventured to broach the subject, one night when they were silently sharing the enormous, mosquito-netting-draped bed, his reply was brusque.

"I had it in mind," was all he said, but Cathy felt inordinately relieved.

The child became more active at night, kicking and squirming until Cathy could hardly rest. Which, she supposed with an inward grin, partly explained why she was so sleepy all day. She knew Jon had to feel the unmistakable signs of life inside her when she curled against his broad back for warmth during the cold desert nights, but he made no mention of it.

Indeed, it was as if he was determined to pretend that the coming child did not exist. He referred to it only when necessity dictated, and when he looked at her Cathy noted that he was careful to keep his eyes above her waist. This cavalier attitude infuriated Cathy, although she was too proud to let her anger show. Whether he wished to acknowledge it or not, she was going through all this discomfort to give life to *his* child. The least he could do, in her opinion, was show a little interest.

The few times he was forced to mention the coming baby, he made it clear that his opinion as to the child's paternity had not changed. He still considered it Harold's, which enraged Cathy all the more. "If that's what he thinks, then bully for him," she thought furiously more than once. "He has no legal claim to me or the child, and as soon as we get somewhere civilized he can go his way and we'll go ours. And Cray's."

When Cathy did on rare occasions go out in public, it was in Jon's company. After what had happened that first day in port, she was not foolish enough to defy him over this. Dressed like a Berber woman in a flowing white robe that both concealed her pregnancy and covered her hair, she attracted little attention. True to Jon's words, she found that it was the custom for the women to walk humbly behind their men, their heads discreetly covered, and the ends of the enveloping burnooses held up over the lower half of their faces. In response to Jon's terse command, Cathy grudgingly complied with what was expected of her. But she found trailing at Jon's heels like a puppy dog so mortifying that she was glad to stay at home.

It was just as bad when they had guests. She was permitted to join the company—like a good child, she thought resentfully—but she could not eat with the men, and she had to sit deferentially behind Jon all the while, muffled in that ubiquitous white robe as she stared at the marble floor and remained as silent as a grave. After her first experience of this,

Cathy tried to decline any encores. But Jon informed her ruth-lessly that her absence from such gatherings would be viewed as an insult, and so she had to swallow her spleen and do as she was told.

Mustafa Kemal was a frequent guest, and he left Cathy in no doubt that he still saw her as a potential addition to the Sheikh's harem. Once he even made an insinuating inquiry of Jon as to what he planned to do with her after she was deliv-ered of the child. Jon passed it off with a laugh, but Cathy felt uneasy. Suddenly she was not quite as eager to remain on dry land for her lying-in as she had been.

Once Jon took her to visit the ship, and Cathy saw that the repairs were well under way. The *Cristobel* should be sea-worthy again before Cathy herself was, and this realization provided Cathy with a modicum of comfort. Soon, if they had to escape, there would be a way.

While Jon stopped to talk to O'Reilly about some of the finer points of the ship's reconstruction, Cathy came face to face with Sarita. She was taken aback by the naked hatred she saw in the other woman's black eyes.

"Whore!" Sarita hissed in her face. Before Cathy could frame a reply, Jon was turning back to her, and Sarita slunk away. Despite its brevity, the episode left Cathy feeling chilled.

About a week after this encounter, Cathy supped alone, and retired early to bed as had recently become her custom when Jon was away. She shed the white robe that was her in-evitable garment by day with relief. Piling her long hair on top of her head, she started to step into the tiled bath that was built into the floor of the small anteroom adjoining the bedroom she and Jon shared. This bathroom was as opulent as the rest of the house, and Cathy knew that it was one thing she would miss when they left. With servants to fill the deep, wide basin with warm water, provide towels and scented soap, and then discreetly vanish, it was almost sinfully luxurious.

As she stepped down, she caught a glimpse of herself in

the enormous mirror that adorned the opposite wall. It was the first time she had looked at herself naked for quite a while, and she could not like what she saw. With her belly swollen out to there, and her breasts heavy and pendulous with milk, she thought that she could understand why Jon preferred Sarita. She could describe herself by no other word than grotesque, Cathy thought glumly, not seeing the soft sheen of her skin and hair, and the luminescence of her blue eyes. Quickly she sat in the warm water to hide her body from the mirror's all-seeing eyes. To look at herself was only to feel depressed.

As Cathy bathed, her thoughts turned of their own volition to Jon. He had treated her, for the most part, with cool civility ever since they had moved into the house, as if he were a polite stranger who had no desire to further the acquaintance. Even in bed he turned his back, and this indifference nettled Cathy mightily. If he was trying to show her without words that she no longer meant anything to him except as an unwelcome responsibility, then he was succeeding very well. To her surprise, the thought hurt. She had once loved him with all her heart, and not so very long ago, either. But, she reminded herself, "once" was the word to cling to. If he no longer loved her—and she was very sure he did not, his actions made that plain—then she was fiercely glad that her love for him was equally dead. And if it was not quite as simple as that, she vowed that he at least would never know it.

When Cathy finally emerged from the tub, dried herself, and pulled the simple cotton shift that one of the servants had procured for her to use as a nightdress over her head, she was feeling decidedly weepy. She blamed her moroseness on the crotchets which tended to beset females in the last stages of pregnancy, although secretly she knew that it wasn't only that. But she refused to consider the other probable cause, and instead took herself firmly to bed.

She couldn't sleep. She tossed and turned and thumped the pillow, and wished bitchily that Jon was present so that he would be forced to suffer her discomfort with her. It wasn't fair that she had to go through all the misery and pain associated with bearing a child, while he had all the fun, and then refused to acknowledge that child as his! As she thought about it, Cathy got angrier than she had been in weeks. "Loathsome swine," she called him blackly, and sank back down into the too-soft mattress, her arms crossing angrily over her decidedly tender breasts. She would be waiting for him when he came in at last, she planned venomously, and as soon as he walked through the door she would let him have it with both barrels!

It was some time later when she at last heard the unmistakable sounds of Jon letting himself quietly into the house. The fine edge of her anger had somewhat dulled, but she was still determined to let him know of her displeasure. To be totally abandoned for hours on end, day after day, was too much, and so she would tell him! Not that she particularly wanted his company—in fact, quite the opposite!—but she could see no reason why Angie should not be permitted to bear her company. After all, it was highly unlikely that the girl would cause any trouble with the sphinx-like Berbers, and besides. . . .

This thought was interrupted by the opening of the bedroom door. Cathy, sitting bolt upright in the bed, her arms crossed over her chest and her eyes snapping militantly, had already parted her lips to deliver her opening salvo when she perceived, to her amazement, that it was not Jon who was slipping cautiously through the door. It was Sarita!

"What are you doing here?" she gasped as soon as surprise let her speak. Really, if Jon had dared to bring his doxy to this house, she would slay him bare-handed! How dared he . . . !

Sarita smiled at her, her black eyes glittering malevolently in the darkness of the room.

"I have a little surprise for you," she murmured, and then over her shoulder into the shadowy hall, she called softly. "Hurry up! She's in here, you fools!"

Cathy was by this time beginning to feel alarmed. Whoever Sarita was talking to, it certainly was not Jon. She had addressed the unseen persons in the plural, and besides, the woman would never dare to refer to Jon as a fool! Whatever Sarita had planned, Cathy was sure that it was nothing that she would enjoy. All at once, with a great thumping of her heart, she began to fear for her life. If she and her coming baby were to die, Sarita might imagine that she would be left a clear field with Jon!

No sooner had the thought occurred to Cathy than she was opening her mouth to scream for help while at the same time struggling into a crouching position in the middle of the big bed. She would fight. . . . But there was no time. The first shrill notes of her scream had barely left her throat when two men burst through the door and leapt toward her. Cathy barely recognized one of them as that repulsive Grogan when they were upon her, one large hand clamping roughly over her mouth while her arms were strained behind her and secured with some sort of silken rope. Before she could do more than give a token kick, her legs had suffered the same treatment. She lay helplessly on the bed, her eyes staring apprehensively over the top of the gag that had been thrust into her mouth. Dear God, what could they mean to do with her? Perhaps throw her, gagged and bound, into the bay to drown?

"Scared, Lady?" Grogan leaned over to whisper tauntingly in her face while Sarita laughed maliciously in the background. "No need to be. We don't aim to hurt you none. It's just that Sarita here has made a little deal with that man of the Sheikh's."

"You'll like living in a harem, won't you, deary?" Sarita joined Grogan to hiss down at her. "Just the place for a whore like you! Jonny won't even know what happened to you—not that he'll care! I mean to keep him too busy to even remember your name!"

Cathy blanched beneath the suffocating gag as she began

to perceive what Sarita had done. Somehow she had arranged to give her to the Sheikh!

"That Kemal man promised me a whole chest of jewels when I told him that I could deliver you! Seems that the Sheikh is fascinated by the notion of bedding a woman with hair the color of yours—not that I think it's anything special! But that's sure the only reason he'd want you. There's nothing else about you to make a man hot with desire. You're fat as a pig!"

Cathy would have been furious at these taunting words if she had not been so frightened. Once locked away in the Sheikh's harem, there would be no escape, she knew. His women were kept out of sight of the world, and well guarded. Even if Jon should somehow discover what had happened, and want to free her, she did not see how he could. Once she had become the Sheikh's property, she would be as good as dead as far as Jon was concerned. He would never even be allowed to see her. . . .

"All clear." Grogan came back from where he had been peering down the hall. Looming over her where she lay on the bed, he reached for her and scooped her up in his arms. His movements were rough, as though he would enjoy hurting her. Certainly he seemed to spare no thoughts for the delicacy of her condition. Cathy felt the large mound of her stomach being crushed against Grogan's ape-like chest, and moaned with fear and pain. Much of this, and she might lose the child!

She squirmed and kicked as well as she could as they bore her out of the house, but she knew as she was doing it that it was useless. The most she could hope for was to attract the attention of the servants, who might summon help. Or they might not. They were, after all, the Sheikh's minions above all else, and to them, Cathy was sure that she was just a woman whom the Sheikh desired. Even if they heard her muffled cries they would likely turn deaf ears. In Rabat, the Sheikh was all-powerful, and to offend him would be to bring down on the hapless one's head the literal wrath of a god.

The house was one of many in the complex surrounding the Sheikh's enormous palace. There wasn't far to go. With Grogan's huge strides eating up the distance, it seemed just minutes before they had reached a side door cut into the palace wall, a door that opened as they approached it. On the other side three men waited: Cathy recognized Mustafa Kemal, and shuddered. He was flanked by two huge, hairless eunuchs.

"We got her," Sarita announced unnecessarily as they entered and the door shut behind them. Cathy saw that they were in a narrow stone passage lit by flaming torches set into the wall.

"You have done well," Kemal said gravely, his hand coming out to finger Cathy's trailing hair before being quickly withdrawn. "There was no trouble with Captain Hale?"

"None," Grogan answered briefly. Sarita, tossing her head, added: "I told you there wouldn't be. He has already grown tired of her. Now that she is gone, he will be thankful."

"I hope you are right. I do not desire any trouble," Kemal said, and motioned to the eunuch standing at his shoulder. "You may give her to Muhammed. She is no longer your concern."

Cathy was transferred like an unwanted parcel from Grogan's huge arms to the eunuch's just as massive hold.

"But what about our reward? You promised. . . ." Sarita whined.

"I have not forgotten," said Kemal with just a touch of scorn. Over his shoulder to the eunuch, he ordered: "Take her to the Women's Quarters. Salina-Begum awaits her."

As Cathy was borne off, writhing uselessly in the huge eunuch's arms, she heard Sarita's ecstatic exclamations as she was handed the promised casket of jewels.

The palace seemed to Cathy's fright-dazed eyes to be a veritable rabbit warren of rooms and passages, all filled with brilliantly colored oriental carpets, dusty tapestries, and

hand-beaten, bejeweled gold and silver ornaments. A trea-
sure in furnishings alone must lie between these walls, she
thought abstractedly as she concentrated on trying to memo-
rize the way they had come just in case she should somehow
manage to break away. It was a forlorn hope, she knew. The
man carrying her would overtake her effortlessly, and even if
she should be able to elude him, stiff and silent servants lined
every wall. There would be no escape.

The eunuch paused outside an ornately carved wooden
door set beneath an arch. Guarding it on either side were two
more of the huge, hairless men.

He said something in Arabic to them, and they stood obediently aside. Then he carried her in and across the dimly lit
room to lay her gently on a cushioned divan. With a small bow
to someone beyond Cathy's line of vision, he turned on his
heel and melted silently away.

"Ahh, they have been rough with you," an old woman
crooned in rusty-sounding English. Cathy, gazing up at her
fearfully, saw that she was clad in a *bourka*, as she had learned
was required of the Sheikh's female servants when they were
in a position to be viewed by men. Did eunuchs count as men?
Cathy wondered absurdly. Then surprise drove every other
thought from her mind. Because, as the woman began to gently loosen her bonds, she saw that the eyes just visible through
the thick veil were faded blue.

"Who are you?" Cathy gasped, as the woman removed
her gag.

"I am Salina," the woman answered simply, freeing
Cathy's hands and moving down to untie the rope that bound
her legs.

"You—you're English!" Cathy exclaimed, still not believing what her eyes and ears told her was true.

"Once, long ago, I was English," Salina said sadly. "Now I
am Berber. As you will be."

"No!" Cathy protested instinctively, shuddering at the thought. Salina smiled.

"That was my reaction, too, but as you see it did me no good," she said, rubbing Cathy's ankles where the rope had cut into them. Cathy pushed herself into a sitting position, curiosity banishing even fear from her mind.

"How did you come to be here?" Cathy asked.

"Like you, I was purchased by the Sheikh. But my life has been very different than yours will be. Even as a girl I was very plain, you see, and he did not desire me for his concubine. So I became the *dai*—midwife—to the women. Which is why they have sent me to care for you. You will not be permitted to join the others until after the babe is born, nor will the Sheikh honor you with his presence until then. But I will care for you, and things will be very well. You will see. You need have no fear."

"Please—you must help me! I don't want to be the Sheikh's concubine!" Cathy said desperately, thinking that as her countrywoman Salina just might take pity on her. "I have another child, a little boy who waits for me in England. And there is a man. . . ."

"The American captain, is it not?" Salina asked knowledgeably, surprising Cathy. Seeing Cathy's astonishment that she should have even heard of Jon in the seclusion in which all the palace women were kept, she smiled again. "Oh, we hear much, even in *purdah*. And it is said that the American captain—a most handsome, manly man—has for his woman one with hair the color of purest gold, whom the Sheikh greatly desires. We have expected your coming for some time, little one."

"My name is Cathy," Cathy said automatically, her mind on Salina's revelations.

"And mine was once Sarah," the old woman told her. "But since I came to live in the Sheikh's palace, I have been known as Salina at his pleasure. I am sure he will find a new name for you, too—something soft and beautiful, as you are."

"I must get away!" Cathy moaned, horror reclaiming her as she pictured being forever imprisoned in the Sheikh's harem, living only to serve his pleasure, even renamed at his whim.

"You will never get away." Salina was patient but inexorable, as if she was pointing out an incontrovertible but slightly unpalatable fact to a child. "No one does—or even wants to, after a while. You will be well treated, and much honored among the women. No doubt your beauty will win the Sheikh's favor, and he will summon you often to his bed."

"Oh, dear God!" Cathy felt ill as she considered this. "Please—please let me go! I beg of you! I could slip away. . . ."

"I am sorry, little one, but if you should disappear I would be severely punished—probably blinded. I cannot risk it. And your life will not be bad with us. Trust me." Salina, seeing Cathy's agitation, patted her arm soothingly. Cathy pushed her hand away.

"I won't stay here!" she half sobbed. As Salina leaned consolingly over her, Cathy saw her opportunity. With one hard shove, she sent the old woman reeling across the small room. In an instant Cathy was on her feet, dashing for the door. Desperately she pulled at it, and felt it open under her hands. She jerked it wide—and froze. The two enormous eunuchs were blocking the door, staring down at her evilly.

"Ahmad, Radi, the little one is foolishly upset. You will bring her back to me, and I will give her a little drink to make her feel better. Tomorrow she will be more sensible, we will hope."

Ahmad and Radi each grasped one of Cathy's arms, and bore her back into the room. Cathy didn't waste her strength trying to resist. It would be useless, as she saw all too clearly. Even if she got beyond the room, she would not get more than a few steps down the passageway before dozens of the Sheikh's servants were upon her.

As the eunuchs pushed her down onto the soft divan, Cathy turned desperate eyes on Salina.

"Please. . . ."

Salina clucked pityingly.

"Poor little one, you must not upset yourself so. Consider the child. Everything will be all right, you will see. Now, you must drink this. . . ."

She held what looked to be a solid gold goblet to Cathy's lips. Cathy, held on either side by the eunuchs, had no choice. As she swallowed, she thought that the liquid tasted slightly bitter, like bad wine. Then the room began to spin around in sickening swirls. With a chill of horror chasing down her spine, Cathy realized that she had been drugged.

❧

The next twenty-four hours were forever blurred in Cathy's memory. Salina re-administered the drug, which she assured Cathy was only a harmless potion designed to keep her from doing herself or her child an injury, at regular intervals. Cathy slept most of the time, rousing only to eat. Salina apparently was constantly in attendance on her, bathing her and brushing her hair even as she slept. Cathy, troubled by nightmares of black dungeons and sinister men in long white robes, felt tears trickling down her cheeks.

It was during one of her brief periods of semi-wakefulness that Cathy heard a commotion in the passageway. Dulled by the drug, she didn't even trouble to wonder at it, just noticing without concern that Salina had left her side and was listening, with her ear pressed to the door.

Cathy's eyes were closing again as she heard as if through a thick fog the sound of the door being opened, and then Salina screaming. The shriek was abruptly cut short. Cathy, feeling vaguely alarmed, forced her heavy eyelids to open. She thought the dark face bending over her was merely a figment of her dreams, but she smiled drowsily at it anyway.

"Cathy, wake up!" a voice commanded harshly, and a hurting hand grasped her arm and shook it. Cathy blinked as her head lolled limply back and forth. If she didn't know better, she'd think that this too-rough vision really was Jon. . . .

"Jon . . . ?" she murmured testingly, and squinted as his face came into focus.

"Good God, they've drugged her," she heard him mutter furiously, and then he was bending over her. She felt his hard arms slide around her and lift her carefully. Then it seemed as if he was carrying her away, down through the labyrinthine rooms and passages of the palace. As if in a dream Cathy saw the prone figure of Salina lying just inside the door of the room where she had been imprisoned, and, a little further down the hall, the sprawled and bloodied bodies of the eunuchs Ahmad and Radi. But her head was too fuzzy to give these visions any credence. It was not until the bitterly cold night air hit her face that Cathy began to realize that Jon had, miraculously, found and freed her.

"How—how . . . ?" she stuttered, as he lifted her up onto a horse and then mounted swiftly behind her.

"So you're waking up, are you, Sleeping Beauty?" he sounded grimly amused. "God, you've given me the worst twenty-four hours of my life! But we don't have time to talk now. I'll tell you all about it when we're safely away."

He spurred the horse to a gallop as he spoke, one hand on the reins and the other holding Cathy firmly before him. She rested tiredly back against the iron wall of his chest, still too much under the influence of the drug to do more than feel vaguely thankful for her deliverance. As they clattered down onto the dock, and Jon leapt from the saddle and then reached up to swing her once again into his arms, Cathy saw to her puzzlement that the sky above the northern side of the Sheikh's palace seemed curiously alight.

"Look. . . ." she told Jon bemusedly, lifting her arm and pointing at the strange orangey glow. Jon laughed harshly.

"I fear the Sheikh's palace is burning, my love, and if we don't get the hell out of here we may soon burn with it," he told her, striding along the dock to where a small boat waited. O'Reilly was in the boat, and Jon handed Cathy to him before jumping in himself.

"She's drugged," he said briefly to O'Reilly. Then, to the men who waited at the oars, added, "For the love of God, get a move on! It won't take them long to figure out what happened."

Thus adjured, the men set to with what looked to Cathy to be almost a frenzy. The little boat fairly shot through the waves. In less time than it takes to tell, they were beside the *Cristobel*, and the men were hurriedly climbing a rope ladder.

"This may hurt, but I don't have time to think of anything else," Jon told Cathy hurriedly, and while she was still trying to comprehend this remark he hauled her onto his back and tied her hands around his neck.

"Hang on," he said over his shoulder, and then as Cathy was still puzzling at his meaning he climbed the ladder with her dangling helplessly from his neck.

When they had almost reached the deck, hands reached down from above to support Cathy's weight, and at the same time drag both her and Jon over the rail.

"How is she, Captain?" Cathy recognized Angie's anxious voice as Jon quickly untied her hands.

"Well enough, I think," he answered tersely. Then, turning to the hovering men, he added: "For God's sake, don't just stand there! Set sail!"

twelve

❦

Jon knew that the way he felt was contradictory, but he couldn't help it. On the one hand, he hated Cathy with a bitter, gnawing hatred for her betrayal of him, and their love. But on the other—he had been half out of his mind when she had disappeared back there in Rabat. It had been indeed the worst twenty-four hours of his life. The Berber servants had ever so circuitously hinted that perhaps the Begum, in one of the fits of despondency so common to an expectant mother, had drowned herself in the bay. Certainly they seemed convinced that looking for her was a waste of time, as she was nowhere to be found. Something in their faces, their very reluctance to discuss the matter, had roused Jon's suspicions. They knew more than they were willing to tell. Never at any moment had he believed that Cathy might have killed herself. Not his Cathy, with her fighting spirit! (Here Jon grimaced wryly as he noticed the possessive, which was how he still thought of her, despite everything.) And certainly not while she was with child. She was an excellent, loving mother, fiercely protective of both Cray and the coming infant. He could visualize no depression black enough to induce her to harm either herself or her child. If she felt herself to be neglected, or misused, as the servants delicately implied, then she was far more likely to harm *him!*

He had scoured the city, thinking that perhaps the little minx was hiding, hoping to give him a fright. Stymied at every turn, he had gone in desperation to the *Cristobel.* Maybe Angie knew something. . . . But even before he had a chance to talk to Angie, he had come face to face with Sarita. The woman's knowing smile had caught his attention. Then, when he had curtly demanded of her whether she had knowledge of Cathy's whereabouts, she had looked both guilty and frightened. It had been enough to convince him that, whatever had befallen Cathy, Sarita had been involved. Cringing in the face of his terrible anger, she had denied everything. Jon had never thought that he would enjoy hitting a woman, but he was wrong. He had taken savage delight in slapping the truth from Sarita, leaving her a sprawled, sobbing heap on the floor of his cabin when he had at last forced her to confess what she had done. But at that, she was lucky. If she had been a man, he would have killed her. As he would have killed Grogan and Meade, her helpers, if there had been time.

Rescuing Cathy by storming the Sheikh's palace, as had been his first, furious intention, was clearly impossible. The building was a veritable fortress, protected by hundreds of guards. No, his only hope for getting in there and getting out alive again with Cathy had been to create a diversion. Which he had done very nicely, thank you, by planting crude bombs against the far wall of the palace. As he had hoped, the explosions had sent everyone running to see what had happened, and they had stayed to fight the mushrooming fire. He had only had to contend with a few eunuchs.

The Sheikh would be livid when he discovered what had happened, Jon knew. Maybe livid enough to send boats in pursuit of what he would call the murdering infidel dogs. Which was why Jon thought it wise to discard his original plan of stopping off at Tenerife. Best to get safely back to America, where they would be beyond the reach of the Sheikh's minions and the Royal British Navy alike.

The one flaw in this plan was Cathy. She was far gone with child, at least seven months, according to Jon's calculations, and more if he believed what she insisted was true. Which he didn't, of course. He remembered very clearly how enormous she had been just before she gave birth to Cray, and she was nowhere near so cumbersome now. Her own body, among other things, gave the lie to her tale. Still, seven months was pretty far along, and he would not breathe freely again until he had her safe on dry land, with a doctor in attendance. He could not conceive of anything more horrible than to have her go into labor on the *Cristobel*, in the middle of the high seas, with one of the few females left on board to act as midwife. The very thought made him break out into a cold sweat. His own mother had died in child-bed, and he had always had a dread of it. And Cathy had suffered so terribly with Cray. . . .

But at the most it should take four weeks to cross the Atlantic, less if he piled on plenty of canvas and headed straight for Newfoundland, via the Azores. If she showed signs of being near her time, they could even berth in the Azores until the child was born. Deciding on that, Jon felt greatly relieved. He did not stop to consider why he should be so worried at the idea of Cathy suffering, perhaps dying, in child-bed. After all, it was only what she deserved, giving birth to another man's child.

Cathy, for her part, was worried herself, although she tried not to let Jon know it. She was much nearer nine than seven months along, despite what Jon thought. It seemed very likely that she would have the baby in the middle of the Atlantic Ocean. But there was Angie to tend her, and Clara, who assured her that she had brought many a child into the world, as the former madam of a whorehouse. Which was some comfort, the scandalous nature of her experience notwithstanding.

Cathy knew that Jon was still convinced that the coming baby was Harold's, and despised her for it. Still, he was kind to her, now that they were back aboard ship, and always inquired solicitously after her health. She still had the exclusive use of his cabin, but she no longer had to worry about where he was spending his nights. Sarita, along with Grogan and the other man, had been left behind in Rabat. The knowledge warmed Cathy mightily.

Another thing that cheered her was the realization that Jon would very soon be convinced that he was the father of this new baby. When the child put in an appearance, all he would have to do was count back nine months to be left in no doubt. The infant had been conceived before she had left Woodham, and when it was born Jon would be forced to admit that there was no possible way that it could be Harold's. Cathy pictured his abject apologies with intense satisfaction. It would do him good to humbly beg her pardon, then sweat for a while to see if she was willing to forgive him. Which she might, or might not, do. That he thought so ill of her rankled mightily, and she was not sure whether or not she wanted to spend the rest of her life with a man who considered her capable of such behavior. Was she prepared to put up with his jealousies for years on end? She would have to think about it. . . . Besides, there was always the possibility that, even after realizing that this new child was his, Jon might not want her.

Days turned into a week, and the *Cristobel* was well away from Rabat, sailing a northwesterly course. The weather was fine, but hot. Jon had set some of the crew to rigging up a shelter for Cathy on the quarterdeck, so that she could be out in the fresh air but at the same time protected from the broiling sun, and under his eyes. Cathy spent most of her time beneath this makeshift canopy, too lethargic to do more than recline sleepily upon the hammock he had had hung for her, and watch the constantly-changing sea. From time to time she would catch Jon's eye, as he tended to the sailing of the ship. Almost reluctantly he would smile at her, and sometimes even come across to chat. They spoke mainly of the weather, and everyday happenings aboard ship, carefully avoiding any topic that might precipitate a quarrel. Both were content to let their relationship drift along in this guardedly friendly fashion for the time being.

One morning Cathy awoke and went out on deck to find the world shrouded in a fog as thick as molasses. Long combers of mist rolled in from the east, enveloping the *Cristobel* like a cocoon. At first it felt good to be free of the blazing sun for a while, but after a couple of hours the dampness grew uncomfortable. Cathy, ensconced in her hammock, shivered. Jon, seeing the involuntary movement and noting the drops of moisture on her face and hair, sent her inside. Cathy went without demur.

When she emerged again, it was afternoon, and the fog seemed to be lifting slightly. Certainly it was warmer, and as Cathy breathed deeply of the gray mist she thought that it was almost like inhaling steam. Eddies of vapor swirled about her full black skirts as she climbed the stairs to the quarterdeck.

Instead of going directly to her hammock, as was her custom, she decided on the spur of the moment to join Jon at the rail. He was busy charting their position on an enormous map, alternating between looking at the compass which he held in one hand, squinting up at the sky in a vain attempt to pinpoint the location of the sun, and drawing lines on the map with a ruler and pencil. As she crossed to stand beside him, she nodded casually at Mick Frazier, who was at the wheel. In such fog, she would have thought that steering was useless, as there was no possible way to see where they were going. Still, she realized that Jon, as always, knew what he was about. She had no fear that he would get the *Cristobel* lost, or see her run aground.

"Should you be out in this?" he asked, frowning slightly, when he at last became aware of her presence beside him. Cathy smiled at him, thinking how handsome he looked with his dark face clean-shaven for once to show the lean, hard lines of his jaw and chin and his eyes as silvery-gray as the mist around them. Moisture had coaxed his black hair into deep waves. One unruly lock curled down across his forehead. On impulse, Cathy stood on tiptoe and gently smoothed it back. His eyes narrowed slightly at her action, and then he, too, smiled.

"Softening me up for something?" he mocked lightly. Cathy shook her head, dimpling. It felt good to banter in this light-hearted fashion, as they once had.

"I wouldn't dare," she answered pertly. "You're far too frightening."

"And you shake on your little pink toes every time I come near you," he said dryly. "You're no more afraid of me than a fish is of the water."

Cathy chuckled, admitting the truth of this.

"Should I be?" she asked provocatively, her eyes glinting mischievously up at him.

"You tell me," he answered, sounding suddenly enigmatic, and turned back to his map.

"Where are we?" she asked idly after a moment, seeing that he was determined to ignore her.

"As near as I can figure, about halfway to the Azores. Another ten days, and we should be sighting them. Think you can hang on until then?" This was accompanied by a slanting look at her bulging midriff, and sounded part sarcastic, part worried. Cathy chose to ignore the sarcastic part. She wasn't in the mood for a quarrel.

"I'll do my best," she said gravely, and his frown deepened.

"You haven't been feeling—uh—unwell?" His voice was sharp, and Cathy could tell that it was more a demand for reassurance than a question. Remembering his dread of childbirth, Cathy sighed inwardly. If she wasn't able to hold out for another ten days, until they sighted land again—and she might not be, if the earliest of her possible due dates was the right one—Jon would likely suffer more than she would herself. She remembered Petersham's account of how upset Jon had been while she had labored with Cray, and wished she could spare him this time. But she couldn't, and anyway she didn't know why she should want to. A little suffering, after all he had put her through, would do him good! Besides, maybe he wouldn't be too concerned about what she had to endure bringing this child into the world. After all, he didn't believe it was his.

"Do you care?" she asked, the words tinged with bitterness. She wished them unsaid as soon as she uttered them, but it was too late. His mouth tightened, and his eyes took on a thin film of ice.

"I should be distressed if you suffered any ill effects while you're in my care," he drawled nastily. "Harold might not like it if his heir were to be stillborn."

"That's a dreadful thing to suggest!" Cathy gasped, her hand flying automatically to cover her stomach in a protective gesture. Jon noted the movement with narrowed eyes. His mouth tightened even more.

"What, that Harold might not like it?" he questioned coldly.

"That the baby might be stillborn," Cathy corrected, her eyes beginning to snap. "As you know very well, you swine! How you can suggest such a thing about your own child?"

"Which you'll never persuade me to believe," Jon interpolated, his voice hard.

"Won't I?" Cathy's head was tilted way back as she stood glaring angrily up into his set face. Her hair flowed in a rippling golden river down her back, and her pale skin glistened with the sheen put on it by the mist. Her eyes had brightened with temper to a sparkling cobalt, and her arms were akimbo as she faced him down. Jon, growing angrier by the minute, admired her nevertheless. Big with child, dressed in garments that were little better than rags, her nose shining and her bright hair dulled by the day's dampness, she was beautiful. His heart suddenly speeded up, and he cursed it silently. Would she always affect him this way? Would he never be free of the hold she had on his senses?

"No, you won't," he growled, madder at himself than her. "You. . . ."

What he had been going to say was never uttered. It was buried forever by a ringing cry from somewhere high in the rigging.

"Sail, ho!"

"Where away?" Jon instantly bellowed in reply, all thought of his ongoing quarrel with Cathy vanishing in an instant. Any sail was a cause for anxiety. If it was not the Sheikh, it could well be the Royal Navy, or even a pirate vessel, although God knew that pickings on the *Cristobel* would be slim.

"Off to starboard!"

Jon immediately swung around to stare off to his right, as did everyone else on the deck. He, and they, could see nothing but an endless expanse of dull silver water, broken up by dense patches of darker gray like thick wads of cotton wool. The ship, or ships, if indeed they existed, were totally hidden by the fog.

"Where are you going?" Cathy demanded, grabbing at his arm as he would have moved away from her. Jon looked down at her with a frown, clearly abstracted.

"Up in the rigging. I have to see. . . ." his voice trailed off, but Cathy let him go. She suddenly realized the danger of their position. She didn't know which would be worse, to be overtaken by the Sheikh's men, or the Royal Navy. At least, in the latter case, she would be spared, and perhaps she could help Jon and the others. . . . But it was more than likely that she was growing unnecessarily alarmed, Cathy comforted herself. If there was a ship, it was probably a harmless freighter.

Pulling himself to a vantage point high atop the main mast, Jon stared off to starboard. He was above the mist, and he could see. . . . There it was—one, no, two of them, frigates both, less than three hours away, he would figure at a guess. The fog had allowed them to draw close. And the worst thing about it was that they were flying the unmistakable red, white, and blue emblem of Her Britannic Majesty's navy.

Lowering himself hand over hand down the pole, Jon thought furiously. There was little doubt that the *Cristobel* had been spotted. Victoria's sailors were some of the finest in the world, not like his own lackadaisical crew. And they would be equipped with the most up-to-date of spyglasses— to say nothing of guns. The next question was, would they recognize the *Cristobel* as a mutineed prison ship? It was possible, after all, that their presence in this part of the world was mere coincidence. But not likely. Jon admitted the fact to himself with a tightening of all his muscles. No, it was best to acknowledge it: the way those frigates were heading straight toward her, it was more than likely that the *Cristobel* was their prey.

All right, given that, what was best to do? As he saw it, they had three choices: surrender, flight, or fight. With the *Cristobel*'s few guns and inexperienced crew, fighting the heavily armed frigates would be tantamount to suicide, and with Cathy aboard it was something that he couldn't contemplate with any degree of fortitude. If the frigates had a mind to do it, they could blow the *Cristobel* out of the water with one salvo, and all aboard her would die. Fighting was out of the question. But surrender also had little appeal, not only for himself but for the men. They would hang along with him, and not for the crimes for which they had been sentenced. Mutiny was punishable by death, and Jon didn't think that the frigates' captain would be content to wait until he got them back to England to have the sentence carried out. No, he would be far more likely to order them strung up at once, from the rigging, using as his judge and jury the law of the sea.

Clearly the only thing to do was to outrun their pursuers. If they could. Jon, remembering the *Cristobel*'s unwieldy lines, felt a sinking sensation in the pit of his stomach. He didn't think they could do it.

But he tried. With a few terse words he told the men what they faced, and then rigged up as much canvas as she could carry. Using every ounce of sailing knowledge he possessed, he sent the *Cristobel* scuttling before the wind. The fog was a blessing, he thought, concealing their exact whereabouts. But even as Jon thanked God for it, the fog began to lift.

Cathy, white-faced, stayed on the quarterdeck throughout the afternoon, although Jon tried more than once to send her below. She knew by the silent desperation in the movements of the men that the *Cristobel*'s chances of escape were not good. Jon had forborne to tell her the almost certain fate he and the rest of the men faced if captured, so Cathy was spared worrying about that. She was able to comfort herself with the thought that she was an English lady of quality, after all, and if they should be taken, she had only to do what she could to ease Jon's imprisonment until they reached England, when she could hopefully turn to her father—or even, if necessary, Harold—for aid.

The fog lifted as suddenly as it had arisen. One moment they were shrouded in a dense gray cloak, and the next the sun shone down on water veiled by only a few thin wisps. Cathy, following Jon's grim glance, was surprised to see the frigates so close. Suddenly she was quite, quite certain that the *Cristobel* was not going to be able to get away.

"Go to my cabin, and stay there," Jon ordered grimly, his

eyes expressionless. "Don't come out for any reason. If there's need, I'll fetch you myself."

"Jon. . . ." Cathy began softly, wanting to let him know that he could count on her help if they should be taken. He silenced her with a fierce frown.

"I said, go to the cabin!" he ordered harshly. Cathy forgave his tone because of the bleakness of his face. He was worried. She started to do as he said, then hesitated. Swiftly she stood on tiptoe, her hand against his sandpaper cheek as she pressed her lips to his hard mouth. For just an instant he was motionless under the soft caress, and then his arms came around her, crushing her to him in a desperate embrace. His mouth moved hotly on hers, seeming to want to record its imprint for all time. Cathy returned his kiss with fervor, knowing all at once that she loved him despite everything. Then, suddenly, he pushed her almost roughly away.

"Get to the cabin!" he said again, his eyes wintry, and then turned on his heel and strode away.

Cathy did as he ordered—for a little while. But it wasn't long before waiting, not knowing what was going on, became more than she could stand. She had to see. Stealthily she left the cabin, taking care to stay in the shadow of the overhang so that Jon couldn't see her from the quarterdeck. She would stay outside for just a minute, and then she would go back.

The frigates were almost directly astern now, and closing fast. Cathy stared at the huge, flatbottomed ships, her eyes widening as she saw and recognized the dozens of cannon set along their sides. The *Cristobel* would be helpless against such adversaries! She thought about the inevitable taking of Jon and the others, and wanted to cry.

Jon, on the quarterdeck, watched the rapidly approaching warships with a face that could have been carved from granite. It was not the first time that he had watched an enemy in a faster, better-armed vessel drawing ever closer like a shark for the kill, but, with Cathy on board and the lives of all those on the *Cristobel* dependent upon what he decided to do, it was the worst. Not that there was much of a decision to make: if they fought, all aboard would perish, while if they surrendered, at least Cathy and the other women would survive.

Never before in his life had Jon surrendered without a fight, and it went very much against the grain for him to do so. But with three ancient cannon and only two men, besides himself, who knew how to fire them, the cause was hopeless before it was launched. He knew the men would disagree, since, like himself, they faced certain death if they were taken prisoner. But it was his decision, as captain, to make, and he knew that he had already made it: for Cathy's sake, the *Cristobel* would not fight.

One of the frigates, separated from the *Cristobel* by perhaps a quarter mile of sea, began to draw alongside. Jon noted the name *Four Winds* emblazoned on her side. She was close enough that he could see men scurrying like ants across her deck. He saw what looked like preparations to fire cannon, and frowned. Probably they just intended to pop a warning shot across the *Cristobel*'s bow as a way of telling her to give up quietly. But still, it never hurt to take precautions. . . .

"O'Reilly, tell Logan and Berry to prepare those cannon for firing. Quickly, and as unobtrusively as possible."

"Aye, Captain!"

The men were unaware that he had decided to surrender, and they were not likely to be overjoyed, Jon reflected grimly, setting himself up so that he could shoot any who tried to storm the quarterdeck. A mutiny attempt was entirely to be expected. Not that it had any chance of succeeding. He had been in this position before, and he knew what he was about.

Jon primed both pistols, and thrust them into his belt. He placed two more, loaded and ready, on a barrel within easy reach. He would have no compunction about shooting these men, whether or not they were under his command. One way or another, they were already as good as dead. He had Cathy to think about. And think about her he did, as he stared with steely eyes at the steadily approaching vessels.

One frigate was still well astern when the other drew directly alongside. The time for fight or flight was at hand, and Jon prepared to order a white flag to be run up the mast.

A cannon boomed. Jon, watching the arching trajectory designed to show them that resistance was useless, thought grimly that the time was upon him. He opened his mouth to roar out their surrender—and it stayed open in sheer surprise. Because that deadly black sphere was not arching harmlessly past the *Cristobel*'s bow, as he had expected. Instead, it was headed right for her crowded deck!

It landed with a burst of fire. The sound of the explosion mingled with the screams of the *Cristobel*'s crew. Jon, cursing steadily under his breath, headed for the main deck at a dead run. It looked as if the frigates weren't going to give them a choice: they clearly meant to blow the *Cristobel* out of the water!

"Logan, Berry, man those cannon!" Jon roared, heading for the forward one himself. "Frazier, to the wheel! O'Reilly, you take about half the men and be ready to put out fires! The rest of you gather up any kind of iron you can find—nails, anything!—that we can use to load these cannon! Move! For your lives!"

Sweating, cursing, he was loading the forward cannon, ramming home the charge, when the side of the *Four Winds* seemed to explode in a burst of black smoke as perhaps half-a-dozen cannon fired. The balls found their target in the *Cristobel*'s starboard side. The prison ship screamed as the missiles tore through her flesh with a roar like thunder. The men caught below screamed, too.

Jon closed his ears to the piteous cries of the wounded, and set his own cannon alight. It coughed, belching smoke, as it expelled its shell, kicking back so hard in its leather harness that it almost knocked him down. Grimly he wrestled it back into position, barely remarking that his first ball had done slight damage to the *Four Winds'* prow. Again he rammed home the shot and set the cannon alight. Again it fired.

Behind him men were yelling, some screaming in pain, running hither and yon across the deck as they tried to put out the fires caused by the warship's salvos. Jon knew the scene would be mass confusion, but he determinedly closed his mind to it. For now, his job was that of gunner, not captain. O'Reilly would have to direct the men. He concentrated on blowing the *Four Winds* to hell.

The huge frigate was getting into position for another broadside. Jon knew what she was about, and signalled to Logan and Berry at the other cannon. They had to coordinate their shots. He loaded his cannon, looked down and saw that the two men were ready, then lowered his hand. The three cannon boomed, simultaneously. Jon, watching their effect out of the corner of his eye as he struggled to get his gun ready to fire again, saw that one ball missed, one hit and caused slight damage, and the other tore a hole in the *Four Winds'* side.

The frigate was not long in replying. The full force of her dozen side cannon roared louder than any thunder clap Jon had ever heard. The missiles caught the *Cristobel* broadside. One brought down the mizzen. Jon could hear it crashing to the deck, hear the shrieks of men crushed by its weight. Jon scooped up the scrap brought him by his men, and rammed it into the cannon's mouth. By damn, if they wanted carnage, he'd give them carnage!

A savage smile curved his mouth as he set the charge alight. He'd seen this trick—peppering the deck of an enemy ship with shrapnel, each sliver of metal having the force of a bullet—used by the canniest pirates ever to sail the sea. He'd even used it a time or two himself. Now it was worth its weight in gold.

The cannon crashed, and he didn't even bother to check on any damage he might have caused the frigate. Instead he got the cannon in position and reloaded. Just as he was setting the charge alight he happened to glance around. He couldn't believe what his eyes were telling him. There, moving about the open deck, apparently bent on succoring the wounded, was Cathy!

"Holy Christ!" he yelled, incensed and frightened out of his wits at the same time. Stupid, mule-headed, defiant bitch, didn't she know she could be killed? She looked up at his bellow, her blue eyes meeting his. He saw tears streaking her face.

Behind him his cannon exploded. The force of it sent him flying across the deck to land with a crash against the opposite side of the prow. A horrible stinging sensation attacked the right side of his face and neck. He clawed at it, howling. He was on fire!

"Jon!" he heard Cathy screaming his name as if from a great distance. He was beating at his clothes by instinct, unable to see anything because of the black gunpowder that had been blown into his eyes.

Cold water dashed over him like a benediction from heaven, putting out the licking flames that had tried to eat his flesh. He rested for a moment in the aftermath of terror, his body limp against the hard boards of the deck. He felt his head lifted, and pillowed on something soft and sweet smelling. . . .

It might have been an instant or an eternity before he opened his eyes. His vision was still blurred from the after-effects of the gunpowder, but mercifully he seemed to be in one piece. What pain as there was he disregarded. He saw Cathy looking down at him, her lovely little face blackened with smoke and streaked with tears.

"I'm—all right," he croaked, and immediately her expression lightened. Jon realized that his head was cradled on her lap. Then he bethought himself of the abandoned cannon, and struggled into a sitting position. He had to get back to the gun. . . .

"It's blown up," Cathy said calmly, as if she could read his mind. Jon, following the direction of her eyes, finally understood what had happened. The ancient cannon, instead of firing as it was supposed to, had been unable to withstand the force of the charge. It had exploded, and now lay broken in half on the deck. He could consider himself lucky to be alive.

Cannon boomed, and the *Cristobel* shuddered from the impact. Jon rose shakily to his feet. As long as he still could, he would fight to the death. What other choice was there?

"Where are you going?" Cathy stood up with him, sounding on the verge of hysteria, her hands clutching at him as if she would never let him go. It was as if they were alone, stranded together on some quiet backwater while guns boomed and men screamed around them.

"Get back to the cabin, and for God's sake, stay there," he growled, disregarding her question and trying not to think that this might be the last time he would ever see her in this world.

"No!" Cathy's voice rose on the word, and she clutched him tighter. Jon's hands closed around the fingers that bit into his arm, gently prying them loose. For just a moment he stood with her hands in his, looking down into her woebegone little face.

"Cathy. . . ." he began, alarmed at the choking of his own voice. But there was no time left for pretty speeches, no time for sentiment. Firmly, jaw set, he put her from him. "Get back to the cabin."

He started to turn away. Her hands reached for him, then there came a roar more deafening than the opening of the gates of wrath on Judgement Day. Bright sheets of flame shot out of the open hatchway, coming from the *Cristobel*'s bowels. The ship leaped into the air with the impact of the explosion, shuddering in her death throes.

The powder! A cannonball from the warship had struck the gunpowder! Even as Jon registered it, the whole ship was ablaze. Tongues of fire shot up the two remaining masts, turning the fluttering sails into great crimson lakes. He stared, aghast, as the *Cristobel* was transformed in an instant into a blazing inferno. Screams of the terrified wounded, trapped by the racing conflagration, assaulted his ears; the smell of burning seared his nostrils.

"Come on!" he yelled, grabbing Cathy by the hand and dragging her after him. Acting more by instinct than reason, knowing only that he had to get them both out of this hell that threatened at any moment to surround and consume them, he took the only path open to him. A barrier of fire closed the prow off from the rest of the ship: impossible to reach beyond it. Crouching beside the scant protection of the port bulwark, he ran forward to where he knew a gig was secured. Reaching it, releasing Cathy's hand to free it and swing it up and over the side with demoniacal strength, he saw that the intense heat was already beginning to blister its paint.

The smoke was thick and black, its oily fingers reaching up his nose and down his throat. Cathy was coughing, he saw as he turned back to her.

"Get down!" he ordered hoarsely, pushing her into a crouching position. There was more air close to the deck, and less chance of either of them being hit by flying bits and pieces. Hot ashes from the blazing sails were beginning to drift down in great smoldering flakes, burning the skin where they touched. They had to get off the ship. At once, while they still could. The gig waited for them below, bobbing patiently in the water. Alone, he would have leapt over the side, and swum to safety. But there was Cathy, far gone with child, to consider. She was certainly a capable swimmer, but the fall to the water, in her condition, might do her serious injury.

Another explosion, rocking the ship, settled the question. They were out of time. Unless they were to be roasted like peanuts in the shell, they had to get out of here now. Standing up, Jon caught Cathy's hand in his, pulling her with him to a point just above and to the right of the gig. They were on the *Cristobel*'s port side, protected from the rampaging frigates' view by an enveloping pall of dense smoke.

"What are you doing?" Cathy cried as he ripped at her skirt. He had no time to explain that he was afraid the heavy folds would, when wet, drag her down.

"We're going to jump!" he yelled back, his hands spanning her waist from behind and lifting her to stand on the rocking bulwark. "And swim to the gig! Go! I'll be right behind you!"

Cathy turned to look at him, wide-eyed with fright, her small face pale under its covering of soot. Then she jumped. Jon watched her fall, the thin white skirt of her petticoat billowing over her head, careful to note her position so that he would not land on top of her. Then as he saw her hit the water and disappear beneath the waves, he threw himself from the ship.

He hit the water in a rough-and-ready dive, feeling its impact slap hard against his chest and belly. The breath was knocked from his lungs in a gasp, he clawed for the surface. He had to find Cathy . . . had to find Cathy . . . had to. . . .

She was there beside him when he surfaced, treading water, her hair trailing around her like long strands of seaweed. Shaking the water from his eyes, he could have laughed with relief if the need for movement hadn't been so urgent.

"Hurry!" he gasped, gesturing toward the gig which was floating amidst a sea of debris some thirty feet away. The *Cristobel* could sink like a stone at any moment, creating a terrifying whirlpool that would suck them down with her. Before that happened, they had to get clear!

Despite her pregnancy, Cathy swam strongly, keeping pace with him as he struck out for the gig. In a short time he was grasping the little boat's side, then pulling himself up and over. Wordlessly he reached down to grasp the hand that Cathy extended to him, hauling her over the side. She was soaking wet, shivering, and half-naked, but he had no time to worry about her now. Turning, he saw to his relief that the oars were still secured in their proper place along the gig's side. Freeing them, he grabbed a pair and sat amidships, rowing with all his might.

He didn't stop until they were safely away. Finally, when he judged them to be beyond the reach of both the *Cristobel*'s death tide and the frigates' line of vision, he shipped the oars for a much-needed breather. Dragging in great gulping breaths of air, he turned to look at Cathy, who sat huddled in the stern. Her slender legs, wrapped in the soggy folds of her nearly transparent petticoat, were drawn up to her chest, and her arms were wrapped around them for warmth. Her drying hair curled wildly around her small face. Big tears trickled down her salt and grime streaked cheeks. Her huge eyes, pain-shadowed, were fixed beyond him on the burning hulk of the *Cristobel.*

"Cathy," he said hoarsely, aching for her pain. She turned those drowned eyes on him.

"Angie," she croaked. "The others. . . ."

Her lips trembled as she contemplated their nearly-certain fate.

Jon's jaw tightened. More than anything in the world his instincts urged him to close the space between them, taking her in his arms and letting her weep out her grief on his shoulder. But there was no time yet for such softness. They were not yet safe.

"The frigates will pick up any survivors," he told her matter-of-factly. "If we got off the ship, so did others."

"Yes," Cathy said quietly, and he was relieved to see that his words seemed to have given her some comfort. Then he noticed that her lips were blue with cold, and her teeth chattered. Dusk was falling, which would greatly aid their escape, but the night would be cold, and she was wet and shocked.

He crawled to the locker set into the prow, opened it, and found to his relief that it was stocked with the essentials of survival. Apparently the *Cristobel*'s former masters had been as doubtful of her seaworthiness as he had been himself, and had prepared just in case circumstances should set them adrift. Among other items, he found a blanket, several twists of dried beef jerky, a couple of canteens of water, and a bottle of whiskey. He grinned wryly as he pulled out this last. Whoever had provisioned the gig had meant to entertain himself while at sea. Then a hard, round object came under his hand. As he identified it his grin widened. A compass! So they would not be totally lost.

"Here, wrap this around you," he said to Cathy, passing her the blanket. "But first take off the rest of those wet clothes. You'll catch pneumonia if you sit around like that for long."

He moved back to his seat amidships, passing her the blanket. She took it apathetically, her eyes still focused on the orange-and-red funeral pyre behind them.

"Don't look at it," he advised quietly, hating the horror that haunted her face. "There's nothing we can do for them. We have to think of ourselves—and the baby. Understand?"

To his relief, she nodded, then started to undress. As she dried herself with the blanket, then wrapped it around her to ward off the cold, he began again to row.

The night, as he predicted, was cold. But the water was relatively smooth, and a full white moon rose to light their path. Cathy came to huddle at his feet, and went to sleep with her head in his lap. As he continued to row, he watched her sleeping face with a tenderness that made his throat ache. Today he had almost lost her forever. . . .

It was nearly dawn when she stirred, and sat up. The sky over the eastern horizon was just beginning to pinken. Jon, dead tired, stiff, and aching from his long night of rowing, was just about to ask her to pass him the whiskey when he noticed that her face seemed unnaturally drawn.

"What's wrong?" he asked sharply, a nameless dread beginning to creep along his veins. Against his legs he could feel her stiffen suddenly. She whimpered, a low, moaning sound dredged up from deep inside her; her hand rose to press tightly against her bulging belly.

thirteen

⤝⤞

Cathy was having her baby. It hurt, oh, God, it hurt! She tried her best to hold back her screams of pain, conscious of Jon's white face bending over her, but she could not. The agony had gone on too long. . . . One day, was it, or two? She had lost track of time, consumed by the torment of her own body. Instead of minutes, she counted knife-thrusts of anguish. She was barely aware of the rocking of the small boat, of the canopy Jon had rigged for her from his tattered shirt to protect her from the blinding sun. Her whole being was focused on the heaving mound of her belly, on this thing that threatened to rend her in two as it thrust forth into the world.

"Bear down one more time, sweetheart, please!"

Jon's hoarse, urgent voice seemed to float to her from a distance. "Bear down," he kept telling her. She wanted to shriek at him that bearing down hurt, that it made the dreadful throes of childbirth just that much more excruciating. But she didn't have the strength.

"Cathy, bear down!"

It was a command this time. Resentfully, Cathy obeyed.

The grinding, twisting torment shot up through her vitals as all her muscles strained to eject her burden. Her nails dug deep into Jon's leg, drawing blood. Neither of them noticed. Jon, ashen-faced, sweating profusely, watched for some sign that the child was indeed ready to be born. Cathy writhed, groaning piteously. Her throat was so raw and sore from crying out that it hurt to make even that sound.

Nothing happened. Cathy, sobbing, twisting from side to side, prayed for a surcease from pain. Jon witnessed her silent torment, and prayed himself. God, this was worse than anything he could have imagined in his worst nightmare! She had been laboring for nearly twenty-four hours in this open boat with only himself, with his memories of birthing colts and calves, to help her. He was hideously afraid that she was going to die. He had done everything he knew how to make her more comfortable, but she was clearly in agony. Gritting his teeth, he wished vainly that he could bear the pain himself. Anything rather than see her suffer so! But he could not. He could only watch, and help her as best he could. The rest was up to her, and to God!

His mouth twisted in a reflection of her suffering as another spasm contorted her face, dragging from her a tortured moan. She was being so brave! He knew she was doing her best to muffle her cries, wanting to spare him full knowledge of what she was going through. His heart bled for her.

"Scream, Cathy," he had told her early on, when he realized that she was trying to bite back the sounds that wanted to tear from her throat. "Scream, sweetheart, if it makes you feel better."

Finally she had, simply because, he suspected, she could hold out no longer. Each scream had torn through him like a sword thrust. Wincing, he had held her hands helplessly, not even feeling it when her nails dug bloody furrows along his wrists and upper arms.

"Rest now," he told her as her latest spasm eased. She lay panting, her face as white as death, her bright hair tangled and sweat-darkened, fanning out in a snarled mass around her face. Jon knelt between her drawn up knees, watching, waiting for the first signs of the child. So far there had been none. He was sore afraid that if her labor went on much longer, Cathy would be too weak to fight for her life. Grinding his teeth, he felt a surge of hatred for this thing that was killing her right before his eyes. If it had sprung from his own seed, then he was a murderer as well. If it was Harold's—Jon's eyes flashed bitterly. If Cathy died, he would kill Harold.

"Oh, God!" she moaned, another contraction hitting her. Jon watched her huge belly convulse, and with some hazy knowledge of having once seen Petersham do the same thing to a mare in difficulties, he placed his hand on the mound and pushed downward. Her head thrashed from side to side and she groaned, the sound making him wince. The one ray of hope lay in the fact that her spasms were getting closer together, and harder. Surely this meant that the child was on the verge of emerging? He prayed that it was so. Tears of pain and weakness coursed down Cathy's white cheeks. Seeing them, Jon felt moisture in his own eyes.

"Try one more time, sweetheart," he encouraged her when she seemed on the verge of giving up. "Just one more time. Cathy, you have to try!"

Cathy, dazed by pain, nevertheless heard his voice with some tiny corner of her mind that was still functioning rationally. Why did he keep pestering her? she thought resentfully. When all she wanted to do was just lie here, and quietly fall asleep. . . .

Her own body refused to let her. It convulsed agonizingly, and she screamed before she could stop herself. The sound ripped through the bright, sparkling peace of the afternoon, bounced across the gently rolling waves, and was gone for lack of an audience. In all this vast, wide ocean, there seemed to be only herself and Jon—and the monster pain. It was devouring her like a sea serpent, and she was growing so weary of fighting it that she was ready to give up and let it pull her beneath the waves. Only Jon, with his urgent, coaxing voice and strong hands, wouldn't let her. Couldn't he see that she was tired . . . ?

Another stab of fiery torment racked her. Cathy tensed, screaming, feeling as if she would be split in half. Between her legs Jon gave a hoarse cry of triumph.

"It's coming! Cathy, it's coming! Keep pushing, sweetheart, we're almost there!"

She could feel his hands on her, trying to help her, and she no longer had to worry about obeying his commands. Her body was doing it for her. Without her volition, it strained to expel the intruder in her womb. Gasping, sobbing, tears rolling down her cheeks, she pushed with all her might. Suddenly the thing seemed to be forced from her like a cork from a bottle of champagne. Sagging with relief, she went limp. She could feel a sticky warmth spreading between her legs.

"Cathy, you did it! God, you did it!" Jon was exultant, a beaming smile splitting his dark face, as he caught the emerging child in his hands. He saw that Cathy was pale and limp, totally unaware of what he was doing. For a moment his heart stopped. Then he noted the swift rise and fall of her breasts and was reassured. She had merely fainted with the last excruciating pains, he told himself. And it was best to let her rest until he had her squared away. Thinking that, he looked down anxiously at the tiny form in his arms, still attached to its mother by the cord. What did one do with a baby now? he wondered frantically. Vague memories of himself bursting into the room just after Cray's birth returned to him. The doctor had held the boy up by the heels, slapping his little rear, and Cray had screamed his head off. That was what he must do now—to this tiny girl, Jon realized as he really looked at the newborn child for the first time. But first he had to cut the cord. Laying the infant rather awkwardly on his leg, he reached into the scabbard at his belt for his knife. Pulling it out, he stared at it with a frown. He would have to sterilize it as best he could. . . . Sparingly he poured whiskey over it, and when that was done looked rather longingly at the bottle. He could have done with a hearty swig, but there wasn't much left, and he might need it for Cathy. He put the bottle aside, and with a single swift movement cut the cord. Knotting it at both ends in a sturdy sailor's knot, he caught the child by the heels, feeling cruel as he administered a sound buffet to its minuscule bottom. To his relief, and amazement, the baby opened her prunish little mouth and bawled.

By the time Cathy opened her eyes again, the sun was falling. Deep purple and orange pinwheels swirled out from the enormous ball. The ocean was the color of pansies, broken in long, rhythmic lines by touches of white. The little boat rocked gently up and down, and Cathy felt lulled by the sound of the water lapping softly against the hull. She stirred, lifting her head. Not far away she could see Jon, his big body folded in what must have been a most uncomfortable position as he sat cross-legged in the bottom of the boat. He was rocking back and forth, and a husky crooning sound seemed to be emerging from his throat. She stared. What on earth was he doing? Then she saw the tiny, black-swathed bundle he held in his hands, and memory came flooding back. Her baby! Stretching out her arms with a low, joyous murmur, she reached for the child.

Jon looked up at the sound she made, a smile twisting his long mouth.

"You have a daughter," he told her, placing the child in her arms. Cathy stared down at the wrinkled little face with delight.

"A daughter," she breathed. Then, recalling his words, she

looked up and met his silvery eyes with a slight frown. "*We* have a daughter," she corrected.

Jon met her blue eyes, still shadowed with pain, his own unreadable.

"*We* have a daughter," he agreed expressionlessly.

Reassured, Cathy went back to her rapt contemplation of the infant in her arms. Jon had washed her, and the red, wrinkled little face looked sweet and clean as she slept, oblivious to her mother's inspection. She was wrapped in a bit of cloth torn from the leg of Jon's breeches, and Cathy smiled as she unwrapped it to inspect the child's tiny body. At this rate, Jon would soon be naked. . . . The baby was perfect in every detail, with ten tiny fingers and toes—Cathy counted. Downy tufts of reddish hair covered her head. To Cathy's fond eyes she was gorgeous, and she smiled as she looked up to convey this news to Jon.

"She's perfect," she said happily, and Jon smiled slowly back at her.

"I know," he said.

They sat there smiling rather foolishly at each other, and Cathy felt a surge of love for him. He had his faults, as who didn't? But he was a rock to lean on in times of trouble. How many men could have got her safely away from a burning ship and delivered her baby all in the space of forty-eight hours? Not many. Most that she knew would have been as helpless as she had been herself. Jon was a man to depend on.

She opened her mouth to tell him so, then was interrupted by a small whimper from her daughter. Cathy stared down, entranced, into eyes that were as blue as her own.

"She's hungry," Jon said sparely as the whimper deepened and lengthened into a howl.

"Yes," Cathy acknowledged, then felt her cheeks pinken as she parted the blanket that Jon had apparently wrapped her in after the birth. Beneath it she was naked. It was ridiculous to feel embarrassed, she scolded herself as she put the child to her breast. But she looked up to find Jon's gray eyes, darkened to pewter with some emotion she couldn't read, fixed on her with the child at her breast, and felt her blush deepen. He saw her color, and tactfully turned his gaze away.

While Cathy fed the baby, Jon resumed his long-interrupted rowing. He had let the gig drift while Cathy had been in labor. They had somehow caught on a current that had pulled them due south, which suited him as well as any other direction would have. But now that the child was safely delivered, he had to pull hard for land. Their supplies, including water, were running very low. He was sure that the danger of their position had not yet occurred to Cathy, and he wanted to be safely near shore before she realized what they faced.

When he looked around again, both Cathy and the child were asleep. The infant was cradled in her arms, the blanket wrapped carefully around them both. Jon, shirtless, shivered in the rapidly cooling night air. He hoped that the blanket was enough to keep them warm.

He rowed through the night, pushing himself long past the point of exhaustion. Now was not the time to succumb to the physical limitations of his body. If he was cold, tired, and hungry, then so be it. Cathy and her child—he still had deep reservations about its paternity; that orangey hair had not gone unremarked—were dependent on him for their very lives. He meant to bring them through safely, or die in the attempt.

Dawn was just beginning to light the eastern sky when he could keep exhaustion at bay no longer. His eyelids felt as if they were being forced down by lead weights. Hugely he yawned, shipping the oars as silently as he could so as not to rouse Cathy or the child. Then he spread his arms wide, stretching his cramped muscles. The gig had caught another strong southerly current, which he reckoned should take them toward land. There was a small chain of islands somewhere in the vicinity, if he remembered this stretch of ocean correctly. With luck they would sight them sometime tomorrow. Or maybe not. During Cathy's ordeal, he had been so taken up with her suffering that they could have drifted a hundred miles from where he thought they were and he would never even have noticed.

Moving as carefully as he could so as not to rock the boat more than he had to, Jon settled himself down near Cathy and the baby, thinking that he could share his body heat with them, and perhaps in return garner some of their own. It was bitterly cold.

As he settled himself on his back, he glanced regretfully at the blanket securely insulating Cathy and the child from the blowing wind. Clad only in his ragged black breeches, even his boots having been abandoned in the swim for the gig, he had nothing but his body hair to warm him, and that was hardly sufficient. But he had suffered more, for less reason. Closing his eyes, determinedly ignoring the shivers that racked him, Jon fell almost immediately asleep.

Cathy was roused by a whimper and the feel of a small mouth rooting hungrily against her breast. Groggily, she offered the child her nipple, and as it greedily suckled set herself to waking up. She raised one hand to push the tangled hair from her eyes, and she blinked against the already bright morning sun. Frowning, she realized that the boat seemed to be drifting aimlessly. Where was Jon? she thought, concerned, and struggled into a sitting position, the infant still snuggled to her breast. With her back resting against the gunwale, she saw him. He was sprawled quite near, lying on his back with one arm flung over his head, his long legs draped over the rear seat in what looked to be a most uncomfortable position. He appeared to be deeply asleep. Cathy smiled tenderly, looking at him. He was shirtless, the thick black pelt covering his chest not enough to conceal the deep red of sunburn that even his dark skin had not prevented as he had sat exposed in the sun hour after hour, delivering their daughter. His bronzed face was tinged with red, too, she saw, especially on the right side where flames from the exploding cannon had caught him. Thick black lashes lay with the innocence of childhood against his lean cheeks. Stubble obscured his jaw and chin, and his black hair was wildly disordered. Her eyes swept his long, strong body with the pride of possession; a frown marred the serenity of Cathy's brow as she noted that his steely muscles were ridged with gooseflesh. Looking down at herself, she realized that of course he had given her and the baby the only blanket. He must be freezing! Her eyes searched for her clothing, so that she could dress herself and spare him the blanket. All she had was the linen petticoat and white blouse in which she had leapt from the *Cristobel*. Vaguely she recalled Jon tossing them aside as she had struggled to produce their daughter. Where could they have landed? Then she saw them, wadded into a ball not far away. They would be horribly wrinkled, but at least they would cover her nakedness—she would wear the petticoat and use the blouse to clothe the baby.

The little girl finished her meal and dropped off to sleep as quickly as she had awakened. Cathy put her gently aside, laying her carefully out of harm's way. Then she crawled painfully after her clothes, pulled the loose petticoat over her head, and gathered up the blanket to spread over Jon's recumbent form. He never so much as stirred as she covered him. Smiling, Cathy moved to wrap the baby in her blouse. Then she settled herself as comfortably as possible and began to consider names.

When Jon awoke at last, the mid-day sun was blazing hotly down. He stirred uncomfortably, feeling much like a fish baking on a stone. When he opened his eyes, he saw that only his face was protected from the burning rays by the canopy of his shirt. Cathy was seated quite near him, under the canopy, her knees drawn up and the child cradled in her lap. Her blue eyes were smiling as they met his.

"Good morning," she said gravely.

Jon yawned and sat up, his head brushing the canopy as he ducked from beneath it.

"You gave me the blanket," he said, almost accusingly, as he noticed it for the first time twined around his legs.

"You looked cold," Cathy explained. Jon frowned at her.

"How do you feel?" he asked, anxiety shading his voice.

"A lot better than I did at this time yesterday," she answered with a wry grin.

Jon, remembering her agony, did not grin back. If anything, he looked even more worried.

"You should be resting," he told her sternly. "God, you even got dressed! You're not strong enough. . . ."

"I'm fine," Cathy interrupted quietly. "Really!"

To tell the truth, she still felt quite weak, but that was only to be expected, after all. And she certainly wasn't going to tell Jon. He would be convinced that she was at death's door.

He looked skeptical.

"You should be resting, not moving around," he repeated stubbornly. Cathy sighed, and the baby whimpered at her movement and then was still. Jon fixed the tiny form with his eyes, his frown deepening.

"Is she all right?" he demanded, hazy memories of Cray's lusty bawling flitting through his head. "She seems awfully quiet."

"She's fine, too," Cathy assured him with a smile. "And I've thought of a name: what do you say to Virginia, after your mother?"

Jon said nothing, just stared at her with narrowed gray eyes. If the child really was his—and she could be; her birth date made that possible—that was the name he himself would have chosen. But if she were Harold's, born prematurely from the multiple traumas Cathy had suffered, then. . . . Cathy was staring at him expectantly, waiting for his response. What did it matter? Jon decided silently. They could sort out the child's paternity at some later date. For now, Cathy's well-being was what mattered most to him. If it made her happy to insist that the baby was his, and name it after his mother, then he would not object.

"Virginia suits me," he said. "As long as her middle name is Catherine. For *her* mother."

Cathy beamed at him. "Virginia Catherine," she repeated slowly, glancing down at the sleeping infant. Then she looked quickly back at Jon, her eyes twinkling. "What do you think Cray will say when he finds out he has a sister?"

"I can't imagine," Jon answered dryly, his eyes flickering to the child. Then he decided it was best to leave that topic before it became sticky, and rose to his knees.

"I bet you're hungry." He changed the subject adroitly. Cathy nodded.

"I am," she replied a little hesitantly. "But is there enough food? I can wait. . . ."

She sounded worried, and Jon realized that the true exigencies of their position were beginning to occur to her.

"There's plenty," he said harshly, to cover up the lie. "Jerky, anyway, and if we run low there's always fish."

He jerked his head in the direction of the ocean, his mouth twisting with forced humor. Cathy smiled, as he had intended, her worried expression clearing.

"Somehow I can't see you as an expert fisherman," she murmured teasingly as he crawled to the end of the boat, where their precious supply of jerky and water was stored. Jon grinned at her over his shoulder.

"My accomplishments are legion," he announced, sounding injured that she should doubt it. Cathy's eyes twinkled.

"I know," she murmured roguishly. Jon, returning with the supplies, laughed aloud.

"Eat, you provocative minx," he ordered gruffly, passing her a generous piece of the dried beef. "Before I forget that you're incapacitated. I have other appetites besides food, you know."

"I remember," Cathy replied in the same provocative tone she had used before, her blue eyes sparkling at him. Jon groaned, and tweaked a lock of her golden hair in retaliation. When he said nothing Cathy gnawed hungrily at the jerky. She was almost finished with it before she noticed that Jon was not eating.

"You're not eating," she accused, her eyes round as they searched his face.

"I ate before I went to sleep," Jon lied smoothly. "I'm not hungry. Finish your food."

But Cathy would not. Stubbornly she held what was left of her piece of jerky out to him, insisting he take it.

"If you don't eat, I don't," she told him firmly. Jon had not eaten for more than twenty-four hours, thinking it best to save what food there was for Cathy, who needed it far more than he did. He was hungry, but he refused to take more than a bite to humor her. If he was wrong about their location, they might be at sea for a long time. With his large frame, he could survive without food for quite a while. But Cathy—and the baby. . . . He shuddered to think of what long days at sea without food would do to them. Because, of course, catching fish, without hook, line, or bait, was far easier said than done.

"Where are we?" she asked a little later, after she had sipped from the water jug and settled back comfortably against the gunwale, holding the sleeping Virginia on her lap.

Jon grimaced. "As near as I can make out, we're midway between the Madeira Islands and the Canary Islands. There's another strip of islands through here, small ones, that the Portuguese call Ilhas Desertas—the deserted islands. With luck, we should make landfall on one of them."

"Shouldn't we head for somewhere with people?" Cathy sounded faintly doubtful.

"Beggars can't be choosers, my love, did no one ever tell you that?" Jon responded a shade grimly. Cathy heard only the endearment. His love. More than anything in the world she wanted to be that again. Now that he had accepted Virginia as his daughter, there was really nothing to keep them apart. She would forgive him his earlier suspicions, and even Sarita, and he would admit that he had been totally, stupidly wrong about Harold. The thought of Harold caused her a moment's unease. He was, after all, still her legal husband, and she supposed that made him Virginia's legal, if not biological, father. . . . But she resolutely pushed that thought aside. She could worry about that later. For the moment, she gave Jon her most dazzling smile.

"Am I your love?" she asked softly. Jon's eyes darkened as he looked at her. Hearing, he pretended not to.

Jon rowed steadily for the next few hours, stopping only to take brief sips from the water bottle. The first time Cathy brought this to him, he ordered her fiercely not to move about so. He could tell that she was not feeling as well as she wanted him to think. She needed rest, and so he told her, glaring at her so sternly that she meekly agreed to do as he said.

Cathy dozed, and fed Virginia, who slept like an angel most of the day. The sun beat down mercilessly on the small boat. Without the protection of Jon's shirt-canopy, she knew she would have been burnt to a crisp. She huddled beneath it, doing her best to keep Virginia cool, feeling uncomfortably warm herself. Every time she looked at Jon, his muscles bulging and glistening with sweat as he worked to get them safely ashore, she felt a surge of love. Perspiration poured down his face, and his black hair was wet with it. Rivulets ran down amongst the thick fur covering his chest. The sun had turned his skin a deep red-brown, almost the color of an American Indian Cathy had once seen. She knew he had to be hellishly hot, sore and hungry, for he still refused to eat more than a bite, instead watching her threateningly until she consumed what he decreed she should eat. But he continued to row with tireless strength, and Cathy's admiration grew with every stroke. He was truly a man in a million. She was proud that he was her children's father. He was the strongest, handsomest, bravest man she had ever known!

Every glance she bestowed on him was soft with feeling. Jon had no trouble interpreting the looks she turned on him, but he was wary of her seeming affection. How much of it was genuine and how much brought on by the knowledge that, without him, she and her child would be at the mercy of a merciless fate? he wondered with forced cynicism. As he had learned to his cost, she was entirely capable of succumbing to cupboard love, which would vanish as soon as the need for it did. His heart was in an odd, fluctuating state, his emotions so confused that he didn't know what he felt. Only one thing was perfectly clear to him: loving her openly had brought him nothing but heartache. If love her he still did—and he was admitting nothing, not even to himself—he would take good care that she should never find it out.

The sun went down, and still Jon continued to row. They had sighted nothing, not so much as a coral reef, certainly nothing that could be remotely classed as land. He began to feel worried. If he was wrong about where they were—and it was very possible—they could drift out to sea and eventually die. Jon didn't fool himself that Cathy and the child would last for long in an open boat. Already Cathy's face was flushed a bright pink by the sun even though she had been shaded from it by his shirt. With her fair skin, she wouldn't stand a chance. Jon thought of her dying in such a way, and his resolve stiffened. He would get her safely ashore, please God. . . . And the baby, too, of course.

Toward morning he slept again, sharing the blanket at Cathy's insistence. She had awoken as he lay down by her side, and had cuddled against his chest, her head resting on his shoulder as she drew the blanket over them both. Virginia she had placed between them. Jon had been too tired to pro-test. He was grateful for the warmth, both of the blanket and her affection, however mercurial. Curling one arm around her shoulders, he had brushed her soft hair with his lips before falling asleep with the suddenness of a thunderclap.

The next day was sheer hell. The sun beamed down even hotter than before, so hot as to make the wooden sides of the boat painful to touch. The food was nearly gone, and Jon in-sisted that Cathy should eat what was left. Thinking of her small, fragile body and the child that drew its strength from her, he was easily able to ignore his own emptiness. The water was in short supply as well. Jon consumed his fair share of that, knowing that if he did not, laboring as he was under the broiling sun, he would soon pass out. Then much good would he be to anyone.

Virginia wailed incessantly, a thin, reedy cry that nothing Cathy did could hush. Vainly she offered the child her breast, sponged her down with sea water, sang to her. Still the baby cried. It became as much a background noise as the gentle slurp-slurp of the sea.

"She's so hot," Cathy said to Jon when Virginia had fi-nally fallen asleep. Her tone was a combination of apology and worry. Jon, looking across at her, thought that she looked as if she were suffering from the heat herself. Every inch of her skin not covered by that loose white petticoat was red-dened. Her blue eyes were huge and appeared unfocused; her mouth was slightly swollen by the sun. Golden wisps of hair escaped from the thick braid she had secured with a strip torn from her petticoat to frame her small face. Suddenly Jon was struck by the fact that she no longer seemed to be sweating. Alarmed, he reached out a hand to her, feeling her forehead and cheeks and hands. She was burning hot, and not from the sun. It was fever!

If Jon had thought the past four days were a nightmare, he had no words to describe what happened next. Cathy was desperately ill, with what he suspected was child-bed fever. His own mother had died with it after giving birth to him, and he was mortally afraid that it would claim Cathy too. She lapsed in and out of consciousness, sometimes knowing him, sometimes not. He cared for her as best he could, sponging her fiery body with sea water, forcing sips of what fresh water remained between her lips, even managing to spear a fish with his knife and feed her its tender flesh. He cared for Virginia, too, out of necessity. It was not in him simply to let the child die, although sometimes, when it seemed as if he would lose Cathy at any moment, he wished with all the strength left in him that she had never been conceived. Grimly he pictured his life without Cathy in it, and knew it for an empty vessel. She was all the world to him, and she was slipping away. . . .

Jon prayed as he had never prayed before in his life. He made God impossible promises if He would only let Cathy live. But as he grimly held Virginia to Cathy's fever-hot breast, he began to prepare himself for the worst. No one could burn so, and survive.

That night she was delirious, calling out his name and yet not seeming to see him as he loomed above her. She thrashed wildly, sobbing with pain and fear. Jon, restraining her as gently as he could, felt tears roll down his own cheeks. God, he loved her—he couldn't hide from the knowledge any longer. And she was dying. . . .

The moon rose high above them, casting its silvery light down over the small boat and its occupants. Jon, looking down with anguish into Cathy's unconscious face, thought that she looked like a ghost already. Under his hands, she was small and helpless, as small and helpless as the infant who lay sleeping fitfully at her side. He felt fiercely protective of her, wanting to gather her up in his arms and howl at the cruel fate that seemed determined to snatch her away. She had no one but him to save her, and he could not. The realization was tearing him apart.

"Hot—so hot," Cathy breathed fretfully, her shadow-filled blue eyes opening wide and gazing directly into his, seeming to see him. Jon tenderly smoothed the tangled hair back away from her forehead, wiping the sizzling surface of her skin with a damp cloth.

"I know, sweetheart," he murmured consolingly, barely able to get the words out past the lump in his throat. Beside him, Virginia stirred, whimpering. Jon barely noticed the baby's cries; all his attention centered on Cathy.

"Cray," she whispered, turning her head blindly as she searched for the source of the sound. "Cray," she said again, more firmly this time, and reached out her hands toward the wailing infant. Her arms were too weak to support even that small movement, and her hands fell helplessly to her sides. Still she yearned toward the child, until Jon, his throat working, picked the baby up and placed her on Cathy's belly. Cathy's hands came up again to gently rub her tiny back. Virginia quieted almost at once. Cathy's eyes closed then, and she seemed to smile. Her hands fell limply back.

"Cathy," Jon groaned, agony tearing at his chest as he felt that she was on the very verge of death. "Cathy, darling, please don't leave me! Cathy, I need you. Cray needs you. The baby needs you. Please don't leave us, Cathy. Cathy, I love you!"

She was oblivious to his words, her breath seeming to barely move her ribs. Jon bowed his head over her still form, his tears dropping onto her white face.

"Please, God," he prayed over and over again. "Let her live. Please!"

He could feel heat rising from her body in radiant bursts, heat which threatened to kill her. If he could just bring down her fever a little bit. . . . He raised his head, thinking hard, and cool salt spray, borne on the light wind, hit him in the face.

The sea! Nearly her killer, perhaps it could be turned into her salvation! Before the thought was even completed, Jon was straightening, unwrapping the blanket from about her, stripping her of the thin petticoat. He would dip her bodily in the sea!

Not even bothering to divest himself of his breeches, Jon picked Cathy up in his arms and carefully rolled over the side of the gig with her, holding her tightly as the waves closed over their heads. He kept one hand clamped over her nose and mouth in case she should try to inhale, and kicked strongly for the surface. When their heads were above the water, he turned over onto his back, letting her limp body rest against his chest as he treaded water. He stayed close to the side of the boat, moving just enough to keep the two of them afloat.

It was nearly dawn by the time he hauled first her and then himself back aboard. He shivered convulsively, but paid no heed to his own discomfort. Instead he knelt beside Cathy's pale, naked body, his hands moving over her first with dread and then with hope. She had been so still against him in the water that he had begun to fear that the shock had killed her. But now he saw that she was still breathing, her breasts rising and falling rhythmically as she drew in air. And her skin was cool to the touch. . . . Dear God, he might have done the trick! She might live! The thought was intoxicating. Jon wanted to laugh, to cry, to sing hosannas aloud from sheer relief. But, he cautioned himself, nothing was a certainty yet, and if he did not want her to come down with pneumonia on top of everything else he had better get her dry, and out of the night air.

He wiped the moisture from her body with her petticoat, using it to towel her hair and then wrapping it turban-fashion around her head. Finally he wrapped her and the baby carefully in the blanket and lay down beside her, taking her wool-shrouded shape in his arms. She sighed, settling against him, and Jon's arms tightened protectively around her. She seemed to be sleeping. . . .

Jon pressed a gentle kiss to her forehead, noting that the skin felt cool to the touch.

"Thank you, God," he murmured as he closed his eyes, and then he, too, slept.

When he awoke, it was to the reedy sound of Virginia crying. It was broad daylight, but the sky was clouded over. Rain later, Jon prophesied with a grimace, but for now at least the cloud cover would serve to keep the sun off Cathy. He turned to look at her, still lying cradled in his arms. Her eyes were closed, and her skin was very pale, but it was cool to the touch, and her breathing was deep and regular. She looked to be sleeping, a natural, healing sleep. She needed it. He would not disturb her, not even for Virginia. The child would have to make do with him until her mother awoke.

Carefully he put Cathy aside, pillowing her head on a fold of the blanket. She sighed, turning over to snuggle on her side, one hand beneath her head. Long, golden strands of hair, having freed themselves from the turban in the night, fanned out from her head. Jon, looking at her, felt a wave of love so intense as to make him feel physically weak. Whatever she was, whatever she had done, he loved her. The rest of his life would have to be worked around that fact.

Virginia's cries had subsided to watery hiccups by the time Jon picked her up. He held her awkwardly, looking down with mixed emotions at the squirming bundle in his arms. On the one hand, she was Cathy's daughter, and possibly his own. But then again, she could just as possibly be Harold's, and she had certainly nearly cost her mother her life. A surge of resentment died as he watched her wave her tiny fists and kick her little feet, to be replaced by pity, and a sense of protectiveness. She was so tiny, so completely at his mercy. What could he do but be kind to her?

He laid her along his knee, amused to find her blue eyes open and seeming to regard him. He smiled, and she watched him gravely. He frowned, and her expression didn't change. He thought, she looks like Cathy, and felt the first faint wave of affection for this small scrap of humanity. Then, as he gently joggled his knee up and down for her entertainment, his eyes widened. A trickle of moisture seeped through what was left of his breeches. For a moment he stared down at Virginia, stupefied.

"By damn, she's wet on me!" he thought, and began to laugh.

By the time he had rather gingerly cleaned Virginia up, and taken another dip in the sea to rid himself of lingering traces of her presence, the little girl was crying again. She was hungry, Jon knew, but there was nothing he could do about that. He tried to ignore the pitiful wails, setting himself to rowing as hard as he could for where he guessed the nearest land to be. But the child's cries battered at him ceaselessly. Finally he could stand it no longer. Getting up, he moved carefully to where Virginia lay, and picked her up. She stared up at him balefully, her little face crimson with temper. Jon, thinking of Cathy in a tantrum, had to grin. Unless he was very much mistaken, this one was going to be a chip off the old block!

Doing his best not to wake Cathy, he gently pulled the blanket aside and set Virginia to her breast, holding the child while she nursed. Cathy stirred, and smiled, her hand coming up to cradle the baby's head before falling weakly back. Her eyes fluttered, and then were still. Jon realized with a sinking sensation in the pit of his stomach that she still had a long, long way to go before she was well again.

Late that afternoon the rain started. It was just a gentle drizzle, not a downpour, but it soon soaked through the shirt-canopy to fall on Cathy's face in tiny silvery droplets. Soon he saw that she was shivering. Cursing, he stopped rowing and crossed to lie beside her, drawing her into his arms and wrapping the blanket around the three of them. His body shielded Cathy and Virginia from the rain, and his body heat warmed them. That he himself was growing cold, and wet, he disregarded.

As he lay there, his arms wrapped around the one person who meant more to him than he had ever thought another human being could, Jon nearly gave way to despair. Unless they reached land soon, they would die. The food was gone, and catching fish was a very iffy business. He himself was growing used to constant hunger pangs, but in her weakened state Jon was afraid that lack of food could kill Cathy. If her milk dried up, as he had seen signs of it doing, then Virginia would die, too. And this constant exposure to the weather— first baking sun, then rain. Next, with his luck, it would snow. He couldn't believe that God had saved Cathy from the fever only to let her die now!

Jon was making another deal with God when a sound rolled to him over the swelling waves. At first he couldn't believe his ears, but then he sat up with a yelp of joy. The sound startled Virginia, who began to whimper, but Jon paid her no mind; instead, his eyes strained frantically to see through the mist surrounding them. Because what he thought he heard were breakers. And breakers meant land ahead.

fourteen

❧

Ever afterward, Cathy had only the vaguest recollections of the days immediately following Virginia's birth. Of the impressions that did stay with her, it was hard to separate dreams from reality. Had Jon really cried, bending over her, when she had lain so sick in the bottom of the boat? Had he told her that he loved her and needed her, and prayed to a God she hadn't known he believed in when he had thought she might die? She wasn't sure. But if those were dreams, they were lovely ones, and she clung to them. Remembering them, as she struggled to regain her strength, heartened her. Her smiles at Jon were slow and sweet, and tenderness shone from her eyes whenever they touched him.

She distinctly remembered him carrying her and Virginia ashore through rolling waves, then going back for the boat. He had worked hard to make a shelter to get them out of the rain, using the upended boat as one side and a sandy cliff as the other. It was this shelter in which she was lying now. They had been on the island for perhaps five days, and she was able to sit up without his help, and to nurse Virginia. Poor baby, she was thin from her ordeal, but we'll soon fix that, Cathy thought, looking over to where the little girl lay sleeping not far away. Cathy knew that she had grown thin herself. But after the porpoise-shape she had sported for what seemed like years, it was a welcome change.

Jon had gone out to find food, and Cathy did not expect him back for some time. They had been fortunate enough to be washed up on an island lush with tropical vegetation, including fruit trees. After the diet of jerky that had sustained her for nearly ten days, Cathy was ready to gorge herself on bananas and mangos, oranges and papayas. But Jon insisted that she needed protein if she was going to get well, and Cathy wasn't up to arguing with him. Besides, he was probably right, and she meekly ate what fish he managed to spear, and the birds' eggs he found and boiled for her. Virginia too benefited from this improved diet, and it did Cathy's heart good to see her daughter beginning to thrive as she should. Thanks to Jon, they were surviving very well, Cathy thought with a surge of pride.

He had issued strict orders that she was not to move around, and so far Cathy had followed these to the letter. But now, looking at the sun pouring in through the V-shaped opening at the front of the crude shelter, she was conscious of a desire to have a look around outside.

"I must be feeling better," Cathy thought humorously, "if I'm starting to get curious about where we are." Just a few days ago she hadn't even much cared whether or not she was alive.

Jon would have a fit, she knew, if he should return and catch her, but Cathy thought that was unlikely. He had only been gone about three-quarters of an hour, and at the rate he caught fish, fetching supper should take him quite a while.

Thus reassuring herself, Cathy crawled to the door of the shelter, which was not tall enough to permit her to stand upright. As she reached the entrance, the bright sun bouncing off the sparkling white sand momentarily blinded her. She shut her eyes, opening them only gradually so that they could adjust to the dazzling light. Finally she could look upon the scene before her without pain, and she stared, entranced.

They had come ashore on a small, semicircular beach surrounding a deep blue bay. White-capped waves whispered gently as they brushed the shore perhaps thirty yards away. Behind her the beach rose in sandy white cliffs, and it was against one of these that Jon had propped the boat to form the basis of their hut. She saw now that he had covered it with branches and other vegetation to keep out the rain and heat alike. No wonder the inside had been shadowy and cool, Cathy thought, and marveled at Jon's resourcefulness before returning to her contemplation of the scene. Down by the water's edge gulls ran to and fro, playing a kind of game with the lapping ocean. Occasionally one would wheel into the air, calling raucously to its fellows. Further out in the water, tall pink flamingos waded, their long bills dipping quickly in and out of the sea as they searched for food. The air was sweet with the scent of wild-growing fruit and immense tropical flowers, and Cathy breathed deeply of it. From her vantage point, the whole world looked dazzlingly clean, as if it had just been freshly bathed.

Speaking of bathing, Cathy thought, emerging from the shelter and getting rather shakily to her feet, she could use a bath herself. The white petticoat that was the only item of clothing left to her was filthy, and her skin wasn't in much better shape. Even her hair felt unclean. She risked a quick look around, checking for any signs of Jon's presence. There were none. It was a safe bet that he had gone into the steamy tropical forest that led back inland from the crest of the cliffs to the freshwater pool he had told her about. There were fish in that pool, said Jon, who would find it a trifle harder to escape than their saltwater brothers. Cathy's lips twitched. Catching their supper had become a point of honor with him, and like a small boy he was almost shamefaced if he had to return to her side with only fruit and eggs.

With a quick glance back inside the shelter to assure herself that Virginia was still peacefully asleep, Cathy made her way rather slowly down to the water's edge. She was still not as strong as she could be, she discovered. In fact, her knees had a distinct tendency to shake. But that was only to be expected after so many days of inactivity, and the best way to get over it was to make use of the lazy muscles.

Feeling slightly guilty as she thought of what Jon's reaction would be if he could see what she was doing, Cathy waded into the bay. She stopped when the water sloshed just above her knees, deciding it was wisest not to go too far until she was stronger. Sitting, enjoying the luxurious feel of the cool water lapping around her breasts, she scooped up handfuls of sand to use as soap. Not bothering to remove the petticoat, she washed it as well as her skin, and finally worked the sand into her hair. Not the most pleasant of soaps, perhaps, but certainly effective! Leaning back in the water to let the waves wash away the last of the sand, Cathy felt wonderfully clean.

"Just what the hell do you think you're doing?" Jon's voice growled from shore, and Cathy turned her head to find him staring at her, alarm and anger combining in his expression. He looked like a tall, bronzed pagan standing there, fists on hips, against the background of white sand and bright blue skies. Clad only in the black breeches, shortened now to the point where they hit him at mid-thigh, he was every inch the arrogant male. Feet planted slightly apart as if he were once again on the deck of a ship, mahogany flesh hair-roughened and stretched tautly over muscles like steel cords, his black hair waving carelessly back from his lean dark face, he was incredibly handsome. Cathy, staring, absorbed this fact, and then, very slowly, smiled at him.

"What does it look like? I'm taking a bath," she called

back pertly. Even at a distance she could see his jaw tighten. With an impatient oath, he waded into the bay, heading purposefully toward her.

Cathy floated, hair trailing wetly around her, as she watched him approach. When he was just a few feet away, she splashed him playfully. He didn't smile. Instead, he stood towering over her, his big body almost completely blocking her view of the beach.

"Good God, girl, don't you have any sense?" he demanded explosively as she just lay there, smiling sunnily up at him. "Not a week ago it was touch and go whether or not you were going to die! And now, the minute my back's turned, you sneak out for a swim, of all the stupid things! What am I going to have to do, mount guard over you to keep you still?"

"I came out for a bath, not a swim," Cathy pointed out mildly. Jon's frown blackened at this non-sequitur.

"I don't give a damn what you came out for," Jon said between clenched teeth. "The point is, you're not to come out at all. I thought that was understood."

"I'm better now." Cathy was beginning to feel a trifle sulky. "And I wanted a bath. I felt dirty."

"Oh, for God's sake," Jon muttered under his breath. Before Cathy had guessed his intention, he swooped, gathering her up in his arms and straightening. She lay cradled against his chest as he waded back toward shore, water streaming from her soaked hair and petticoat, getting him almost as wet as she. He didn't appear to mind. Suddenly, the absurdity of the situation struck her, and she gurgled with laughter, her hands coming up to teasingly stroke his strong nape.

"Bully," she called him softly. His gray eyes flashed to her, narrowing on her pale little face.

"You need to be bullied," he shot back impatiently. "Of all the stupid stunts, this has to take the cake. For your information, there's a strong riptide in this bay, and you're not strong enough to fight it. If you'd gone out very far, it likely would have pulled you out to sea and you would have drowned."

"Would you have been sorry?" Cathy asked provocatively, her blue eyes gleaming at him from beneath the demure shield of her lowered black lashes. Her hands continued to play idly with the thick black curls at his nape, twining them around her slender fingers, tugging at them. He shot her a quick, penetrating glance, seemingly trying to judge how much seriousness there was in the question. The slight smile on her soft pink lips gave him his answer. She was playing games with him, as she had been ever since she had begun to recover her strength. It was as if she was trying to provoke him into making a confession of his feelings, which he was damned if he was going to do. Love her he might, but he wasn't fool enough to take the risk of telling her so. Not again. Uncomfortably Jon remembered the words he had uttered that night in the boat, when he had thought her on the verge of death. Every time he thought of the way he had broken down, he felt almost ridiculously embarrassed. If she had any memory of that night at all, he thought grimly, she would no longer have any need to tease him about what he felt for her. She would know beyond the shadow of a doubt, and the knowledge would be a razor-sharp sword poised over his head.

"Well, yes," he drawled in reply. "You see, I haven't quite got the knack of handling Virginia."

"Oh, you!" Cathy exclaimed, exasperated, and pulled his black hair punishingly in retaliation.

❧❧❧

Over the next few weeks, Jon watched over her like a mother hen, making a ridiculous fuss when she did anything he felt might tax her strength. If he had his way, Cathy thought, annoyed, I'd spend the rest of my life on my back in the shade! Determinedly ignoring him, which was easier by far when he wasn't around, she at first took daily walks along the beach, carrying Virginia with her. Gradually she worked up to a regular afternoon swim. Jon had flat-out forbidden her to swim without him, in case she should get caught in the riptide, or get a cramp, but Cathy, tossing her head, refused to bow to his wishes. Not that she openly defied him. If she had, she knew he would find some way of enforcing her obedience to his command. Instead, she operated on the principle that what he didn't know wouldn't hurt him—or her—and while he made his daily forays for food, or to explore the island, Cathy did just as she pleased.

The long days of sunshine and flawless, balmy weather were just what she needed to recover her strength, Cathy thought one afternoon as she lay on the beach with Virginia. The little girl was contentedly sucking on her toe, a habit Cathy had given up trying to discourage, while Cathy herself was laughing at the antics of a pair of land crabs. They scuttled back and forth, battling over a bit of discarded fish, for all the world like two old-world swordists caught up in a duel. Jon had decided to try his luck catching fish in the bay for once. He stood thigh-deep perhaps forty feet away, knife glinting between his teeth as he watched for a silver flash in the deep blue water that would tell him of the presence of a fish. Earlier, he had bragged to Cathy about how he had learned to catch the slippery creatures with his bare hands; when Cathy's eyes had twinkled, he had volunteered to show her. If she would sit on the beach, and watch, he would catch their supper. So far he had been out there nearly half an hour. He was soaking wet, cursing steadily under his breath, and after several abortive tries, empty-handed. It was all Cathy could do not to chuckle aloud. If she did, she feared he might turn murderous. He had already cast several darkling looks in her direction, which she had returned with bland innocence.

"Maybe all the fish have drowned," she called to him with a grin, able to restrain herself no longer. He threw her a glittering look over his bronzed shoulder, clearly in no mood for her sauciness. Cathy chuckled. Standing, she gathered Virginia up in her arms, and started in the direction of the shelter.

"Where are you going?" he demanded, his sharp eyes observing her movement as she had known he would.

"First I'm going to put Virginia down for her nap. Then I'm going to go looking for some gull's eggs to cook for supper. I fear I'll starve to death, if I wait for your fish."

She was laughing at him, her blonde head thrown back and her lovely eyes alight with it. The sight of her carefree mirth went a long way toward soothing Jon's chagrin. It was a long time since he had seen her looking so well.

"Minx," he said without heat, abandoning his fishing to come after her, his movements purposeful. Cathy backed, grinning, as he sloshed toward her, his glinting gray eyes promising retribution for her teasing. "I'll teach you to show a little respect!"

Cathy's eyes widened to enormous blue pools during this speech, and not because of his words. He was out of the water now, stalking her, his bare brown feet dark against the gleaming white sand. And she was not the only one to notice the startling contrast. Scuttling nearer, so apparently did the larger of the two land crabs. . . .

"Ouch!" Jon howled, leaping a good yard straight up into the air. When he came down, he was holding his foot. A drop of bright red blood welled from the tip of his big toe. He stared down at it, looking so shocked that Cathy went off into paroxysms of giggles. Sinking down into the sand with the force of her mirth, she rocked helplessly back and forth, Virginia clutched to her breast. Jon looked at her, still seeming nonplussed, which made Cathy laugh even more. Speechless, she pointed after the rapidly vanishing crab.

"Damned thing . . . !" Jon muttered half under his breath, watching as the crab disappeared into a hole in the sand. Then his eyes swivelled back toward Cathy.

"Laugh, will you?" he growled, and advanced on her. His limping gait brought tears of mirth to Cathy's eyes. Gasping for breath, she could only wait defenselessly for whatever punishment he chose to visit on her. In just instants he stood towering over her, his big body throwing its shadow over her small one. Still Cathy could not control her giggles.

"I'll wager you planned the whole thing," he accused, smiling despite himself in the face of her rippling laughter. "You need schooling, my girl."

With that he caught her upper arms, hauling her mercilessly to her feet. Cathy clutched Virginia frantically, terrified of dropping her. Still she could not hold back the giggles that seemed to have a life of their own.

"Watch . . . Virginia," she gasped out warningly as he hauled her against his chest. His iron-thewed arm imprisoned her back; she could feel the knife he had replaced in its scabbard digging into her side. Virginia was wedged between them, surprisingly docile in the face of this unaccustomed rough treatment. Jon, thus prevented from coming too close, stared down into Cathy's small upturned face, his eyebrows trying to frown blackly while his eyes smiled. Cathy's own eyes were dancing with laughter, he saw, and her face was alight with it. A faint pink color had come up under her skin, making her cheeks seem to glow. Her long hair rippled in deep golden waves down her back; long strands of it, caught up on the gentle breeze blowing in from the bay, rose to caress his face. He looked down at her, and his eyes were caught by her smiling mouth. It was as fresh and appealing as the ripest of cherries, open now as she laughed cheekily up at him, framing her teeth which gleamed in the brilliant sunlight like twin rows of small perfect white pearls. Jon was suddenly consumed with an overwhelming compulsion to taste those sweet lips. It had been so long. . . .

Cathy saw him bend his dark head, and felt her heart give a curious excited flutter. He was going to kiss her, she realized without any shadow of a doubt, and she was suddenly hungry for it. Shameless to acknowledge that she wanted him, this man who was both the joy and the bane of her existence, lover, tormentor, devil, father to her two children. But want him she did, and he, conceited animal that he was, was probably well aware of it. Her blue eyes deepened almost to purple; her small hand reached up behind his neck to draw his head down. She heard a sharp in-drawing of breath when their mouths met with the heat of an explosion, and was unsure whether it came from him, or was her own.

His mouth devoured hers hotly, his lips and tongue doing delicious things to her insides. Cathy kissed him back without reserve, standing on tiptoe as she held on to him with her hand at the back of his strong neck. Her nails dug into his nape with the force of her passion, but neither of them noticed. Jon's hands slid down from her waist to fasten intimately on the soft round cheeks of her buttocks, grinding her lower body closely against his. Cathy could feel the iron hardness of him pressing urgently against her, and her toes curled into the sun-warmed sand.

Between them Virginia wriggled protestingly. When that brought no results, she let loose an indignant wail. Cathy seemed to hear the sound from a far distance; only gradually did she realize its source. By then, Jon was already releasing her, his every movement betraying his reluctance. Cathy, staring bemusedly up into his lean face, saw that his eyes were dark with desire. His breathing was labored. He wanted me, too, she realized with a quick flush of happiness. Her lips, slightly swollen from his kiss, smiled tremulously up at him. Her blue eyes shone like stars.

"Virginia. . . ." he said huskily, his eyes never leaving Cathy's face. Cathy blinked, swallowed, and took a step backward. With Virginia wailing for her supper, now was definitely not the time. But later. . . .

"She's hungry," Cathy explained with a self-conscious

laugh, suddenly aware of the way her eyes were eating him. Blushing a little, she glanced quickly down at her squalling daughter. Jon grimaced, and turned away.

"I know exactly how she feels," Cathy heard Jon mutter under his breath, and smiled a slow, secret smile.

After that, Jon found it almost impossible to keep his hands off her. She was his, his woman despite everything, and he wanted her with a single-mindedness that left room in his head for thoughts of little else. He tried to keep away from her, because just the sight of her slender yet voluptuous body, barely covered by that ridiculously thin petticoat, was enough to set his senses aflame. He could not like leaving her on her own. His knowledge of Cathy was such that he had a lively fear of what scrapes she might get into if he left her long out of his sight. But to be near her was torture of a different sort. Jon compromised, spending many of the hours when he was supposedly off exploring the island for signs of human habitation lying on his belly on top of one of the cliffs overlooking the bay, watching her playing on the beach with Virginia. There he could look, and yearn, but be safely too far away to be unexpectedly consumed by the heat of his own passion. However enchanting her body appeared to him, he had to remind himself—forcibly, if necessary—that she had not yet had time to recover from what he knew only too well had been a hellishly difficult childbirth. It would be criminal of him to touch her as she was, but she was driving him crazy. He couldn't make up his mind whether or not she was doing it purposely. He rather thought not. There was no way she could know how the least of her smiles could send his temperature soaring skyward, or how the slightest brush of her hand against his body could make his mouth go dry with longing. Being a woman, she could not possibly gauge the strength of his craving for her. . . .

If the days were bad, the nights were nothing less than an endurance contest for Jon. After the sun went down, the air grew uncomfortably cold. Lying beside Cathy, in the tiny shelter he had erected for the three of them, with her snuggled close against his side, her arms more often than not cozily around his neck and his arm wrapping her shoulders, it was all he could do not to pitch her over onto her delectable little backside and take her then and there. He could feel cold sweat pop out on his forehead with the force of his longing, and more than once long tremors racked his limbs until he felt as if he was afflicted with palsy. Through it all she slept on, blissfully unaware. Jon, gritting his teeth, fought to control his impulses, and so far he had succeeded. The one thing saving him was the fear that, while he was renewing his possession of her, the strength of his passion would make him lose control of his tongue and he would babble out his love for her. He meant to keep her—he had finally come to terms with the realization that, without her at his side, his life would not be worth the living—but on his own terms, not hers. Never again would he figuratively kneel at her feet, kissing the hem of her gown with the reverence more properly reserved for a celestial being. No, she was a woman, flesh and blood, with all a woman's failings. And he had to accept the fact that to expect faithfulness from a woman was as useless as expecting it from the weather. Only as long as he kept her close under his eyes could he be assured of her fidelity. So that was what he meant to do. If ever they got off this infernal island, he would take her back with him to Woodham, as his wife or mistress, however matters worked themselves out. He would take Virginia too, and accept her as his daughter whether she was or not. After all, he and Cathy would have many more children, children whose paternity he meant to make damned certain was not in question. And of course, there was Cray. . . . Cray was, without a doubt, his son. The three of them had been happy as a family at Woodham before, and they could all be happy there again. He had been stupid to get so insanely jealous because of Cathy's liaison with Harold, stupid to expect more of her than she had it in her to give. . . .

Jon gritted his teeth. The thought of Harold in bed with Cathy was still enough to send him slightly out of his head. So he forced himself to dismiss the all-too-vivid images from his mind. What she had done, she had done. It was over now, and there was nothing either of them could do to change it even if they had wished to. Virginia existed as living proof of that. If he wanted Cathy—and he did, as he was grudgingly forced to admit—he had to accept her as she was. An imperfect, fallible human being, like himself.

While Jon was going through his own private version of hell, Cathy was lazily content. Their days on the island seemed to her like golden moments stolen from time. There was no past, no future, only the sun-drenched present. She was surrounded by miracles: plenty of food, shelter, warmth; the presence of her daughter, and the man she loved. The only cloud in her sky was Cray's absence, but she refused to dwell on that. He was being well cared for, she knew. The thought that Jon had any further questions concerning Virginia's parentage never even crossed her mind. She had heard him accept the child as his, and she never doubted that Virginia's birth date had finally convinced him. And he was so careful of them both, fussing over them like a hen with two chicks. Making sure they were safe. . . .

He wanted her badly, she knew, yet still he held off out of concern for her health. Cathy was warmed by this evidence of his regard. Many men would have taken her regardless. After all, it had been over a month now since her lying-in, and it would have been easy for him to presume that she was well in the interests of gratifying his own desires. But he was prepared to wait, and she loved him for it. He was kind, and thoughtful . . . and she was in no hurry. They had time. All the time in the world.

The island was a constant source of delight to her, although Jon had forbidden her to leave the beach without his escort and she had sense enough to know that, in this instance at least, his concern was well-founded. There were snakes in the forest, huge snakes capable of crushing and then swallowing someone as small as herself, but besides the snakes there were monkeys, with their funny little faces and hilarious ways, and birds of all sizes and descriptions, winging about through the trees, running along the beach, stalking proudly across the bay. Brilliantly colored birds, ranging from the gorgeous vivid blues and greens of the parrots to the scarlet macaws to the pink-crested white cockatoos to the pink and red flamingos. And there were flowers whose perfume wafted deliciously on the air. Banks of white, pink, and yellow jasmine contrasted against the mysterious dark green of tropical foliage around the perimeters of the forest. Sometimes Jon, with an almost sheepish smile, would bring her a large bunch of these along with the food he gathered, or escort her along the windy path up the cliffs to pick them for herself. On these occasions Cathy would reward him with a light kiss, and delight in the response that he found impossible to hide.

Parrot Island, as Cathy had laughingly dubbed it after its noisiest inhabitants, appeared to be devoid of any human life except for themselves. At least, for the present. Jon had found evidence that people did from time to time visit it, although nothing to indicate their purpose in doing so. Not that it mattered. If people came even occasionally to this tiny atoll just barely lifting its head from the Atlantic, then their chances of eventual rescue were greatly enhanced. Jon piled a huge amount of dry wood and brush on top of the tallest cliff, to be set afire as a signal when a ship should appear. Then, as there seemed nothing more he could do, he settled down to enjoy life on the island.

One bright morning perhaps two months after they had landed on the island, Cathy awoke to the noisy bird chorus that had become so much a part of her life. Jon had already left the shelter, which wasn't unusual. He was often gone when she awoke. Virginia still slept soundly on, and Cathy hovered for a fond moment over the tiny crib Jon had fashioned for their daughter out of wood whittled to size by his knife and lashings of vine. She was so small, so perfect in every respect, and yet already so much of an individual. Cathy touched the pink little cheek lightly, then as the baby didn't stir she sighed, and left the shelter.

The morning sunshine was dazzling, and Cathy had to close her eyes for a moment against its glare. When she opened them again, she perceived Jon crouched down by the edge of the bay, seeming to peer intently into its depths. What on earth . . . ? she thought, amused, and walked toward him. He heard her soft footsteps on the sand behind him, and turned, smiling.

"Good morning, sweet slug-a-bed," he teased lightly, quoting a nonsensical poem about a fashionable young lady. Cathy saw that a trickle of bright red blood flowed freely from his chin. Her eyes widened in consternation, and then she took note of the knife in his hand, and the half-bearded, half-not condition of his face.

"You've cut yourself," she told him.

"I'm well aware, believe me," he grimaced, putting a rueful hand to where the blood began. "And not just in the one place, either. The whole right side of my face is raw! And all to please my lady."

Cathy grinned at that.

"Liar," she said, making a face at him. "You probably just found out that a beard itches! Anyway, I rather liked it on you. You looked so wonderfully wicked!"

"You should have told me sooner," he groaned, his gray eyes glinting humorously. "To think I've scarred myself for life to no purpose!"

"More fool you," she retorted unsympathetically.

"Ah, hard-hearted!" he mourned, and stood up, his big

body towering head and shoulders above her. Cathy tilted her head way back to see his eyes, reminding him of a lovely but inquisitive small bird. He bent to place a quick hard kiss on her mouth, his action automatic. Cathy's hand came up to rest, palm down, against his furry bare chest. He was as solid as a slab of granite.

"Let me finish the job for you," she offered when he lifted his head, hating to think of him perhaps slipping and cutting his own throat with only the water for a very wavery mirror. Jon grinned down at her, his eyes twinkling.

"I was hoping you would offer," he admitted, handing her the knife. She looked up at him, frowning.

"You're too tall," she complained. "You'll have to sit down."

"As my lady commands," he replied, obligingly sinking down cross-legged on the sand. Cathy squatted in front of him, hesitated, and moved around behind him.

"Put your head on my lap," she directed, thinking that this approach would be easier.

"Isn't there some legend about a unicorn that I should be remembering about now?" he wondered aloud, his black head lowering to rest in her lap as she had directed. "Ah, yes, now I have it: to catch a unicorn, one must first provide oneself with a young maiden. The beast will lay his head on the lady's lap, no doubt hoping for a tender reward, and while he is in that position he may be captured."

"Stop talking," Cathy advised severely, leaning over him so that her long golden hair brushed his bare chest. As she set the blade to the hard plane of his bearded cheek, she frowned, concentrating. Jon lifted a finger to gently smooth away the furrow between her silky brows.

"And hold still," she added, moving her face back out of his reach. "Unless you want a matched pair of cuts. This is tricky business."

"Don't I know it," Jon muttered half under his breath, and

then was prudently silent as Cathy painstakingly scraped the blade over his face. She worked as carefully as she could, but still she nicked him several times. When she was finished at last, Jon let out a sigh of relief.

"You can get up now," Cathy told him, straightening. He grinned up at her, his teeth a mocking white slash in his brown face. His head was very dark against her white petticoat.

"I'm comfortable," he demurred plaintively, his hand coming up to suggestively stroke her bare calf under the skirt of her petticoat. Cathy, looking down at him, saw something that was not laughter flare into life in his eyes at the contact. She shivered as they blazed hotly over her face, her breathing quickening. His hand was so hard, so warm, against the silkiness of her leg. . . . She held very still, scarcely breathing, as it slid higher, brushing intimately along her thigh. Then he was touching her as she had wanted him to for so long. . . .

"God," she heard him mutter as she closed her eyes, gasping. Then suddenly his hand was removed and he was getting rather jerkily to his feet. Cathy, her eyes flying open, watched him with a disbelief that rapidly turned to frustration. He was carrying chivalry a bit too far!

"Jon," she murmured achingly, then bit her lip. She would not beg!

At the sound of his name he turned to look down at her, his expression unreadable.

"Help me up," she said, holding up her hand to him.

For the rest of that day, while she swam and fed Virginia and played, desire was like an ache inside her. She was beginning to understand the urgency that drove men to such rash acts. She wanted him with an intensity that was with her constantly. Even when he took himself off, as he did nearly every afternoon, there was no relief from the gnawing torment. She didn't even have to close her eyes to picture his handsome face, his hard, strong body that she knew could take her to heaven and back. She felt as if her body were on fire.

When he came back, shadows were lengthening over the bay. The sun would soon go down, and night would be upon them. When she thought of spending this night chastely at Jon's side, Cathy clenched her teeth. It would be impossible!

Frustration made her cross, and the few looks and words she bestowed on him were snappish. That he was equally short with her she welcomed. She was spoiling for a fight, and by the way he was acting so was he.

"Oh, go to hell!" she finally screeched at him, when he demanded, most unreasonably, why she didn't take her foul temper and go to bed.

"With pleasure!" he snarled, jumping to his feet from where he had been sitting not far from the entrance to the shelter. The remains of their fire still glowed redly, and his big body looked tall and menacing, silhouetted as it was against the smoldering flames. "At least I'd be free from your shrewish tongue!"

"Well, if it bothers you so much, I suggest you sleep elsewhere!" Cathy threw at him, incensed. With the firelight catching in her hair and her blue eyes flashing like swords, she looked like a very beautiful fishwife as she stood, fists on hips, hurling abuse at him. Jon was both aroused and infuriated by the sight.

"Bitch!" he grated, his hands reaching out of their own accord to grab her hurtfully by her shoulders and shake her. Cathy's hands curved into claws and went for his eyes.

"Oh, no, you don't!" He sounded really angry now, as his hands caught hers before they could inflict any damage, almost crushing them with the pressure of his grip.

"Let me go!" she cried furiously. Then, as his fingers tightened even more, she was betrayed into gasping out, "Oh, you're hurting me!"

"I want to hurt you," he said between clenched teeth. "I want to. . . ."

His words were cut off as he brought his mouth down on

hers, hard, brutally grinding against her soft lips. Cathy felt passion flare along with her anger. Not caring that his kiss was meant as a punishment, she swayed against him, feeling a flame race along her flesh where the softness of her body brushed the iron tautness of his. Groaning at the unexpectedness of her response, he released his vise-grip on her hands to slide his arms around her waist and back, pulling her tightly against him. Her own hands curling around his neck, Cathy rose on tiptoe to meet his kiss, her mouth opening submissively under his hungry onslaught. He was rough, his kiss a violent rape, and she loved it. She quivered in his hold, her knees feeling as if they would no longer support her. As if he felt her shudder, his hold tightened until she feared he might break her in two. His breath was hot in her mouth, his tongue a fiery torment. Cathy clung to him, pressing shamelessly against his big body, trembling.

Through the thin material of her petticoat, she could feel the heat of his bare chest burning against her breasts. She heard a sound, a low, aching moan, and realized that it came from her own throat. Blindly she pressed closer to him, feeling his hands begin to move over her body as if he couldn't get enough of the feel of her. One of his hands slid from her back to cup her breast. . . .

"No!" The protest was torn from her as he thrust her harshly away from him. "Jon . . . !"

He stood for a moment staring at her, his chest heaving as he fought to control his breathing. His fists were clenched into hard balls at his sides.

"For God's sake, go to bed!" he muttered thickly, sounding as if he could hardly get the words out. "Before I go completely crazy!"

"But I want. . . ." Cathy began, all thoughts of pride banished by the heat of her longing. She might as well have saved her breath. Even as she spoke he had turned on his heel, pivoting and striding away into the night.

"Where are you going?" she wailed after him, stomping her foot. Her every pore seethed with rage and frustration. He didn't answer.

Cathy spent the better part of the next hour pacing around what was left of the campfire. Virginia was sound asleep, settled down for the night, and there was nothing to distract her attention from the flames that still licked at her body. He had wanted her too, she thought furiously, and yet he had thrust her away! What ailed him? If he thought that it was too soon after Virginia's birth, then it was time she disabused him of the notion. She was fully recovered now, and she was a grown woman with a woman's need of him. His misguided concern for her welfare was doing her more harm than his possession ever could! Blind, stubborn idiot! She would like to wring his neck!

Eventually she crawled into the shelter and tried to sleep. After tossing and turning for what seemed like hours, she gave up, and crawled back into the open air again. This is ridiculous, she thought furiously. And she wondered where Jon was. She was beginning to feel worried about him, and this infuriated her almost more than anything else.

Finally, without ever consciously deciding that she was going to, she found herself climbing the path up the side of the cliff and then walking along the trail that Jon had hacked through the forest. She would walk down to the pool, she told herself, and then come back and go to sleep. And she tried not to think that the pool where he fished was a very likely place for Jon to be.

It was dark going through the forest, a heavy black darkness alive with sounds. Cathy, her bare feet moving rather gingerly over the coolness of the vines covering the ground, refused to allow herself to speculate on what might be causing the various noises. Jon would be livid, she knew, at the idea that she had dared to walk through the jungle by herself. Even during the day, he refused to allow her to venture off the beach without his protection. While as for at night . . . !

Just when Cathy thought she would have to turn around and go back, she saw the silvery gleam of moonlight on the dark waters of the pool. Breathing a sigh of relief, she approached on noiseless feet, stopping before she was out of the protection of the overhanging foliage. This way she could see, and not be seen.

As she had more than half expected, Jon was there. She was immediately aware of that. He was in the pool, his dark head cleaving the surface like a seal's. As she watched him, he executed a shallow dive, and disappeared beneath the water. The moon touched the long length of his body as he twisted in the dive. Cathy's breath caught in her throat, and her heart speeded up, as she realized that he was swimming naked.

fifteen

◆❦◆

Cathy stepped out into the moonlight. Jon, surfacing, saw her standing there, and the passion he had been battling all evening flared anew. The moon turned her hair to shimmering silver-gilt fire. Bathed in its light, her skin seemed incandescent. Her eyes looked huge and mysterious in her small face, deceptively quiet sapphire pools that a man could drown in.

He opened his mouth to call to her, but as he saw what she was about the words died in his throat. Her hands caught up the hem of her petticoat, lifting it over her head with a single graceful movement and letting it drop to one side. For a moment she stood there, her lovely pale body glowing against the whispering dark background of the jungle surrounding the pool. Then she stepped into the water.

Jon, watching her wade toward him, her breasts and hips and thighs gleaming above the rippling night-dark water, felt his heart begin to thud in his chest. His mouth went dry with the force of his longing. God, she was beautiful, and he wanted her . . . !

Cathy felt the cool water rise to cover her hips, her waist, and finally, when she was nearly to Jon, her breasts. What she was doing was shameless, she knew, but she didn't care. If she had to seduce him, then so be it. After all, how many times in the past had he seduced her?

His eyes were fixed on her, and even from where she was, still a yard or so away, Cathy could hear the stentorian rasp of his breathing. She smiled, her hands reaching toward him through the water. His eyes glinted silver as they stared at her. For a moment she thought he would resist, but then he was reaching for her, his hands closing around her wrists, pulling her hard against the jutting contours of his body.

"This is stupid," he growled against her throat, his hands already running over her slender curved back as if he couldn't hold her closely enough. Cathy laughed, the sound husky, seductive. As his mouth lifted from its ravagement of her neck, she tilted her head back so that she could see into his face.

"I love being stupid," she whispered, and saw his eyes darken almost to black before he bent his head and his lips took her mouth.

Cathy's mouth opened to him endlessly, hot with desire, returning his kisses with a feverishness that fanned the flames of his passion to a white heat. She was on tiptoe, feeling weightless in the buoyant water, her hands locked behind his strong neck. The iron wall of his chest was crushing her breasts; she could feel the roughness of his body hair scraping her soft skin, and she moved sensuously against the rasping pelt, loving the feel of it. Jon was shaking. She could feel the long tremors that racked him. His steel-muscled arms and legs quivered with the force of his wanting. Cathy pulled her mouth free of his to press soft, adoring kisses along the strong lines of his neck and shoulder. Beneath her ear she could hear his heart beating like a kettle-drum.

"Oh, God, I want you," he groaned, his voice unsteady. Cathy brushed another line of nibbling kisses down his chest, her tongue licking over the curling hairs that tickled her nose and chin.

"Then take me," she breathed, her fingers sliding down to follow the trail blazed by her mouth. When they reached the surface of the water, her hands did not stop. Instead, they moved deeper, touching him, arousing him to the point where he was in actual physical pain. When she reached up finally to kiss his mouth, he was groaning.

"Take me," she whispered again, and his eyes opened to blaze down into hers.

"I have to," he muttered as if it were a death sentence. Then his arms were sliding beneath her knees and around her shoulders and he was lifting her, wading with her to the edge of the pool. Cathy's own arms were locked tightly around his neck. He was kissing her devouringly, and she felt as if she were drowning.

Gently he lowered her to the vine-covered bank, following her down. Cathy felt the cool, slippery surface of the leaves beneath her back, saw the overhanging foliage enclosing them like a shadowy green cave. Then his big body was moving over hers, blotting out everything except himself, and the way she wanted him.

His hands were on her breasts, his fingers unsteady as they caressed her quivering nipples. Cathy arched her back as he replaced his fingers with his mouth. The hot, devouring warmth of his kisses on her breasts made her wild with desire. She was writhing snake-like under his expert hands, her eyes shut tightly, a low sobbing moan coming from deep in her throat. Her hands clutched at his broad, sweat-filmed back, trying to pull him down.

"If I hurt you, tell me. I'll try to stop," he growled in her ear. Cathy, gasping, her nails digging punishingly into his back, barely heard. Her whole being was focused on the hairy thigh she felt parting her legs, then the hot, throbbing staff that was probing her softness.

When he possessed her at last, Cathy cried out with the sheer ecstasy of it. Immediately Jon froze, still deeply imbedded in her flesh.

"What is it? Did I hurt you?" he demanded hoarsely, lifting himself up on his elbows and staring down into her white, passion-contorted face.

"No. Oh, no! Oh, God, don't stop. Please don't stop!" She clutched at him frantically, her eyes opening to stare blindly into his.

"Please. . . ." she begged, beyond knowing that she was doing so. His eyes darkened, and then he was bending to her, his mouth taking hers in a way that set her to shaking helplessly. He was moving, gently at first as if trying not to hurt her, but as she sobbed, and writhed, and moaned, gentleness flew out the window along with all of his good intentions. She was exciting him wildly, beyond anything he had ever imagined, and he was losing control. . . .

"I love you," he groaned in the last earth-shattering moment, the words torn from him before he could stop them. "Love you, love you!"

"Darling," Cathy breathed, and then she was spiralling away, claimed by her own shuddering rapture.

Jon lay across her for long moments afterward, his breathing slowly resuming a more normal rhythm. Inwardly he was cursing himself with a steady, scathing stream of profanities. His final, mindless confession haunted him like an avenging ghost. Damn it, he'd known it would happen, and should have guarded more closely against it! Now she knew beyond a doubt how he felt about her; he had condemned himself out of his own mouth. She could laugh at him, mock him, torment him at will, and it was only what he deserved for being so damned loose-tongued!

"Darling, I adore you, but could you shift yourself? You're crushing me," she murmured from beneath him. Jon, recalled to the present, obligingly rolled onto his side. He lay flat on his back, unspeaking, staring up at the intertwining branches above them, his hands crossed behind his neck. He felt immensely tired, sated—and wary.

Cathy propped herself up on one elbow to look down into his dark countenance. His eyes flickered once over her small face, then returned to their contemplation of what he could see of the sky. A small, satisfied smile curved her lips; he thought savagely that she looked like a smug little cat about to finish off a particularly plump mouse.

"Did I hurt you?" he asked gruffly, partly from concern and partly to stave off the discussion he was sure was coming.

Cathy shook her head, her eyes dreamy, that infuriating little smile still hovering on her mouth.

"Ummm, no," she purred. Her free hand came out to gently stroke his bare chest, idly twisting the sweat-drenched black curls. "So you love me, do you?"

Jon stiffened as if from a blow. His eyes returned guardedly to her face. It was shadowed, hiding much of her expression from him, but as he watched he could see an unmistakable dimple quiver in her cheek. Grimly he sought for some glib answer that would save him, and could think of nothing.

"Yes," he answered, the word sounding almost angry. Above him he could see Cathy's smile widen. His stomach muscles tensed, and he gritted his teeth. So she found his humbling amusing, did she? Very funny, in fact! Ha, ha!

"It's about time you admitted it, you fool," she whispered, bending close, and before he could make sense of that remark she was kissing him, her little mouth sweet as honey. Jon kissed her back because he couldn't help himself. To his chagrin, he felt his muscles tighten hungrily once more. All right, he told himself, all right! Now that you've made an utter ass out of yourself, you may as well make the most of it!

This time his taking of her was merciless, almost brutal. He was angry, at himself as well as her, and it showed in every movement he made. Cathy didn't mind in the least.

His violence touched off an answering fierceness in her. They coupled like a pair of savage tigers, Cathy clawing and biting and hissing, Jon spearing her time and again with his passion. When at last the explosion came, it was as a flame-streaked frenzy, a gasping, fiery kind of death.

They both fell into an exhausted sleep almost immediately afterward, worn out by their labors. When Jon wakened, it was still dark, the night-sounds loud around them. A chill breeze caressed the right side of his body, and he shivered. His left side, with Cathy curled snugly against it, was toasty warm. Like him, she was naked, her slender body defenseless in sleep. Mentally Jon compared her to a tired child; then, with another look at her tempting curves, revised his description.

"Cathy." He shook her gently, knowing that they had to get back. They had been away from the shelter too long already, with Virginia left there alone. Cathy stirred, muttered, and as he removed himself from her curled into a tight little ball. Jon, looking down at her, felt a wave of possessive, rueful tenderness. She had led him a merry chase, but he had caught her again at last. And he meant to keep her. Woe betide anyone who tried to wrest her from him a second time, and that included Cathy herself!

He found his shortened breeches, still hanging from the branch where he had left them, and pulled them on. Then he picked up Cathy's petticoat, lying in a discarded heap not far from where she lay sleeping. Not bothering to dress her, he merely wrapped the garment around her to afford her some protection from the cold, and lifted her in his arms. She opened her eyes as he swung her up against his chest, and murmured something incoherent.

"Go back to sleep," he hushed her, and when she obediently closed her eyes again, he set off with her along the trail leading to the shelter.

The next morning Cathy wakened to the sound of Virginia bawling. Still groggy with sleep, she crawled over to the child's crib, changed her automatically, and then picked the little girl up and set her to her breast. As Virginia suckled greedily, appeased now that she had what she wanted, Cathy's mind began gradually to function. Memories of the night before returned to her, and she blushed hotly. Her behavior had been nothing short of wanton, she had to admit. Then she smiled. Jon hadn't appeared to be disgusted by it. In fact, he had taken her as though he couldn't get enough.

And he loved her! His words seemed to dance through her head. He loved her, he'd admitted it, not once but twice! She felt like singing. All was once again right with her world.

Where was Jon? At the thought Cathy frowned. He was certainly not in the shelter. Perhaps he was on the beach, or fishing in the bay. . . . Impatient now, she waited until Virginia had finished her meal, then lay the child back in her crib. A full belly always made her sleepy. Quickly Cathy pulled the crumpled petticoat over her head, and crawled to the entrance of the shelter. As far as she could see, she was alone.

She crawled outside to make sure. The beach was awash with sunlight, bits of shells sparkling like diamonds among the sand. Flamingos waded in the bay and gulls strutted along the water's edge, but other than that the beach was deserted. Cathy frowned. She was impatient to see Jon again, to see his face when she told him that she loved him, too. He knew it already, of course. He would have to be blind, deaf, and dumb not to. But last night she had neglected to mention it, and she wanted to say it aloud so much that her throat hurt with the effort of holding it back.

The day lengthened, growing hotter, but still Jon didn't return. Cathy began to worry about him, knowing that it was ridiculous to do so. Jon was a big, strong man, and he could assuredly take care of himself. Still, as the afternoon melted away, she gathered Virginia up and walked with her along the trail to the pool. It was the only place she could think of for Jon to be.

He wasn't there. Cathy retraced her steps, no longer frightened of this particular section of jungle. Last night, she and Jon had exorcised all the demons. She had a gruesome picture of Jon being crushed and swallowed by a huge snake, and impatiently banished it. The creature would have to be as big as a dragon to kill a man as large and muscular as Jon. No, more than likely he was exploring somewhere, or doing something else equally useless. As the afternoon wore on, and Cathy sat disconsolately on the beach with Virginia, she grew steadily angrier. He had better be lying dead or mangled somewhere, she thought furiously, because if he returned in one piece, she was going to kill him!

Jon spent the day at the top of the cliffs, watching Cathy and Virginia from that safe vantage point. He knew that his removal of himself smacked of cowardice, but he couldn't help it. He couldn't face her, and read victory in her eyes, until he had himself well in hand. It galled him to admit that she had defeated him, but defeat him she had. Despite her whoring with Harold—and he refused to call it by any other name—and her bearing of a child that could just as easily be Harold's as his own, he, Jon, was still mooning over her like a lovesick schoolboy! She was no longer his wife, had no hold on him except the one he himself had given her, and yet he was as bound to her as Prometheus to his rock. If he had any sense left, he would leave her to her own devices as soon as they reached civilization again, and find himself another woman to bed. What was a female, after all, but a hank of long hair, a few meters of silky skin, and a warm wet cave to give a man ease?

Watching Cathy as she moved about on the beach, he could read her growing temper as easily as if he was standing there beside her. Just as he had suspected, now that she had gotten him to admit he loved her, she expected him to dance to her tune. Well, he might have done it once, but never again! He wasn't a man to make the same mistake twice. He had loved her once without reservation, with a grand wild tide of feeling so intense that he'd thought he would die when she betrayed him. He loved her still, he had to admit, but he would never be such a blind, besotted fool again.

By the time the sun crept down behind the horizon, Jon had his barriers well in place. He wasn't going to take any nonsense from the little vixen, and so he meant her to realize. If she thought to rule him now that he had revealed his Achilles heel, then she would have to think again.

When he strolled onto the beach at last, it was almost completely dark. Cathy had crawled into the shelter, and as he entered himself he could see that she was nursing Virginia. She glared at him, her eyes shining like a cat's through the gloom. If not for the nearly sleeping child at her breast, Jon knew that she would have launched a tirade at him. He smiled mockingly at her, and lay down on the bed of leaves and vines he had fashioned for the two of them to share, stretching lazily at full length, his hands linking behind his head.

He watched her as she finished feeding the little girl, and despite himself felt a tug of tenderness. The two of them made a beautiful picture. Cathy looked like a golden-haired, half-naked madonna, with her thin white garment pulled down to allow the baby access to her breast. She held the child cradled in her arms, rocking gently back and forth, crooning to her. The only thing that spoiled the image of motherly bliss was the occasional dagger-look she shot at him.

Finally Virginia's mouth fell away from Cathy's breast, and she slept. Cathy carefully crept across to the tiny crib, and put the little girl in it. For a moment she hovered, waiting to see if a wail would summon her to resume her rocking and crooning. Nothing happened, and Jon could sense Cathy's attention swinging to himself. He was right. She crawled across to him, pent up anger emanating from every pore.

"Where have you been?" she hissed, the words no less virulent for being whispered.

"I wasn't aware that I had to account to you for my movements," Jon answered coolly, his eyes closing as if bored with the conversation. He could hear Cathy spluttering, apparently at a loss for words. It was all he could do not to grin.

"I was worried about you!" she managed finally.

"Then you shouldn't have been." His answer was the epitome of indifference. Knowing Cathy as he did, he could feel her itching to pick up something and hit him over the head. Only the lack of a suitable object, and the sleeping child, saved him.

"You can be sure I won't be again!" she spat finally, and turning her back flounced away. The effect of this gesture was somewhat spoiled by the confined space available to her, and the fact that it had to be carried out on her knees. Even at the opposite side of the shelter, she was still within easy reach of his hand.

Jon let her sulk for a while, and then, when he thought she was thoroughly enraged, drawled lazily, "Come to bed."

"No!"

"You weren't so reluctant last night," he taunted softly. This brought her whirling to face him.

"That's just the kind of thing I would have expected a cad like you to say!"

"Do you deny it?"

Knowing she couldn't, Cathy ground her teeth. Arrogant, mocking devil! She would take him down a peg or two, or die in the attempt!

"No, I don't," she said. "But then, last night I wanted a man. *Any* man. You were all that was available, so I had to make do."

He laughed harshly at that. Little bitch, she was doing her best to provoke him.

"Liar," he said softly.

"What about you?" she accused furiously. "Last night you said you loved me!"

The words hovered between them for a moment, flicking Jon on the raw.

"Ah, yes," he drawled finally. "But you see, last night, like you, I wanted a woman. I would have said the same to anyone."

She gasped at this blatant insult. Before she thought, she was launching herself forward, her hand swinging back to slap his face with all the force she could muster. The blow never connected. He caught her hand, and, using it as a lever, jerked her forward into his arms.

Cathy fell hard against his chest. The breath was temporarily knocked from her lungs. When she recovered, he had imprisoned both her hands in one of his. His other arm was wrapped around her waist, holding her in place. She was lying full length on top of him, her skirts askew, and his dark mocking face was just inches from her own.

"Brute!" she said, glaring at him.

"Bitch," he returned equably, and in the darkness she saw his mouth twist in a smile.

"Let me go!"

"Never," he answered huskily, the word just barely audible. Then, before Cathy had time to ponder his meaning, he was kissing her. The hot contact wiped every conscious thought from her mind. Despising herself, she was helpless against the potent appeal of his mouth. Unable to resist, she kissed him back. When at last he released her hands, they cradled his dark head.

He was gone again when Cathy awoke. She was so mad she wanted to spit. Vile, arrogant bastard! she called him mentally. Last night he had wrung from her every last drop of response, and all without uttering a single tender word. She should have kicked him where it would have hurt, should have bitten and scratched . . . but what had she done? She had melted in the swine's arms!

It was early afternoon when Cathy first saw the flutter of white on the horizon. She was playing in the shallows with Virginia, and she lifted the little girl into her arms, straining to see. Was it—could it be—a sail? She stared out toward where it had been, but this time she didn't see a thing.

Suddenly Cathy saw a shadow fall across the water. It was unmistakably human, and male, and Cathy turned toward it with excited words falling from her lips. For once Jon was around when he was needed. . . . Then her jaw dropped. Facing her was not one but two men, and neither of them was Jon!

Swallowing, Cathy backed, Virginia held tightly in her arms. The man closest to her—a big, burly fellow, dressed in breeches and a vest, with a red bandanna tied around his head—grinned at her, showing a gold front tooth.

"Well, well, hello, pretty lady," he said amiably, his eyes sweeping over her lightly clad form as if he could see right through the petticoat to what lay beneath. "All alone?"

Cathy shook her head, taking another step backward. Who were these men, and where on earth had they come from? And where, oh, where, was Jon?

"Don't be afraid, lady. We don't aim to hurt you," the man said soothingly, taking a step toward her. "Cute little baby you got there."

The other man chortled. Cathy licked her suddenly dry lips. She was frightened, not only for herself but for Virginia. These two looked like the scum of the earth. Silently she debated whether or not to risk a scream. It would almost surely bring Jon running, but on the other hand it might provoke the men into taking action. Her dilemma was resolved when the second of the two men, a little shorter than the first but just as broad, began to move around behind her. With Virginia in her arms, Cathy could not swim to safety, and they were blocking her only other avenue of escape. She was well and truly trapped. Opening her mouth, she screamed to wake the dead. Virginia, startled, began to cry.

Jon was some distance away when he heard Cathy's scream. He had been to the other side of the island, more to get away from the problems set him by Cathy than for any real need to be there, and had come across a small ship anchored in a shallow cove. He had hidden himself, and watched, caution urging him not to make his presence known until he had thoroughly spied out the lay of the land. And as usual caution paid off. It didn't take much observation to convince him that the ship was a pirate vessel. Perhaps she had ducked into the cove to hide from a pursuer, or perhaps she had needed to make repairs. He didn't know, and it didn't matter. He had to get back to Cathy, and keep her and Virginia hidden until the ship left. It didn't take much imagination to guess what men such as the ones on that ship would make of Cathy.

Jon was more than halfway back to the beach when Cathy's scream froze him in his tracks. It was high and frightened-sounding, and it made his blood run cold. All manner of hideous possibilities occurred to him as he set off toward the sound at a dead run, but, as he saw when he burst panting onto the top of the cliffs, none of them had been correct.

Two men, from the pirate ship he had just seen by the look of them, were dragging Cathy out of the bay and onto the beach. One had his hand over her mouth to prevent any further outcry. She was barely resisting. Jon puzzled at that for an instant, then as the man blocking his view of her moved a little, he saw the reason. A squirming Virginia was held tightly in her arms.

Rage rose in Jon like a thick red tide. They dared to manhandle what was his. . . . He would kill them for it! As swiftly and silently as a panther he moved down the path bisecting the face of the cliff. The two men, intent on their sport, didn't notice him. Cathy, her eyes huge in her white face, didn't either.

When they had dragged her some few yards up the beach, one of them wrested Virginia from her, holding the baby carelessly by the arms as he grinned at Cathy. Virginia screamed shrilly, and Jon felt the blood begin to pump hotly through his temple. Surely the bastards wouldn't harm an infant? But even as he thought it, the man holding Virginia flung her casually to one side. The baby lay where she had landed in the white sand, looking like a small, pathetic doll. She didn't move, or make a sound.

Cathy turned into a wildcat. She kicked and clawed and bit, trying to get to Virginia's side. The men were clearly having trouble holding her. But hold her they did, chuckling, making bawdy comments. They were forcing her down onto her back in the sand. Even as Jon watched, moving toward them as quickly as he dared, she buried her teeth in one of her assailants' legs. He screamed, hopping about on his uninjured limb, his hand clapped to the wound. The other man lifted his fist and dealt Cathy a blow in the face that sent her spinning backward. And with that, Jon promised the man grimly, he had just signed his death warrant.

He was crossing the beach now, moving up behind the man who was kneeling over Cathy, holding her pinioned to the ground as he tried with one hand to paw up her billowing white skirt. She was fighting him with every inch of her body, writhing and bucking and kicking as she tried to throw him off. The other man was sitting in the sand not far away, one leg hiked up over the other as he gingerly examined the tooth marks on his grimy calf.

They were two to his one, both armed with long sabers thrust into their belts as well as knives. This was no time for Marquis of Queensbury rules. As silently as a shadow, Jon slipped up behind the man who was now bent over, attempting to force a kiss on Cathy's elusive mouth. Jon's hand closed brutally on a hank of his greasy reddish hair. The man looked around, surprise and then fear written plainly on his face. He tried to lunge to his feet, calling hoarsely to his companion. Jon smiled at him, his gray eyes deadly, then as efficiently as a butcher brought his knife up and cut the fellow's throat.

"Jon, look out!" Cathy cried as blood splattered over her like rain. Jon saw that her eyes were fixed on something beyond him, and whirled. The other man was charging like an enraged bull, his saber drawn and held high over his head.

"Stay back out of the way!" he said fiercely to Cathy as he crouched, his own knife ready in his hand, prepared to meet the man's rush. As the saber slashed in a whistling arc over his head, and he ducked, pivoting to meet the next onslaught, he saw to his relief that she was obeying, scrambling over the sand to Virginia.

All his attention had to focus on his opponent. The man was coming back for another charge. Jon knew that his only hope was to stay out of reach of that murderous long sword until he could get in close enough to gut the man with his knife. Still he feinted, not wanting the pirate to know what he was about. Then, as the saber chopped down toward his head, he whirled out of range. The blade whistled harmlessly past.

Jon crouched again, the blade of his knife held stiffly before him. He was ready for anything the other might try. The pirate was circling, looking for an opening, his lips drawn back in a snarl. The sun glinted off his gold front tooth.

"I aim to kill you, friend," he grunted, his eyes never leaving Jon. "And then take your woman!"

Jon smiled, his eyes as hard as agates.

"I don't think so," he said slowly, and then as the other man rushed him, he struck out with his knife, at the same time pivoting away.

Cathy, the unconscious Virginia cradled in her arms, felt

her heart leap into her throat as she watched. The other man was easily as big as Jon, and he had the advantage of weapons. Every time that gleaming sword whistled around Jon's head she felt her breath stop. She was sure he would be killed. She had never seen him fight before, not like this, meaning to kill. His gray eyes were cold as death, his face intent. A savage smile split his dark face. He looked almost as if he were enjoying himself.

The men were circling each other like big, blood-hungry dogs, both crouched low, both with the same deadly intent in their eyes. Then the pirate made another lunge, and she saw Jon's knife slice the underside of his arm as Jon ducked beneath it.

The pirate was rushing again, the long sword raised threateningly over his head. Blood dripped from his wound. Jon crouched, feinting with his knife, as the other man closed on him. Cathy held her breath, sure that Jon's head would be severed from his shoulders at any second. Why did he not jump out of the way? Then, as the sword slashed down beside him, she saw Jon crouch even lower, his big hand scooping up sand—and then he was flinging the sand into the pirate's bulging eyes.

"Arrgghh!" the pirate howled, clawing at his eyes. Jon took the opportunity to lunge forward, his knife aiming for the other man's belly. But the pirate was clearly the veteran of many a fight. Half-blinded or no, he managed to jump out of the way. At the same time his booted foot kicked out, catching Jon behind the knees. Cathy, eyes huge with horror, watched Jon go down.

Before Jon could leap to his feet, the pirate, blinking and shaking his head to clear his eyes, pressed his advantage. Savagely he slashed downward with his saber, the blade missing Jon by just inches as it bit deeply into the sand. Time after time the blow was repeated. Jon, scrambling backward, just managed to stay out of reach. In such circumstances, his knife was almost as useless as a toothpick.

"Jon!" he heard Cathy cry from somewhere close on his left hand. Daring to turn his head for just an instant, he saw that she had retrieved the dead pirate's sword. As she saw his eyes register what she intended, she tossed it to him. His eyes fixed on it, his hand rose to catch it and it fell into his hand just as he felt the blade of his opponent's sword dig deep into his shoulder. Pain rocketed through him, but there was no time now to feel—not if he wanted to live. Blood pouring from the wound, he planted his feet under him just as the pirate drew back for another savage blow. Grinning tigerishly, Jon used his legs to propel him upward in a fierce lunge. The saber penetrated the man's stomach, its tip thrusting out through his back.

Jon withdrew the sword in a rush of crimson. The pirate, both hands clapped to the pouring wound, staggered backward. His eyes fixed on Jon, glazed over. His knees buckled under him, and he fell to the sand, rolling onto his back. Then, grunting, he died.

Panting heavily, his hand moving to close over his injured shoulder, Jon sank down on his knees on the sand. Cathy ran across to him, her blue eyes burning in a face that was as white as her petticoat. Daubs of blood covered her like droplets of brilliant red paint.

"Oh, dear God, how badly are you hurt?" she sobbed, falling to her knees beside him. Sweat rolling from his brow into his eyes half-blinded Jon, but he could see the terror staring out from her face.

"I'll live," he managed, then gritted his teeth as a searing pain shot through his shoulder. Turning his head, he saw blood oozing up between his fingers that were clapped to the wound.

"Let me see that," she ordered shakily, her hand coming

up to gently set his aside. The saber had opened a gash the length of his shoulder. Blood welled from it to run down over his chest and back. It looked to be perhaps half an inch deep. Quickly Cathy caught up the skirt of her petticoat, gnawing at its hem with her teeth. When she felt the material give, she ripped it with both hands. A wide swath of material tore free all around the hem, leaving her standing in a garment that was just a little longer than knee-length.

"Good God, if this keeps up we'll both be naked!" Jon sounded suddenly amused. Cathy cast him a sharp look, then pressed the pad to the wound, bearing down hard to stem the flow of blood.

"Ouch!" he said, wincing. Then he turned his head to watch what she was doing, his expression quite dispassionate.

"Did they hurt you?" he asked after a moment, his eyes on the smears of blood that streaked her face and neck and what was left of her petticoat. Cathy, seeing where his eyes rested, shook her head.

"That isn't my blood," she explained. "When you cut that man's throat. . . ." She broke off, shuddering. Jon, seeing her face turn even whiter than it had been, hastened to distract her thoughts.

"How is Virginia?"

Cathy frowned, sending a worried look over his shoulder to where she had put the child down on the sand.

"I don't think she's badly hurt," she said slowly, biting her lower lip. "She's breathing normally, and none of her bones seem to be broken. But she won't wake up. I think she must have hit her head on something, when that man threw her down."

"Bind up my shoulder and then go and get her," Jon directed, grimacing a little at the pain as Cathy started to do as he said. "We've got to get out of here before they send someone looking for those two."

"Before *who* sends someone looking?" Cathy asked, puzzled. Jon, realizing that she didn't know about the ship he'd seen in the cove, quickly told her.

"Then that must have been the sail I saw. . . ." she said half to herself. Jon looked at her sharply.

"You saw a sail? When?" .

Cathy told him about the flash of white she'd seen on the horizon just before the two men had accosted her. Even as she talked, she realized that it couldn't possibly have been the same ship.

"The ship in the cove has been at anchor at least overnight," Jon confirmed her conclusion. "That means there's another ship out there. We've got to try to get to it. Once those bastards find two of their crew dead, they'll come looking for whoever did it. Leave me, and go get Virginia."

Cathy tied the last knot in the bandage she had made for his shoulder, then moved to obey. Behind her, Jon got rather slowly to his feet. After a moment he walked on unsteady legs toward the shelter.

To get to Virginia, Cathy had to pass the body of the gold-toothed pirate. He lay flat on his back, his eyes staring sightlessly at the sky, his mouth open in a silent scream of pain. His blood had soaked into the sand, framing him in a dark crimson pool. Cathy tried not to look at the other man, but she couldn't help but get a glimpse of him out of the corner of her eye. He, too, lay on the beach where he had fallen, his grotesquely splayed limbs obscene against the gleaming white sand. His split throat gaped open like a second mouth, the blood already congealing. . . .

To Cathy's relief, Virginia whimpered slightly when she picked her up.

"Poor baby," Cathy crooned tenderly, cradling the child against her breast. She could see a bruise just beginning to form above the child's right eye. A harsh scraping noise brought her swinging nervously around. Her muscles relaxed as she saw that it was caused by Jon dragging the boat across the sand. Cathy followed him down to the water's edge.

"Get in," he said, when he had the gig all the way in the water, its prow pointing out toward the open sea. Cathy did as he told her. When she was seated, with Virginia held gently across her knees, he waded out into the bay, pushing the boat before him.

sixteen

◦❧❧◦

*H*er Majesty's ship *Victoria* was a brigantine, part of the Royal Navy fleet. She had been sent to patrol the seas off the African coast after British merchants had complained of suffering heavy losses of ships and cargos in that area. The merchants were inclined to be hysterical and blame the missing ships on pirates, said Miles Davis, the *Victoria*'s captain, but so far his men had spotted nothing that even remotely resembled a pirate vessel. Personally he felt that the whole thing was pretty much a bag of moonshine, and he had already directed his crew to put about and head for England and home when a keen-eyed sailor had spotted Jon's small boat. Both Cathy and Jon forbore to contradict him, or to mention that the very prey the *Victoria* sought was anchored off a little island less than half a day's sailing from where they had been picked up—Cathy because she was heartily sick of bloodshed, and Jon because, after so many close calls, his only desire was to get Cathy safely home again.

Neither Captain Davis nor any of his crew had apparently heard of the mutinied *Cristobel*, or of an escaped convict named Jonathan Hale. For safety's sake, Jon introduced himself as plain John Hale, a merchant, who had been delivering a cargo of molasses to Saint Vincent in the Cape Verde Islands when his ship had gone down in a storm. His wife and infant daughter had been traveling with him, and as far as he knew the three of them were the only ones to survive his ship's loss. But it was clear from the first that no one on the *Victoria* was inclined to be suspicious, so Cathy and Jon were able to settle down to life aboard ship with relatively few worries.

Virginia, except for a bruise on her forehead, was soon as well as ever. The ship's crew made much of her, and of Cathy, which didn't go down too well with Jon. Cathy also sported a bruise on her jaw where the pirate had struck her while Jon wore his left arm in a black silk sling which, in Cathy's opinion, made him look very dashing. These wounds were explained as having happened while trying to escape the sinking ship. Beyond a great deal of solicitous comment lavished on Cathy by the sailors, they occasioned no remark.

Cathy and Jon were given the first mate's cabin. It was small, and extremely spartan, but Cathy was grateful for the privacy and very prettily thanked Mr. Corrigan, who had turned out for them. Bed sheets were obligingly donated to diaper and clothe Virginia, and Jon was able to wear the best dress uniform of the bosun, who was a tall man, though quite a bit larger in girth than Jon. Still, belted, the uniform jacket did very well, and if the pantaloons beneath were held in place by a belt, the whole effect was to make Jon look breathtakingly handsome, to Cathy's eyes at least. Cathy herself presented something of a problem. There were, quite simply, no dresses aboard the ship. Finally she was forced to make do with the cabin boy's best going-ashore outfit. The breeches were of dark blue broadcloth, and they fitted loosely about Cathy's hips and legs. The shirt was of plain white linen, without frills or ornamentation of any kind. Beneath the thin material Cathy's full breasts jutted very noticeably. Jon's eyes popped when he saw her outfit, and he absolutely forbade her to go outside their cabin dressed in such garb. Cathy, to tease him, pretended to pout, but in reality she had no intention of going out amongst so many men in such immodest apparel. Finally the captain hit upon the idea of loaning her his voluminous cloak. With that all-enveloping garment fastened about her shoulders, even Jon could make no objection to her taking the air on deck.

The sailors were dazzled by their luck at having such a beauty as Cathy dropped in their midst. Whenever she appeared on deck, she was the object of much gallantry and many admiring glances. Virginia too came in for a great deal of attention. When the two of them were out of the cabin, Jon was usually never far from their side. Just his presence in the vicinity was enough to send most of the men about their business. Those gray eyes had a way of resting on a man that made him feel as if death was breathing down his neck, as Cathy overheard one sailor tell another. She repeated the remark to Jon with a gurgle of laughter, but Jon didn't even grin.

He was polite when they were alone, but not particularly communicative, or affectionate. Cathy began to wonder if she had imagined him telling her, in such passionate tones, that he loved her. Or if, as he had said, his words had been motivated by nothing more or less than sheer physical need. She wanted to ask him, but somehow the opportunity never seemed to arise. She would wait until they were safely back in England, she decided, and then they would have it out.

The one place where Jon was not coolly courteous was in the narrow bunk they shared. There he was as hot and passionate as Cathy could have wished. His lovemaking had the power to wipe every other consideration from her mind. Each time she was caught up on the tidal wave of his passion, sweeping along with him to scale incredible heights. And when they slept, afterward, he would hold her close, his arms wrapped protectively around her, her head cradled on his uninjured shoulder. But never once, though she strained to catch them, did words of love fall from his lips.

As the *Victoria* drew ever nearer to England, Cathy found herself thinking of things that she had long forced to the back of her mind. First, of course, was Cray. She was feverish to see him again, to hold him in her arms, to assure him that she loved him. It had been eight long months since she had married Harold and left on that fateful honeymoon cruise. Would he understand that she had left him because she had to, not because she wanted to? Would he even remember her? And what would he think of baby Virginia? It would be such fun introducing them. . . .

And her father. How, she wondered, was he? She refused to dwell on the possibility that he might no longer be alive. With Mason's devoted nursing, she was sure he must have pulled through.

Harold's pudgy face loomed larger in her mind the nearer she got to land. He was like an evil genie, haunting her dreams. She was reluctant to mention even so much as his name to Jon, for fear of seeing those gray eyes film over with ice, and that long mouth harden. Still, it was a problem that had to be dealt with. Like it or not, she was Harold's legal wife. Until that difficulty was eliminated, there remained an enormous barrier between her and Jon. More than anything in the world she wanted to be Jon's wife, to have both her children legally recognized as his, and to return with him to live quietly and happily at Woodham. But Harold stood squarely in her path.

An annulment shouldn't be hard to obtain, she thought optimistically. The problem was, she would have to be in England to get it, or so she assumed, and she wanted to get Jon safely back on American soil as soon as possible. As long as there was the possibility that he could be dragged off again to prison and have the whole horrible nightmare start up once more, she wouldn't feel secure. Perhaps it would be best if he went ahead to Woodham, and she and the children joined him when everything was settled. But she hated the prospect of another lengthy separation. It was something she needed to talk over with Jon. Still, she couldn't quite bring herself to broach the subject. Despite the fact that Virginia's birthdate had finally, she thought, convinced Jon she was his daughter, the whole fiasco of Cathy's marriage to Harold was a sensitive topic. She dreaded bringing it up. It was something else that could wait until they reached England. . . . .

Deliberately turning her mind to more pleasant matters, Cathy realized with a sense of amazement that she had missed her own birthday. She had turned twenty on February 21, but so many things had been happening in her life at that time that she hadn't even realized. Jon, too, was a year older than when they had left Woodham. He had turned thirty-seven this past November, while he was a prisoner on the *Cristobel*.

Thirty-seven! From the perspective of twenty, that sounded almost old. Cathy, closely studying Jon as he lay sleeping in the bunk next to her, noticed as if for the first time the harsh lines carved by time and experience on the bronzed planes of his face. His hair, that thick wavy black hair that she loved to caress, was just beginning to be touched by silver at the temples. Discovering this, Cathy felt a fierce rush of tenderness for him. In twenty years' time, she realized, he would be an old man. But what an old man! She pictured him, his silver head leonine, his big body still strong and erect, but possibly a trifle leaner. The gray eyes would be unchanged, still fierce and twinkling by turns beneath silvering dark brows. He would be incredibly handsome even then, and she would love him madly. Of that she had no doubt.

Now that she was really looking at him, she saw that he had collected quite a number of scars over the years since she had first met him. There was the long, jagged tear on his right thigh, caused by a viciously wielded broken bottle on the night nearly three years ago when he had rescued her from the bar in Cadiz. It was white and puckered now, running like a piece of yellowed ribbon along the inside of his leg from just below his manhood to just above his knee. Criss-cross marks, the legacy of countless prison beatings during his first confinement in Newgate, formed faint ridges on his broad back. More recent disfigurements included the reddish puckered circle just below his left shoulder where she had shot him. Touching it with a penitent finger, she bit her lower lip. She still felt guilty about that. And, of course, there was the saber slash just above it. . . .

"You're making me feel like an underweight steer at a cattle auction," Jon murmured dryly, the gray eyes opening to stare straight at her. Cathy started. It was still very early in the morning and she hadn't expected him to be awake. She flushed a little as she realized that her absorbed inspection of his long naked body, gleaming darkly against the white sheet as he lay on his side facing her, must have wakened him.

"I was just—looking," she stammered. His eyes darkened to the deep gray of storm clouds. He turned over onto his back, his hand coming out to catch hers and draw her down beside him.

"Look as long as you like," he invited, his voice a soft, slow drawl. "As long as I'm allowed the same privilege."

Cradling her against his side, he lifted his free hand to gently squeeze her breast. It swelled into instant life under his hands. Cathy, her lips parting, felt a languorous warmth begin to steal upward from the pit of her stomach. She made no protest when he started to unbutton the too-big nightshirt donated to her wardrobe by one of the *Victoria*'s crew. Soon she was as naked as he, and his mouth was sending shivers chasing up and down her spine as it crawled over her skin. By the time he possessed her, she was moaning, nearly out of her mind with pleasure.

When it was over, he lay across her still quivering body. Cathy could feel perspiration dropping from his flesh onto hers. Slowly, slowly, she was coming back to reality, her hands still clutching his back, loving him. . . .

"God, you drive me crazy," he muttered into her ear. Cathy smiled, her eyes still closed, her toes curling at his words. It was wonderful to hear him say such things. Maybe now was the time to get him to say even more. . . .

"Tell me you love me," she whispered shamelessly, her eyes opening to fix him with a pleading blue stare. To her bewilderment she felt him stiffen. Then he was lifting himself away from her, rolling onto his side of the bunk and then sitting up, his legs over the edge, his back to her.

"Jon!" she protested, hurt puzzlement in her voice as she, too, sat up, the sheet pulled up under her armpits to hide her nakedness.

"Does it give you a thrill, to hear me admit it?" he demanded, casting her a glinting look over his shoulder. "All right, I love you: I love your soft, squirming little body and the way it jumps and quivers under my hands; I love the wild little mewling noises you make deep in your throat when I take you. But every time I love you, something funny happens: I find myself wondering how many other men have loved you in the exact same way!"

His voice was cruel, his words deliberately calculated to hurt. Cathy's eyes widened at the shock of his attack. For a moment she just sat staring at him, stunned.

"What are you talking about?" she asked at last. "You know you're the only man I've ever—who's ever. . . ."

"Oh, for God's sake, can't you be honest for once?" His voice was harsh, his gray eyes as bleak as a wintry sea. "I know about Harold, and I've come to terms with it. Maybe you even did what you did for love of me, as you kept insisting not so long ago. But what I can't take is watching you smile and bat your eyelashes at every man who comes within arm's length of you! You've flirted with every horny bastard on this ship, and I'm getting damned tired of playing watchdog! I realized long ago that women are naturally about as faithful as alley-cats, but I'm warning you now that I won't put up with it any longer: if I catch you bedding another man, I'll kill him. And then I'll take a great deal of pleasure in making you wish that you'd never been born!"

Cathy was gasping at the ferocity in his face and voice.

"How dare you accuse me in such a way?" she said furiously, when she had at last recovered her powers of speech. "Just who the hell do you think you are, anyway? You're not my husband, you know! I don't have to listen to that from you any longer, thank God! You're sick, Jonathan Hale, and I feel sorry for you! You're so jealous of any man who so much as asks me the time of day that you're pathetic!"

"Pathetic, am I?" he growled, his gray eyes beginning to blaze as he swivelled fully to face her. "You didn't seem to think so just a few minutes ago!"

Cathy's face flushed a deep pink at the undeniable truth of this.

"You're a conceited swine, aren't you?" she spat. "Did it ever occur to you that I might respond to every one of my legions of lovers the same way?"

Rage had forced the remark from her. As soon as it was uttered, she would have given anything to recall it. But it was too late. The gray eyes fairly leapt with fury, and Jon's jaw clenched as he glared at her.

"So you're admitting it at last, are you?" he snarled unpleasantly. "The truth will out, as they say. How many men have you had, Cathy? Besides me, and Harold? Tell me, did you cuckold me every chance you got when we were living at Woodham?"

"You unspeakable bastard!" Cathy gasped, her hands clenching over the edge of the sheet that covered her. She looked fragile and very feminine sitting there, her golden hair a wild riot of curls around her small, pink-flushed face, her eyes shooting sapphire flames. Jon regarded her almost with hatred. The way he felt about her was making his life a hell!

"Get out of my sight," she ordered, her voice shaking. "I have nothing further to say to you: you can believe what you like. Thank God I'm not married to you any longer! I can't imagine anything worse than being tied for the rest of my life to such a jealous brute!"

Jon's eyes narrowed until they were no more than icy gray slits in his face. He got jerkily to his feet, his big hands clenching and unclenching at his sides as if he was having a struggle to keep them from closing about Cathy's slender neck.

"Can't you?" he drawled unpleasantly. "Well, I can: believe me, it's far worse to be married to a chit of a girl who'll spread her legs for anything in sight. And I speak from experience!"

Cathy felt her cheeks turn fiery crimson. She was almost beside herself with temper, so furious she could hardly speak.

"You certainly don't believe in practicing what you preach, do you?" she hissed finally, her eyes glittering with homicidal intent. "Haven't you heard that what's sauce for the goose is sauce for the gander? You're a fine one to prate on and on about fidelity! Or have you very conveniently forgotten about Sarita?"

Her tone was one of angry triumph. Jon stared at her for a moment without speaking. Then a hard smile curved his lips.

"Ah, Sarita," he murmured reminiscently. "Now there was a fine, warm armful. . . ."

"Get out!" Cathy practically screamed the words at him. Insufferable beast, she would like to kill him! It would give her more pleasure than anything in the world to carve him up for bait with a dull knife!

He stood there grinning at her, malice snapping from those gray eyes.

"How does it feel to be jealous, my sweet?" he taunted softly. He was watching her with a certain amount of savage satisfaction. Naked, fists resting lightly on his hips, his body hair like a thick dark shadow against his bronzed skin, he looked big and dangerous.

"Get out!" Cathy flounced into a kneeling position in the center of the bunk, the sheet still clutched protectively before her, her eyes wild with fury. More than anything in the world she longed to do him an injury. . . . Her eyes darted feverishly about the tiny cabin, looking for something that would make a satisfying dent when brought into hard contact with his arrogant black head. Jon, angrily pulling on his borrowed pantaloons, correctly interpreted the murderous gleam in her eye.

"I wouldn't advise it," he growled, his mouth curling in a nasty smile. "It would give me too much pleasure to retaliate. Right at this moment I could happily break your cheating little neck."

"Swine!" Cathy flared, giving up her search for a suitable hard object and reaching instead for the nearest thing to hand. This just happened to be her feather pillow. Snatching it up, she flung it at him with every ounce of her strength. He dodged, laughed derisively, and slammed out of the cabin, his uniform jacket in his hand.

"I hate you!" Cathy screeched at the closed door. She gritted her teeth in impotent fury, dwelling with considerable pleasure on the various gory details of such methods of slaying him as ocurred to her. She hated him, she told herself, hated him, hated him! It would serve him right if what he thought was true, and she was momentarily tempted to take a lover just to teach Captain Jonathan Hale a much-needed lesson. She pictured his towering rage if she should flaunt the *Victoria*'s nice young captain under his nose. He would be fit to kill. . . . And that was probably literally true, she realized. In a jealous fury, he was quite capable of summarily disposing of any man he believed to be her lover. Which would hardly be fair to Captain Davis. Still. . . .

These reflections were brought to an abrupt halt by Virginia's lusty wail. Cathy, her cheeks still hot with temper, pulled the discarded nightshirt over her head and went to pick up her child, who lay in a makeshift cradle on the floor nearby.

"Hush, darling," she soothed the little girl, sitting down in the one straight chair and setting her to nurse. "Hush, my lamb, while Mama thinks up ways to kill your Papa!"

Over the next few days, a state of icy warfare existed between Jon and Cathy. When they were in the company of the ship's crew, they spoke to each other when it would have been awkward not to. On one occasion, Cathy even brought herself to smile at Jon for the benefit of Mr. Corrigan's interested eyes. But when they were alone they were coldly silent. They shared the bunk, but only to sleep. At night, Cathy would turn her back to Jon pointedly, not even saying so much as a chilly good-night. Jon, for his part, did the same thing. It was difficult, to share such cramped quarters without touching, but Cathy did her best and thought that she succeeded pretty well. Jon did nothing to indicate that he found the sudden cessation of sexual relations bothersome. In fact, if Cathy hadn't known better, she would have sworn that he was almost unaware of her existence.

It was a cool, misty morning in late July when they sighted Plymouth at last. The *Victoria* had only to sail up the English Channel, and they would be in London. Cathy, standing on the deck with Virginia in her arms, Captain Davis' dark blue cloak fastened around her neck, realized that their journey would be ended before another day had passed. And still nothing had been settled with Jon! She was much inclined just to walk out of his life forever when they were safely arrived in London. If it weren't for Cray, and Virginia, that was precisely what she would do, she told herself, her little chin tilting proudly. But for their sakes, she would give him one final chance to make amends. If he apologized with sufficient humility, and swore that he had only accused her of such dreadful things in the heat of anger without meaning a word of it, and told her he loved her, she might possibly consider forgiving him. . . .

Jon, standing further along the rail, was nonetheless aware of Cathy's presence downwind. She looked very beautiful standing there, Virginia sleeping in her arms, her golden hair caught by the brisk sea air to ripple like a bright golden banner behind her. Captain Davis' voluminous dark blue cloak, with its epaulettes and gold frogging, became her vastly. Huddled inside it, she looked to be little more than a child herself. But as he knew all too well, and to his extreme discomfort over the past few days, she was very much a woman.

He had to get things straight between them today. As he had decided before, despite her typically female untrustworthiness, he meant to keep her. Quarreling with her had been a mistake, both because it was futile to keep raking up the past and because it had cost him sorely in terms of physical discomfort. Despite what she was, he had not been able to stop himself from wanting her. Her presence in that hellishly narrow bunk beside him, when he had promised himself he would keep his hands off her, had been pure Purgatory.

When she had demanded that he confess his love, it had flicked him on the raw. He did love her, and that was the trouble. He despised himself for his weakness, but he couldn't seem to do anything about it. The little witch had him hopelessly in her thrall. During their pseudo-marriage, he had been as putty in her hands; she had played with him and twisted him as she chose. He had even begun to trust in her love, telling himself that all women were not after all like Isobelle, his father's whore of a second wife who had taken pleasure in openly flaunting her many affairs, carried on right under the old man's nose. No, he'd almost managed to convince himself that Cathy was different, that she was as sweet and innocent and devoted to him as she seemed. Then she had left for England, and his carefully rebuilt life had seemed to collapse around him like a house of cards.

He would keep her, but this time he meant to be very much the master in his own house. She would do as she was told, and he meant to make it very clear that if she so much as looked sideways at another man he would beat her to within an inch of her life. Like some dogs, women had to be taught how to behave by fear of the consequences if they stepped out of line. Before, he had been too soft with her; he didn't mean to make the same mistake again.

Jon spent the rest of that day out on deck, turning his hand to the hundred and one chores that had to be performed before the *Victoria* arrived at her destination. An experienced seaman, he knew what he was about, and had spent most of the trip helping out where he could. The sailors had come to hold him in considerable respect. His seamanship was one reason, but Jon was not such a fool as to discount the benefits accruing to being taller and stronger than most of the ship's crew—and having a very beautiful so-called wife. To a man, they envied him. Jon grimaced wryly: little did they know. . . .

Cathy, once she had made up her mind to give Jon one last chance to apologize, felt the usual feminine urge to look her best while he did it. Rather shyly, she asked Mr. Corrigan if it would be possible for her to have a bath. The man assured her gallantly that it would be a pleasure to arrange, and not long afterward two burly sailors were knocking on the cabin door, one carrying a serviceable porcelain hip bath and the other lugging steaming buckets of water.

When the bath was filled, Cathy stripped, and sank down into the warm water with a sigh of pure bliss. She soaked luxuriously for a while, and then sat up and began to scrub herself vigorously with soap. When every inch of her skin was pink and glowing, she washed her hair. It felt wonderful to massage the thick white suds through the long strands, then to sink down beneath the water for a rinse and know that her hair was squeaky clean. Virginia whimpered a little, wanting attention, as she wrung the water from her hair. Cathy stood up, wrapping a towel turban-fashion around her head, then, still dripping, went to pick up her daughter. She brought the little girl back into the tub with her, and held her carefully on her knees while the two of them played a watery version of ten little pigs.

Later, when Virginia had settled down for a nap, Cathy went out on deck to dry her hair in the sun. She took a small straight chair with her, and placed it in an out of the way spot near the rail. Dressed in breeches and shirt, with the blue cloak around her shoulders, she seated herself, and began to run her fingers through the long damp strands, spreading them out so they would dry. She was aware of Jon watching her throughout this operation, but determinedly ignored his narrowed gray eyes. If he thought to keep her immured for the rest of her life like a nun in a convent, then he could just think again!

Her hair was almost dry, fanning out around her shoulders like shimmering gold silk, when Captain Davis came to stand beside her. He was a nice, rather nondescript young man, perhaps in his middle twenties, with fair hair and hazel eyes. He had been unfailingly kind, and Cathy rather liked him. As he joined her, she smiled welcomingly at him, unaware of the effect her radiant beauty could have. He was clearly dazzled by the warmth of her smile. A watching pair of gray eyes, seeing this, glinted dangerously.

"Would you think me presumptuous if I said that you have the most beautiful hair I've ever seen in my life?" Captain Davis asked deeply. Cathy dimpled. Compared to Jon, he was very much a boy. He meant no harm, she knew.

"It's always nice to receive compliments," she said demurely, but her smile was kind.

"You must receive dozens—no, hundreds!" he murmured, enthused. "You're the loveliest lady I've ever met. If I...."

"I thank you on behalf of my wife," a cool voice said behind them, with a faint biting emphasis on the last two words. Captain Davis started guiltily, his face reddening. Cathy, recognizing those gravelly tones very well, slanted a glittering look up at their possessor.

"Oh, uh, hello, Hale. I was just—uh...." Captain Davis squirmed uncomfortably. Cathy, taking pity on him, said sweetly to Jon, "Captain Davis was kind enough to bear me company for a few moments while I dried my hair. It was most considerate of him."

"Indeed," Jon murmured dryly, his eyes flickering meaningfully over Cathy. "Then I must thank you doubly for your care of my wife when I was busy elsewhere. But now that I'm here, I will of course bear her company myself."

Again he placed that slight but unmistakable emphasis on the phrase "my wife." Captain Davis cleared his throat.

"Uh, yes," he said. "Well, if you'll excuse me, Hale, Mistress Hale, I must be getting on. I have duties about the ship...."

"Don't let us detain you," Jon murmured satirically. Captain Davis stammered, blushed, then prudently took himself off.

"Oh, go away," Cathy said crossly to Jon after Captain Davis had left. "There was not the slightest need for you to act like a heavy-handed husband! He's a very nice man, and he merely stopped for a moment to pass the time of day. And you can take that frown off your face: it doesn't impress me the least little bit! What I do is absolutely no concern of yours. If I want to talk—or anything else, for that matter—with a man, I will. And if you don't like it, then that's just too bad. Need I remind you that I'm *not* your wife?"

Cathy repeated the last two words in mocking imitation of the way he had claimed her to Captain Davis. Dark red color crept up along Jon's brown cheekbones as he absorbed this speech. His jaw hardened. The sunlight striking his eyes made them look almost silver as they glinted down at her. His hand reached out and grasped her upper arm beneath the enveloping cloak, not hard enough to hurt but with just enough pressure so that she could feel his steely strength. A humorless smile curving his mouth for the benefit of onlookers, he lifted her easily to her feet.

"I think we need to talk," he gritted through that stiff smile. Cathy tossed her head, tilting her chin until she could look him squarely in the eyes. His tone, grip, stance were clearly intended to intimidate her. That'll be the day, Cathy promised herself grimly. Her lips curved in a mock-sweet smile.

"I agree," she said clearly. His hand still on her arm, he turned her about. Catching up the chair she had been sitting in in his other hand, he escorted her firmly to their cabin.

"I'm ready to hear your apology," Cathy announced cheekily when they were alone.

Jon snorted, leaning back against the closed door and crossing his arms over his chest. He regarded her for a moment in silence, his gray eyes calculating.

"I think we need to get a few things straight," he drawled finally. Cathy lifted her eyebrows at him in haughty inquiry.

"I'm prepared to take you back to Woodham with me," he said, when it became apparent that she wasn't going to say anything. "And I'll provide a home for you and Cray and even Virginia. And, of course, any other children that we may have. But I'm not putting up with your constant flirting—or worse. I want that clearly understood."

"What makes you think I want to go back to Woodham with you?" Cathy demanded icily, feeling her temper soar at the condescending tone of his offer.

"You should be grateful for the opportunity," he told her grimly. "With two children and no husband, if I left you to your own devices as you deserve, you'd be a social outcast."

"You forget—I *have* a husband," she said very sweetly, only her sparking blue eyes revealing her anger. Jon's lips tightened into a hard, straight line.

"I don't forget anything," he grated. "But I am prepared to overlook your past behavior, provided that it isn't repeated. Hell, I'll even marry you, if you can get rid of Harold."

"Are you proposing, Captain?" Cathy mocked lightly, all the while feeling furious blood pounding in her veins. She was so furious that she could have slain him there and then. Far from apologizing, he was repeating his insults, even adding to them! And then to inform her in such a lordly fashion that he was prepared to marry her . . . ! Cathy silently ground her teeth.

"If you want to take it that way," he said, sounding suddenly better humored. "But from now on you're to confine your feminine wiles solely to me. If you give me reason to even suspect otherwise, I won't be answerable for the consequences, I warn you! You really can't expect me to put up with having another bastard foisted on me!"

"What do you mean, 'another bastard'?" Cathy's voice was ominously quiet, although all her nerve-ends were screaming.

"We'll never be sure of Virginia's paternity," he said reasonably. "She could be Harold's just as easily as mine. In fact, easier. She was very small to be a full-term infant. . . ."

"You—can—go—to—hell!" Cathy uttered the words very slowly, to make certain he got the message. A red haze of fury seemed to descend over her eyes, bathing everything in its glow. "I wouldn't marry you if you got down on your knees and begged me! I won't go back to Woodham with you, either, so you can stick that in your pipe and smoke it! When I leave this ship, I never want to see you again! My children and I will do very well without your noble sacrifice. Who knows, I might even stay married to Harold! He may not be as handsome as you, but as Martha always said, handsome is as handsome does, and that leaves you at the starting gate. And he's certainly of far higher birth! Maybe he'll even adopt Cray. Think of it, Jon: your son may one day be Lord Stanhope!"

"You can, of course, come back to Woodham or not just as you wish." Jon straightened away from the door, his hands clenched at his sides and a muscle twitching at the corner of his mouth. "But if you choose not to, you're not keeping my son."

"*My* son," Cathy corrected between clenched teeth. "And just how do you propose to take him from me? There's not a court in England that would award his custody to you. A convicted felon, who just managed to escape the gallows by the skin of his teeth!"

"You think that a judge might decide he'd be better off with his whore of a mother?" Jon grated, the way he was clenching and unclenching his fists indicating that he was now as angry as she. "You may be right, at that!"

They stood glaring at each other while tension crackled like lightning between them. In her crib, Virginia broke the quivering silence with a whimpering cry.

"Your bastard's calling you," Jon snarled, and turning abruptly on his heel stalked from the cabin.

Pure, simple, unadulterated rage was Cathy's only bedfellow that night. Jon didn't return to the cabin, and for that she was heartily glad. When she'd said she never wanted to set eyes on him again, she'd meant it. She would never forgive him for his insults, never!

Sometime during the night they docked at London's harbor. Cathy, up at the crack of dawn with a cranky Virginia, saw the pier from a porthole. Even at such an early hour, the wharf was busy. . . .

She dressed, and gathered up what few possessions she and Virginia had. As soon as possible, they would be going ashore. She would put up at an inn, and send at once for Martha and Cray, and her father. Then she would sort out the tangled mess that was her life. She'd just been sniping at Jon when she'd said she might stay married to Harold. She still despised him as much as ever. But she certainly was not going back to Woodham with Jon! She would die first, after the unspeakable things he believed of her! What she would do was start an entirely new life; preferably, one that was completely devoid of men!

She was just getting ready to leave the cabin when a knock sounded at the door. Virginia in her arms, Cathy went to answer it. Most likely it was Captain Davis, wanting to know when she would be leaving the ship. Certainly it would not be Jon. Knocking was a piece of good manners he'd never practiced!

When Cathy swung open the door, she stood staring, dumbfounded.

"Good morning, Cathy," Harold said affably, his pudgy face every bit as unattractive as she'd remembered.

"What are you doing here?" she gasped, making no move to invite him in out of the passage.

"I received a most interesting caller last night—or should I say this morning," Harold told her with every evidence of enjoyment. "Your pirate, to be precise. At first I was in fear of my life, thinking that his purpose was to make you a widow. But he assured me that that was the furthest thing from his mind!"

"I presume there is a point you're trying to make?" Cathy grated, when he paused dramatically.

"Is that any way to talk to your long-lost husband?" he reproached, his beady blue eyes snapping maliciously. "Yes, I do have a point: your pirate came to me to make a deal. He said that he would be happy to give me my wife and daughter," here Harold snickered, shooting a droll look at Virginia, "in return for his son!"

seventeen

❧❦❧

By the time the tall ship sailed into Charleston's harbor, Cathy's rage had cooled and hardened into icy implacability. It was little more than three months since Jon had left her on the *Victoria*, catching the next vessel bound for the States and taking Cray with him. Although she had been in little doubt as to Jon's destination from the time Harold had smirkingly brought her word of what he had done, Cathy had hired a couple of Bow Street Runners just to make certain, using money drawn from her trust fund with a sense of savage satisfaction. She was no longer Jon's wife, and she could spend her money as she chose without fear of angering him. And she chose to use it to recover her son! Jon may have thought to neatly spike her guns by absconding with Cray, but he was soon going to learn that he had made a mistake: Cray was her son as well as his, and she would have him back if she had to spend every penny she possessed to do it, by fair means or foul!

The one thought that slightly mitigated Cathy's fury was that Jon had at least had the decency to take Martha with them. How Jon had managed to persuade the woman to let him take Cray she couldn't imagine, but knowing Jon she guessed that he hadn't bothered with much persuasion. More than likely he had just scooped the boy up under his arm and walked out, leaving Martha to follow or not, as she chose. And of course Martha would never leave Cray. Cathy took what comfort she could from the knowledge that her son was being well cared for, and hoped that he wasn't missing her too much. Which he probably wasn't, she acknowledged wryly. She had been away from him for such a long time, especially in the eyes of so little a boy, and Cray had always adored Jon. With Martha to see to his creature comforts, Cray was probably as happy as a clam at low tide. Which should have made Cathy feel better, but, perversely, didn't.

Harold had been ridiculously easy to deal with. He had come aboard the *Victoria* plainly thinking to bully her into returning with him, as his wife, to the life he had mapped out for them. The steely-eyed, grim-jawed woman who turned on him with such scorn clearly took him aback. Gasping, he had floundered, had even tried to use physical force to put her in what he termed her proper place. Cathy had routed him with fierce enjoyment, refusing to even so much as accompany him to her Aunt Elizabeth's townhouse to talk things over. When he saw that he had not a hope of persuading her to live with him, Harold had changed his tactics. Whining with frustration, he had told her that she had a duty to support him, as he was, after all, her husband. Cathy had laughed at this. Not for long, she promised him grimly.

Her father, quite recovered and able to walk with the aid of a stick, was a great help to her in the matter of obtaining an annulment. Harold, fueled by malice, had at first refused to give the sworn statement necessary for the granting of such a decree. But the promise of a handsome settlement, if he did as she asked, promptly inspired him to a positive fever of co-operation. After that, it needed only to get the written testimony of certain members of the *Tamarind*'s crew, now safely returned to England. They swore that, due to Cathy's constant indisposition from the time she and Harold had boarded the ship, there was no possible way the marriage could have been consummated. Armed with these documents, and greatly assisted by her father's influence at Court, Cathy encountered little difficulty in obtaining both legal and ecclesiastical annulments of her marriage to Harold.

Sir Thomas had insisted on accompanying her on the voyage to the States. He wanted to be in at the kill, he said grimly. Cathy, mindful of his still precarious health, had done her best to dissuade him, but he would not budge from his stand. Mason had privately whispered in her ear that it would probably do him more harm to be left behind to fret than it would to go, so Cathy at last gave in. Now, standing at his side at the rail as the ship dropped anchor in Charleston's harbor, Cathy was glad of his presence. He and Mason had been her bulwarks throughout the voyage, cosseting her and doing their utmost to cheer her when she teetered on the verge of giving way to depression. They, along with Alice, the nurse-maid she had engaged to care for Virginia, and Martha, and of course the children, would be the nucleus of the household she intended to set up when she had Cray safe and they had returned once again to England.

Cathy was dressed as befitted the weather, which was sunny but crisp, as October usually was in South Carolina. From the tips of her elegantly-heeled little shoes to her dashing feathered bonnet, she looked every inch the great lady, which was just as she had intended. Before she took Cray away, she intended to impress on Jon exactly what he had lost. Not only his son, and daughter, but herself.

Her dress was of peacock blue silk, the bodice shaped close to her slender figure and slightly elongated as was the fashion, the skirt flaring out in an enormous bell from her tiny waist, the sleeves full and caught in at the wrists to fall over her hands in a froth of white lace. More lace cascaded from her throat to where the silk of the dress formed a deep V between her rounded breasts. Her bonnet was a frivolous and vastly becoming confection of the same shade of blue silk, ruched to frame her small face enchantingly, and set off with an emerald green peacock feather which trembled as it just brushed her cheek. Wide, flat, emerald green ribbons were tied in a saucy bow beneath one shell-like ear. The color of the dress made her eyes glow like twin sapphires set aslant beneath sooty black fringes of lashes; her hair, worn in a soft roll at the back of her head, framed her features like gleaming gold floss. With temper at the thought of seeing Jon again putting a spark in her eyes and flushing her cheeks a becoming shade of rose, she was a vision to bedazzle the most hardened of men. The sailors, busy with chores about the deck, could hardly keep their eyes off her.

It was mid-afternoon before they were at last able to go ashore. On the dock, Cathy hesitated before climbing into the carriage hired to transport them to a hotel.

"I would really prefer to go directly out to Woodham," she told her father. He looked down at her, the expression in his blue eyes, so like Cathy's own, grave.

"Don't you think you should rest first?" he asked mildly. "After all, Hale and the boy aren't going anywhere. They'll still be there tomorrow."

"I know," Cathy said, "But. . . ."

She couldn't put into words this sudden compulsion she had to go at once, to see Cray and hold him in her arms, to be enfolded in Martha's warm embrace—and to tell Jon exactly what a bastard she thought he was before taking his son away! She would even show him the sworn statements attesting to the truth of her relationship with Harold, just to watch his face as he realized what a stubborn, stupid fool he had been. And when she took Cray and left—how she wished she could watch him then! The biggest ambition in her life was to see Jonathan Hale bleed to death right before her eyes. He had taken her love and trampled it, turning it to an intense, burning hatred in the process. She hoped viciously that it hurt when he discovered his mistake. She hoped he hurt enough to die. . . .

"I would really rather go at once," she told her father again. "But the rest of you must go on to the inn. I'll fetch Cray myself, and join you in a few hours."

"Don't be ridiculous," her father said crisply, sounding so much like his old self that Cathy started. "If you are determined to go at once, then I will of course accompany you. I wouldn't dream of letting you face Hale alone. Mason can look after Alice and Virginia."

"I'm not afraid of Jon, Papa," Cathy answered, the light of battle gleaming in her eyes. She was already anticipating with savage pleasure the upcoming confrontation with Jon. Her inward vision so engrossed her that she completely failed to notice the interested stares fixed on her and her father, both dressed in the height of London fashion, standing amidst the piles of their obviously expensive luggage while Mason and Alice, holding Virginia, waited patiently nearby.

"Lady Catherine! So good to see you back home again!" The voice belonged to Eunice Struthers, a flighty maiden lady who lived with her widowed sister in the heart of Charleston. The pair of them had been frequent callers at Woodham. "Does Captain Hale know you're arriving today? He said nothing about it, when I visited your dear little boy. In fact, Captain Hale indicated that you might be away for quite a long while, since your father is so ill. . . ."

Here the woman trailed off, her eyes on Sir Thomas. Clearly she was puzzling over his identity. His dress, bearing, and manner all proclaimed him to be a man of standing.

"Miss Struthers, I'd like to present my father, Sir Thomas Aldley, Earl of Badstoke," Cathy said, seeing nothing for it but to perform the introduction the woman was obviously expecting. "Papa, this is Miss Eunice Struthers."

Sir Thomas murmured something civil, while Cathy added: "As you can see, my father has recovered from his illness. And no, Jon didn't know we were arriving. I wanted to give him a—surprise."

Cathy's slight hesitation before the last word was lost on Miss Struthers. She giggled, a high-pitched, girlish sound that went oddly with her prim dress and manners.

"I'm sure he'll be delighted," she gurgled, already backing away in her eagerness to spread the news. "It was such a pleasure meeting you, Sir Thomas, and seeing you again, of course, Lady Catherine. We must have a little supper party soon, to celebrate your return home. . . ."

"Now I have to go to Woodham immediately," Cathy said wryly, watching her leave. "She'll have the news of our arrival spread all over town before dark. And if Jon hears that I've come before I have Cray safe. . . ."

Sir Thomas nodded grimly. He understood that Jon was unlikely to let Cray go without a fight. They had already decided that the best thing to do was to get Cray away while Jon was in the fields.

Mason and Alice were hustled into the waiting carriage, not without some protest from Mason, who felt he should accompany them. But Sir Thomas told him that he could be most useful by looking after the little girl, and assuring them all of comfortable accommodations. The Charleston Arms was reputed to be the best inn in town, and Mason was to secure rooms for them there.

When the carriage had gone, Sir Thomas set himself to obtaining transportation for himself and Cathy. In a very short period of time he had managed to procure a curricle and driver. Soon they were moving smartly along the cobbled streets through the town, and finally out along the winding road that passed eventually by Woodham.

Cathy, seated silently beside her father, drank deeply of the crisp air. She loved South Carolina in the autumn, loved the bright reds and golds that turned the trees into brilliant splashes of color against the still green grass and the halcyon blue sky, loved the sweet smells of freshly cut hay and open fires and limitless space. She loved the gently rolling countryside and the tall trees that lined the road and protected them from the bright afternoon sun. The thought came to her unbidden that, if she carried through on what she intended, she would soon be returning to England, never to see all this beauty again.

Seated in the back of the open carriage, Cathy strained for a glimpse of Woodham while trying to seem nonchalant. With every clop of the horses' hooves she was drawing closer and closer to home. Cathy bit the inside of her lower lip, vexed at herself. Woodham wasn't her home any longer, and she must remember that.

"Daughter, are you sure you want to go through with this?" Sir Thomas, speaking for the first time since they had set out, sounded troubled. Cathy, turning to look at him, saw that a frown wrinkled his brow.

"Get Cray, do you mean? Of course I'm sure." Deliberately she made her voice light. Sir Thomas was not fooled.

"You know I mean leave Hale—and don't tell me he left you first, which I see is on the tip of your tongue. I would be the first to agree that he has treated you badly over this business with Harold, and now Cray. And you know that I always thought you could have married someone more— suitable. But before all this came up, you were happy with him. And, Cathy—I think you love him." This last was said quietly.

Cathy stiffened. "I do not!" she protested fiercely. Then, more calmly, "Papa, you must allow me to know my own mind! I loved Jon once, I admit. But he killed what I felt for him very effectively. I will be quite happy never to set eyes on him again once I have Cray."

"But. . . ." Sir Thomas began.

"Please don't let's talk about it anymore," Cathy said almost desperately, and then, "Oh, look, there's the drive! Driver, turn right up there!"

Sir Thomas said nothing more as they bowled along the dirt road leading up to the white-pillared brick house. But he was troubled.

When the curricle rocked to a halt before the circular stone steps leading to Woodham's front door, Cathy was out of her seat almost before the carriage stopped. Already the oak front door was opening.

"Miss Cathy! Miss Cathy!" Petersham was running down the steps, closely followed by Martha with Cray by the hand. Cathy, smiling with tears in her eyes, jumped lightly down from the carriage without waiting for Sir Thomas to alight and assist her. Immediately she was enveloped by three pairs of arms, all bestowing crushing hugs. She hugged them back impartially.

"Oh, lovey, it's good to see you!"

"Mama! Mama, where have you been? Daddy said you were coming soon, but this isn't very soon, I think!"

Cathy laughed at this without taking time to consider the implications. Freeing herself from Petersham and Martha, she took Cray in her arms. The little boy's arms closed tightly around her neck. She kissed the top of his silky black head, so absurdly like Jon's. At the thought tears began to rain freely down her cheeks.

"Mama, you're making me wet!" This wriggling protest from Cray made Cathy laugh again. Giving him another kiss on his soft little cheek, she turned around with him in her arms so that he could see Sir Thomas, who had alighted rather stiffly from the curricle and was regarding the scene with a thoughtful expression.

"Cray, do you know who this is?" Cathy prompted with a smile. Cray stared hard at Sir Thomas, who smiled at him.

"It's Grandfather," Cathy told him. Cray nodded doubtfully, then said audibly in Cathy's ear, "Mama, I don't see why you call him that. He's nowhere near as grand as my real father. My real father's much bigger!"

Everybody chuckled at this, including Sir Thomas. Then they were all moving inside. The center hallway with its polished wood floors and hanging mirror was so familiar that Cathy felt her throat tighten up all over again. Home! her wayward senses cried. You've come home!

"Miss Cathy, would you like to go upstairs and freshen up? I'll have hot water sent up." Petersham was beaming foolishly at her. "We're all so glad you've come home! Master Jon will be so pleased!"

Before Cathy could answer, Martha broke in.

"Where's the little girl? Master Jon said there was a little girl! He said she looks like you, lovey. I can't wait to see her!"

They were both staring expectantly at Cathy. She looked rather desperately to her father for assistance. He returned her look stolidly, without making a move to help her out.

"Yes, Martha, there is a little girl. I've named her Virginia, and she's with her nursemaid in town." She took a deep breath. "Petersham, I'm sorry, but we won't be staying. I've only come for Cray. Martha, will you please go and pack his things? We'll be going back to town."

"Miss Cathy, you can't!"

"Lovey, you're not serious!"

"I am deadly serious," Cathy said quietly. "Please, Martha, would you just pack his things? I'll explain everything later."

Cray, hearing the sounds of trouble in their voices, looked from one to the other. His small face began to pucker.

"Don't cry, darling, it'll be all right," Cathy whispered to him swiftly, tickling him to make him laugh before passing him across to Martha. Martha took his hand, then shot a troubled look at Sir Thomas. Sir Thomas nodded slowly, and Martha went reluctantly off to do as she was bidden.

"Miss Cathy, I can't let you take Master Cray! Master Jon would take me apart!" Petersham sounded anguished.

"I'll handle Master Jon," Cathy said, with more assurance than she felt. "Don't worry, Petersham, I don't mean to leave without seeing him. Where is he, please?"

"He's in the west field." Petersham's eyes were worried as they fixed her. "But, please, Miss Cathy, whatever's wrong between you two—and I've known all along there's something, he's been down in the dumps ever since he got home again—don't just leave him like this! You'll break his heart! He loves you, Miss Cathy!"

Cathy laughed.

"Please have the trap brought around, Petersham. I want to drive out to the west field." Then, to Sir Thomas, she added, "Papa, I'm going to drive myself out there. I want to speak to Jon alone."

Sir Thomas stared at her hard for a moment, then slowly inclined his head. "I'll escort Martha and Cray into Charleston and then come back for you," he said.

"Oh, Papa, there's no need! I can drive into town very well!"

"There's every need," her father said heavily. Then, as Petersham reluctantly departed to do her bidding, his tone gentled. "Cathy, I think you ought to think about this. If Hale is prepared to marry you. . . ."

"I wouldn't marry him if he was the only man left on earth," Cathy broke in fiercely. "Papa, my mind is made up! I don't want to discuss it any more!"

Sir Thomas bowed his head, and said nothing further. It wasn't long before the trap was brought around, and Cathy, scorning assistance, climbed into it.

"I won't be gone long," she told Sir Thomas and Petersham impartially as they watched her, varying degrees of concern on their faces. Then she snapped the reins briskly and the horse moved off.

The west field was further along the road, down a little dirt track that led over small hillocks and a trickling stream. Cathy drove at a good pace, wishing vainly that she had worn gloves as the leather reins chafed her hands. The late afternoon air, warmed by the still bright sun, caressed her face gently, bringing a glow to her cheeks. Her blue eyes sparkled with the light of approaching battle. She sat very straight in the narrow padded seat, her head protected from the sun by a fringed canopy, her bottom protected from unexpected jolts by well-sprung wheels. Her gorgeous dress with its matching little bonnet looked completely out of place in that homely setting, but she didn't care. She also didn't care, or know, that, set within the frame of the dusty black trap, she looked a trifle absurd but wholly beautiful.

As the trap crested the last rise before reaching the west field, Cathy pulled to a halt. For just a moment she sat drinking in the scene below her. The field was waist deep in tall, golden grass that swayed in the gentle wind. The sun shone warmly down on the backs of the slaves, who were wielding long scythes as they cut the grass in rhythmic rows. Directing the operation was Jon. She would know that tall form in the dark a mile away. As she watched, he too picked up a scythe, and set to work.

Cathy felt her throat suddenly go dry, and her heart speed up. The showdown was at hand. Now he would pay—pay in blood for the insults, humiliation, and final outrage he had dealt her!

With a smart snap of her wrists she set the horse in motion. As the trap moved down the hillock to the edge of the field, she felt the eyes of the men turning to stare at her. Jon, busy with his work, was one of the last to look around. After one incredulous glance, she saw him straighten, turn, and start toward her.

Cathy pulled up, and sat waiting for him to reach her. He was leaner than she remembered, but so brown and fit that he looked invincible. Dressed in a loose white shirt and formfitting buff-colored breeches, a wide-brimmed hat set carelessly on the back of his dark head, he exuded earthy male virility. As he drew closer, Cathy could see the black stubble on that iron jaw, and the odd gleam in the gray eyes as they moved over her. A faint, half-wry smile twisted his mouth. Cathy felt a sudden rush of joy at the sight of him, but fiercely tramped it down. She was here for a purpose, she reminded herself: to teach the black-hearted wretch a lesson that he would never forget!

"Lady Stanhope, I presume?" he drawled with a touch of mocking humor as he came to a halt beside the trap, one foot raised to rest negligently on the step. When he rested his arm on his raised knee, the movement brought him close. So close Cathy could see every individual pore in his dark face. Gulping, she tried to present an outward facade of cool hauteur. Inwardly, she was a trembling mass of nerves.

"Not any longer," she replied composedly, forcing herself to meet those gleaming gray eyes. "The marriage was annulled. I'm Lady Catherine Aldley again."

"I see." The smile playing on his hard mouth widened a little.

"The papers are in my bag. You can look at them, if you like. As I told you, they all attest to the grounds for the annulment: non-consummation." Despite her best intentions, Cathy could not prevent a touch of asperity from entering her voice.

"I don't doubt it."

Cathy stared at him incredulously, hardly able to believe her ears. He didn't doubt it? Then what in God's name had he been playing at all this time?

Jon correctly interpreted the disbelieving expression flitting across her face. One corner of his mouth tilted up in a self-mocking grin.

"As soon as I got away from the situation, and had time to think, I knew I'd been a blind fool. Can you forgive me?"

Cathy was so taken aback that she could only gape at him. After everything he had put her through, he was now prepared to simply admit he had been wrong? Without proof of any kind? It was incredible! She wasn't going to stand for it! He had put her through an emotional wringer for months, and now he thought he could just apologize, and all would be forgotten? Not on his life!

"How do you feel about exchanging plain Lady Catherine Aldley for Mistress Hale again?" The tone of the question was light, but those gray eyes were not. They were warmly sensuous as they moved over her. Cathy felt rather like an actress who had learned her part by heart, then walked onstage into the wrong play. Nothing was going as she had expected.

When she didn't answer, Jon cast a quick, impatient glance around.

"We can't talk here," he said. "Move over."

Stepping lightly up into the trap, he took the reins from her nerveless hands. Cathy obediently scooted over as he sat beside her, clucking to the horse. Her mind was in such a turmoil that she hardly felt the trap begin to move. He had apologized—and proposed. It would be so easy to forgive him—until the next time. Cathy, remembering how he had refused to listen to her, refused to believe her when she had told him nothing but the truth, remembering how he had used and abused her, labeling Virginia a bastard and stealing Cray, felt her heart harden.

"I don't want to marry you." Cathy's voice was jerky.

Jon cast a quick, appraising look across at her, but said nothing until he pulled the buggy to a stop. They were in the midst of another tall, golden field, not far from the stream, with a lone oak tree standing sentinel some little distance away. All around them the land rose in a gentle slope, cutting them off from the rest of the world. They were completely alone.

"Why not?" Jon asked calmly, turning to look at her.

Cathy began to feel a trifle annoyed at his coolly reasonable tone. It was as if he were an indulgent father, giving in to the whims of a fractious child. Well, she was no child, and so she meant to make him well aware!

"Where shall I start?" She looked him fully in the eyes. "First, I'm sick and tired of living with your jealousy. I've never given you the least cause to suspect me of anything at all out of the way, yet you're always accusing me of having lovers. Second, you have a vile, nasty temper, and you can be violent. I'm sick of that, too. Three, talk about being unfaithful! What about Sarita? I refuse to put up with that sort of thing, and if it happened once I don't doubt it will happen again. Four, you suspected that Virginia wasn't your child. How do I know you won't capriciously decide the same about any other children we might have if I was misguided enough to marry you? And five, you stole Cray from me! I find that harder to forgive than anything!"

Jon's jaw hardened as he listened to this speech. Without a word, when she was finished and sat glaring at him belligerently, he jumped down from the trap, then turned to look at her.

"Get down," he said sparely, and when she made no move to do as he had said he reached up and caught her under the armpits, lifting her down beside him. Cathy didn't physically resist. Instead she allowed him to pull her arm through his, and walk her away from the trap toward the stream.

"I'll answer that point by point." His voice was even, and this irritated Cathy more than ever. "You're right: I do tend to be somewhat jealous, but you must admit you've given me provocation!" Here Cathy threw a fiery glance at him, and he backtracked a little. "By that I mean that I found you in some pretty damning circumstances. What other man wouldn't have thought the same thing I did, if he had found his wife naked in bed with another man? A lot of men would have throttled you on the spot!"

"Instead of which you, generous, kind soul that you are,

merely raped me!" Cathy broke in heatedly. Jon had the grace to look faintly shamefaced.

"It wasn't rape," he began sulkily, but prudently decided to abandon this argument in the face of Cathy's clearly rising temper. "Anyway, I'm working on not being jealous. I promise I'll do my best to control it. If I get out of line, you have my permission to brain me with something. Knowing you, you will, anyway."

Here he grinned briefly, but encountering Cathy's fulminating glance hastily wiped it away.

"As to my temper, may I point out that I *didn't* throttle you? I've never laid a violent hand on you, and you know it, so I think we can dismiss that point."

"And Sarita?" Cathy prompted coldly.

"Ahh, Sarita," Jon drawled teasingly, but seeing Cathy's eyes flame quickly abandoned the joke. He stopped walking and turned to face her, his hands lightly resting on her upper arms. "She didn't mean a thing to me, and you know it. I just took her to get back at you."

"You were just unfaithful, as you were constantly accusing me of being," Cathy interjected waspishly. Jon's eyes narrowed as he looked down at her.

"You can't accuse me of being unfaithful if we weren't even married," he pointed out, then as Cathy's eyes widened and her soft pink lips parted for what he was certain would be a pithy retort, he added: "You know damned well that I never so much as looked at another woman from the time I first saw you, screeching your fool head off in your cabin on the *Anna Greer*, to that one time with Sarita. And it will never happen again, I give you my word. Good God, you're going to throw that up at me for the rest of our lives, aren't you?"

"No, I'm not," Cathy told him icily. "Because I'm not going to be around for the rest of your life. Let me go! I'm leaving!"

She tried to jerk her arms free of his grasp as she spoke. Going over all his many misdeeds in her mind had effectively stiffened her resolve to teach him a lesson. He had rent the fabric of their love apart with his jealousy, and now he thought he could blithely stitch up the tears and make whole cloth again. Well, she didn't even intend him to have so much as the tattered pieces!

"You can't leave me. I won't let you." Jon's grip on her arms was iron-hard, and his voice was even harder. He towered over her small form, his dark face menacing.

"And just how do you propose to stop me? Lock me up and keep me a prisoner for the next twenty years?" Cathy was furious, and it showed in her face and tone.

"I can think of better ways." Jon was smiling, but the gesture was not pleasant. Cathy, staring up at him with fire leaping from her eyes, felt a shiver of apprehension run along her spine. He was so very big, and he looked bent on something violent. . . .

"Let me go!" He was pulling her into his arms, laughing softly under his breath as he did so. Cathy kicked him, her little foot coming into bruising contact with his very solid shin-bone. Jon didn't even flinch. Instead, his arms went around her, imprisoning her against the hard wall of his body. Then he was bending over her, his head and shoulder blocking out the sun.

From the first touch of his mouth on hers, Cathy knew that she was lost. Blindly, like a child seeking comfort, she returned his kisses, her arms going up to curve around his neck, her fingers entwining in the thick dark hair. She knew in some deep recess of her being that this was what she had been born for, this man, this moment.

He was bending her back over his arm, muttering her name over and over as his mouth pressed against her soft flesh beneath its silken covering. Cathy moaned as his lips found the quivering peak of her breast, parting over the swelling softness. She could feel the moist heat of his mouth burning her skin through the layers of silk.

Her dress was falling away from her shoulders, and he was pulling it down, loosening her arms from about his neck so that he could free them from its folds. Vaguely Cathy realized that he was undressing her, in the middle of an open field, with the sun shining down on their heads and a party of men just over the rise. But she didn't care. She didn't care about anything except this fever that was in her blood, scorching her, turning her to fire beneath his hands. Like a kitten wanting to be rubbed she arched herself against him as he sent her petticoats the way of the dress. Then she was standing in nothing but her chemise and pantalets, her fingers shamelessly unbuttoning his shirt, laying hot little kisses on the bronzed skin thus exposed.

He groaned at the touch of her lips, his hands not quite steady as they slid the straps of the chemise down her arms, then untied the drawstring of her pantalets and let them drop to the ground. Then he was lifting her free of the little circlet of clothes, laying her on her back amidst the tall, waving golden grass. Cathy, looking up at him with searing desire as he divested himself of his clothing, saw the wide naked shoulders, gleaming beneath the sun, the curling black pelt that covered his body, the flat belly and long, powerful-looking legs, and felt weak with longing. He was so handsome it hurt, and she wanted him. And from the look of him, there could be no doubt that he wanted her.

He came down beside her, naked, leaning over her, his black head framed against an expanse of untroubled blue sky. Those gray eyes, that long, hard mouth tempted her. . . . Shuddering, she reached up and slid a hand behind his neck, pulling him down. Just before his mouth touched hers again she closed her eyes, shutting out the light.

"Oh, God, you're beautiful," he groaned just before he took her, his voice shaken. Cathy opened her eyes to see him staring down at her, his eyes dark with passion as they eagerly watched the hunger build in her small flushed face.

"Love me," she moaned, her nails digging punishingly into the nape of his neck. "Oh, Jon . . . !"

This last subsided into an aching gasp as he possessed her, the throbbing heat of his desire impaling her fiercely. Cathy writhed, moaning, her nails raking deep furrows down his broad, sweat-slick back. Her eyes shut tight, her breath coming in little pants, she met thrust with thrust, responding to his bruising ardor with a clamoring need of her own.

"Oh, darling!" she cried when she felt she could stand his hot-sweet torture no longer. His mouth closed over one aching nipple and his final hard thrust began to throb deep inside her. She felt him shudder, gasping, in her arms, and then was whirled away into a dark, timeless void.

When she came to at last, she was surprised to find that the sky was the same bright blue it had been minutes before, the grass was still tall and golden and sweet, surrounding them like whispering guards, the sun was shining, and the air was cool. Somehow she had expected it all to be changed.

Jon was lying on his side next to her, his long, naked body dark against the rustling grass, his hand propping his head as he looked down at her. A lazy smile curved his mouth. His black hair was wildly mussed, and Cathy felt color stain her cheeks as she recalled running her fingers through it mindlessly. At her blush, his eyes warmed on her face.

"Now tell me you don't love me," he murmured complacently. Cathy, staring at him, said nothing. He looked so smug, so supremely self-satisfied. . . . She sat up abruptly. He was so certain that his lovemaking had settled everything!

"I have a confession to make," he said idly, turning over to lie on his back with his hands crossed under his head, clearly unconcerned with his nakedness. Cathy rose to her feet and began to pull on her clothes with hands that were still not quite steady. He watched her, his expression both admiring and possessive.

"When I took Cray, I knew you'd come after him," he told

her, smiling a little at the memory of his own cleverness. "As angry as I was, I still couldn't bear to lose you forever. I even told him that Mama would be coming soon, when he asked. I've been expecting you for weeks."

Cathy, struggling to fasten her dress, felt a welcome dart of anger. So he had manipulated her again! He thought her so easy to bend to his wishes, did he? Well, he was in for a surprise!

She tied her bonnet beneath her chin, not caring if the bow was slightly awry. Then she turned, and walked purposefully in the direction of the trap. Behind her, she heard the grass rustle as he suddenly sat up.

"Where are you going?" The question was sharp. Cathy smiled grimly. Ah, maybe he was at last beginning to get the idea! Reaching the trap, she stepped quickly into it, gathering up the reins. Then she turned to look at him.

He was standing, looking slightly ludicrous as he stared at her, hands balled and resting on his hips, feet planted apart, as naked as the day he was born.

"I'm leaving you," she said sweetly, and clucked to the horse. Obediently the animal moved forward. As she turned the trap around, she heard Jon cursing, a steady, furious stream of profanity. Her last glimpse of him as she rolled out of the meadow found him hopping about on one leg, hurrying madly to pull on his breeches so that he could come after her. Her action had caught him totally unawares.

Cathy smiled, her blue eyes gleaming triumphantly. She had her revenge at last. So why was it that she couldn't shake the conviction that she had just cut off her nose to spite her face?

eighteen

~⚬~

"Miss Cathy, I am positively ashamed of you!" Martha said severely, dragging the brush through her mistress' long hair so hard that it actually pulled out a few silky golden strands.

"Ouch! Martha, if you don't hush, I swear I'll turn you out without a character! As I've told you a dozen times, it's none of your business what I choose to do!" Cathy jerked her head away from the woman's vengeful brush. She was getting sick and tired of hearing Martha's views on poor, mistreated Jon! What about poor, mistreated Cathy? Was no one concerned about her wrongs? Even her father seemed inclined to feel that Jon had suffered a little too much at her hands.

"That poor man," Martha continued, ignoring Cathy's threat as Cathy had known she would. "All the way across the ocean on that benighted boat, you were all he talked about. Cathy this and Cathy that, it was. He even told me how like you Virginia is! And when I explained to him how it happened that you married Lord Harold, he was most understanding. Said he saw it all now, and couldn't understand why he hadn't seen it before. Proper apologetic, he was."

"Not to me!" Cathy murmured resentfully. Martha, busy arranging her hair in a becoming topknot, paid this interjection no heed.

"I tell you, Miss Cathy, if you take those poor children away from their papa for no better reason than spite, I'll have to take shame on the way Sir Thomas and I have raised you! Master Jon loves you, and you won't find a finer gentleman the length and breadth of this heathen country. Not even in England! Why, he. . . ."

"If he loves me so much, then why hasn't he come after me?" Cathy interjected unanswerably. "We've been here for a week—a *week*—and he hasn't come near us. Answer that, pray!"

Martha couldn't, and both she and Cathy knew it. She hemmed and hawed, but the simple truth was that there was no acceptable answer. She and Cathy and the children, along with Sir Thomas and Mason, had been staying at the Charleston Arms. Every day since Cathy had returned with Sir Thomas and little Cray, Martha had expected Master Jon to come battering down the door, demanding that they come home to Woodham with him. But so far, it hadn't happened, and even Martha's faith in him was being shaken.

Cathy, too, had expected Jon almost hourly since she had left him half-naked and cursing in the meadow. When she pictured his coming, she was filled with a pleasurable sense of anticipation mixed with fear. He would be so angry . . . ! But as the days passed, and he didn't come, that shivery feeling that possessed her whenever she thought of his rage began gradually to be replaced by dull resignation. Apparently he had accepted that it was over between them. The ship taking them back to England sailed in another ten days. Once she was on that boat, Cathy knew that she would have lost Jon forever.

"That's good enough, Martha. Help me get dressed," Cathy said irritably, pulling her head away from Martha's fingers as they coaxed a few ringlets to fall becomingly around her face. After all, who was there now to care how she looked?

Cathy turned away from the dressing table mirror and got to her feet. Martha, blessedly silent now, went to retrieve Cathy's dress from the tall wardrobe. It was a beautiful autumn morning, with the sun streaming in through the long windows and a light breeze rustling the brightly-colored leaves on the maple tree nearby. In keeping with the weather, Martha selected a wine-colored velvet two-piece outfit, consisting of a short, fitted jacket and a sweeping, full skirt. Beneath the jacket went a white silk shirtwaist, with a high neck and stock. It was a severe garment, almost masculine in style. It heightened Cathy's fragile beauty, making her seem the very epitome of femininity.

Both women were silent as Martha helped her into the dress. When the last heavy fold had been twitched into place, Cathy turned to survey herself in the long cheval glass without interest. Today her appearance held no charms for her. She would rather by far have been wearing the tattered petticoat of Parrot Island days, as long as she had all that went with it. . . .

As Martha tidied up the room, a knock sounded on the door. Cathy looked at it with some impatience as Martha went to answer it. Most likely it was her father, come to add his harangue to Martha's.

It was Petersham. Cathy stared at the wiry little man in some surprise. He looked both ill at ease, and determined.

"Is something wrong with Jon?" The question burst from her before she could catch it. Petersham stepped inside the room, twisting and untwisting the hat he held in his hands. Martha stood back to admit him, then closed the door, a peculiarly satisfied expression crossing her face.

"Yes, ma'am," Petersham said, wetting his lips. Then, coming closer, the words fell from him like a torrent.

"Miss Cathy, you have to come home! Master Jon is killing himself! Ever since you left with Master Cray, he's been so drunk he can't walk! I'm afraid he'll drink himself into his grave!"

Petersham's eyes were imploring on her face. Cathy, looking from him to Martha's smug expression, felt immediately suspicious. Were they trying to put something over on her?

"Petersham, are you telling me the truth?" she demanded, her eyes probing as they met his.

"Yes, Miss Cathy, I am!" he said huskily. "Master Jon is swilling down whiskey like it's water. He hasn't been out of your bedroom since that day he got home and found you'd left with Master Cray. He won't eat, he hardly sleeps, and last night, when I tried to get him to take a little soup, he told me to get out and let him be! Then, when I did, he locked the door! He hasn't been out since, Miss Cathy, nor will he open it when I knock. Miss Cathy, I'm sore afraid for him!"

Cathy felt her heart constrict as she pictured Jon in these circumstances. Why she should care, she didn't know, but she found to her surprise that she did. Still she eyed Petersham suspiciously.

"What makes you think I can do something about it?" she asked. Petersham made an impatient gesture.

"Miss Cathy, I told you before you took Master Cray that you'd break his heart if you left him. You know he loves you, and you know better than anybody why he is the way he is. I've been with the two of you from the first, and I know for a fact that he's been good to you. You're just letting pride stand in your way now, and your pride may be Master Jon's death!"

Cathy stared at Petersham's impassioned face for a long moment. What he said was true, as far as it went. Jon had been good to her, from the first moments of their acquaintance, when he had stolen her off the ship that was carrying her to London and her first Season. Even when he had taken her body, it had never really been against her will. She had wanted him from the first time she had seen him, only then she had been too young and naive to realize what wanting a man meant. Jon had taught her, gently and tenderly initiating her into womanhood. Oh, they had quarreled, but that was inevitable in a mating between two people as hot-tempered as they both were. And making up had been sweet. . . .

He was drinking himself to death for love of her. Cathy found the notion warmed emotions that had been slowly freezing to death. If he loved her—if he loved her. . . .

"All right, Petersham, I'll ride back with you to Woodham and I'll talk to him. I'm not promising anything, mind. But I'll talk to him."

"Oh, thank you, Miss Cathy," Petersham beamed his relief. "If you can just get him to sober up, and eat something. . . ."

"He's more likely to throw me out on my ear," Cathy said dryly, but she didn't believe that any more than either Petersham or Martha did.

During the ride out to Woodham, Petersham drove and Cathy was largely silent. She was surprised to find butterflies in her stomach at the idea of facing Jon again. If Petersham had lied to her—she shot him a killing look. She would never forgive him—or Jon!

Petersham had not lied. The house was silent as a tomb, the servants moving about mournfully, speaking in whispers, as though there had been a death in the family. Even from the foot of the stairs, Cathy could smell the sickly odor of whiskey. Upstairs, not a sound came from the direction of the master bedroom.

"I'll bring up a big pot of coffee and some sandwiches, in a few minutes," Petersham said softly as she started up the stairs.

Cathy gave him a wry look.

"First you'd better wait and see if he'll let me in."

From Petersham's answering smile, it was obvious that he had no doubts about that. Cathy wished that she were as confident, as she stood in the hallway, hesitating outside the bedroom door.

Finally she gathered up enough courage to knock. The sound echoed hollowly through the hall. There was no answer.

"Jon?" she called, pressing her ear against the thick panel, the better to hear any movement from inside.

"Jon?" she called again, knocking, when there was no response. This time she heard a crash, as though something made of glass had fallen to the floor and broken. The sound was followed by a steady stream of curses, uttered in a thick but clearly recognizable voice.

"God, now I'm hearing things," she thought she heard him mutter from just beyond the door. Before she could ponder the meaning of that, the portal was jerked open. Leaning against it, she almost fell into the room. Immediately a steely hand closed about her arm, gripping it punishingly as it kept her from falling.

"I thought I told you to keep the hell away from here!" Jon began harshly, then broke off, his bloodshot eyes widening as they fastened on Cathy's face.

"Oh, God!" he said on a queer, strangled groan, thrusting her away from him with what she could have sworn was revulsion. Cathy staggered backward, only to find the door being slammed in her face. She blinked at the closed panel bemusedly for a moment. Whatever reception she had expected, it had certainly been nothing like this! How dare he be so rude, when she had driven all this way just to see him!

Anger sparking from her eyes, she marched up to the door again and boldly knocked.

"Jonathan Hale, you open this door!" she demanded furiously, rattling the knob.

It opened almost at once. Before Cathy could do more than glare hotly at him, he was pulling her into his arms, holding her so tightly that she could feel every hard muscle and sinew of his body.

"Oh, God, it is you," he muttered thickly, pressing his lips to the silken cord of her neck. "I thought I was imagining things again!"

Cathy found herself enveloped in a haze of whiskey fumes, but just at the moment she didn't care. She wrapped her arms around his strong back, hugging him fiercely. He returned her hug, murmuring endearments she couldn't quite make out into the curve between her shoulder and neck.

After a moment he let her go, only to pull her into the bedroom and close the door behind them. He stood leaning rather unsteadily against the panel, regarding her with red-rimmed eyes that seemed to devour her. After a few moments his gaze sharpened, hardened.

"What are you doing here?" he demanded as brusquely as the drunken thickness of his tongue would allow. "If you've come to gloat, you can just go away again. I don't need you! I don't need anyone. . . ."

Cathy was somewhat taken aback by the abrupt change in his manner. He was glowering at her, his expression fierce. She got the impression that he almost hated her.

"Petersham. . . ." she faltered before she thought. His face darkened.

"Did that old goat fetch you?" he asked fiercely. "Damn, I'll kill him! I suppose he told you some nonsensical tale about me drinking myself to death for love of you?"

His tone was a sad parody of mockery. Under the influence of so much whiskey, he couldn't quite control the grain of truth that was evident in his words.

"He did tell me something like that, yes," Cathy admitted, watching him closely. She saw hot red color wash into his cheekbones. Those gray eyes looked away from hers.

"Damn it, I *will* kill him!" he growled. "Hell, if that's why you came, you might just as well leave again! I don't want your pity!"

"You don't have it," Cathy answered steadily, her eyes never leaving his dark face. "You have my love instead, you dolt. That's why I came."

Jon's eyes swung back to her face, a mixture of hope and doubting in his eyes. Before she could say any more, he was coming away from the door in a lunge, catching her against him. This time his kiss found her mouth. Cathy returned it freely, her hands sliding up around his neck, ignoring the sour taste of whiskey against her lips. She felt him sway suddenly, and braced herself to steady him.

"You'd better sit down before you fall down," she told him humorously as he freed her mouth at last.

"Yes, I. . . ."

A knock at the door interrupted him.

"Just a minute," Cathy called, and helped Jon to a chair before answering it. He sank down into the chair gratefully, his long legs sprawling out in front of him.

"Who the hell is that?" he demanded irritably.

"Probably Petersham, with coffee and some food," Cathy answered, her face serene as she went to answer the door. Behind her she heard Jon grumble, "Interfering old fool!"

Petersham, when she opened the door to admit him, looked anxious. Cathy smiled reassuringly at him as he crossed the room to place the food on the table. Jon watched him balefully, and when Petersham cast him a quick, appraising look, he growled, "Remind me to fire you later."

"Yes, Captain," Petersham replied woodenly, then winked broadly at Cathy before leaving them alone again.

Cathy pulled the little table to stand at Jon's elbow, then poured him a cup of black coffee. He took it impatiently, his eyes never leaving her face.

"Cathy . . ." he began. She silenced him with a gesture.

"Eat first," she ordered sternly, passing him a sandwich. "Then we'll talk."

As he complied, gnawing hungrily at the sandwich, Cathy glanced around the room. It was complete chaos, she saw, wrinkling her nose at the whiskey fumes rising from a half-full bottle that had apparently broken when he had come to answer her knock. Besides that mess, dust lay visibly over every available item of furniture. Clearly Petersham had not been exaggerating when he had said that Jon had refused to allow anyone into the room. It hadn't been dusted for at least a week. The bed was unmade, its pillows lying on the floor on the opposite side of the room where Jon had apparently flung them, whether in a temper or an effort to get comfortable Cathy couldn't tell. The curtains were drawn, enveloping the room in a thick gloom. Shaking her head, she jumped up to open them. Sunlight streamed in, its light brightening every corner. Behind her, Cathy heard Jon groan.

"Oh, my eyes," he mumbled, shielding them with his hand from the light. Cathy crossed to his side, looking down at him with affectionate chiding.

"Serves you right," she said unsympathetically. "After all that whiskey, your hangover should last for weeks. If you're feeling better, I think I might call Petersham in to help you get cleaned up. Quite frankly, my darling, you wouldn't be out of place in a pigsty."

Jon grinned a little at that.

"I must stink to high heaven," he murmured, lowering his protective hand a little to peer up at her.

"You do," she said frankly. "Never mind, Petersham will soon have you feeling very much more the thing."

As Cathy moved toward the door, Jon caught at a fold of her velvet skirt.

"You won't go away?" he asked huskily. Smiling down at him tenderly, Cathy shook her head.

"I won't go away," she promised, and went to call Petersham.

She waited downstairs in the back parlor while Petersham assisted Jon with his toilette. When Petersham had finished, she meant to go up again, to continue that most interesting conversation where it had been broken off. She hummed as she waited, her heart lighter than it had been for months. She had made the right decision, she knew. She would stay. In spite of everything, she loved him, and he loved her. That was all that mattered.

To her surprise, she heard Jon's booted feet on the wooden floor outside the back parlor door. She was just turning to face the door when he entered. He was looking very much better, she saw, as he halted just inside the room, his hands thrust into his breeches' pockets, his expression guarded as he looked at her. He was freshly shaved, and bathed, his black hair neatly brushed, and dressed in a clean white shirt and dove gray breeches. His eyes were still a trifle red, but Cathy supposed that that was only to be expected.

She smiled at him somewhat hesitantly. He didn't return her smile. If anything, his expression hardened.

"You're free to go, if you like," he said stiffly. "I assure you, I'm in no danger of dying from over-consumption of whiskey, despite what Petersham may have told you."

Cathy looked at him closely. Dull red crept up his neck under her scrutiny. Satisfied, her smile widened.

"You sound as if you're anxious to be rid of me," she said lightly. His jaw tightened.

"For God's sake, don't tease me," he said harshly, crossing the room so that he stood looking out the window, his back to her.

"I'm not teasing." Her voice was soft as she came to stand behind him, her arms sliding around his muscular waist. She felt him stiffen at her touch, then slowly he relaxed.

"I love you, you know," he said gruffly to the window. Pressed closely against his back, Cathy smiled.

"Enough to marry me?" she asked. He turned slowly in her arms, his own sliding around her. She saw that he was smiling a little uncertainly.

"Are you proposing to me?" His voice was husky.

"Yes." She smiled shamelessly up at him, her eyes alight with love. His gray eyes started to return her smile, glinting warmly down into hers.

"Does that include two children, and possibly a dozen more in the future?" he asked, as if considering.

"Yes."

"Then I accept, with pleasure," he said, and his mouth coming down on hers sealed the bargain. When he lifted his head at last, Cathy twinkled mistily up at him. His eyes were soft with love as he cupped her small, radiant face in his two big hands, smiling down at her.

"We'll be married as soon as I can beg, borrow, or steal a preacher," he told her, his head descending again.

And they were.

Gallery Books proudly presents

Sleepwalker

KAREN ROBARDS

Available now in hardcover from Gallery Books!

Turn the page for a preview of *Sleepwalker* . . .

one

∽⟊∾

Sometimes terrible things happen in the middle of the night. Sometimes the monster under the bed is real. Sometimes there truly is a bogeyman hiding in the closet.

Sometimes people die.

"Do you think they saw us?" Jenny Lange gasped as she fled across the overgrown vacant lot in Detroit's rough Eight Mile area. Moonlight silvered the bright banner of the fifteen-year-old's long blond hair, turned her face into a pale beacon as she glanced back over her shoulder. Dressed in a ski jacket, jeans and boots, she was little more than a slim shadow in the darkness. The night was black and cold. A biting wind whistled through the canyon made by the surrounding apartment buildings, whipping sparkling whirlwinds of snow from the crusty layer on the ground.

"Don't know." Lori Penski snorted with laughter. Also fifteen, she ran a couple of steps behind her best friend, Jenny, her flight slowed by an intermittent attack of the giggles. "Did you see what they were *doing*?"

"What? What were they doing?" Micayla Lange's heart

pounded so hard that she could hear it thudding in her ears even over the rapid-fire crunch of their feet punching through the snow. Slip-sliding along behind, she almost begged for an answer, knowing even as the words left her mouth that she was probably going to be ignored just like always. Only eleven and undersized, she was having trouble keeping up. Having hurried so as not to have been left behind when her big sister and her sister's friend had sneaked out of the apartment where they'd been babysitting her and she'd supposedly been asleep, she'd grabbed her coat and stuck her bare feet in the sneakers she'd worn to basketball practice earlier. The sneakers were proving no match for ten inches of snow: icy wet, they kept threatening to slide off with every step she took. Her feet and ankles burned from churning as fast as they could through the frozen slush, and her pajamas were wet almost to the knees. Even with her coat zipped clear to her throat, she was so cold that her skin stung.

And scared. She was so, so scared. She and Jenny were never, ever supposed to leave the apartment at night while their mother was at work. They weren't even supposed to answer the door. This run-down section of Detroit was dangerous, riddled with crime even in broad daylight. They'd only lived there for two months, since their parents had split up, and already they'd gotten used to the sound of gunfire at night and learned to rush straight in from the school bus so that they would spend as little time as possible on the street.

"Here they come!" Jenny's eyes went wide as she looked past the other girls, back toward the sixteen-story brick tenement that backed up to the vacant lot. With much shushing and giggling, Jenny and Lori had peeped in the windows of the basement apartment, where a bunch of boys the older girls knew had been—what? Micayla had no clue. She hadn't made it all the way to the building before Lori had slipped and banged a knee into a window with a loud *clank* and the girls, choking with laughter, had bolted for home.

"No way," Lori gasped as she and Micayla glanced back, too. Sure enough, Micayla saw three or four boys tearing around the corner of the building, shouting and pointing as they spotted the girls. But they weren't the only ones in the vacant lot in the middle of this frigid night. Off to the right, in the shadow of another of the boxlike apartment buildings, a lone figure stood watching. A man, Micayla thought, too big and bulky to be a teenager. Unlike the boys, who were loudly and enthusiastically giving chase, he melted into the darkness even as Micayla caught sight of him. A stray beam of moonlight slid over him to catch on something he was carrying: a pole? An aluminum baseball bat? Whatever it was was black, but it had a shiny metallic gleam that showed up as a quick, glittery flash as he stepped into the light spilling from an apartment window above him, then just as quickly moved into the dark again. Micayla didn't know why, but something about the man made the hair stand up on the back of her neck.

There's somebody else here, she wanted to tell her sister. But she was too winded to say it out loud. Plus Jenny was too far ahead. And Jenny never paid attention to her, anyway.

"Jenny! Micayla!"

At the sound of the familiar voice, sharp now with angry surprise, Micayla's attention riveted on the source. Wendy Lange, blond and slender like Jenny, stood wrapped in her shabby blue coat on the sidewalk in front of their apartment building, which was directly across the street from the vacant lot. The car she'd just gotten out of pulled off down the street, engine rattling, taillights reflecting red off the knee-high piles of snow that lined the curb.

"Oh, no, it's Mom!" Sounding horrified, Jenny slowed down, glancing around at her friend and her little sister in dismay, while Lori made a face and muttered, "Busted," out of the side of her mouth.

"Mom! Mom!" Micayla shrieked, waving. Unlike Jenny,

she was so glad to see their mother that the gladness felt as warm as a little ball of sunshine forming inside her. Mom meant safety, and she hadn't felt safe from the moment she'd left the apartment. Now, suddenly, with their mother's eyes on them, she did. Stepping off the curb, Wendy waved back specifically at Micayla as she started across the street toward them. Despite the wave, Micayla could tell from the way she was walking that she was mad.

At Jenny, though. Not at her. Her mother rarely got mad at her. Micayla's my good girl, was what she always said.

Because Micayla always was.

"We went out to get some milk," Jenny hissed, backtracking to grab Micayla's hand. "Hear? We were just going to walk down to the little all-night grocery on Hines because you wanted milk, but we got scared and decided to come back. Got that? Don't you dare say anything about us spying on the guys."

"She's gonna know—"

Jenny squeezed her hand so hard that Micayla yelped. "Not if you don't tell her, she won't."

"*Okay.* You don't have to *hurt* me."

"You just better not tell."

"I *won't.*"

"You girls get over here right now!" It was their mother's stern voice. Micayla felt sorry for Jenny. Jenny got in trouble a lot, and Micayla hated it every time, whether Jenny deserved it or not.

"The guys took off," Lori muttered to Jenny, who glanced back.

Micayla glanced back, too, and saw that the boys were indeed nowhere in sight. Only she, Jenny and Lori were left to face Wendy's wrath. Micayla felt a sinking sensation in the pit of her stomach. Jenny would probably get her face slapped at the very least, and the prospect made Micayla feel sick. She hated it when Mom and Jenny fought. Wendy would say that Jenny was the one who'd been left in charge, and Jenny was *older*. Sometimes Micayla felt bad because, according to their mother, nothing was ever her fault. Although if she lied like Jenny wanted her to and got caught, this time it might be her fault and this time she might get her face slapped, too.

That wasn't so good, either.

"Come *on*." Jenny yanked on her hand. Lori had dropped back, obviously glad she wasn't the one whose mom was furiously marching toward them. By this time, Wendy had almost reached their side of the street. Stumbling a little because of the relentlessness with which Jenny was pulling her, Micayla kept her eyes on their mother as Wendy stepped carefully up onto the packed-snow path between the drifts that led to the sidewalk. Head bent, Wendy was watching her feet. The moonlight brightened her short blond hair, gleamed off the slick wet blackness of the street behind her, sent her long shadow stretching out toward the hurrying girls.

That moment—the sight of her mother bathed in moonlight, the feel of Jenny's warm hand clamped on her own, the wet smell of the snow, the sounds of the retreating car and their crunching footsteps, and the bite of the icy, blowing wind on her cheeks—was frozen forever in Micayla's mind. The last tick of *before*. If only she could stop time right there. . . .

Because the *after* began a heartbeat later, when shots exploded through the night.

Crack! Crack!

The sound still bounced off the buildings, still reverberated in Micayla's ears, when Wendy crumpled. Just like that, like her bones had suddenly turned to dust. She toppled face-first into the snow, which instantly began to turn scarlet around her.

Micayla screamed.

And woke up.

As cold as if she'd actually been outside on that frigid night again.

Which of course she wasn't.

She was inside. The air around her was warm. The cold she was experiencing came from the frosty window glass she was doing a full-body press against. The curtain had been pulled back, and beyond the window—actually one section of a wall of sliding glass doors—the pool area glistened under the fresh layer of pristine white snow that had been falling since she'd arrived at her uncle Nicco's lakeside mansion shortly after 5:00 p.m. Except for the pale gleam of moonlight reflecting off the snow, the world beyond the window was black as ink. Earlier, at the stroke of midnight, an explosion of fireworks had lit up the night sky as cash-strapped Motor City had thrown its cares aside and celebrated the New Year. She'd watched, alone, through a downstairs window, then gone to bed.

If it hadn't been for the glass, I would have been out there wandering barefoot in the snow right now, Mick thought, and she felt her stomach knot.

At least, from the absence of sound echoing around her, she felt safe in assuming that this time the soul-shaking scream she'd let loose had been all in her head.

Please God.

She didn't need to see a clock to know that the time was right around 2:30 a.m. Just like it had been then. Plus it wasn't long after Christmas, as cold as a meat locker outside, spurting snow. And she'd been upset when she'd fallen asleep.

Of course she'd been sleepwalking again.

I'm twenty-seven fricking years old. Am I never going to outgrow this?

Peeling herself away from the window, Mick ignored the mild vertigo that she always experienced when she woke up abruptly under these conditions, then took a deep, hopefully steadying, breath. Her heart, which had been pounding like a SWAT team at an unsub's door, started to slow down. Looking around, she tried to get her bearings.

Having gone to sleep in one of the eight second-floor bedrooms, she was now two stories below, in the part of the vast, elaborately finished walk-out basement that led to the pool and tennis court. With no memory at all of how she had gotten there.

Carefully she closed the curtain, blocking out the night.

Her hands shook, but she chose to ignore that. Just like she ignored the ringing in her ears, the dryness of her mouth and the racing of her pulse.

With the curtain closed, she was left standing in the dark. A pinpoint-size red glow up near the ceiling reminded her that security cameras were everywhere. At the thought that her unconscious perambulation might have been witnessed by one or more of the security guards manning the monitors from the gatehouse out front, she felt a slow flush of embarrassment creep over her body. The good news was, it chased away the last of the chill.

She slept in flannel pajama bottoms and a tank top. The bottoms were red and loose, the top white and snug. Her long, horsetail-thick chestnut hair trailed over her shoulders in two braids. Not a look meant for public consumption, and not the image she wanted to project to the security guards. At five foot six, she was as lean as a whippet and superbly fit. Hard-bodied. Cool, competent, tough as nails. Right now, though, to anybody who happened to be watching, she probably looked the exact opposite.

Current appearances notwithstanding, girly and vulnerable she was not.

Mentally flipping the bird at the invisible watcher who might or might not be behind the camera, depending on the degree of slacking that was going on, she padded back down the carpeted hallway. There was an elevator, but she preferred to take the stairs. A little exercise was what she needed to take the edge off. She didn't sleepwalk much anymore, maybe two or three times a year, but she knew the drill: her thought processes would be cobwebby for hours if she didn't do something to shake them out.

By the time she made it up the semicircular marble staircase to the second floor, her head was on straight and she felt normal again. Which wasn't necessarily a good thing. The anger and sense of betrayal that had been with her for almost twenty-four hours now had come back, and had once again settled into her stomach like a rock.

"Bastard," she said out loud to her absent ex-boyfriend. She'd said it to his face before she'd left, along with a lot of other things. She didn't know why she'd been so surprised to learn he'd been cheating on her. She knew men. She knew cops.

What was surprising was how much it hurt to find out that Homicide Investigator Nate Horacki of the Detroit PD was no better than the rest of them.

This time yesterday, she would have said she was in love with him.

But now . . . no way. She wasn't that big of a . . .

Clink.

Mick never would have heard the slight sound if she hadn't been right where she was, striding along the open second-floor gallery that ran across the top of the enormous, eye-popping entry hall, nearly at the doorway of the bedroom she was using, the one she always used, which she'd come to think of as her way-luxurious home away from home. But she *was* there, and she *did* hear it. Stopping dead, she listened. To nothing at all except the hum of the heating system. Except for the faint glow of moonlight streaming through the windows, the house was dark. Not wanting to advertise her movements to anyone outside who might be interested, she hadn't turned on a light on her way back to her bedroom. Now every sense she possessed focused on the shadow-filled spaces stretching out all around her. The house was huge, and tonight, except for her, it was empty. At least, it was supposed to be.

Clink.

There it was again. Mick went taut as a bowstring, every sense on the alert. The smell of pine from the Christmas garlands tied to the gallery's wrought-iron railing wafted in the air. Shimmery gold ornaments in a glass bowl on the console table to her left glinted as a shaft of moonlight played over them. Trying to remember how the house had looked before darkness had swallowed it up, she concluded that the tall, menacing shapes in the corners were the human-size toy soldiers and nutcrackers her aunt Hope, Uncle Nicco's wife, had used as Christmas decorations. She relaxed a little even as she listened hard.

Silence once again blanketed everything. But she knew she hadn't imagined the sound. And it hadn't been a random creak that she could put down to the settling of floor joists or something equally innocent; it had been sharper and metallic. Purposeful, was how she characterized it. Which meant she needed to check it out.

She embraced the thought with relish. Checking it out was something to do, something to think about, something she was good at. And it was a whole hell of a lot better than lying sleepless in her bed trying not to think, which she knew was the fate that awaited her for the rest of the night.

Uncle Nicco had hired her to house-sit while he, his wife, five grown children and their families spent New Year's and the week after at their place in Palm Beach. Because of the bust up with Nate, she had arrived a day early, just a couple of hours after the family left. The house should have been empty for this one night.

New Year's Eve.

So if the house was empty except for herself, what was the source of that sound?

Moving swiftly, Mick slipped into her bedroom and retrieved her gun from the nightstand. The familiar, solid weight of the Glock 22 felt good in her hand. Her handcuffs were on the nightstand, too. She grabbed them, tucked them into her pocket just in case, and thrust her feet into terry flip-flops, which had been part of the spa basket her longtime best friend, Angela Marino Knox—Nicco's daughter—had left on her bed as a Christmas present and which she had been using for slippers after painting her toenails with the hot pink Passion Fruit polish that had also been in the basket. Then she retraced her steps, quiet as a whisper, moving cautiously but quickly back along the gallery, listening.

Clink.

There it was again. Probably it was nothing. Still, her heart rate accelerated as she focused in on the location of the sound: first floor, toward the rear. Padding down the stairs, the marble hard and silent beneath her feet, she tried to pinpoint the location more exactly. Left, past the huge formal living and dining rooms and the music room and the library. Slinking purposefully along, moving from shadow to shadow, she gave a fleeting thought to hitting one of the panic buttons that had been placed in strategic locations for the purpose of instantly summoning the security guards. The odds were high that the sharp, metallic sound she was hearing was something entirely innocent, but backup was always a good thing. Then Mick considered who had pulled security guard duty on this icy New Year's Eve and made a face.

She didn't need backup, anyway.

No longer hearing anything out of the ordinary, she proceeded with quick caution, clearing each dark room as she passed it. As Uncle Nicco was always bragging, the security system was state of the art, not the kind of thing a burglar could easily breach. Plus, given the presence of the guards, the cameras, the fact that the estate was ringed on three sides by a twelve-foot-high fence (the fourth side was secured by the lake) and every outside door had at least two top-of-the-line double bolts, the house was a virtual fortress. What were the chances that . . . ?

Boom.

Okay, that wasn't nothing. It was a soft boom, a muffled, barely audible boom, but a boom nonetheless. As if something had exploded, maybe, only quietly. Mick's eyes widened as she rounded a corner and spied the faintest of yellow glows emanating from a door about twenty feet away. A click, a boom, a glow—good God, could the house be on fire?

The security system included state-of-the-art fire detection. If the house was on fire, by now the system should have been wailing its little heart out.

Unless something had compromised the system.

Adrenaline pumping, Mick glided quickly and silently to the open door, then flattened herself against the wall beside it. The yellow glow was gone. The hall . . . the room . . . the house . . . were once again silent and dark. A quick, careful peek around the door frame revealed exactly nothing: there was just enough moonlight filtering through cracks in the floor-to-ceiling drapes to help her ascertain that the room was empty. But there was a smell: a kind of acrid, smoky scent that reminded her of a detonated cherry bomb. And barely audible sounds—a shuffle, a click, a thunk. Although she liked to think she possessed a highly honed sixth sense, one wasn't required to deduce that she was not alone. Her heart lurched. Her stomach clenched. She wet her lips.

Then professionalism kicked in, and icy calm descended like a curtain.

She was still peeping around the door frame, formulating her next move, when a man, tall and lean, dressed all in black and wearing a black ski mask with one of those miner's lights affixed to a band around his forehead, walked out of an open door on the opposite side of the room as brazenly as could be. She hadn't previously been more than vaguely aware of that door. If she had thought about it at all, which she couldn't recall ever having done, she had probably assumed it led to a closet. Only no burglar—and a burglar this certainly was— would bother to blow open a closet door, and it was clear from the sulfurous smell, from the boom she'd heard, and most of all from the fact that the door appeared to be hanging drunkenly from one hinge, that it had been blown open.

The room was Uncle Nicco's private office, which meant the door almost had to belong to a safe. A closet-size, walk-in safe that held God only knew what in the way of valuables. A safe she'd never even known existed.

Which it was nevertheless her job to protect.

The man was maybe six foot two, broad shouldered and athletically built, with a young man's confident gait. Open military-style jacket over a tee, pants and boots. With—she squinted to be sure—surgical gloves that made his hands look as white as a cadaver's against all that black. Still absolutely unaware that she was anywhere in the vicinity.

Having registered all this in the space of a split second, Mick did what she had to do: she stepped into the doorway, planted her feet and jerked her weapon up.

"Freeze," she barked. "Police."

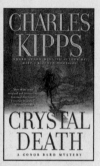